RETRIBUTION

MARK S. WILLIAMS

TITAN BOOKS

Transformers: Retribution is a work of fiction. Names, places, and incidents either are products of the author's imagination or are used fictitiously.

Copyright © 2014 by Hasbro, Inc. All rights reserved.
Based on Hasbro's Transformers® Action Figures

TRANSFORMERS: RETRIBUTION
ISBN: 9781783290697

Published by Titan Books
A division of Titan Publishing Group
144 Southwark Street
London
SE1 0UP

First edition January 2014

1 3 5 7 9 10 8 6 4 2

www.titanbooks.com
www.hasbro.com/transformers

Did you enjoy this book? We love to hear from our readers. Please email us at readerfeedback@titanemail.com or write to us at Reader Feedback at the above address.

To receive advance information, news, competitions, and exclusive offers online, please sign up for the Titan newsletter on our website: www.titanbooks.com

A CIP catalogue record for this title is available from the British Library.

Printed and bound by CPI Group (UK) Ltd, Croydon, CR0 4YY

TRANSFORMERS™
RETRIBUTION

For Bob Budiansky

Acknowledgments

Mark would like to thank: my family, Dr. Luther S. Williams and Constance M. Williams, Dr. Monique M. Williams, and Franklin Stephenson, for all their support. Also much gratitude to Andrew Crown, Mitch Engle, Tony Halasohoris, Pak Mhojadee, Ed Wong, and Gabrielle Kern for always believing.

Dave would like to thank: Sabrina Lloyd, Brian De Groodt, Erin Sheley, Christopher Goddard, Rob Cunningham, Elizabeth Dell, Paul Ruskay, Adam Green, Marc Haimes, Jerry Ellis, Rich Dent, Tom Doyle, James Wang, Frank Parisi, David Pomerico, Howard Morhaim, and most of all the Beasts.

Acknowledgments

Mark would like to thank: my family, Dr. Luther S. Williams and Constance M. Williams, Dr. Monique M. Williams, and Franklin Stephenson, for all their support. Also much gratitude to Andrew Crown, Mitch Engle, Tony Halasohoris, Pak Mhojadee, Ed Wong, and Gabrielle Kern for always believing.

Dave would like to thank: Sabrina Lloyd, Brian De Groodt, Erin Sheley, Christopher Goddard, Rob Cunningham, Elizabeth Dell, Paul Ruskay, Adam Green, Marc Haimes, Jerry Ellis, Rich Dent, Tom Doyle, James Wang, Frank Parisi, David Pomerico, Howard Morhaim, and most of all the Beasts.

Prologue: Alpha Trion

MY TIME HAS COME.

Yesterday Shockwave came to me again. He talked and talked—he is so proud of himself, so arrogant. And yet (as is ever with such hubris) the real meaning was in what he did not say. He claims the Decepticons have almost won control of all Cybertron, but I know better. Ultra Magnus and his fearless Wreckers are unleashing havoc . . . hit and runs on convoys, surprise raids on isolated bases, sudden severing of supply lines . . . guerrilla war gradually intensifying to the point where now only the Decepticon forces in the major cities are secure from attack.

But Shockwave could care less. His lord and master Megatron craves total domination, but Shockwave thrives on chaos. It took me longer than it should have to understand this—to realize that Shockwave now regards all of Cybertron as his laboratory. For him, the Wreckers are simply culling the weaker Decepticons, making the race as a whole that much fitter. His is the most dangerous kind of insanity: the kind that stems from logic run riot. Even as the Wreckers inflict ever more damage, Shockwave cultivates his larger agenda. To him, the Wreckers are unwitting tools.

Whereas I know the role that he expects from me. Again, he would not tell me directly. But here in the Hall of Records, I can hear his Insecticon guards buzz outside *my door, and I know that they will lead me elsewhere very soon, to a place I would rather not go. It is not the impending pain I fear, though I would hardly claim to welcome it. It is the thought of the forces Shockwave might inadvertently unleash. It is disquieting to reflect that there are far worse outcomes than his crushing of all resistance on Cybertron.*

What is happening half a galaxy away is testament to that. So far from where I write this, yet I know enough of it. Even if so many of the mighty space bridges have fallen into disrepair—even if so much of our once-great culture lies in ruins—I am still one of the Thirteen, and I am not deaf to the manifestations of my brethren.

Nor am I unaware of the machinations of ancient enemies. Civil war is the worst kind of war; every shot fired, every blow struck, all of it leaves one's people that much more enfeebled when it is time to face the real foe. Had I been able to spend enough time with Optimus before he left our battered planet in search of the AllSpark, I might have had the chance to tell him that . . . to explain to him what the gladiator who once called himself Megatronus knows intuitively, that an infinite universe contains infinite opponents by definition. To learn to live in peace with this reality: there can be no higher aspiration. And even though Megatron will almost certainly never attain any such serenity, his way of fire and sword has nonetheless granted him the easier path.

At least in the short term.

And though I am a being that measures time in eons, the short term is all I have now.

Because now I hear them: Shockwave's personal guards striding toward the door. They will drag me from the solace of my records, from the Covenant of Primus that I have hidden in a place they never will find, all those pages containing words of the future crashing like ocean on the jagged shore of now. I stand upon that shore and yearn for days when I was younger. Oh, yes, I admit it. Why should I not? Even as I know it for the ultimate temptation . . . and thank Primus himself that I am too old for it to sway me: to stride onto the bridge of a ship plowing across the parsecs, readying weapons with which to rend your foes to pieces. Megatron, I envy you such simplicity of purpose. Would that I could have turned your malice to better ends. Would that I could somehow stop those who now advance to claim me. But all I can do is write these words and hope that somehow they make it past my captors to tell the tale of events heroic and terrible . . . an epic inferno to echo all the way to the day in which you (in a happier time, a sunnier time perhaps) sit here and read and wonder.

Chapter One

AN ENDLESS WALL OF GLITTERING STARS; A SINGLE spaceship sweeping in toward it.

For weeks, the *Nemesis* had traversed the gulf between two of the Milky Way's spiral arms. Now that journey was almost over. Ahead was the edge of the Orion Arm; that of Sagittarius lay far behind. As the *Nemesis* gracefully slipped out of faster-than-light mode, its cloaking systems kicked in automatically. Dozens of sensor dishes bloomed like flowers along the titanic warship's spinal mount, scanning the approaching field of stars, processing everything they saw, and relaying their findings to the ship's bridge.

On the bridge, Starscream and Soundwave studied the readouts. They were the only Decepticons on the flight deck. It didn't take much of a crew to run the ship in standard transit mode, and that was just fine with Starscream. If they found anything, he intended to be the first to know. It wasn't like the ship was going to tell them; the *Nemesis* had sustained considerable damage during its pursuit of the Autobots; not only had it lost the ability to shift out of spaceship mode, it was no longer sentient. The rest of the Decepticons seemed to regard that as a loss, but Starscream relished the fact that the thing had finally shut up. The last thing he needed was a spaceship with its own agenda, for power politics among the Decepticons was complex enough as it was. Let Megatron sulk in his quarters; Starscream would rather watch from the front than give orders from the rear, would rather bide his time, for he knew that after the inevitable victory over the renegade Autobots, the real struggle between him and his master would begin. Until that day arrived, he took what satisfaction he could in bullying those below him. He turned his ruby-red eyes on Soundwave and pointed a long finger at him.

"Proceed to secondary scans."

"At once," Soundwave replied in his usual monotone. Starscream knew there was no need to vocalize what was merely standard operating procedure, but he did it anyway to remind Soundwave that he was second in command on this bridge. He enjoyed reminding all of them every chance he got. Soundwave might be Megatron's loyal pet, but as far as Starscream was concerned, he was nothing more than a jumped-up communications officer with visions of spymaster grandeur, though he was nothing if not obedient: Starscream watched the results from the secondary scans flicker past him. Dozens of screens lit up as the *Nemesis* searched system after system, star after star—a search that now expanded to include substellar material: brown dwarves, burned-out suns, nomad planets, wayward rocks . . .

There.

"Isolate that signal!" Starscream barked. Soundwave was already on it; along one wall, a wraparound screen focused on the system in question, several layers back from the edge of the spiral arm. It was a young star surrounded by a huge cloud of debris. A typical circumstellar disk . . . but Starscream's eyes narrowed, for such debris would be the perfect place for wounded prey to hide. And as the *Nemesis*'s mainframe broke down the signal's composition, Starscream felt an emotion he rarely knew: joy.

For it was unmistakably an echo from the engines of the Autobots' Ark.

Perhaps the Autobots were hoping the various debris and gravitational distortions could hide them. If so, they had underestimated the *Nemesis*'s powerful sensors. Back in orbit around Cybertron, it had been a state-of-the-art scientific station while in its Trypticon mode. And now its sensors were put to the test even further: They picked up a second signal, buried still deeper in the mix . . .

"Autobot distress call," said Soundwave.

That wasn't what Starscream was expecting him to say, but he instinctively hid his surprise. So the Autobots were in desperate straits. So much the better. Apparently they were hoping that someone besides the Decepticons was out there to rescue them from whatever they'd stumbled into. *Pathetic,* Starscream thought. They weren't warriors by trade; they could boast of nothing approaching the instinctive grasp of tactics possessed by every Decepticon. There were times he almost felt sorry for them. It wasn't their fault that they hadn't been born for battle. Yet they'd made matters worse for themselves by entrusting their leadership to a glorified data clerk. That the no-name Orion Pax could become Optimus Prime was offensive to every self-respecting Decepticon. His leading the Autobots to their demise was only a matter of time.

Now that time had arrived.

"Shall I alert Lord Megatron?" Soundwave asked.

Starscream thought for a moment. "No. You stay here and monitor the signal. If it changes in any way, contact me immediately. I shall go and alert Lord Megatron myself."

"As you wish, Air Commander."

*   *   *

MEGATRON HAD LITTLE USE FOR AMENITIES.

He'd declined to use the captain's quarters as his lair, instead opting to set up his command post in a massive observation bubble that sat high atop one of the *Nemesis*'s aft superstructures. In peacetime, that bubble had been the site of telescopes that charted faraway stars, but all such equipment had been jettisoned long ago, making it the perfect place for Megatron to brood and plan high above the troops he commanded deep in the bowels of the vessel. The Decepticon leader had felt the ship drop out of lightspeed and knew that very soon those subordinates would be clamoring for orders.

For they were nothing without orders. There was no way they'd ever have gotten this far without him. Although each Deception was an excellent fighter in his own right, working together just wasn't something that came naturally to them. They needed a strong hand to guide them to victory. Nor was it simply a matter of each Decepticon recognizing where his collective interest lay. It was far more basic than that—it was might makes right, the purest expression of the Decepticon credo, and everything Megatron did reinforced the fact that he was the mightiest of all. There would always be pretenders to the throne, but what was leadership without the occasional opportunity to grind would-be usurpers down to their basic components? It was a part of the game that Megatron relished.

Though such satisfaction fell far short of the pleasure he would know on the day he crushed the Autobots and personally destroyed Optimus Prime. It vexed Megatron greatly that the librarian had escaped his clutches thus far. Only luck had allowed that rebellious bot to escape Cybertron in the first place. But luck could take one only so far. As of late a new factor had entered the equation— after their clash at Junkion, Megatron reluctantly had to admit to himself that the data clerk was fast learning the art of war. No doubt about it, Optimus's possession of the ancient Matrix of Leadership was making a difference. The Autobot leader had grown into his rule; he had led Megatron on quite a chase, but he couldn't run forever. Sooner or later he would have to stand up and fight. And probably sooner . . . The sound of the door chime pulled Megatron back from his thoughts.

"Enter," he said. Starscream strode into Megatron's chambers, dropped down to one knee, and bowed his head to his leader in a gesture that—though technically quite correct—bordered on the mocking.

"Oh mighty Lord Megatron, it is my humble duty to—"

"Dispense with the pleasantries," said Megatron. "And get to the point before I decide your service is no longer required."

"We've found the Autobots, Lord Megatron." Starscream keyed up the data on a screen in the observation module. "The system is awash with debris, but we're sure this is an Autobot transponder."

Megatron studied the display. His traditional scowl shifted to a wry half smile, but he said nothing. As the silence lengthened, Starscream started to get a little anxious.

"What do you think, sire?" he asked.

The half smile became a full one. "I think the Autobots have set a cunning trap," said Megatron.

"A trap? For us? Impossible."

"You've always underestimated the Autobots, Starscream. One day that arrogance will be your undoing. They may not be born warriors, but they are more than capable of deceiving the likes of you." The screen on the wall expanded out into a hologram. "Look more closely; do you see it this time?"

Starscream was definitely nervous now. He had no idea what Megatron was talking about. He shook his head, wishing Megatron would stop talking in riddles. The Decepticon leader let out a low sound that was half growl, half chuckle. He pointed at a series of coordinates around the site of the transponder.

"You forget, the *Nemesis* is purely automated intelligence. It cannot rival my judgment. These *look* like reflections from the primary source, but they are almost certainly heat signatures as well."

"I don't understand," Starscream said.

"They could be *ships*, fool. Using the debris as cover for an ambush. They think if they can trap us between the star and the debris field, they'll be able to maximize their weaker numbers against our stronger force. They know that the Ark is no match for the *Nemesis* and that the radiation in this debris field will play havoc with our targeting systems. So they're trying to even up the odds. And had you been in charge instead of me, it might have worked."

Starscream ignored the barb. "So what should we do, my lord?"

"Spring the trap, of course. Set the ship to condition red. We'll finish this once and for all."

"At once, my lord." Starscream hesitated. "And how shall we spring this trap?"

"*We*? Try *you*. Take a detachment of your best Seekers."

Starscream didn't like the sound of that at all. He tried to think fast.

"My lord, I'm not sure I'm worthy of such an honor."

Megatron laughed. "Don't be so hard on yourself," he said.

Chapter Two

THE NEMESIS'S WARDROOM WAS A POPULAR PLACE FOR the Decepticon warriors to replenish their Energon, talk shop, argue tactics—and, of course, gossip about their leaders. But even away from the front lines, Decepticon hierarchy was very much in evidence. Thundercracker and several others in Starscream's combat air patrol treated the place as their personal lounge. The less hearty of the Decepticons usually cleared out when they appeared in force to crowd around the rechargers and oil kegs. Thrust, Dirge, and Ramjet spent most of their time arguing over who was the better Seeker while Skywarp fine-tuned the circuitry on his teleportation unit. As of late, the scuttlebutt had centered on the increasingly boring system-by-system search for the Autobot enemies: How long would it go on? Would they ever find their quarry?

Not that anyone was so unwise as to express such sentiments to Megatron. The Decepticon leader kept his own counsel, and no one second-guessed it unless he wanted a good old-fashioned laser blast to the head. Though there had been plenty of talk behind his back about what he was up to. Because whatever Megatron had been doing these last few weeks was strange—it was almost as if he'd been told the direction in which to search but not how far out he had to go.

Following a more or less straight line, the *Nemesis* had systematically made its way across the galaxy, all the way to the edge . . . and then it had just kept going, out into the void, crossing to the next spiral arm. Perhaps Megatron was chasing phantoms. Perhaps he had become too obsessed with his hunt. Perhaps he was losing it. No one said that out loud—not even to one another—but it was on all their minds. That was the problem with dictators—it was an efficient way to do business, but it all fell to pieces when they started making poor decisions. More than one bot aboard the *Nemesis* was beginning to wish he'd stayed behind on Cybertron. There were those among the naysayers who hinted at disaster . . .

Thundercracker had no such qualms. He was quite happy to follow Megatron wherever he might lead, particularly since remaining on Cybertron with Shockwave had few attractions. The scientist-regent was about as unpredictable as a Decepticon could get, but if past was prologue, it surely involved experiments on his own kind with little regard for the end result. Thundercracker privately hoped that Shockwave would meet with a reckoning when Megatron returned home in triumph. But those were concerns for another time indeed.

Because now an alarm was sounding throughout the ship.

Thundercracker glanced at the others in the room. Suddenly they were all on edge, like athletes waiting for the signal to go. The intercom buzzed to life.

"This is Air Commander Starscream. All Seekers, prepare for orbital assault."

An excited buzz ran around the wardroom. Surely that meant the Autobots had been found. Thundercracker stood up and spoke to the room in tones that rang down the corridors and that (he hoped) were overheard by their glorious leader.

"It's time to do what we do best! Thanks to Megatron for delivering us this chance at battle! All hail Megatron!"

The answering shout would have deafened anything that wasn't metal. *"ALL HAIL MEGATRON!"*

SOUNDWAVE SNAPPED TO ATTENTION AS MEGATRON strode onto the *Nemesis*'s command deck.

"Status report," Megatron barked.

"We've isolated the transmission's location, Lord Megatron." Soundwave quickly set the ship's viewscreens to display all the information he'd obtained regarding the mysterious system and the signal emanating from it. Megatron frowned.

"And your personal analysis, Soundwave?"

"The signal is of Autobot origin. That being said, I still cannot locate the exact position of the Autobot Ark. The debris serves as effective cover, complicating any effort at triangulation—"

"Yes, yes, yes. I understand." Megatron smiled as he stared at the screen. "Well played, librarian, well played indeed."

"What should we do, my lord?"

"Starscream has volunteered to attack immediately. We will bring the *Nemesis* to the system's edge and prepare to support him."

Soundwave hesitated. "Do you think it wise to send so small a detachment in first, sire?"

"This is what Starscream and his Seekers were built for," Megatron said. "They'll be on top of that signal faster than the Autobots will be able to react. Optimus will have to reveal his precise location, and then we'll move in with the main force and strike."

That made sense to Soundwave. Exposing Starscream to the brunt of the enemy made even more. If he'd had a sense of humor, he would have giggled.

Fortunately for those around him, he didn't.

DOWN IN ONE OF THE *NEMESIS*'S FORWARD LOADING BAYS the Seekers got ready. Starscream, Thundercracker, Skywarp, Thrust, Dirge, and Ramjet were finishing their final weapon checks.

"So let me get this straight," said Ramjet, shrugging his blue steel shoulders. "We're going to go in there and spring what may very well be a trap?"

Thrust laughed. "Feeling nervous, Ramjet?"

"No, I'm just wondering why we have to stick our head into the meat grinder," Ramjet said. "Surely we should lead with a decoy. It hardly seems like the kind of assault work we Seekers merit."

"A far cry from when we ruled the skies of Cybertron," Dirge added. "This sounds almost like we're being used as cannon fodder. I wish to protest—"

"Wish all you like!" Starscream bellowed. He'd resigned himself to the situation—there was no choice other than to get with the program and hope for the best. "We're going in first because we're the elite, okay? When you want something done right, you deploy your finest troops. Agreed?"

"Agreed," said Thundercracker. "Anyway, who wants to sit around here when there's the chance of a good fight? You lot *do* remember how to fight, don't you?"

"You keep talking and I might have to show you," Ramjet answered while powering up his laser blade. Starscream stepped between his two air raiders.

"Enough; save your energy for the real enemy." The bay doors cycled open as the warriors seamlessly switched to jet-attack mode. They swarmed out of the *Nemesis* in tight formation, accelerating through dozens of Gs as they raced toward the signal. Ahead lay a vast cloud of rocks and a sun flickering deep within.

"Wait for my command to resume jet-trooper mode," said Starscream. "Stay on my six, Thundercracker. The rest of you form attack pattern delta." Thundercracker swung in directly behind Starscream, sunlight flitting off the red streaks on his wings. With incredible grace, the whole formation weaved in and out of the dense debris field on vectors that would allow them to respond to any attack from hidden ships. It was a task that would have been impossible for lesser pilots. If there were enemy ships in here, they were well hidden. The Seekers could detect nothing. As they closed on the asteroid that marked the signal's exact coordinates, Starscream gave the final go-ahead; the Seekers fired their thrusters and descended down toward the rock like giant birds of prey.

"*There*," said Thundercracker. He'd just spotted a single small ship tethered against a crater in the asteroid. Starscream and his Seekers switched to jet-trooper mode, firing their retrothrusters to slow their approach, landing in a tight circle around that ship, their guns aimed at what looked like a—

"Lifeboat," Thrust said, sounding disappointed.

"It's not even Autobot design," Dirge added.

"Cover us," Starscream said as he and Thundercracker advanced on the craft.

"Where are all the Autobots?" a puzzled Ramjet asked. "Where's the Ark?"

"Maybe it's been destroyed," said Skywarp.

"Shut up and get this thing open," Starscream snarled. Thundercracker ripped off the hatch to reveal a battered orange and yellow robot, obviously still functional but restrained and hardwired into the ship's systems. The bot looked up at them plaintively.

"Hello, mate," he said. "Be a good 'un and release me, eh?"

"Who the slag are you?" Starscream asked.

"Wreck-Gar is the name; wheeling and dealing junk is my game." He grinned wanly through his goatee. "Or at least it *was*."

"It's one of those Junkion robots," Dirge offered.

"*One* of?" Wreck-Gar looked offended. "Guv'nor of the lot, more like it. Show a little respect"—but that was when Starscream ripped him out of his restraints, grabbed him by the neck, and pressed an arm-mounted laser up to his eyes.

"*Respect* is an interesting word," said the air commander. "But I feel you and I might differ on its meaning."

"No need to get so hot under the collar," Wreck-Gar said.

"So tell me where the Autobots are," Starscream said, his voice dangerously soft.

"No Autobots here. Haven't seen any of those blighters in a fair while."

"Then there's no reason why I shouldn't blast you—"

"Hey, I'm picking up energy readings," Debris said.

Starscream glanced at him. "Where?"

"Um, in every direction."

Asteroids all around them suddenly split open like monstrous eggs, each one shattering to reveal a warship within. Too late, Starscream realized the nature of the trap—so many of those giant rocks were just cleverly constructed shells. And now each warship belched forth hundreds of smaller pirate marauders. Leading the armada was the monstrous catamaran flagship *Tidal Wave*, both of its hulls bristling with guns.

"Not these guys again," Thrust muttered. He figured they'd seen the last of the Star Seekers back at Junkion. Hunting the Autobots was tough enough without a gang of marauders getting in the way, especially when they were led by a relentless psychopath who hated all Cybertronians regardless of faction. And just to make matters worse—

"Hey," Ramjet said, "it's still got the Requiem Blaster."

He was right. The legendary weapon was plainly visible, attached to the underside of the hull like some gigantic growth.

Thanks a lot, Megatron, Starscream thought as he and his Seekers fired their thrusters.

Chapter Three

FROM HIS THRONELIKE COMMAND CHAIR ON THE BRIDGE of the *Nemesis*, Megatron watched the viewscreens as Starscream and his Seekers split up and took off at high speeds in different directions, racing away from the fleet that had just appeared. In his embarrassment at having misjudged the situation so completely, Soundwave leaped to state the obvious.

"Lord Megatron, those aren't Autobots, they're—"

"Star Seekers. Yes. Those marauders we encountered over Junkion." Megatron didn't even try to hide his disappointment. "Little more than scavengers." He watched on the screen as Starscream fled for his life, dodging shots from several pirate pursuers. Now *that* was a vid-clip he'd enjoy putting on repeat view.

"Lord Megatron, the Star Seekers are hailing us. Should I—"

"Go ahead, Soundwave. Put them onscreen and let's see what they have to say."

The *Tidal Wave*'s bridge came into view, revealing the spiny blue scowl of the pirate leader Thundertron, resplendent in blue and gold, a triumphant expression on his face. He was flanked by his tattoo-covered first mate Cannonball and the Decepticon traitor Axer; behind him, Sandstorm manned the ship's helm while Brimstone moved from station to station checking readings, making sure the pirate flotilla was prepared to do its duty.

"We have them exactly where we want them," Brimstone said as if the statement would further demoralize the Decepticons hearing it. Thundertron rose from his captain's chair and pointed his glowing energy cutlass at the screen.

"You Cybertronians are so predictable, 'Lord' Megatron."

The Decepticons on the bridge tensed for Megatron to react with rage. But instead he just leaned back, a sardonic expression on his face. "Permit me to guess. You must be Thundertron."

"You know cursed well who I am."

"Well, that doesn't mean I don't like to observe the formalities. Allow me to express my utmost admiration for your work, Captain. Piracy is a dangerous trade where only the most cunning survive. Your fleet is truly impressive. And your ship? Absolutely first-class."

"False compliments will get you nowhere, Megatron, for today I am the whirlwind and you are the dust doomed to be flung into eternity."

"How poetic," said Megatron. "I appreciate that in an adversary."

"Then you will appreciate this even more: Your destruction will complete my revenge on you Cybertronians. For I have annihilated the Autobots already, and now I shall send you to join them."

That was news to Megatron. Had the Star Seekers really destroyed the Autobots? It had to be some kind of bluff. But then again, they had the Requiem Blaster. They might have made short work of Optimus. Megatron gave Soundwave a sidelong glance, a signal to his subordinate to activate his short-range telepathic ability. Now Megatron would be able to give orders without the pirates realizing it. His first command: Scan that weapon.

"I'm sure we can come to terms," Megatron said. "You talk about revenge: I've caused a lot of damage in my time, but I can't remember doing anything to *you* specifically." He was stalling for time but figured there was no downside to trying. They needed more information on the Blaster. Besides, with every second that passed the fleeing Starscream continued to draw off some of the pirates, spreading out their formation.

"This isn't about you and me," Thundertron said. "This is about Cybertron itself."

"So you keep saying," said Megatron. "Can you be more specific?"

"We were your loyal subjects, curse you. We enjoyed the prosperity of your Golden Age. But you turned inward; your bridges collapsed, and you left us in the cold. My people died by the millions. This fleet is all that's left."

Megatron couldn't believe what he was hearing. "Your grievance against Cybertron is that our *empire collapsed*? This is ancient history."

"For us it is a vendetta that has lived to this day. Which is why you must die."

"I've got a better idea," Megatron said. "Join me."

"Do not jest with me, you puny bot."

"I'm not jesting. The Cybertronian empire is back, and it's under new management: mine. And rest assured, I don't intend to let the place go to seed the way my predecessors did. There's no reason you can't play a role in my Pax Megatronica. Pledge your fleet to me, and together we will restore Cybertron and all its works to their former glory."

"I've got a counteroffer," Thundertron replied.

"I'm all ears."

"If you surrender now, I shall grant you a quick and painless death."

No one talked like that to Megatron. But even now he

appeared more amused than anything else. "Most generous of you," he said. "Let me consider it for a moment."

"No. You'll answer right now," said Thundertron—just as Soundwave signaled to Megatron that his scan was complete. All the data on the Blaster appeared on a nearby screen, out of the pirates' view. It took Megatron less than a femto-second to absorb its meaning.

"I'm afraid I'm going to have to decline," he said.

Thundertron nodded as though that was the reply he'd been hoping for, then signaled to Cannonball. "Prepare to fire the Requiem Blaster," he said.

"At once," said Cannonball. Thundertron turned back to the viewscreen.

"Any last words, Megatron, before I end your pathetic existence?"

"I think not," Megatron replied. "Do your worst." As he said this, the *Nemesis* fired its engines, jetting off to the side and placing one of the larger asteroids between it and the *Tidal Wave*. But Thundertron just laughed.

"That won't save you," he said. "Weapons free!" he yelled.

The Requiem Blaster fired.

A massive surge of energy ripped out and smashed into the asteroid, which disintegrated in a sheet of white light. As the dust cleared, there was nothing left—and nothing now standing between the *Tidal Wave* and the *Nemesis*. The Requiem Blaster took aim once more.

"Lord Megatron, should we take evasive action—"

But Megatron cut Soundwave off with a wave of his hand. "Hold the current course and stand by to return fire."

"But Lord—"

"I said hold our current course and prepare to return fire!" Soundwave watched in horror as the legendary weapon charged up. Megatron stood beside him, his arms crossed and a look on his face that verged on boredom.

"Good-bye and good riddance," Thundertron intoned. *"Fire!"*

The Requiem Blaster was one of the most powerful weapons ever developed by the Primes, perhaps the ultimate weapon of mass destruction ever to see use. But in their zeal, the Star Seekers had overlooked its fatal flaw—it required almost a mythic amount of power to fire and even more energy to keep it from overheating. As soon as Megatron had reviewed the schematics, he knew that they'd get only one shot at full strength. After that—

A thin stream of plasma poured out of the Blaster, but it was a pale shadow of its predecessor. Energy peppered the hull of the *Nemesis* with a force that was little more than intense sunlight. And as it dissipated . . .

"My turn," Megatron said.

The *Nemesis* opened fire. As its long-range shots smashed into the *Tidal Wave*, Thundertron whirled to face Cannonball, who shrugged helplessly.

"The Blaster has overloaded most of our systems, Captain!"

"I'm going to overload yours if you don't fire it again!"

"Captain, we're lucky the ship's still running!"

Thundertron smashed his fist down in rage on his armrest. He should have known better than to think some ancient Cybertronian popgun would work.

"We don't need it!" he yelled. "We'll destroy these fools with our bare hands!"

The *Tidal Wave* jettisoned the Requiem Blaster, engaged its afterburners, and headed directly for the *Nemesis*. As the two ships charged each other, hundreds of Decepticons erupted from hatches on the *Nemesis* while the ship's guns unleashed a withering covering fire. The swarms of pirates still in pursuit of the Seekers turned to rejoin the main force, which came as a welcome relief for Starscream. Thundertron pressed a button on his command chair, which folded into the floor; hydraulic lifts carried him out of the bridge and up onto the ship's top deck as the *Tidal Wave* veered toward the *Nemesis*. Forget the Requiem Blaster. He'd just have to resort to close encounters. Which would make the inevitable victory all the sweeter . . .

AS THE BATTLE RAGED, WRECK-GAR WAS KEEPING BUSY. Now that Starscream had freed him from his restraints, he'd managed to get the podship running again. With everyone distracted, it was simple enough to plot a course back to the *Tidal Wave*; as the huge catamaran took fire from the *Nemesis*, Wreck-Gar flew his ship straight through one of the holes punched in the pirate hull. The crewmen in the vicinity were far too concerned with damage control to notice a single Junkion sneaking to the recently installed space bridge deep within the vessel. And when it came to tinkering with systems, Wreck-Gar was the best; it took him only a few moments to uncover the panels to the power relay systems and drain off just enough of the ship's batteries for a single use of the bridge.

"Easy peasy," Wreck-Gar said to himself as he punched in Junkion's coordinates. He'd almost managed to complete the sequence when the hard barrel of a laser pressed up against the back of his head.

"And what might you be doing?" said a voice.

Wreck-Gar turned to see Axer standing there, a self-satisfied expression on his gleaming blue face.

"I'm making myself scarce," Wreck-Gar replied. "You'd be wise to do the same before the Decepticons give these pirates what for."

"Not just yet." The *Tidal Wave* shook as it absorbed more damage. "I have some unfinished business here."

"With me? Now that's junk; I'm sure we can come to an arrangement—"

"I'm not going to shoot you—*if* you show me how to operate this bridge. Is it true that they're particularly sensitive to Cybertronian artifacts?"

"Well, yes, but—"

"Let's say I was looking for one artifact in particular."

Wreck-Gar didn't reply; instead, he suddenly closed the distance between them while pulling his shield and ax clear of their shoulder mountings. Axer switched his arm to a laser cannon, but Wreck-Gar had already spun past him like an orange steel tornado and slashed his ax through the two Star Seekers who had been creeping up from behind them. They fell to the ground, twitched, and lay still. Wreck-Gar turned back to Axer.

"You were saying?" he asked.

Axer recovered his poise and steadied himself as the ship changed heading suddenly. "If I was looking for a specific artifact, could you show me how to find it?"

Wreck-Gar mulled this over. "Depends on the artifact, guv'nor. One that hasn't been activated for years would be no joke to tease out."

"Say it gets used all the time."

"Then that shouldn't be a problem." Wreck-Gar suddenly realized what Axer was up to. "Wait a minute."

"Beginning to get the picture now?" Axer had to yell as the *Tidal Wave*'s backup drives suddenly came online, powering the ship through a particularly sharp turn. "Hurry up and dial more power into the system. We don't have much time."

"I'd say we're fresh out of it already," Wreck-Gar told him.

Chapter Four

COMBAT RAGED ACROSS THE SYSTEM. VEHICONS AND Star Seekers weaved in and out of the asteroid field, blazing away, chasing one another even as they tried to shake off pursuers. Fleet order on both sides had broken down rapidly, giving way to hundreds of furious dogfights. Clouds of debris testified to the losses both sides had suffered.

But at the center of the mayhem were the two flagships. The *Nemesis* and the *Tidal Wave* unleashed withering broadsides at each other, each ship pounding away at close range, maneuvering furiously to gain an advantage. Any shot that missed inevitably hit one of the myriad asteroids, sending pieces of rock flying in all directions, crushing friend and foe alike. It was the same for any lesser vehicle caught in the path of one of the behemoths. Both ships smashed everything in front of them into roadkill in their eagerness to get at each other.

"Show these cretins no quarter!" Megatron yelled. Soundwave said nothing; he was too busy piloting the *Nemesis*, doing his best to keep it out of the arc of the *Tidal Wave*'s larger guns. The catamaran was larger than the *Nemesis* and possessed significantly more firepower. But the *Nemesis* was more agile, particularly with Soundwave at the helm, coaxing maximum performance from the craft's computers. The *Tidal Wave* was clearly trying to get close enough to board the Decepticon warship, but Soundwave wasn't about to oblige it. Once the two ships locked together, anything could happen. And winning these kinds of duels was all about calculated risk.

"Cowards!" Thundertron yelled from his perch atop the *Tidal Wave*. "Are you afraid to face me, Megatron?"

"What do you call this?" Megatron said as the *Nemesis* spun past the *Tidal Wave*, riddling it with a series of energy blasts.

"I call it not taking things personally enough! Let's do this, Megatron! Right here, right now, and may the best bot win!"

"You're on," Megatron said. A hatch behind the *Nemesis*'s bridge opened, and he roared out in spaceship mode, his disklike shape a stark contrast to the metallic lion that now careered toward him. Thundertron's alt-mode was enough to strike fear in even the hardiest bots: A giant laser protruded from his mouth, and his claws rippled with energy. Blasts ripped past Megatron as he zigged and zagged toward Thundertron. In the background he caught a glimpse of Starscream and his jet troopers conducting strafing runs on the *Tidal Wave,* knocking out gun emplacements and engines. Dueling pirates and Decepticons were everywhere, the battle spilling onto one of the larger asteroids. Megatron landed on that rock, reverted back to his humanoid form, and let fly with his fusion cannon at Thundertron. But Thundertron was nothing if not fast; he dodged the fusillade and alighted nearby, switching out of his lion mode as he charged his foe, swinging his cutlass. Limbs and heads flew as he carved a path straight to the Decepticon leader, who beckoned him forward.

"So glad you could join me," Megatron said.

"This is the way it should be," Thundertron screamed. "You and me, face to face!"

"Do you have to yell so loud?"

"Prepare to have your spark extinguished!" Thundertron's cutlass met Megatron's fists. Sparks flew as the two clashed; lesser bots backed away in all directions to give the main contenders some space. Megatron's expression was one of contempt.

"You may have done well against low-rent stellar trash," he told Thundertron, "but now you're facing Cybertron's greatest gladiator. There's more than a few lessons for you to learn today. And I think we'll start with—"

But he broke off as Thundertron suddenly intensified the speed of his attack. His cutlass was a blur; Megatron was barely able to parry the ferocious onslaught. Thundertron drove him steadily backward, snarling the whole way.

"You Decepticons think you're the only warrior race. But there's a reason your empire collapsed. The universe *wrote you off*, Megatron, just like I'm going to do now." He drew his cutlass back for the killing blow. But as he did so, Megatron stepped past him, grabbed his one good leg, and flipped him onto his back. The Star Seeker leader tried to pull himself to his feet only to realize that Megatron hadn't let go—he was still holding on with one hand while he brought a fist down toward Thundertron's head. The pirate took the shock of the blow with his sword, then swung the weapon in a quick arc; Megatron released his grip, jumping back to save his own arm.

"So quick," said Thundertron. "So far from enough."

"So try this," Megatron said, catching the hilt of Thundertron's cutlass and sending it hurtling from his grasp. But Thundertron grabbed Megatron's wrists, pulling them apart, getting him in an armlock, and twisting.

"How does it feel, Megatron? To know that yours is the setting sun? Would you like to know where I'm going when I'm done here? I'll tell you: *Cybertron itself*. Your planet will pay for all its crimes. It's just too bad you won't be alive to hear the screams."

"Such an active imagination," said Megatron, surging power into his arms—pulling himself free, then whirling back on Thundertron and smashing him in the face so hard that pieces of metal flew. Thundertron staggered backward, and Megatron closed in.

"Let's get back to that lesson," he said.

He grabbed the pirate leader's body and hurled him headlong to the rocky surface, then moved in for the kill. But before Megatron could deliver a killing blow, Thundertron reverted to his lion mode and rolled clear of Megatron's mighty kick. Megatron swung his fusion cannon around for a clear shot, but Thundertron kept moving, staying one step ahead of Megatron's shots and then leaping in, shifting back to his robot form and smashing the side of Megatron's head with the side of his cutlass, sending the Decepticon leader reeling backward.

"What's the matter, Megatron? Not used to fighting a real warrior? That's because you're *weak*." Thundertron raised his glowing blade and swung it at Megatron.

"Don't make me laugh!" Megatron brought his arms up, fending off a dizzying rain of blows.

"What's that? I couldn't hear you over the sound of me beating you senseless!"

Megatron dropped to one knee as a particularly vicious swipe passed over his head. "I'll give you this, pirate: You've lasted longer than most of my opponents."

"But you'll last only a few more minutes," said Thundertron.

"GET US IN CLOSER!" CANNONBALL YELLED. THE *TIDAL WAVE* rocked as rocket and laser fire impacted all along its armored hull. The main viewscreen displayed hundreds of warrior robots darting in and out of the asteroid field. Cannonball cursed under his breath as Sandstorm wrestled the *Tidal Wave* around the *Nemesis*'s flak envelope. Cannonball had lost his leader's signal in the swarm of activity. On the one hand, he admired Thundertron's boundless courage. On the other, sometimes he wished the pirate king would place a greater premium on teamwork than on personal glory.

Brimstone was too busy to ponder such abstractions. His throat was almost hoarse as he barked ceaselessly into the shipwide com, directing damage control teams to where they would do the most good. Frankly, he wasn't sure how much more of this assault the *Tidal Wave* could take. With the Requiem Blaster no longer a factor, the flagships were just too evenly matched and he was acutely aware that the Star Seekers would be doomed without their ship. He turned to Cannonball.

"We can't take much more of this kind of punishment!"

"No surrender!" Cannonball shot back. "No retreat!"

"If we lose the ship—"

"We will *not* lose the ship!"

"We will if we don't withdraw!"

Cannonball took a hard look at the tactical display. The only way they could win was to get close enough to the *Nemesis* for a killing broadside. But the Decepticons were far too disciplined to let them attempt such a move. The only way to destroy them utterly would be to sacrifice the ship in a suicide play, a call that Cannonball was in no position to make. There was only one thing for him to do.

"Transfer reserve power to the communications array. I need to cut through this interference and talk to the captain! Now!"

*   *   *

Megatron sidestepped another one of Thundertron's wild swings with his cutlass.

"You can't beat me, Megatron!" the pirate leader snarled. "You can't win!"

Megatron sent Thundertron flying with a solid head butt. "You have delusions of grandeur, my soon to be disintegrated friend!"

But Thundertron changed back into his lion mode and sprinted at full speed, knocking Megatron off his feet. As Megatron struggled to get back off the ground, Thundertron's tail extended a few meters and wrapped itself around Megatron's neck, and then Thundertron's mighty front paws smashed him in the chest and pinned him to the ground. Megatron's vision was filled with teeth. The giant lion's mouth opened wide to engulf him, but at the last moment, the Decepticon leader managed to jam his forearm under the robot lion's throat, keeping the snapping jaws at bay. Thundertron pushed as hard as he could, straining to shear off the Decepticon's faceplate with his teeth. The two bots strained desperately for advantage, and then suddenly Thundertron heard a familiar ping in his ear. His personal communicator—and with it the panicked voice of his first mate, Cannonball.

"Captain! We can't keep up the fight against the *Nemesis*! There's too great a chance we'll lose the ship!" The words sent a chill down the pirate leader's spine. Without the *Tidal Wave* their operations would be fatally impaired. There would be no way to complete his life's mission of wiping the universe free of the Cybertronian scum he loathed. But to have Megatron at his mercy was an opportunity that might not come again for so long . . . Yet his ship was in peril . . . Even as Thundertron contemplated his options, Megatron twisted in his grip and got loose. Thundertron whirled to face him.

"Luck has favored you today, Megatron, but mark my

words, we will meet again!" And with that, he fired his thruster jets and sped off back toward the *Tidal Wave*. Megatron rose to his feet and carefully aimed his fusion cannon at the departing Star Seeker. As he pulled the trigger, Thundertron darted behind an asteroid, fouling his shot. All Megatron could do was laugh at the irony.

"Yes, pirate," he said, "lucky indeed." Shifting to spaceship mode, he surged back toward the duel between the flagships. The *Tidal Wave* was clearly getting the worse of it. Flame was spewing from multiple points on the pirate flagship's armor. For a moment, Megatron wondered if he should follow Thundertron and finish this. But then he realized that there was still enough gunnery on the *Tidal Wave* to keep lone bots like himself from getting too close. Plasma bolts tore past him; he ducked and weaved and then turned away altogether, speeding back to the *Nemesis*. As he switched back to bot form and stormed onto the bridge, Starscream and Soundwave saluted.

"Congratulations, lord," said Starscream. "You have won a glorious—"

"Shut up, idiot. I won nothing. The craven fool retreated."

"Their fleet is, too," said Soundwave.

He was right. The *Tidal Wave* was breaking off from the combat, turning away from the *Nemesis*, its swarms of Star Seekers adjusting course to follow while several of the lesser surviving warships moved to provide rearguard cover.

"Shall we pursue them?" Starscream asked.

"No," said Megatron. "Let them go."

"Let them *go*?" Starscream was incredulous.

"Would you care to pursue them single-handedly?" Starscream shook his head.

"My lord," Soundwave said, "the *Tidal Wave* is hailing us."

"Put them through," Megatron said with a wave of his hand. A battered Thundertron appeared on the screen. In the background Cannonball and Brimstone could be seen coordinating damage-control efforts.

"I'm surprised you've got the guts to show your face," said Megatron.

"You think you've defeated me?" Thundertron asked.

"You're the one who's running away, aren't you?"

"And I'm the one who'll be back to finish this! You haven't heard the last of the Star Seekers, Megatron! You can count on that!"

"Just tell me one thing, Thundertron."

"What?" the pirate leader snarled.

"You didn't *really* kill Optimus Prime, did you?"

Thundertron broke the connection. The *Tidal Wave* accelerated out of the system, and the Decepticons watched it go. Megatron glanced around the bridge. He knew what they were all thinking: that they should be pursuing the *Tidal Wave* and exterminating every last pirate aboard. He understood the feeling; it ran against every Decepticon instinct to let an opponent survive unscathed. But that was why they were *taking* orders and he was *giving* them. Sometimes a leader had to make tough decisions. Not only were the Star Seekers an annoying distraction, they were tough opponents, meaning that crushing them utterly would exact a heavy price with no strategic gain. No, thought Megatron, he'd shown those pirates who was master of the spaceways, and despite Thundertron's inflated rhetoric, he doubted he'd be seeing the pirates again anytime soon. And even though he hadn't destroyed Thundertron, he'd certainly shown him who was superior in hand-to-hand combat. He sat back in his chair on the bridge.

"What are our casualties?" he asked.

Starscream snapped to attention. "The Vehicons

suffered heavily; however, no essential personnel were lost. But the med-lab is full of wounded, sire."

"And the *Nemesis*?"

"Damaged, but nothing we can't fix while in transit."

"Good. I want to get back on the hunt as soon as possible."

Soundwave stepped forward and double-clicked on a schematic. "This was how they simulated the Autobot distress signal, my lord."

Megatron studied the readout. "I'm disappointed in you, Soundwave. They manipulated a *Junkion*'s circuitry? Which one of them was it?"

"The most annoying one of all," said Starscream. "Wreck-Gar. If it's any consolation, he seems to have perished in the battle."

"Good riddance," Megatron muttered.

"Actually, he's very much alive," a voice said. Megatron turned to see Axer entering the bridge, flanked by two of Starscream's jet troopers. The traitor bot looked as sly as ever. "You see, I helped him escape."

"You helped him *escape*?" Starscream was incredulous.

"Easy, Starscream," Megatron said. "Axer can't help it if he's not as . . . subtle as you or I. I have a feeling there's something he wants to tell us. Certainly he's not here to announce that not only is he a traitor but that he helped one of our enemies make his getaway. I'm sure he has something more than that to say. Something that might actually save his miserable hide. Please, Axer, do continue."

Axer had looked progressively more uncomfortable during this soliloquy. It was only with the greatest difficulty that he kept his voice steady. "I have brought you vital information, my lord. I helped Wreck-Gar escape in exchange for the knowledge of where the Autobots went."

A wash of relief flooded Megatron. "So Thundertron really *was* lying," he said.

"No doubt he claimed he'd destroyed them merely to throw you off guard," said Axer. "He was looking for them, just as you were, my lord. But he found you first."

"And how did the Junkion come across this information as a captive?"

"The space bridge inside the Star Seekers' flagship. Before Wreck-Gar used it to get back to his homeworld, he jury-rigged its systems to locate the Autobot Matrix of Leadership. As you know, the space bridges are very sensitive to Cybertronian artifacts."

"And the Matrix—the current position of the Ark—you have those coordinates?"

"I do, my lord."

He reeled them off to Soundwave, who fed them into a grid. A light in the middle of that grid began flashing.

"That's not far away," Starscream said. "Only a few days' warp."

Axer looked pleased. "You see, my lord? What is the fate of a single miserable Junkion against the acquisition of such priceless information?"

Megatron nodded. "Your logic is sound." And then without warning he let loose a mighty backhand, smashing Axer into a bulkhead. As Axer sprawled on the floor, Megatron turned to his guards. "Take him below. Soundwave, you know what to do."

"Yes, my lord."

"You don't have to torture me!" Axer yelled. "I already told you where they went!"

"Probably. But torture is the only way to be sure you aren't lying just to save your miserable parts."

As Axer was dragged off wailing, Megatron stared at the screens showing the receding asteroid field. So Thundertron had been dissembling after all. The librarian lived. All was not lost. He looked up as Starscream stepped in front of him.

"What are your orders, my lord?" Starscream asked.

"What do you think? Follow them, of course."

With that Megatron turned his back on his troops and stared out into the vast panorama of stars. *Soon, Optimus*, he thought to himself.

Soon . . .

Chapter Five

SOMETIMES OPTIMUS PRIME HAD DIFFICULTY BELIEVING just how far he'd come. As the lowly data clerk Orion Pax, he'd spent countless hours dreaming of making a difference. Now that he was commander of the Autobot forces and a Prime no less, the very future of the Autobots rested squarely on his broad shoulders. Every day he had to put it on the line. Every moment.

Moments like now . . .

Optimus streaked forward through the smoke, his sensors working overtime, the engines on his heavy cargo transport mode pushed up to full throttle. The enemy was somewhere nearby; the fact that he couldn't see him meant that staying mobile was the best defense. The problem was that such a defense could be anticipated—if the enemy could guess your vectors, he would aim just ahead of your path . . . but at the last moment, Optimus slammed on his brakes, letting the incoming rockets streak past him. Through the smoke and fire, he could make out the humanoid shape of his opponent. He gunned his motors and made a beeline for that shape, vectoring past more missiles as the enemy emptied his racks and drew two pulsating energy blades to deal with the onrushing Optimus—who waited until the very last second to shift into robotic form, letting his momentum carry him straight over the head of his adversary as those blades slashed past his wheels, mere inches beneath him. He landed with a resounding thud, quickly rolling to his left as his opponent fired one of the blades. It grazed Optimus, sending chips of red armor flying.

The next moment, the two combatants were too close for ranged weapons. Optimus activated his energy ax and sword as his combat mask slid into place; the creature sprang two more limbs, each one equipped with another glowing blade. Battle was joined in a whirl of light as Optimus's two weapons clashed with his opponent's three. He feinted a blow from his ax; as he expected, his opponent dedicated two spinning blades for defense, leaving the third to deal with what would surely be the inevitable counterthrust from Optimus's sword.

But the blow never came. Instead Optimus kicked out savagely, catching his enemy off balance and knocking him to the floor, exposing for the merest of moments the lightly armored underbelly. His opponent rolled, but it was too late: Optimus's blue fists were already driving deep into the downed robot's guts, clenching and tearing out a large chunk of machinery and wiring. Somehow the bot pulled itself to its feet, attempting to change to its spaceship form—and failed, falling flat onto its face, oil leaking from its perforated innards.

The computerized voice of Teletraan-1 chimed across the battlefield.

"Ending simulation."

Instantly, the smoke and fire disappeared to reveal the spartan walls of the Ark's training room. Optimus's mask slid back; he turned to see Jazz, Ratchet, Perceptor, and Bulkhead applauding.

"See? Less than three minutes against a level ten battle-droid," said Ratchet. "That's almost a record."

"Yeah, just don't forget who set it," Jazz said.

Jazz served as Autobot deputy commander and head of special operations. In a less official capacity, he was Optimus's closest friend. Ratchet was perhaps the finest medical officer Optimus had ever worked with, Perceptor was chief science officer, and the hulking Bulkhead was second to none with machinery. Optimus was grateful to have such comrades in arms; just seeing them together gave him a renewed sense of hope for their mission.

"Looks like all that practice is paying off," Ratchet said.

"I couldn't have done it better myself," Jazz added, clasping Optimus on the shoulder. "You've really come a long way."

"You didn't come down here to watch my workout," said Optimus. "What's the situation?"

Perceptor stepped forward.

"Remember when you asked me and Bulkhead to fine-tune the long-range sensors for Energon detection?" Not long after the battle at Junkion, Optimus had decided that they needed to investigate every possible angle to find the AllSpark, so he'd asked Perceptor to make a number of modifications to the ship's sensor package, dramatically increasing its sensitivity to Cybertronian artifacts. To the Autobots that had seemed like a sensible precaution. But there was more to it than that.

Optimus had a secret. He had no intention of telling anyone lest he fatally affect morale. But the truth of the matter was that the unthinkable was happening.

He was having grave doubts regarding the Matrix of Leadership.

Secure within his chest, it had been so reliable for so long, yet ever since they'd arrived in the Orion Arm, the Matrix had been acting more than a little peculiar. For one thing, it kept showing him blurry scenes from Cybertron's distant past that made no sense, though they filled him with foreboding: Cybertronians shuffling forward, their heads bowed, as though they were being driven somewhere.

As though they were slaves . . .

Yet disquieting as that was, it was the Matrix's present capabilities that were the real problem. As they moved across the galaxy, Optimus would have expected the AllSpark's signal to be growing stronger; instead, it had faded to the point of nonexistence. Had the Matrix somehow led him astray? Was it possible that it was no longer working? The question plagued Optimus night and day; the absence of a reliable guide made him feel very much alone. He wished he could talk with Alpha Trion, for the scribe's knowledge would have been most welcome. But Optimus knew deep down that his mentor had his own road to travel, that he would have to discern the secrets of the Matrix for himself.

And lately that had been getting ever harder.

"We've found something," said Bulkhead.

To say Sideswipe relished his duties as the pilot of the Ark would be to indulge in considerable understatement. Never before had he felt so needed. His duties on the Ark humbled him given how critical the ship was to the continued survival of the Autobots. If they weren't able to find the AllSpark, Cybertron was as good as gone, and the Ark was the only way the Autobots were going to pull it off. Some had said it was the most powerful ship ever built in the history of Cybertron. Unlike so many of the planet's machines, it had no alternative form—just the single function of transporting over three hundred Autobots and destroying any enemy ship that stood in its way. The Ark's four hyperaccelerators achieved superb performance at sublight speeds and in hyperspace. Though the Ark's main computer, Teletraan-1, wasn't sentient, there were days Sideswipe could have sworn it was developing its own preferences—its own personality, however subtle. But Perceptor had assured him that was impossible and had gone on to suggest that maybe Sideswipe should stick to driving and leave the deep thinking to the professionals.

That rankled Sideswipe. So what if his job was being a pilot? He knew deep in his circuits that none of these other scrap heaps could do a better job. It was no secret in the ranks that some Autobots thought they were better than others, a factor that Sideswipe chalked up to the lingering effects of Cybertron's once-rigid caste system. But back in those days all the Autobots were considered relatively unimportant. Now the business at hand was too important for distracting one-upmanship.

Sideswipe glanced up as Optimus, Jazz, Ratchet, Bulkhead, and Perceptor strode onto the bridge. He grinned insouciantly.

"Evening, gents, and thanks for flying Air Sideswipe."

Perceptor scowled as he strode past Sideswipe and activated the science station's viewscreen. "Enough with the jokes," he said. "We have serious business."

"Don't you always?"

"Show us what you found, Perceptor," Ratchet said with some irritation. It wasn't that he didn't have a sense of humor, but the bickering between Perceptor and Sideswipe got old. Especially when there were more pressing matters to discuss. A green world appeared on one of the screens, planetary rings encircling it, holographed statistics scrolling alongside. Perceptor cleared his throat.

"This is right in our path. And it wasn't on any of the charts or databases we have."

"That doesn't mean much," Jazz said. "Much of our exploration data is millions of years old. Maybe somebody just missed it. Or a database got corrupted."

"A possibility, but I'm more inclined to believe that somebody deleted it."

Now *that* was interesting. "Deleted it?" Jazz asked. "When?"

"Obviously not recently. The last update to the Universal Navigation Crystal was maybe two million back. The star charts weren't well maintained during the civil war. But if you scan back far enough—we're talking Golden Age or before—there *was* an update to this area of space, and I think that update might have been a deletion. I get the feeling somebody didn't want us to know that this system was here." He enlarged the magnification, filling the screen with a green hue.

"Tell us more about this planet," said Optimus.

"It's a ringed aquatic world, orbiting a K-class star." Perceptor enlarged the view of the planet on the main viewscreen. "Weather systems cover most of the planet, but as far as we can tell, it seems to be almost entirely water."

"A water world?" Optimus mulled this over. "That's a rare find."

More holographic displays blossomed. "Initial scans indicate robotic populations living under the water in highly concentrated areas."

"Submerged cities," Jazz breathed.

"Presumably. Unfortunately, the depth of the oceans precludes a more detailed analysis."

"What about the system itself?" Ratchet asked.

"The central star seems stable," Perceptor said. "They don't have the same problem as Velocitron, at any rate."

"What do you think, Optimus?" Jazz asked. "Has the Matrix told you anything?"

Optimus closed his optics, concentrated, and felt that fearful sense of being alone again. He had no idea why the Matrix would leave him in the lurch like this. But this was neither the time nor the place to bring it up.

"It's said nothing," he said, trying to sound more casual than he felt.

"Are you sure?" Perceptor asked.

"All I'm sure about is that the Matrix said we take this heading. And that's what we've been doing."

"For a long way," said Perceptor. "You would think that it would have given us a hint—"

"Since it hasn't said much, I can only assume we're still on the right track," Optimus interrupted, maybe a little too sharply. "Perhaps this planet isn't important to finding the AllSpark. But if nothing else it could be a place where we can make some repairs. And its inhabitants might have information that can help us in our quest." He turned to the Ark's pilot. "Sideswipe, put us in orbit."

"Aye, aye," said Sideswipe. As the ship vectored into a polar orbit, Optimus studied the screens and came to a decision.

"Get an away team together," he said.

"You got it," said Jazz.

Chapter Six

CYBERTRON

IACON WAS A BELEAGUERED CITY.

There were no besieging forces. No assault lines surrounding the capital. No attackers in sight. But that didn't mean that the city wasn't under constant pressure, for the Autobot Wreckers dominated the countryside. Only the largest Decepticon forces ventured beyond Iacon's massive walls without fear of ambush. Indeed, the war for Cybertron was proceeding as anyone familiar with the patterns of guerrilla warfare might have anticipated, with the stronger force dominating the cities all across the planet while the areas between those cities were subject to assault at any time by fast-moving Autobots who hit hard and then ran for their lives before the Decepticon commanders could concentrate their strength. Those commanders found the situation frustrating, to say the least.

Still, they couldn't complain about the big picture. Ever since Optimus Prime had left the planet, the Decepticons had had the upper hand. In the wake of the Ark's departure, the remaining Autobot strongholds had fallen quickly. For a while it looked like Iacon would be the site of the Autobots' final stand. But just as the Decepticons were bringing up their reserves for an all-out assault,

Ultra Magnus and the Wreckers had decided that it was better to live to fight another day; they'd withdrawn overnight, retreating across the north pole and into the border regions. From there, they scattered to embark upon the insurgency they'd conducted with such vigor ever since.

But that success had its limits. Guerrilla warfare is by definition the recourse of a force that dare not engage the other in open battle, and that was certainly true for the few Autobots left on the planet. Yet they held on nonetheless, a thorn in the Decepticons' side. The countryside had become a no-man's-land; the population had retreated back into the cities. This was partially because of the martial law the Decepticons had implemented: All able-bodied Cybertronians had to report to the factories to meet the production quotas. But the emptying of the countryside was also an inevitable response to the constant skirmishes, the unceasing Autobot attempts to cut the cities off from one another.

Iacon itself appeared to be relatively untouched by war. The skyline looked almost the same as it had the day the Ark thundered out into deep space. But the city had changed dramatically nonetheless. For one thing, there was hardly any activity visible on the streets and overpasses. They were all inside, counting their blessings and—like the majority of people in any civil war anywhere—hoping they could survive until it was all over.

But it was at night that the real difference became apparent, for Iacon was a mere shadow of its prewar glory. Where once it had had a panoply of shimmering lights to rival the Milky Way itself, now it was virtually dark. The power was rationed, diverted to military bases and those directly involved in the war effort. Yet there were those who whispered that there was more to it than that—that in the face of constant conflict, the Energon reserves of the Decepticons were running low—that they hadn't just cut power to all nonessential areas, they had been forced to deprive even some of their active fighting units of fuel. They were desperate, some said, and all their talk that they would shortly crush the Autobots once and for all was just that: talk. Bravado, plain and simple. Then again, maybe the bravado was simply that of those muttering in the shadows, speculating about the course of a war they dared not participate in, a conflict that when all was said and done they knew very little about. In war, the larger picture is so hard to see. All that was clear right now was that a once-great city lay dark.

But not entirely.

One building was an exception to the general blackout. One building blazed with lights and dwarfed all else. One single structure stood at the very center of Iacon: a massive tower that was the newest addition to Iacon's skyline, the only such improvement, if it could be called that, to be made during the entire war. The tower had been built by Autobot prisoners forced to work at gunpoint in slave-labor conditions. What had happened to those prisoners subsequently, no one knew. But they had constructed the largest building on Cybertron by far, twice the height of any other structure on the planet, stretching up and up until it seemed it might burst through the atmosphere and touch the heavens.

It was the Tower of Shockwave.

Cybertron's master, the Decepticon whom Megatron had personally delegated to be his lieutenant to rule as he saw fit until the day the *Nemesis* returned victorious, with the head of Optimus Prime a trophy in its hold. Until that time the only head that mattered was the one to whom the summit of the tower bore more than a passing resemblance. An enormous elongated oval within which burned a piercing light. That Shockwave would have ordered an edifice built in his own image surprised no one unfortunate enough to deal with him directly.

Right now Shockwave was contemplating the imminent arrival of the latest prisoner to be summoned to his presence. He sat in his personal suite, which encompassed the highest level of the tower. The walls were lined with screens, all of them carefully monitored by Shockwave's single glowing eye. Some of them showed the position of troops across the planetary surface, but most of them depicted subjects far closer to Shockwave's heart: calculations, data, experimental results. The screens without data had been left transparent, providing a breathtaking view of the city and all that lay beyond. One could see all the way to the pole from this room, but Shockwave couldn't have cared less. He wasn't interested in aesthetics. What interested him was the visitor he was about to welcome. He watched as the room's double doors slid open. Insecticon guards entered, trailed by a large hovercart that floated mere inches above the floor.

Strapped to that cart was Alpha Trion.

His arms were secured by reinforced clamps, and electromagnetic spikes driven into his circuitry at select points rendered him immobile below the waist. But the expression above his long white beard was one of utter calm as he met Shockwave's gaze with a serenity that belied his situation.

"Leave us," Shockwave said to his guards. They flitted back through the door they'd come through, which slid shut behind them. Shockwave turned back to Alpha Trion.

"So good of you to join me," he said.

Chapter Seven

RODIMUS, BUMBLEBEE, AND KUP STOOD OUTSIDE THE dropship listening to Prowl's lengthy mission briefing while Ironhide completed the craft's preflight checklist. Jazz had chosen Prowl as the away team leader because of his natural discretion and the investigative skills he had acquired as a police officer on Cybertron. Not only that, but Prowl's experience with the civilian high council back in prewar days spoke well for his ability to address the diplomatic niceties a first contact scenario might require. No doubt about it, Prowl was no-nonsense and business-oriented.

That was good, because the team he led was going to be a handful. Rodimus was quick on his feet; his ability to improvise had been useful in many a tight pinch. Like nearly every Autobot on the ship, he'd seen a few million years of combat. Yet his experience was nowhere near Kup's; though the old-timer was old and dented, his experience dealing with the unknown just might be the edge they needed. Rounding out the team was Bumblebee, who had proved himself to be a first-rate scout many times over.

"So this dropship has been fitted with aquatic capabilities should we need to do any underwater exploration . . ." Ironhide chuckled to himself as he eavesdropped on Prowl's somewhat tedious briefing. He wished he were going. It had been a while since he'd seen some action, and he hated to think that someone else might be seeing it first.

"Remember, I'll be in command of this operation," Prowl continued.

"Second time you've mentioned that," said Rodimus. "I think we get it." Bumblebee beeped in agreement.

"Just as long as you get this: If you have any doubts or questions, run them past me first. It's vital we obtain as much actionable intelligence as we can."

"Yeah, yeah, yeah . . ." Rodimus offered with a bored wave of his hand. Kup pulled out a cy-gar and slapped Rodimus on his orange-plated back.

"Easy, kiddo; knowledge is power, after all. Prowl knows what he's doing. Top-notch operator he is. Nobody better suited for a sneak-and-peak job like this one. Did I ever tell you about the time we tricked a herd of Igyaks into—"

"Only about a million times," Rodimus interrupted. He raised a finger in the air. "I have a question."

"Yes," Prowl said impatiently.

"Who gets to fly the ship down?"

"Nobody," said Ironhide. "Teletraan-1 will be handling the drop."

"Aw, where's the fun in that?" Rodimus said, disappointment written on his face. Ironhide handed the electronic checklist to Prowl and gave him a jaunty salute.

"All systems are green, good buddy."

"Thanks, Ironhide."

"Just remember that if you find any Deceptifools down there, leave a little bit for old Ironhide, all right?"

"Count on it," Kup answered with a thumbs-up.

"Okay," said Prowl. "If there are no more questions, let's get this show on the road." The team members climbed in through the hatch, found their seats, and strapped in.

"Away team ready for drop," said Prowl.

"Green light," Sideswipe said over the radio. The massive flight bay doors opened; the dropship rocketed out of the bay and soared in toward the planet.

"You're in the pipe," Sideswipe said. "Looking great."

"Passing the rings now," Prowl said. They were spectacular, stretching out in both directions. But there was something about them that was a little peculiar . . .

"*Look at that,*" Rodimus said, pointing at one of the rings that was . . . It didn't seem possible, but it was *blinking*, its colors alternating slowly from green to blue to purple and back again.

"Sideswipe," Prowl said as he put the feed through to the Ark's bridge, "you getting this?"

"Roger that," Sideswipe said.

Perceptor broke in. "Initial scans indicate they might be artificial."

"What do you mean artificial?" Kup asked.

"I mean somebody made them. Possibly to shield the planet's equatorial seas from cosmic rays and their radiations. The placement seems very specific indeed. I'm going to have Teletraan-1 slow your descent so we can take a better look."

"Copy that," Prowl said. The dropship fired its retros, rolling right to give the crew a closer view of the planet's ring system. The purple and blue hues reflecting off the rings made for a breathtaking symphony of light.

"This is really quite amazing," said Perceptor. "There seem to be particles in the rings capable of trapping the sun's rays. They might be serving as solar collectors."

Bumblebee chimed in with a series of high-frequency bleeps.

"Same here, kiddo. I don't like it." Kup chomped down hard on his cy-gar. "If it can collect energy, it might be able to discharge it. Would make a heck of a weapon."

Bumblebee sighed in agreement. Sometimes the deadliest things were also the most beautiful.

"Heavy weather brewing," Perceptor said. "We're going to try for insertion at the northern pole. It looks like the storms there are a bit milder."

"Roger that," Prowl said. The ship fired its boosters and descended in toward the clouds that covered the planet.

"This is going to be bumpy," Kup said.

He was right. Turbulence rocked the dropship as it dived through the thick storm clouds. For long moments, they couldn't see a thing; they even temporarily lost contact with the Ark.

"Switch to manual," Prowl said.

That, of course, was what Rodimus had been dying to do the whole time. He fired the thrusters, descending through the rest of the clouds. The churning waves of the planet's great northern ocean came into view. Rodimus had never seen so much water in his entire life. He doubted anybody else on the ship had, either.

"This place is way too wet," he muttered. Far below, the impossibly tall spires of a sprawling metropolis became visible through the fog. It was entirely surrounded by the ocean, a building-packed hub perhaps a mile across. Spiderweb-like transport tubes ran out to the tops of underwater facilities; one couldn't make out the details, but dark shapes loomed in the water. Rodimus couldn't help thinking that there was something familiar about some of the city's architecture. Magnification showed that many of the buildings were covered in runes and etchings.

"Hey, Kup," said Rodimus, "any of this look familiar to you?"

Kup frowned. "Seems like I've seen it before. But not sure where."

"Any idea what those runes mean?"

"Not a clue, sonny. I just know they have to be old."

"I thought *you* were old."

"Old enough not to find you funny."

That was when the Ark regained contact. "Glad you guys are okay," Perceptor said. "Want to give control back to Teletraan-1?"

"Not particularly," Rodimus said. He made a wide circle around the metropolis and then swooped in toward what had to be a landing pad of some kind: a raised platform that protruded out over the sea, evidently capable of handling heavy freight. There was no doubt that whoever lived there had to have a high level of interstellar traffic to justify a facility like that.

"Here we go," said Rodimus. The dropship reverberated as it touched down on the platform. Automatic clamps rose up and gently held the ship in place while long sinewy hoses reached out and connected the ship to clean and refuel it. There were no other ships on the jetway, and most of the nearby hangars looked empty. But the facilities sparkled as if they had been built yesterday.

"Up and at 'em," Prowl said. He opened the rear cargo hatch. The away team trooped out and took in the scene.

"Okay, let me be the first to say that this is pretty creepy," Rodimus said. "Where is everybody?"

"Stay alert," Prowl ordered.

"You don't have to tell me twice," Kup said as he started a long-range scan.

"It's like a ghost town," said Rodimus.

"Enough with the back chatter," Prowl said. "Bumblebee, give us a quick recon. Stay in com range and alert us the moment you find anything." Bumblebee gave a hearty salute, shifted into his scout-vehicle mode, and took off at a high speed, roaring away into the city itself. As his feed merged with that from Kup's scan, Prowl sent the data back to the Ark.

"Perceptor," he said, "you getting all this?"

"Copy that. The Ark's adjusting for the interference; we've got the uplink locked in. Looks like extensive Energon-mining facilities on the seabed around you."

"What about these structures? The architecture looks . . . well, almost Cybertronian."

"I'm running the images through Teletraan-1. Hopefully we'll have some more data within the hour."

"I've got this funny feeling we're being watched," Rodimus said as he took a closer look at an engraving on a nearby wall. It showed giant fish with huge teeth battling one another.

"Remind me not to go swimming," said Kup.

As THE AUTOBOTS CONTINUED THEIR RECON, THE BEING known as the Curator watched with satisfaction from his command center. In the time that had elapsed since he'd first detected the approaching Ark, he had been working quickly to get used to his new form. It was far uglier and much less mobile than what he was used to, but it was a necessary step. He flexed his chubby fingers, then touched his new face. At least the new parts all functioned properly. He had designed this body to be as close to perfect as possible. It was so primitive that he wanted to retch, but it was a key part of the charade he was about to play. The Curator was disappointed that so few of the Autobots had elected to come down to the planet initially, but his calculations indicated that more would follow. They just needed to be given a little space. The Curator knew that some things couldn't be rushed. Some things just needed patience.

Problem was, his masters had none.

The voices from beyond filled the Curator with terror and dread, but he knew he was singularly fortunate to serve them. There was no greater honor than being the instrument of their will. And to refuse—to dissemble, to disobey in even the slightest way—well, he had heard the stories and had no intention of being a participant in any of them. So now he rose heavily (this new form was most ungainly) and made his way to the chamber of supplication, activating the ancient communication array. Even after millions of years, it still functioned without problems. The receivers of his message were a vast distance away; sometimes it took up to several hours to establish the link fully. But this time they must have been waiting for him, for they responded to his call within moments. A swirling darkness filled the screen.

"Speak, Curator." The voice was cold, dispassionate.

The Curator steeled himself. "Masters, the Autobots have arrived."

"Go on," the voice said in a tone of barely restrained excitement.

"They have landed at the Energon production facility near the north pole," said the Curator. "We manipulated the weather to increase the likelihood that they would touch down there. They just dispatched one of their scouts on reconnaissance. We are shadowing their every move."

"Excellent," said another of the voices. "Our calculations show their scans have less than a 3 percent chance of detecting the southern continent."

"I make that less than 2 percent," the Curator said.

"You dare contradict us?"

"With respect, my data is more immediate. Hydratron City and the machinery below it will remain cloaked. All security protocols are holding."

"Make sure that continues," said the first voice.

"Is there a Prime with them?" the second asked.

"It is more than 80 percent likely," the Curator replied. "This many Autobots, so long a distance from their home—they would surely not venture so far without the leadership of a Prime. But we shall know more once I've made contact."

"Be careful, Curator. If a Prime is not involved, then we reap but small rewards from this situation. Several hundred lost Autobots and one wayward ship barely justifies the cost of this communications link. But if a Prime *is* involved—well, should he become aware of your subterfuge, you will have to assume a more aggressive posture. Bringing a Prime into the equation too soon could contaminate the original algorithms."

"I am prepared for all eventualities, masters. There are certain accounts that must be settled."

"You speak truth. We have waited a very long time for this and placed great faith in you."

"*Great* faith," said the second voice, though it sounded far more threat than praise. "Keep us apprised of your progress."

"Our goal is within our grasp," the Curator said, but the screen had already gone blank. For a long moment he stared at it, breathing heavily. Then he pulled himself to his feet and retreated from the chamber of supplication. It seemed like it had been eons since the last time they had revealed their faces to him. Perhaps it had been. He had placed himself in cryogenic hibernation while the planet's installations ran automatically and had configured the deep-space sensors so that only the most extraordinary contingencies would justify his waking. The detection of the Autobot ship was just such a contingency. Nor was it an accident. He had set up the mechanisms that would lure the ship to him, and he had succeeded. A few more correct moves and the ultimate prize would be his.

Venturing back into his laboratory, he looked around. All was ready. Every instrument had been reconfigured to his new body's specifications to maximize his ability to conduct the experiments that would be taking place here very soon. He flexed his new hand again and for the first time began to feel at ease with the new fingers. If he had known how to smile with his new face, he would have. Right now the best he could manage was a rather shaky grin. It was enough, though. He pressed a button; there was a rumbling in the floor as a hatch irised open. A pedestal rose slowly from within.

Atop it was a glowing device that looked exactly like the Matrix of Leadership.

Chapter Eight

CYBERTRON

THERE'S A STORM BREWING OVER CYBERTRON TONIGHT. Acid rain drenches the streets of Iacon. Lightning flares so brightly that it might as well be day. Thunder crashes so loudly that you might think Unicron himself had returned.

But in the Tower of Shockwave you wouldn't hear a thing. The walls are too thick, the armor too strong. And your peril is probably too great. You wouldn't hear a thing in the Tower of Shockwave much as you might wish to. Chances are that all you're wishing for is for it to all be over. Because very few who enter his building are ever seen again.

A sadist would have enjoyed such a reputation. But Shockwave was no sadist. He was something far worse. To him the pain of others was just one more data point— one more method of eliciting information or simply one more by-product of whatever process the subject was undergoing. And it was usually inevitable.

But sometimes it was best to start off with conversation.

"I've been looking forward to this," Shockwave said.

Alpha Trion gazed up from his shackles. "I understand that," he replied calmly.

"You are a traitor."

"So you have said. May I ask to what?"

"To this planet. To your kind."

Alpha Trion smiled sadly. "My kind is long gone."

"I have my doubts about that."

"You are entitled to them."

Shockwave frowned. "Solus Prime was destroyed by the Fallen. But I have no evidence that any of the other Primes met with a similar fate."

"I will clarify," Alpha Trion told him. "When I said my brethren were gone, I did not mean to assert that all of them were *dead*. They simply left. In all directions, I might add. Vector Prime retreated to an enclave of his own devising. I suspect the Fallen and Liege Maximo are in faraway prisons. Or perhaps they went the way of Solus Prime. It would be fitting. But I do not know for certain."

"You know more than you're telling."

"So tell me what you want to know."

"Which one of the Thirteen did you last speak to?"

"Alchemist Prime. Just before he left in search of Liege Maximo."

"And what did he say?" Shockwave asked eagerly. "What did he confide in you?"

"He showed no interest in anything save his quarry."

"What was he armed with?"

"His own knowledge. Believe me, that was usually enough."

"What I would give for that knowledge," said Shockwave.

Alpha Trion laughed. "It would do you no good."

"Why is that?"

"Because you have no moral compass. You are a sociopath, Shockwave. It sickens me that Cybertron has passed into your custody."

Shockwave looked amused. "Now we see your true colors, Alpha Trion. You sit in your archives and pretend that you are above all this, yet you cannot hide your contempt for me."

"Can it really be said I ever tried?"

"You are pathetic. You and your fellow Primes could have ruled the cosmos, yet you fell out over trivialities."

Alpha Trion shook his head. "What divided us was anything but trivial."

"When we Decepticons gain such power, we will not make the same mistakes."

"You're already making them."

"Clarify that," Shockwave said.

"Megatron entrusted you to rule this planet, yet no sooner had he left than you began plotting to make yourself his master."

Shockwave looked genuinely affronted. "I am his loyal servant."

"Did Megatron not give you orders I was to be left alone until his return?"

"I could no longer ignore the aid and comfort you have been furnishing to the Autobot cause. Why, just last week the Wreckers destroyed another of my laboratories."

"I have had no contact with the Wreckers since they left Iacon."

"But you *have* had contact with Optimus Prime."

Alpha Trion said nothing.

Shockwave stepped closer. "Oh, don't think I'm not aware you sent a courier to him. As well as a cargo. Fragments of the Blades of Time. Do you deny it?"

"I merely acted as I had to."

"And so I had to take you into custody."

"But you mean to go further than that," Alpha Trion said.

"Because science demands it."

"What you call science is really just a craving to play god."

"You *were* a god once, Alpha Trion. The Thirteen together acted as such. And then you threw it away."

"And if you have any sense, you will leave it where it fell."

"Now, that is something I can never do," Shockwave said. He pressed a button. There was a whirring noise, and the floor began to descend. The room was one large elevator; Iacon's skyline quickly slid from view. But the interior walls of each level were transparent, and through them Alpha Trion could see sights he would have preferred not to see. In one room an Autobot hung from the ceiling while a clawed machine pulled him apart. In another an Autobot was slowly dissolving as acid dripped over him. And in still another, a bot that looked half Autobot and half Decepticon was battering its head against the wall in a way that suggested it was anything but sane. The sights got even worse as the room reached the bottom of the tower and dropped down through subterranean levels.

"You are a monster," Alpha Trion said.

"I passed beyond labels a long time ago," said Shockwave. "All that interests me now is results. You contain within you the knowledge of the ancients. It is churlish to deny that power to we who must dwell in the desolation of today." The last of the levels was left behind as the elevator accelerated seamlessly toward supersonic speeds. They were in a maglev chute now, plunging ever farther downward.

"I know where you are taking me," said Alpha Trion.

"I would expect nothing less."

"You should not do this."

"And why is that?"

"Because you are meddling with forces far beyond your understanding."

"Do not presume to set limits on my understanding," Shockwave replied.

After several more minutes, the room halted. The doors opened onto a huge underground chamber whose ceiling vaulted upward like a cathedral. The far wall was covered with dials and instruments arranged around a glowing orb that seemed to grow out of the wall itself. If it had been possible for Shockwave to smile, he would have.

"Welcome to Vector Sigma," he said.

Chapter Nine

MEGATRON STORMED ONTO THE BRIDGE OF THE *NEMESIS* and dismissed the Decepticon guards with a wave of his hand. Even though his lust for battle had been somewhat satiated in the clash with the pirates, it couldn't come close to that rush he got when crushing Autobots. He had bested Thundertron, but he would have far preferred it to be Optimus Prime.

Starscream and Soundwave bowed as he approached. Usually Megatron couldn't get enough of their deference, but for some reason today it only filled him with more rage.

"This had better be good," he said.

"Oh, it is, my master," said Soundwave, bowing even lower. "Very good indeed."

"Rise and speak."

Soundwave stepped forward.

"Lord Megatron, I have completed my interrogation of the traitor Axer and have obtained the precise location of the Autobots. Would you like to see the playback of the questioning?" He said it with enough unrestrained relish that Megatron waved his hand wearily in assent. Sometimes you had to indulge your subordinates.

"Certainly. Let's see it." Soundwave switched the video feed over to the holding cells where Axer was secured, spread-eagled on a giant X-shaped rack. His screams filled the speakers.

"Please! I've already told you everything! You don't have to do this!" Soundwave came into the picture holding a plasma torch and a pair of tongs. Axer's eyes went wide.

"What are you going to do? Please! Have mercy!"

But mercy wasn't on the menu. Soundwave's chest opened to reveal one of his more diabolical mini-cons: Ravage, who crawled up Axer's leg until he reached Axer's chest cavity, whereupon he proceeded to rip it open and systematically pull out components one by one. When Axer's screams grew loud enough to drown out Soundwave's questions, Megatron decided that it was time to move things along. There was no doubt in his mind that Soundwave could watch this video over and over again—and that he probably already had.

"Enough of this," Megatron said. "What did you learn from the traitor?"

Soundwave switched off the vid and replaced it with a map of the local sector of space. "The coordinates he gave us were accurate. And now that we're only a day's journey out, we're doing a more precise scan of—"

"*Nothing*," said Megatron, staring at the map. "There's nothing there. What kind of trickery is this?"

"No trickery, my lord. What you're seeing are our own data archives, which do indeed show empty space. But after careful personal scrutiny of the quadrant via long-range optics, I found this." Soundwave manipulated the screen to bring something into focus. "See, master? This planet isn't on any of our charts, but there it is anyway." Megatron took a closer look; it was certainly out of the way and a fine place to hide if one was interested in keeping a low profile.

"And the Autobots?" he asked.

"I took the liberty of having Skywarp perform an advanced recon. He was able to use his teleportation abilities to get just close enough to obtain detailed imagery."

There was a burst of static, and then the Autobot Ark appeared, sunlight glinting off its hull as it orbited the ringed green world. A round of applause broke out on the bridge as the Decepticons cheered.

"Now that's a welcome sight," said Megatron.

Soundwave nodded. "This time we know for certain exactly where they are—*and* we maintain the element of complete surprise."

"Do we know what they're doing there?"

Starscream broke in. He'd been chafing impatiently while Soundwave hogged all the glory, but now he'd had enough. "Knowing Optimus Prime as we do, we can assume that he is still following the guidance of the Matrix of Leadership. Presumably it guided them to the planet for some reason. The most reasonable hypothesis is that there is an artifact nearby or another clue to the location of the AllSpark—or the AllSpark itself. And the planet is inhabited."

"By what?" Megatron asked.

"Readings indicate some kind of robot life-form."

"Do they seem like a threat?"

Soundwave shoved past Starscream. "No, my lord, they do not. Skywarp was not able to detect any surface weapon systems, though that doesn't mean there aren't any. There are certainly no active offensive capabilities, though. On the other hand, Skywarp *was* able to determine they have an active Energon production in operation."

"Energon," Megatron said with the tone of someone licking his lips.

"Giant stores of it," Starscream said.

"All ripe for the taking," added Soundwave.

Megatron smiled. "The two of you have done well. Very well indeed. Send Skywarp back to keep an eye on the situation. I want to know every move the Autobots make.

Tell him that he is to do nothing aggressive. He should not reveal himself; his job is strictly intelligence gathering."

"Yes, lord," said Starscream. He turned to go, but Soundwave stood his ground.

"Yes?" Megatron asked impatiently. "What is it?"

"Just one more question, my lord. Now that we have extracted the information from Axer, what do you want us to do with him?"

"You know as well as I do: There is no mercy for traitors. Find some use for him while I think up a suitable death."

"As you command." Soundwave strode off, leaving Megatron to stare at the imagery of the Ark and marvel at his luck. But then he shook his head. *Luck?* He was a military genius and had surrounded himself with the finest soldiers ever assembled. Deep in his heart he'd always known that luck simply wasn't a factor—nor would there be any for the librarian on the day when he was caught.

And now that day was finally here.

Chapter Ten

"I THOUGHT THIS PLANET WAS TEEMING WITH LIFE," Rodimus said.

"That's what the Ark said." Prowl double-checked his own scans of the area.

"Well, where are they exactly?"

Prowl was silent. Kup could tell that Rodimus was grating on the away-team leader's nerves. He chuckled to himself at the way these youngsters ran hot and cold.

Perceptor broke in. "To repeat, the scans showed considerable life under the water. If you're not finding anything in that city—"

There was a burst of static as storm activity cut off the link to the Ark.

"Great," Kup said.

"Hey," said Rodimus, "here comes Bumblebee. Let's see if he's found anything."

Bumblebee sped up the ramp back to his comrades and shifted back into his bipedal form, making a series of bleeps, blips, and high-pitched whines.

"Slow down, son," Kup said. Bumblebee did so, calming down and giving them a more coherent report. The city seemed empty. He hadn't seen anybody, nor had anyone made themselves known to him. Lights were on, and walkways were running; all the elements of a living, breathing metropolis were in place. All that was missing was the population. Curiously, the city had more than its share of surveillance cameras, all of which seemed to be fully operational.

"Told you," said Rodimus. "We're being watched."

"Maybe we should go to the northern pole when the storms die down," Kup said.

"I say we wait here," Prowl said.

"What kind of plan is that?" Rodimus asked.

"Well, you're right; we're obviously being studied. Sooner or later they're going to come to us."

"Probably sooner," Kup said. He pointed at water churning offshore. An enormous fin broke the surface and headed toward them.

"Everybody stay calm," Prowl said. Kup popped his antique wrist cannons, and Rodimus unfolded his rocket bow. Three torpedo arrows locked into place with a resounding clack. Bumblebee's fists collapsed back into his wrists to expose his twin particle decelerators.

"You call that staying calm?" Prowl asked.

Kup laughed. "I call it being prepared, youngster!"

As the fin reached shallow water, more of the creature beneath it became visible: a silver fish-bot, several meters long. The Autobots were even more surprised when that creature changed into a humanoid-shaped robot, stepping onto the lower platform and making the universal greeting: *I come in peace.*

"Hello," Prowl said to the robot. It was short and was covered in blue-white metallic scales, each one highlighted with a slight golden tint. The eyes were bright green. There was a burst of static, and then its translators kicked in.

"Hello, hello, hello. So very glad to meet you. So wonderful to have visitors, so very, very wonderful indeed!" It advanced toward them.

"Stop right there!" Prowl barked.

"No need for weapons!" the bot said as it came to a halt

in front of them. "I come in peace and all that!" The three Autobots lowered their weapons, and the robot smiled. "Splendid, splendid, splendid. Allow me to introduce myself; I am the Curator, and I am charged with overseeing this planet. Might I have the honor of your names?"

"I am Prowl, and this is my team: Bumblebee, Rodimus, and Kup. We are from the planet Cybertron."

"Oh, very good. Very good. We've been waiting a long time for visitors from Cybertron."

"Oh, really? You've heard of Cybertron?" Prowl asked.

"Why, yes. Yes, of course. Hasn't everybody?"

"Are you one of the lost colony worlds?"

"No, we are just a world. Tell me, are you Autobot or Decepticon?"

"Autobot," Rodimus said with pride.

"Yes, indeed. I can see it now. Right there on your chest the insignia is. It has been a very, very long time since I've seen that. I am so very glad you are here."

"Sure, of course you are." Rodimus leaned in close to Kup. "Are you buying this guy?"

"Just keep your optics peeled and your audio receptors open, sonny. I got a feeling this fella's got all kinds of things to say. We'd do well to listen."

"Where are the rest of your people, Curator?" Prowl asked.

"Out to sea. Since we are amphibious, there are times when we live solely under the oceans. You might think of us as schools of fish, no? Right now many of us have migrated to the underwater facilities in the southern hemisphere. All of our cities have a high degree of automation. This outpost alerted us to your landing, and I was dispatched to see to your needs."

"And who is 'us' exactly?" Rodimus asked.

"Why, the citizens of Aquatron of course. Let me show you around."

*   *   *

OPTIMUS FELT IT AGAIN AS RATCHET RAN A SYSTEMS diagnostic: that terrible isolation. Optimus recalled the times he had traveled halfway across Cybertron delivering messages to members of the civilian council. He had felt alone then, too, but free on the open roads of Cybertron. Alive and in control of his own destiny.

Yet right now he felt an acute sense of dread bound up in the feeling that somehow, somewhere along the line he had lost his independence by becoming so reliant on the Matrix of Leadership. He wondered if, by its silence, the Matrix was trying to tell him something. Or maybe the problem was within him—he was somehow resisting the awesome responsibilities that had been thrust upon him. After all, he had never asked to be Prime. He had assumed the mantle out of duty and respect for the council. Never in his wildest thoughts as a data clerk had Orion Pax seen himself as a leader or even a warrior. Those titles had been handed to him, along with the power of the Matrix. What was the Matrix trying to show him now? Why wasn't it just telling him what he needed to do? Was it telling him that maybe his time as Autobot leader was over?

"Well, there don't seem to be any problems with your systems," Ratchet said as the tests ended. "In fact, you're operating at peak efficiency."

"I see. Good."

"Is there any reason why you wanted me to run these tests, Optimus?"

"I just felt I needed a checkup before going down to the planet. So you're sure there were no anomalies?"

"No particular reason why you're concerned?" asked Ratchet.

"Not at all."

"Optimus, if you don't mind me saying, you are a

terrible liar. If you tell me what's really wrong, I might be able to help you. A patient who doesn't share all his information with his doctor risks a faulty diagnosis."

Optimus shrugged. There was no hiding from Ratchet. "I think the Matrix of Leadership is malfunctioning," he said.

Ratchet considered this. "Malfunctioning? How?"

"I'm not sure. I was hoping that maybe my own systems were the problem, but now you're telling me they're fine."

"I am. You've got a clean bill of health."

"Are you sure? When was the last time you checked your diagnostic equipment?"

"I can assure you that my equipment is in top working order," Ratchet said. He hesitated, then continued: "Tell me more about what's going on with the Matrix."

"It's gone almost silent."

"Hmm." Worry flickered across Ratchet's face, only to subside beneath his professional demeanor. "Anything else?"

"I've been having these strange feelings. They're tough to describe."

"Try."

"It's sort of like . . . Well, one moment I'm free, and the next moment I'm in a cage."

Ratchet frowned. "You feel like somebody is putting you in a cage?"

"Not exactly. It's as though I'm constrained by something I can't put my finger on. Almost like I've had this feeling before but I can't quite remember all the circumstances."

"Hmmm." Ratchet looked concerned.

"It goes without saying I need you to keep this between us."

"You know you can rely on me for complete confidentiality, Optimus. It wouldn't do for this to get out."

Suddenly, the med-lab door slid open and Jazz rushed in.

"Optimus! I've been looking all over for you. Didn't you hear us calling?"

"Oops," said Ratchet. "I must have accidently shut down the lab's com-system. Blame me. Sorry."

"What's going on, Jazz?" Optimus asked.

"We just got the away team's report."

"And?"

"It's complicated."

OPTIMUS AND JAZZ JOINED PERCEPTOR BACK ON THE Ark's bridge. Prowl's silver face glared at them from the main viewscreen.

"Report," Optimus said as he took his position on the bridge.

"We've made contact with an administrator-leader type who calls himself the Curator," Prowl said. "He says the name of the planet is Aquatron." Images of the Curator appeared on the screen. Perceptor stepped in and took over the briefing.

"As you can see from his construction, this 'Curator' is a highly advanced form of robotic life geared toward survival on an aquatic world. He is capable of taking on both fish and humanoid form. It's very possible that these machines evolved amphibious shapes in order to gain access to all of this planet's resources. It would be fascinating to run a study that allowed us to cross-compare our own evolution with theirs. There are several ramifications that I think might be particularly—"

"Get to the point," Optimus said impatiently.

"I'm just saying it's amazing to think that they paralleled our own development in so many ways, yet they aren't one of the colony worlds. Robotic life that evolved on its own."

"Or it *is* a colony world and they've forgotten," said Jazz.

"There were stories that Primus created other forms of life," Optimus said. "This planet might prove that hypothesis."

"Like I said, I'd love to do some tests," Perceptor said. "At one point in time, these robots might have dwelled solely on land, but as their technology advanced and they found themselves spending more time underwater, their form adapted to those efforts. Possibly they didn't start on this planet but migrated here instead. Take a look at this video footage the Curator provided the away team with—some of the local fauna."

The screens began to show more images. "What you're looking at here is what they call a school of Cleaners," Perceptor explained. "These groups can reach into the thousands and function as microsocieties. They deal with garbage buildups along the underwater pumps; their bodies ingest it, then reprocess the waste as solvents to help clean other systems. However, there are larger units that service facilities like these." A series of pictures of seabed mining units followed.

"The Curator claims their entire society is dedicated to the production and long-term storage of Energon," Perceptor continued. "As you can see from these projections, they've been steadily producing a 20 percent surplus every refinement cycle. There's enough Energon here to last several thousand years."

"Wow," said Jazz.

"It gets even more intriguing," Perceptor said as Teletraan-1 displayed a comprehensive breakdown of what appeared to be an Energon cube. "Thanks to samples the Curator gave the away team, I've had a chance to analyze the Energon they produce. It's a highly oxygenated mixture; no doubt that's because of their environment, but that makes it highly compatible with what we use. In fact, it might even be more efficient."

"Interesting," Jazz said.

"And they've said they're willing to sell it to us. Cheaply, too. The entity who calls himself the Curator wants to meet you, Optimus. He says it's very important that he speak with you face to face."

"Does he now? Did he give any more information than that?"

"No," Prowl said. "But he did make it clear that he has some knowledge of Cybertron and our conflict with the Decepticons."

"How would he know about that?" Jazz asked skeptically. "Is there any sign they've ever been in contact with the Decepticons?"

"None," Prowl replied.

"According to the Curator," Perceptor said, "there used to be a fairly active space bridge in the planet's orbit that they used to sell their Energon to a variety of races. But he hasn't dealt with an actual Cybertronian for thousands of years."

Optimus punched up Bumblebee's reconnaissance photos of the city. Optimus thought some of the Aquatronian architecture looked vaguely familiar. He could have sworn he'd seen such patterns and designs on Cybertron, but for the life of him he could not remember where. He found that fact unsettling.

"What happened to the bridge?" Jazz asked.

Prowl broke in. "The Curator said that when it stopped functioning a few million years ago, they broke down what was left and used its components to build the ring system."

"Which seems plausible enough," said Perceptor. "Optimus, I would like to take samples of their Energon and see what its exact effect is on Autobots. All the simulations indicate it ought to be compatible. I would like permission to conduct the tests on myself."

"Request denied, Perceptor. Let's learn more about this planet first."

"As you wish, Commander." Perceptor never called Optimus by his rank unless he was irritated. But at this point, Optimus felt that a peeved Perceptor was a small price to pay given the risks. Since the Matrix still wasn't offering any kind of guidance, he turned to his oldest friend, Jazz, and took him aside to talk privately.

"What does your gut tell you, Jazz?"

"My gut says we go down there but we go in force."

"Agreed," but even as he said this, Optimus grimaced as though he'd been struck. The Matrix flared to life, then went dark again.

"Optimus?" Jazz looked concerned. "What is it?"

"I don't know. I just felt—the Matrix—it was almost like a cry for help."

"From whom?"

"I don't know. Somewhere far away yet very dear to me. Almost as though our home is in grave danger."

"Cybertron," Jazz whispered.

"Let's hope not," Optimus said, but he was badly shaken. And he hated to think of what was really happening back on the world from which he'd traveled so far.

Especially when the one they were orbiting seemed to hold so many secrets.

Chapter Eleven

CYBERTRON

THE ORB IN THE CENTER OF THE FAR WALL IS LIKE nothing you've ever seen. Whirling blades of light, an incandescence as bright as the sun itself—so intense that you'd better adjust your optics if you wish to preserve them. Officially, no one knows this orb exists.

In practice, matters are a little more complicated.

"So you found it," Alpha Trion said.

"So I did," Shockwave replied. He patted Alpha Trion's head in the most patronizing manner possible. "You thought to spread rumors that Vector Sigma was somewhere in the Sonic Canyons."

"I thought to spread rumors that Vector Sigma didn't *exist*," Alpha Trion told him.

"And nearly everybody believed you that it was just one more legend. But to a logical mind like mine, legends are a *code*. It's simply a matter of deciphering them. Even those who thought they were in the know weren't strictly correct. Some said Vector Sigma was beneath Iacon, but we are so far down in the planetary core, we're actually closer to Kaon."

"So what do you intend to do now?"

"Activate it, of course."

"Cleverness without wisdom is mere stupidity," Alpha

Trion said. "You cannot activate Vector Sigma unless you have the—"

"Key? The one that Optimus Prime carries without knowing it? How cunning you must think you've been. Your handpicked hero, spoon-fed everything, given every tool he might need—even the ones he doesn't know about."

"It's not just a matter of giving Optimus the things he needs; it's about keeping them away from you."

"And that you have surely done. Optimus is on the other side of the galaxy, so how could I possibly reach him?"

There was something in Shockwave's tone that made Alpha Trion nervous.

"You cannot," he said. "It is impossible."

"Unless I could find a way to reactivate the space bridge."

"Are you saying you've done so?"

"I'm working on it."

Alpha Trion relaxed. "Work all you like; it's impossible unless—"

"Unless I had access to Vector Sigma," Shockwave said. "Exactly. And so you think me boxed in. I cannot control the space bridge without access to Vector Sigma, and without a space bridge I cannot reach Optimus Prime and somehow deprive him of the key. But computers are like fortresses—they always have more than one entrance. Back doors, side doors, hatches through which the subtle might sneak. What makes you think that Vector Sigma is an exception?"

"You are mad, Shockwave."

"Do you think I rose to power by daring too little?"

"All you're going to do is destroy yourself."

"Perhaps. But not before I destroy *you*." Shockwave gestured to his guards, who pushed Alpha Trion toward Vector Sigma. Simultaneously, diagnostic drones floated forward, interfacing with the instrument panels along the wall. "You are a *Prime*, Alpha Trion. You may have long ago forgotten all your pride, but you are still a Prime and you were created by Primus himself. And so was Vector Sigma. Each of you is stamped indelibly with the mark of your maker. Your circuitry's patterns will thus serve as a most precise skeleton key."

The guards halted just in front of Vector Sigma. More diagnostic drones swarmed forward. The room filled with a low buzzing noise. Alpha Trion stared into the orb's glowing maw, and for the first time in a long time he knew an emotion he had almost forgotten.

Fear.

"Listen to me, Shockwave," he said. The buzzing was getting louder. "There *may* be some way to use my circuitry to gain access to some of Vector Sigma's powers. I say 'may,' because I truly do not know. And neither do you. But if there is a way, you'd need the right settings, the correct calibrations, and your chances of achieving that through guesswork are—"

"Who said anything about guesswork?" Shockwave asked.

"What else would you base it on?"

"The Covenant of Primus."

"I hid that."

"In pieces, no less. You tore it apart and scattered its pages in anticipation of your arrest. But my Insecticons found a tantalizing fragment." Shockwave held out a hand, and one of his Insecticons placed a scrap of paper in it. Shockwave read aloud: "'Pity my Remaining Child, for he will be cast into the Mind of My Own Creation, He shall be used to engineer Dark and Wondrous Artifices . . .'" Shockwave looked up at Alpha Trion. "Any of this ring a bell?"

"That leaves more than a little room for interpretation," Alpha Trion said.

"Perhaps," Shockwave replied. "But what about this?" He held up a second piece of paper. On it were two illustrations. The first showed a bot that looked a lot like Alpha Trion in front of an effulgent orb that was clearly intended to be Vector Sigma. The second picture depicted a crystalline object that bore a distinct resemblance to Optimus's Matrix of Leadership. But whereas the Matrix glowed, this crystal was colored so dark as to be almost black. The edges of both illustrations were decorated with abstract patterns that seemed merely decorative until one compared them against . . .

"Vector Sigma's instrument settings," Shockwave said. "Yes. Do not try to hide the fact that you see it. This is a precise manual for how one might interface your circuitry with that of Vector Sigma. Do you really think I'm so foolish as to not use it?"

"But you *are* foolish enough to take pages out of context."

"Namely?"

"That Primus warns against this process."

"I don't doubt he did." The buzzing was now a rumbling. The entire room was beginning to shake. Vector Sigma was glowing ever brighter, and its rotation was accelerating by the moment. Shockwave's finger stabbed down on the image of the darkened crystal. "Because it creates a Decepticon Matrix of Leadership," he added.

"There is no such thing," Alpha Trion said.

"That's about to change."

"And what would you do with such a thing?"

"What *wouldn't* I do? All things would be possible."

"Optimus's Matrix of Leadership has hardly made him all-powerful."

"No, but it *has* allowed him to rule the Autobots, has it not? When was the last time you heard one of them question him? No matter how stupid his demands, no matter how weak his objectives. Think of what such power could do in the hands of one with true insight."

"So with a Decepticon Matrix, you would turn the tables on Megatron."

"Only if he insisted on not seeing reason upon his return. But it's more immediate matters that interest me. Crushing the Wrecker resistance, for example. Keeping them away from my research. Not to mention augmenting that research with the fruits of everything Vector Sigma contains. The secrets of the ancestors, Alpha Trion. The artifacts of the Primes. The weapons Primus never allowed his creation to wield. As your mind melts inside that of Vector Sigma, take comfort in knowing that you have handed me such strength."

The rumbling that filled the room had become deafening. The orb that was Vector Sigma was whirling like a dynamo, burning white-hot. Diagnostic drones pulled cables from the wall and prepared to plug them into Alpha Trion.

"I am begging you, Shockwave. Do not do this."

Shockwave smiled. "I always knew this day would come," he said. "The day when the great Alpha Trion finally came to his senses and *begged*."

He turned to the drones.

"Integrate him," he said.

Light engulfed Alpha Trion.

Chapter Twelve

OPTIMUS, RATCHET, IRONHIDE, BULKHEAD, PERCEPTOR, and several dozen others rolled out of the strike shuttle that had just touched down. They were ready for anything, though so far no one had detected any defenses. Things might be a different story underwater, but the Ark's artillery had this section of the planet covered from space. As the newcomers spread out around the shuttle, reverting back to bot form, Rodimus straightened up and checked himself for debris. He always wanted to appear his best in front of his hero, Optimus.

"How do I look?" he asked Kup.

"There's grease on that phoenix of yours," Kup said, pointing at Rodimus's insignia.

"*What?!*" Rodimus looked down, saw nothing, and looked back up to see Kup grinning.

"Just kidding. Believe me, kid, the commander doesn't care how you look; he cares about how you do the job. And what *I* care about is that somebody remembered to bring old Kup a fresh cy-gar."

As Optimus made his way across the tarmac to his comrades, he saw the familiar rune-covered buildings and felt those feelings of strangeness building up again. If the others were unsettled by their new surroundings, they certainly didn't show it. Prowl stepped forward, offering Optimus a crisp salute.

"The area is secure, Commander."

"Good job, Prowl."

"Welcome to the waterworks, gang!" Kup called out as they approached. Ironhide handed Kup a new cy-gar, then looked around disdainfully.

"Can you believe all this ocean? Just doesn't seem right. Me, I need good old metal under these feet."

"There's metal here," Kup said.

"Sure," said Ironhide, "and those guys are making the most of it."

He gestured at the Aquatronians, who now swarmed across the island facility; they'd come out of the sea and were busy opening up trading posts and preparing all kinds of kiosks for their new visitors. Most were humanoid, but a few had remained in their fish forms. Apparently they could function above the surface in either form.

"What's going on here?" Jazz asked.

"They're trying to make us welcome," Prowl answered. "Whatever we need, they say they can supply. They're bending over backward to please us. I think they're even setting up some kind of parade to welcome us to their world."

"Yeah," Ironhide said. "I remember the entertainment for us on Velocitron. Remember how well that worked out?"

"Hard to forget," Optimus said. "Ironhide, I want you to stay with the ships just in case. They seem peaceful enough, but you never know." Ironhide nodded and snapped his pressure cannon into place on top of his shoulder mount.

"Don't worry, Optimus. Any of these fish-bots makes a wrong move, I'll hose it down with liquid nitrogen and hit it with a really big hammer."

"Show-off," Bulkhead muttered.

"The rest of you follow me," Optimus said. "Let's see

what else we can learn before this Curator returns to meet us." He led the Autobots from the landing platform and over to the city's edge, his optics scanning the runes covering the buildings.

"Are we any closer to figuring out what these mean, Perceptor?"

"I'm still running it through the universal translator. So far there's no match with anything we have on record."

"What about the building designs?"

"Nothing, although since we're dealing with robotic life, it's entirely possible that similarities in form and style are just a function of use. That might explain some of the resemblance. Especially when it comes to Energon storage and fuel disbursement."

Prowl broke in. "Speaking of Energon storage, there's something you should see, Optimus." He led the group a few blocks into the city to a group of warehouses. Prowl walked up to one of the hangar-size doors and slid it open to reveal tons upon tons of Energon.

"By the AllSpark!" Ratchet exclaimed. "I don't think I've ever seen this much in one place before."

"And this is just one warehouse," Prowl said.

"The Energon in here alone could recharge every Autobot on the Ark," Optimus said, "and refuel the ship three times over."

"The Curator said he was willing to do a deal," Prowl told them.

Optimus shook his head. "Let's see if we can find out more about these Aquatronians before we start making trade agreements."

"Agreed," Jazz said pointedly, looking at Perceptor. "And this must be that parade you were mentioning earlier." A stream of Aquatronians marched down the street in perfect formation, a joyous marching tune playing through their loudspeakers.

"Optimus, there he is," Prowl said.

"Who?"

"The chief weirdo—I mean, the Curator." The blue-white Aquatronian leader emerged from a nearby building flanked by ceremonial guards carrying banners and sporting a color scheme similar to their leader's. The Curator approached them with open arms and a wide, toothy smile.

"Friends, friends, friends; welcome to our humble planet. We of the planet Aquatron salute you one and all."

Optimus stepped forward. "I am Optimus Prime, commander of the Autobot forces. It's a pleasure to meet you." The Curator bowed deeply and grasped Optimus's giant armored hand.

"Oh, yes, it most certainly is. It's been so long since we've had any visitors of note, let alone an actual Prime! I have so very, very many questions to ask." The Curator positively beamed with excitement as he vigorously shook Optimus's hand—and kept on shaking it. It started to get a little awkward. Optimus tactfully withdrew his hand.

"I hope I will be able to provide you with the answers you seek," he said.

"I am sure that you will," replied the Curator. "And please, please, please—do not hesitate to let me know whatever I can do to make your stay as comfortable as possible."

"Well, we hadn't exactly planned on—"

"Staying? Certainly you must be tired from spending so much time in space. Doesn't it feel good to have such solid ground beneath your feet?"

"Funny definition of solid," Bulkhead muttered in a low voice.

The Curator ignored him and gestured at the warehouse. "And I know that you will want to take us up on our ability to replenish your ships and provide you with all the fuel that you require."

"Thank you," Optimus said. "We greatly appreciate it."

"Then permit me to show you around."

The Curator proceeded to lead Optimus and a few of the Autobots on a tour of the island facility. Optimus was impressed with the sophistication of the operation and the symbiotic way in which the Aquatronians lived with their ocean. The Curator explained that they had stopped selling Energon long ago because of a lack of buyers. But now they were locked into their traditional ways, and even though they didn't have customers, they had simply waited for a time when they would. Hence their jubilation at the appearance of the Autobots.

Despite his misgivings about the Aquatronian leader, Optimus found the planet's way of life orderly and efficient. He couldn't help thinking that if the Cybertronians had been more focused on peace, maybe they could have built a society such as this. *Until all are one*—it seemed to him that the Aquatronians had perfected that principle, all working toward a common cause without malice or tyranny. These machines indeed had much to be proud of.

"We Aquatronians are a humble people," said the Curator. "What little ambition we have centers on living in harmony with our ecosphere. As you can see, we have no war here, no hunger, no disease. We have been able to dedicate our existence to helping others like ourselves."

"So you've encountered Cybertronians before?" Optimus asked.

"Millions of years ago, yes. Back when our space bridge was functioning, perhaps even before your Golden Age. Some say not long after your Thirteen Primes left, your world found us. We were such grand friends then. We all prospered from the Energon trade."

That might explain the similarity in architecture, Optimus thought. "You know of the Thirteen?"

"Of course we do," the Curator said. "Anybody who knows anything about you Cybertronians knows of the legendary Thirteen. That being said, we have never actually seen a Prime until now. I cannot begin to tell you how honored we are that you have found us again."

"Yes, well, the honor is all ours. Perhaps this exchange of ideas and knowledge will bring our two races together in ways that benefit us both."

"Indeed," said the Curator, "that is as it should be. Once we served as a hub for trade for many worlds. The galaxy was different then. Now all the planets have fallen into isolation, alas."

"We are doing our best to pick up the pieces," Optimus said. "Our head scientist, Perceptor, would be most interested in conducting some tests to see if our species are related. After all, there are few mechanoid races at this level of sophistication."

"We would welcome whatever testing you would like to perform," the Curator replied. "Though I assure you we are not one of your lost colonies. Which does not mean we cannot be brothers, no? Tell me, Optimus, what of events on Cybertron?"

"Civil war rages there now."

The Curator shook his head slowly. "We had heard rumors, but I had hoped they weren't true."

"They are. In fact, the Decepticons have driven us into exile." Optimus decided not to mention the AllSpark to the Curator. It didn't seem prudent. Maybe after they had gotten to know each other a little better but not right now. Nor did the Curator seem to notice his reticence; instead, the bot waved his hands expansively.

"Well," he said, "even though our star charts are old and outdated, you are welcome to them. We also possess the charts of many of the races we used to trade with. As you didn't know our planet was here, maybe they will fill in the gaps in your own."

"That would be most welcome assistance."

"Perhaps our help should not stop there." For a moment the Curator almost looked sly. "Since we once had so much contact with other worlds and other species, we are quite proficient at the art of negotiation. Might it be that we can aid you in finding peace with these Decepticons?"

"Peace with the Decepticreeps?" Jazz said. "I wouldn't bet my racing stripes on it."

"Easy, Jazz," Optimus said. He turned back to the Curator. "Though his words are harsh, I fear that my comrade Jazz may be right. The Decepticons do not want peace; they want total dominion over all the races they encounter. You should bear that in mind should they ever find your planet."

The Curator shrugged. "Well, should you change your mind, we will of course do everything we can to assist you, Autobot friends."

"Perhaps there is—" But Optimus stopped in midsentence as an image filled his mind. It was the clearest image yet and the most disturbing. He was still Orion Pax working in the data labs, but he found himself overwhelmed by a singular feeling—a fear of a savage invader bent on enslaving him . . . an unrelenting force seeking to become his master and make him its eternal servant. For the briefest of moments he was deep in the bowels of Cybertron with some implacable predator bearing down on him. Was the vision the product of the Matrix? Was it an actual memory? Was he nothing more than a puppet of the Matrix? Was that the true nature of being a Prime? A giant shadowy figure loomed over him, intoning words that chilled him to the bone:

You rejected us once, but we never turned our back on you. The gift we have bestowed upon you will forever bind us. By the time you realize your error and folly, it will be far too late. You belong to us now and forever, Optimus Prime. Your destiny lies in our hands, and our hands are around your throat . . .

That was when he saw Megatron's laughing face.

"Megatron!" Optimus cried out as he fell heavily to the floor.

There was a moment's shocked silence. Then Ratchet rushed to his side and popped his external diagnostic panel.

"Optimus! What's wrong? What do you see?"

Optimus tried to speak but could not form words.

"Whatever is the matter?" the Curator asked with what seemed to be deep concern.

"I don't know," Perceptor said. "We should get him back to the Ark."

"That'll take too long," Ratchet said. "I'll examine him in the dropship's med-lab."

"That lab is nowhere near as sophisticated as the one we have on the Ark," said Perceptor.

"I'm telling you, there may not be time."

The Curator stepped in. "If time is of the essence, then by all means use our medical facilities. We have a fully equipped lab scarcely a few blocks away, thank goodness."

Perceptor and Ratchet exchanged a concerned look. They knew they had to act fast.

"Okay," said Ratchet. "Your med-lab it is, then."

Perceptor shifted into his science-vehicle mode; the others loaded Optimus aboard. None of them noticed the smirk on the Curator's face.

Chapter Thirteen

RODIMUS, KUP, AND BUMBLEBEE WATCHED WITH concern from the launch pad while Perceptor, Ratchet, Bulkhead, and a few others went with the Curator to the Aquatronian med-lab, disappearing through the door to one of the towers. Rodimus paced back and forth while Kup fired up his new cy-gar and filled Ironhide in on what had happened to Optimus. Bumblebee seemed content to sit back and calibrate his sensors as he scanned the water around them.

"No, sir, I don't like it," Ironhide said as he checked the dropship's security systems. Any unauthorized intruder who had the ill-advised idea of trying to steal the ship would be in for a big surprise.

"What do you think is wrong with Optimus?" Rodimus asked.

"No clue, kiddo," Kup said. "Hopefully the sawbones will figure it all out." Then, seeing how worried Rodimus looked: "Honestly, it's probably nothing."

"Of course it's nothing," Ironhide said with his usual bluster. "Optimus is a Prime, and there's nothing that can stop a Prime. You can take that to the credit depository!"

"There's something about this place that rankles my olfactory sensors," Rodimus said.

"These fish-bots seem friendly enough," Kup offered.

"Sure they seem friendly, but what do we really know

about them? How do we know they aren't the reason Optimus collapsed?"

"Well, we don't, kiddo. But so far we have no reason to suspect them of being duplicitous, now, do we? So keep an open mind."

"Don't tell me what kind of mind to keep," Rodimus said. Bumblebee blipped and beeped in assent. Rodimus nodded. "See, even Bumblebee thinks there's something fishy going on here. Um, no pun intended."

Ironhide nodded. "I have to admit, I think Bumblebee and Rodimus might have a point. I'm not sure how keen I am on these fish types either."

"Yeah," said Kup, "but you're suspicious of everybody."

"So? Somebody has to be."

"So you three don't trust the Aquatronians. What do you recommend we do about it?"

Ironhide smashed his fist into his palm. "Easy. We grab one of these fish fellas and squeeze him until he tells us everything."

"Not so fast," Rodimus said. "We don't know if they have some way of communicating distress to each other. Putting the question to one of them might tip our hand."

"You got a better idea?" Ironhide asked.

"I say we go on our own little intelligence-gathering expedition. Take a closer look around here and see just exactly what it is these people are hiding."

Ironhide thought about it. "Okay, that is a better idea," he admitted.

"And what if they aren't hiding anything?" Kup asked.

Rodimus shrugged. "Well, then I'll admit I was wrong, you can say I told you so, and we'll call it a day. But doesn't this all seem a little odd to you? A little too convenient? If you ask me, these people are too friendly by half. I mean, do you really believe they've just been sitting on all this Energon for millions of years simply waiting for us to show up again and take it off their hands?"

"If there's one thing I know for sure, it's that there's no such thing as a free lunch," Ironhide said.

"Exactly," said Rodimus. "This whole place makes no sense. I'm telling you these robots are up to something, I just don't know what it is."

Bumblebee stepped forward and issued a series of low-pitched beeps. "See?" Rodimus asked. "Bumblebee says—"

"I heard him," Ironhide said. "Yes, our scans picked up elaborate undersea structures beneath here, but chances are they use them to store more Energon."

"How do you know that for sure?"

"Because they're right next to the Energon-mining facilities."

"You mean they're right next to what we've been *told* are Energon-mining facilities."

Ironhide frowned. "And you think we should go down there uninvited and snoop around?"

"As a matter of fact, I do."

Kup threw the remains of his cy-gar on the ground. "Okay, say I'm with you on this, kid. What's the plan?"

"The plan is we sneak into the undercity and find out what these bots are really up to," Rodimus said.

"And what about the chain of command?"

"Optimus will forgive us if we're wrong."

"And if we're right?" Kup asked.

"Well, then we're going to have much bigger problems than not having followed the chain of command. Ironhide, will you cover for us?"

"Will I . . . Wait a second. You mean I don't get to go?"

"Well, if you disappear as well, Optimus won't know where we went."

Kup was mulling things over. "In order for us to do this quickly, we'll have to take the dropship."

"What? *No*." Ironhide crossed his arms across his barrel chest. Kup stepped forward and placed his hand on his old friend's shoulder.

"If this plan is going to work, we need an edge. If we take the dropship, we can scoot out to the seabed and take a closer look at this operation from a new angle. Maybe one these fish-bots aren't expecting."

"And with these sensors we can cover a lot more ground a lot sooner," Rodimus added. "We'll be back before you know it."

Ironhide's metal brow furled at the notion, but he knew deep down that they were right; there was no sense in going halfway on a caper like this. Sure, he knew Jazz would read him the riot act, but every ounce of his combat experience told him that the only way to be sure about anything was to see it with one's own optics. And in a situation like this, Kup's eyes were as good as his own.

"Fine," he said. "You go ahead and I'll keep a lookout here."

"Thanks, old buddy," Kup said.

"Not a scratch on that dropship, you hear?"

As Rodimus, Kup, and Bumblebee piled inside, Ironhide couldn't help thinking that this was the second time that day he had been left behind. He wished he was speeding off to do some exploring, but deep in his circuits he knew somebody had to mind the store. Through the ship's forward viewports, he watched Rodimus climbing into the pilot's acceleration chair while Bumblebee joined him at the navigator's station. Then Rodimus shot him a crisp salute; the next moment, the engines roared as the ship lifted off the pad, swerved to the side, and then plunged into the gray ocean. All Ironhide could do was thank Primus that Kup was going with them.

The kids these days were getting harder and harder to reason with.

* * *

THE CURATOR LED THE AUTOBOTS DEEPER INTO THE city, along ramps and down elevators, to an area that he described as their social service complex, a group of buildings that apparently served as one of many energy distribution hubs when the city was fully inhabited. At the center of the annex stood a huge hospital. Ratchet, Perceptor, and Jazz escorted Bulkhead as he carried Optimus's body inside; Prowl and the rest of the Autobots stood guard out on the streets. It wasn't as if there were any other bots in sight, but as far as Prowl was concerned, that was all the more reason to stay vigilant. His optics swept over empty roads and buildings while he wondered what the hospital looked like inside.

The answer was impressive, to say the least. It was all Ratchet could do not to stare in awe at the scope of the Aquatronian infirmary. With its high ceilings and flying buttresses, the medical lab looked more like a house of worship than a place of healing. It was only upon closer inspection of the rows of medical bays and transorganic medical computers that its true function became apparent. Channels of water cut through the room; through them could be seen an additional, underwater level.

"This is really quite a facility you've got here," Ratchet said with a slight twinge of envy. The Curator waved them over to a pool from which climbed a puffer fish-bot covered with spines—as they watched, it shifted into a medium-size greenish robot with an enormous black mustache. The Curator cleared his throat.

"Allow me to introduce our planet's senior medical physician, Doctor Xeros."

The doctor bowed. "Always a pleasure to meet another practitioner of the medical arts," he said to Ratchet.

"Very pleased to meet you indeed."

"Well," said Ratchet, "allow me to complement you on this facility." But as he spoke, he was scanning the equipment, trying to decide whether they could entrust Optimus to it. "Most impressive."

"You're too kind," said Doctor Xeros. "Most of what you see here is millions of years old. I daresay that most of the technological advances we've made over the years have been geared toward the Energon trade."

"Where should I put Optimus?" Bulkhead broke in impatiently.

"Oh, yes, over here. Over here." Xeros led him to a med-bay and gently lowered Optimus down into it while the Curator drew back, watching intently.

"You're conversant with Cybertronian physiology?" Perceptor asked the doctor.

"Have no fears on that score," Xeros said as he warmed up the med-bay. "We have a comprehensive codex of over three thousand different species. Some aren't even robotic in nature, if you can imagine. Did you know that there are some places in the galaxy where carbon is the primary building block of life?"

"Carbon-based life-forms?" Perceptor said. "That sounds incredible."

"It's true. Purely organic beings. With life spans that don't even last for a fraction of ours. In some cases they never actually leave their larval state and exist only for a matter of days before their spark terminates."

Ratchet pondered this while the robotic arms of the med-bay whirred to life, reaching out with a multitude of wires, probes, and contact sensors that slotted into parts of Optimus's body. "First things first," Xeros said. "We'll run a class-one diagnostic."

"I just did that a few days ago," Ratchet admitted.

"And the results?"

"Nothing out of the ordinary."

"Well," Xeros said, "so far it would seem that all of his systems are functioning at high capability. Curious. Let's take a closer look." He leaned over Optimus and began gingerly prying open a few of the chest plates, only to let out an exclamation at what was revealed.

"I hope you don't mind me asking, but is that a Matrix of Leadership?"

"*The* Matrix of Leadership," Jazz said with a hint of trepidation. "Yes. That's exactly what it is."

"Amazing. I heard that such a thing existed. Simply amazing. But this could be the problem. Were you able to do a diagnostic on whether it's functioning correctly?"

"The diagnostic said it was."

"Did you remove the Matrix to ensure an isolated environment without interference from the host bot?"

"Of course not. Look, Doctor, I appreciate your efforts, but the Matrix has built-in safeguards. It's intended to be self-diagnosing. And if there's a problem with it, it should let Optimus or his potential successor know."

The doctor mulled that over. "Are you that successor?" he asked a little too casually.

"The Matrix will make the decision when the time is right," Jazz said curtly.

"But how do you know that decision is right if you can't be sure the Matrix is functioning properly?"

Jazz looked flummoxed. "Well, now that you put it that way . . . I'm not sure."

"Perhaps if I were to attach my instruments directly to it." As Xeros's hands moved toward the Matrix, Optimus's hand shot up and grabbed the doctor's wrist.

"That will not be necessary," Optimus said.

"It appears that your leader is awake," the Curator said superfluously.

"Where am I?" Optimus asked.

"The Aquatronian medical lab," Ratchet said. "We didn't know what else to do."

Optimus stood up, albeit a little unsteadily.

"I don't know if that's a good idea," said Xeros.

"Who are you?"

"I'm Doctor Xeros. Your friends brought you to me after you became unresponsive. You had us all very worried."

Jazz placed his hand on Optimus's shoulder. "Optimus, are you—"

"I'm fine, old friend."

"You mean you *feel* fine," Ratchet said.

"What's the last thing you recall, Optimus?" Xeros asked.

Optimus shook his head, still obviously a bit dazed.

"We were walking through the city . . ." His voice trailed off. "That's all I can remember. What happened then?"

"Then you screamed out Megatron's name and blacked out," said Jazz.

"I did?" Optimus asked.

"Who is this Megatron?" Xeros inquired.

"The leader of the Decepticons," Jazz said. "Our sworn enemy."

"Then maybe he had something to do with this," said the Curator.

"Impossible," Perceptor insisted.

"How can you be so sure?"

"Because Megatron doesn't have any *mental control* over me," Optimus said. "If he did, we'd have lost long ago." But even as he said those words, something was pressing at the fringes of his memory. *Mental control . . . lost . . . long ago . . .* It didn't make any sense. Or did it? Had Megatron found some way to undermine him from afar? He heard Xeros cough tactfully.

"Well, since there appears to be nothing wrong with

you physically—and since you seem convinced that the issue is not the Matrix—then perhaps there might be another explanation."

"And that is?"

"You might be suffering from a neurological issue."

"What kind of junk statement is that?" Jazz towered over Xeros, looking both offended and alarmed.

"I'm a physician. It's my job to assess the condition of my patients. And I'm simply raising the possibility that a lot of what we're seeing here might be due to an imbalance in Optimus Prime's cognitive circuitry. Neurological, processing, psychological—call it what you like. But it would explain a lot."

"Armchair quackery," Jazz said, getting more incensed by the moment.

"Patient resistance to diagnoses is something I'm used to," Xeros said icily. "I'm simply inviting you to consider the possibility. The pressures of leadership can weigh heavily on even the strongest mind. I might even say that part of the duty of leadership is for a leader to assess how much strain he's under. The very least you can do is be alert for any related symptoms."

"What kinds of related symptoms?" Optimus asked.

"They would vary," Xeros said. "Sudden mood swings. Impulsive rage. Buried trauma. Repressed memories." As he said the last two words, a cold chill ran down Ratchet's spine. He had been thinking along the same line himself. And if Xeros was right, it meant that more surprises were almost certainly in store. Ratchet cleared his throat, forcing himself to sound matter-of-fact.

"An interesting prognosis."

"It is indeed," Xeros said in a tone that made Jazz want to slug him. "But for now all we can do is wait. Optimus, I'd recommend a good Energon recharge. And you're only too welcome to stay here where we can keep you under careful observation."

"Thank you," Optimus said. "I appreciate the courtesy, but you've already done enough."

"Well," said the Curator, "in that case, you'll excuse me while I attend to some details for tonight's celebration. I certainly look forward to seeing you at our Coliseum shortly."

"Of course." As Jazz watched the Curator leave, he couldn't help thinking that there was something disconcertingly familiar about him. Something that—far down in the depths of his circuits—he disliked immensely.

Chapter Fourteen

ALL IN ALL, THE CURATOR WAS QUITE PLEASED WITH himself.

Certainly these Autobots were not as clever as they believed. Tricking them was easier than he'd expected. His initial predictions had put his chances for immediate success at just above 65 percent, but the gambit had paid off in spades. The Curator made a mental note to himself to revisit his underlying algorithms; perhaps they had been too pessimistic.

Because right now he felt only optimism. By the time he got back to his inner sanctum, the data was awaiting him: a comprehensive set of Optimus's medical scans freshly downloaded from Xeros's medical facilities. The Curator would have preferred the actual Matrix of Leadership itself—or at least detailed specs of that Matrix—but precise data on Optimus Prime was the next best thing. He hoped the scans would show how the Autobot was able to interface with the Matrix. Did the Matrix create new connections? Or were old ones simply rerouted?

The Curator loaded up the schematics and projected them onto his viewscreen. Optimus's systems lit up, the only blank spot being the core where the Matrix of Leadership was situated. The Matrix was the key, of course. It was probably the most powerful of all the Cybertronian artifacts, certainly the most powerful known to actually still exist. And as to its actual powers . . . The ancient legends said that the Matrix contained the essence of Primus himself and allowed its possessor to converse with former Primes. The Curator could barely restrain his excitement. To think he was so close. There was nothing he couldn't achieve with such knowledge. Some rumors even said that the Matrix possessed the power to restore life itself. No wonder that among the Autobots the Matrix was held to be little short of divine. The Curator viewed it somewhat more pragmatically: a weapon of pure science. Now he had an opportunity to discover its true nature.

"Incredible," he said to no one in particular as he examined the Autobot leader's systems. The Curator could not contain his awe at the way the Matrix was integrated into Optimus. Most tantalizing of all, the connection seemed to eschew traditional physical contact. In fact, the interface resembled something along the lines of telepathy, a type of robot empathy that allowed direct contact with the deepest part of the Cybertronian's brain. If only the Curator could hack the Matrix itself—or seize it altogether . . . As it was, the data on the interfaces would make the job of interfering with it even easier than it had been already. Certainly far more so than tampering with it when the Ark had been out in the depths of space. The Curator smiled at the thought of how lost Optimus must be feeling. Once again he activated his own Matrix-simulation protocol; the facsimile rose up out of the floor, filling the room with its intense red glow. A broad smile spread across his face.

But it quickly faded as he noticed the alert flashing on the secure command channel. The Curator waved his hands over the isomorphic controls set to his command circuit. A hologram of one of his guards appeared and bowed in a military salute.

"Report," the Curator stated crisply.

"A group of Autobots have taken one of their ships into the Kraken Sea. How would you like us to proceed?"

"Show me the video."

The Autobot dropship came into focus, cruising through the underwater depths. Alongside it were coordinates. They were vectoring in toward the seabed and had started scans of various underwater facilities adjacent to the city. But so far they had found nothing of significance.

"Keep them under close surveillance," the Curator said.

"What if they venture into the restricted zones?"

The Curator sighed in frustration. As though he were going to issue any categorical rules to his subordinates in advance of that eventuality. Yet it was in the nature of his underlings to welcome precise orders and be uncomfortable with ambiguity. It was a necessary price of not programming them to see the big picture. Besides, the Curator knew that the Autobots' chance of stumbling onto anything of consequence was less than 6 percent. He met his guard's eyes.

"If and when that happens, I will take care of the situation personally," he said.

The guard saluted; the holograph winked out. The Curator turned back to his facsimile of the Matrix and made some adjustments.

"YE-HAAAAAAAAAA!" RODIMUS EXCLAIMED AS HE TOOK the dropship into a power dive. The green sea churned behind them as the ship picked up speed, a trail of bubbles obscuring the huge complex they were leaving behind. For long minutes they thundered down through blue water that quickly turned black. Lights in the cramped cockpit showed false-color imagery of the seafloor below: long stretches of underwater fissures, endless sprawled reefs, all of it shot through with—

"Machinery," Kup breathed.

The ocean floor was covered with a complex spiderweb of conduits, ministations, and full-blown refineries. As they got closer, they could see pipes running back the way they'd come, presumably connecting this underwater infrastructure with that above the surface. Schools of fish-bots moved gracefully along the seabed, apparently conducting maintenance work across the various installations. At the last moment, Rodimus leveled out the ship, bringing it to an abrupt stop over a refinery of some kind.

"This baby handles like a dream underwater," he said.

Kup looked less enthused. "Easy on the stick there, junior; we don't want to crash this thing."

"Look, the faster we get down there, the faster we get back. What do you make of the activity on the scanners, Bee?" Bumblebee chirped and pointed out the window at a small school of mecha-fish that had just finished cleaning the refinery's walls and were moving away to the north, along the seabed. "Sure, I see them," Rodimus said. "What are you suggesting?" Bumblebee made a series of low blurps punctuated by a high-pitched tone. Rodimus whistled.

"You want to track them, huh? I'm game."

"So now we're just gonna follow these freaky fish-bots around?" There was more than a hint of foreboding in Kup's voice.

"Look," said Rodimus, "I don't know what it is exactly we're looking for, but if we follow these bots to their home, we might get a better idea of what these Aquatronians are up to."

"That's thin, sonny."

"Well, for right now it's all we've got." Rodimus

cranked the underwater drives up to quarter speed and proceeded to trail after the school, following a pipe farther and farther out along the seabed. The mecha-fish paid no attention to the dropship a few hundred meters behind them. Maybe they weren't programmed to notice.

"You might want to keep an eye on that fuel gauge, kiddo."

Bumblebee beeped agitatedly. Almost as one, the fish were diving out of sight. Rodimus increased the dropship's speed ever so slightly, and suddenly the seafloor dropped away beneath, tumbling down a cliff into—

"*Nothing*," Rodimus breathed.

They were looking down on an incredibly deep system of trenches. It was a veritable maze, and it seemed to stretch on forever, filled with canyons several dozen kilometers across. Along the walls of the trench over which they were floating were more facilities, protruding out like barnacles. Rodimus peered down into the abyss.

"Bumblebee, scan that trench. I want to know how far down it goes." Bumblebee quickly came back with an answer that made Rodimus grin and Kup cringe.

"You're not thinking of taking us down there, are you?" the veteran asked.

"We've got nothing to worry about."

"See, when you say things like that, that's when I start to worry."

"This dropship can handle the pressure," Rodimus insisted, adjusting the ship's ballast to initiate a slow descent into the darkness. He switched on the dropship's floodlights, illuminating the structures clinging to the side of the cliff wall. Out the window Kup could see all manner of facilities. It was almost as though they were in some underwater city and the cliffs were the skyscrapers. But in between the rows of pipes and conduits, he could make out more of the strange runes they had seen in the city above, only these were carved directly into the rock past which they were dropping. They must have been etched there millions of years ago, he thought, long before the Aquatronians had covered the walls with their complex machines and automated factories.

Suddenly the ship's collision Klaxon sounded. Alarm lights flashed.

"What's going on?" Kup demanded.

"Sonar picking up a contact below. Closing on us. Something big."

"How big?" All three Autobots stared at the sonar screen as the data scrolled past: well over forty meters in length and heading right toward the dropship. Bumblebee bleeped frantically.

"Hang on!" Rodimus yelled. He blew the remaining ballast in a desperate attempt to rise out of the trench and gain maneuvering room. But the signal kept closing. It was almost on them . . .

"*Brace for impact!*" Kup yelled. Rodimus threw the ship to the left in a last-ditch evasive maneuver, and then the entire dropship shuddered under the impact of a titanic force. Rodimus's reflexes ensured that it was only a glancing blow, a mere fraction of what it might have been, but that was small consolation as the structural integrity of a portion of the hull gave way and water poured in. Rodimus sealed off the bridge from the flooded compartments, doing his best to regain control of the ship. But whatever had hit them had knocked out too many of the key systems. For a moment everything went dark, and then the emergency lighting kicked in. Rodimus felt the stick go dead.

"Okay, guys, maybe it's time to worry," he muttered. Kup peered out the window just in time to see the tail of the biggest fish-bot he had ever seen disappearing back into the depths. The crippled dropship rolled over and started to float back down like a falling leaf, gradually spiraling out of control into the dark of the trench, gaining speed . . .

"Scrap me," Kup said.

Everything went black.

OPTIMUS AND THE REST OF THE AUTOBOTS SAT IN PLACES of honor in the Aquatronians' Coliseum as honor guards marched by with their streaming pennants. The Curator had just finished a long, boring speech on the theme of kinship lost and found. He'd expressed his fervent hope that now that the two species had found each other again, they would be able to fulfill their mutual destinies. Indulging in a rather poetic rhetorical flourish, the Curator suggested that perhaps the great Primus himself had stopped by their world during his long journey at the beginning of time.

None of that stopped Optimus from having grave misgivings about this planet. But if the Matrix really *was* malfunctioning—however slightly—maybe that was also the cause of his suspicions. Maybe he was jumping at shadows. Yet even as he watched the ceremony, Optimus felt like he had seen it all before, like he'd witnessed a similar procession long ago, back on Cybertron. But wasn't that the nature of déjà vu—that feeling that a thing had happened before even when it hadn't? There was very little he was sure of now. The Coliseum's walls were adorned with that script Optimus *knew* he had seen someplace back on Cybertron. Memory was one thing, giant block letters carved in stone was another, and he couldn't help thinking that the Aquatronians and the Autobots were much more closely related than this "Curator" was willing to admit. When Optimus had asked earlier about the nature of the Coliseum, the

Curator had replied that it wasn't used for games, that it stood as a testament to the Aquatronian legal system, which required the participation of a large proportion of the populace to ensure that justice was properly served.

Justice.

There was something in the way the Curator used that word that was odd, a peculiar emphasis. Optimus couldn't help noticing the precision in the robot's cadences, the careful way he always chose his words. Optimus now felt it was a mistake to have let the Curator's doctor examine him. Sure, Xeros had claimed merely to have confirmed what Ratchet had already discovered, that physically there was nothing wrong with him. But if they had found something, would they have told him? And if his robotics really *were* fine, that meant the unthinkable was still a possibility: There was something wrong with the Matrix of Leadership and they had no way to fix it or even to find out what it was.

There was another possibility, though, and it was the one Optimus found the most disquieting. Maybe he had done something to fall out of favor with the Matrix. Maybe the sparks of the great leaders contained within it felt that Optimus was failing them as a Prime. After all, what had he done so far? Fight a losing war on Cybertron and then career halfway around the galaxy looking for the AllSpark that he himself had ejected into space, all the while being pursued by a vastly superior force of Decepticons, even as—he felt it in the depths of his circuitry—unspeakable events occurred on Cybertron. He truly believed that at every step of the way he had made the best of a series of bad options. But perhaps a real leader would have found a better way. Perhaps the Matrix had judged him and found him wanting. Perhaps the spirits of past Primes were saying that he just didn't have what it took.

But if that was the case, why didn't they just tell him?

"Optimus," Ratchet said, stepping up behind him. "Can I have a word in private?"

"Of course." Optimus rose and walked with Ratchet to an empty section of seats. It looked like the two of them were simply enjoying a better view, but Ratchet obviously had something to say.

"I've been studying the diagnostics I did earlier," the physician said. "Trying to cross-correlate them against the seizure you had."

"Seizure?" Optimus grinned ruefully. "Is that what you're calling it?"

"I don't know how else to refer to it."

"Go on."

"Well, earlier you were talking about being in a cage. That may involve the problems you've been having with the Matrix. But Xeros may be right—it also may be linked to dormant memories."

Optimus frowned. "I take *your* opinions far more seriously than that so-called doctor. Tell me more."

"Well, you know that our life spans can be very long. But the Cybertronian brain can only store a finite amount of information. There have been some studies that suggest our brains take key information and compress it, storing it for later use. How much do you remember of your time as Orion Pax?"

"I know I spent much of that time in the Hall of Records."

"But you don't remember every single second of that time, do you?"

"I suppose I don't."

"Well, that's what might be happening here. Your brain is trying to alert you to something. But as to what that something is, perhaps time will reveal the fuller picture."

"We may not have that time."

"I realize that."

"But from what you're saying, you don't think this involves the Matrix."

"I didn't say that. Actually, I'm sure the Matrix *is* involved with this."

"Well, then you should take a look at it."

But Ratchet shook his head. "I wouldn't be able to tell you anything useful. The artifacts of the Primes, the way they work, all that; that's not a medical problem *per se*."

"That's what has me worried," Optimus said. But even as he spoke, his internal communicator buzzed to life, alerting him to an urgent message on his emergency channel:

"Ironhide to Optimus, come in, Optimus."

"Go ahead, Ironhide, I read you."

"We have a situation back here at the landing pads. Rodimus, Kup, and Bumblebee took the dropship out a few hours ago, and now I can't raise them on the communicator."

"They took it back into space?"

"No, Optimus." Ironhide hesitated. "They took it underwater."

For a moment Optimus was too stunned to reply. "Why?"

"They wanted to do some more exploration. I know I should have told them no, but—"

"Where was the last known contact location?"

"Last check-in was near a series of deep sea trenches in the southern sea. Then they fell right off the grid. That's why I'm calling."

"Hold your position. I'll be there in a few minutes."

"Thanks, Optimus. I'm really sorry."

As Ironhide disconnected, Jazz leaned over and nudged Optimus.

"Is there a problem, boss?"

"Some of the scouting party has gone missing."

Observing the agitated conversation, the Curator turned his attention from the parade.

"Is everything all right, Optimus?"

Optimus decided he might as well come clean. "It looks like some of our people might have gone exploring and gotten themselves lost."

"My word. That's terrible."

"What can you tell us about the trench system around here?"

"Oh, my. Well, we have a few older facilities kept out there as reserve production units should our main ones go offline, but the currents above those trenches are treacherous. And then there are still some . . . er, ah . . ."

"Go on," Optimus said.

"Well . . . there are still some creatures from our prehistoric age that evolved much more slowly than the rest of us—that became much larger than us—and that make their homes deep in those trenches."

"So not every mechanoid on the planet is as evolved as you," Perceptor said.

"Well, no. I never claimed they were. And there *have* been instances over the years of them occasionally coming up out of the trenches to hunt."

"Well, isn't that just great," Jazz added with extra sarcasm.

"Your tone implies criticism," said the Curator. "And I understand that you're upset. But your bots ought to have consulted me before they went out exploring."

"Too late now," Jazz said.

"What's done is done," the Curator said. "But you have my word that we'll do everything in our power to help you find your people, Optimus Prime."

Optimus gave him a hard stare. "You can start now," he said.

Chapter Fifteen

KUP BLINKED AND ADJUSTED HIS OPTICS AS THE INSIDE of the dropship came back into focus. They were no longer in motion, and the control panel was flickering. Had they sunk all the way to the bottom of the trench? How close were they to being crushed? He was sitting in a shallow pool of water, staring up at the floor overhead. Above him, Rodimus and Bumblebee were hanging upside down in their acceleration chairs, their arms dangling, their systems still coming back online. Kup quickly checked himself for serious dents or breaches in his armor; satisfied that everything was still functioning, he proceeded to cut his two comrades out of their harnesses. As he sliced away, Rodimus came to with a groan.

"Easy there," said Kup.

"I guess . . . you were right," Rodimus said.

"I was *right*?" Even now, Kup kept his trademark sense of humor. "Wow, you really must have taken a bang on the head." He eased Rodimus gently onto the floor. "Easy, kid. You're just a little banged up." Kup turned to Bee and started cutting him down.

"How's Bee?"

"Still out, but I don't see any major damage. He should be up and at 'em in a few moments."

"So we're all okay."

"Depends how you define *okay*," Kup said. As he spoke, a seam gave way and jets of water sprayed into the room. The dropship shifted noticeably; metal creaked alarmingly. Rodimus eased slowly over to another viewport. This one provided more of a vantage point and made the reality of their perilous situation all too clear: They were tangled in a network of pipes along the trench's clifflike wall. That was all that had saved them, and it wouldn't keep doing so for long. Sooner or later, the whole twisted mess was going to give way and they would continue their inexorable descent to the bottom of the trench. Long before they reached it, they would be crushed by millions of tons of pressure. In the meantime, the crippled ship was rapidly filling up with water. Rodimus tried to activate the engines, but they didn't respond; the dashboard flickered, but there was nowhere near enough power.

"We need to get out of here," he said.

"Good idea, but where?"

"I'm still working on that," Rodimus said as he looked back out the viewport. They were several kilometers down, so the idea of swimming back to the surface didn't seem feasible. But that was when he saw it just beyond the tangled mess of conduits and smashed metal: a hatch set in the cliff wall amid the pipes. Its iris doors were sealed tight. He turned back to the control console.

"Grab Bee and get ready to move," he said.

"You want to give me a hint as to what the plan is?" Kup asked.

"There's some kind of service hatch over there, I'm trying to hack into it and get it open. Then we open our main hatch, jump, and hope the current carries us in."

"Hope?" Kup asked.

"Look at what all that junk is doing," Rodimus said. Out the viewport, pieces of debris were being swept against the side of the cliff by the unseen current. "So we're at least going to be heading in the right general direction."

"You do realize that debris is pieces of our hull, don't you?"

"All the more reason to move now. I'm going to set both doors to stay open for exactly five seconds."

Kup shook his head. "For the record, I hate this plan."

"I'm not too crazy about it either, but—" Still another seam gave way. The jets of water intensified into a flood. The ship started to lean to the side.

"Primus help us," Kup exclaimed. He grabbed on to Bumblebee.

"Here we go," Rodimus said. He simultaneously opened the ship's hatch and the one in the side of the cliff. Water poured in, smashed him back into the rear of the craft, then tore him out into the ocean as though it were a living thing. He caught a quick glimpse of Kup struggling to hold on to Bumblebee and saw the various pipes and fittings give way and snap off the cliff face as the weight of the dropship dragged the wreckage free. For a moment, Rodimus was caught in that inexorable undertow. He was on the point of being swept downward. The abyss was pulling him in, and his last thought was at least he'd given it his all . . .

But suddenly a steel hand clasped around his wrist, yanking him forward just as the iris valve squeezed shut behind him with a resounding clang. Water drained out through sluice gates in the floor. Rodimus looked up to find himself staring at Kup.

"Cutting it a bit close there, junior."

Rodimus was too shaken to reply. Beside him, Bumblebee stood up, emitted a series of beeps, and then expelled water from his various sockets. Rodimus looked around.

"Where are we?"

"Your guess is as good as mine," Kup said, helping him to his feet. The room they were in was at least thirty meters high, its vaulted ceilings covered in more of the weird runes they had seen in the city. Auxiliary parts and components were stacked all around, but there were no signs that this place had seen much use. At the far side of the room sat a large industrial cargo elevator, though the only direction it could go was down.

"Try your communication systems," Kup said. "Can you reach Ironhide?"

Rodimus tried, but all he could hear was static. "I'm not getting anything," Kup said. Bumblebee bleeped plaintively; he was striking out, too.

"We must be too far down to transmit," Rodimus said as he retracted his antenna. They were just going to have to do this the old-fashioned way. He turned back to Bumblebee.

"Bee, do you think you can find us a way out of here?"

Bumblebee saluted, then began running scans. If anyone could get them clear of this place, Rodimus thought, it would be Bumblebee and his state-of-the-art mapping gear and natural sense of direction. A few more moments and Bumblebee emitted a series of chirps. According to him, their best bet for getting back to the island-city was to take the elevator.

"And go farther *down*?" Rodimus asked as though Bumblebee had just stepped on his toe.

Bumblebee explained through whirs and beeps: His sensors were picking up heavy concentrations of Energon storage below and a short distance off, near where some of the seabed pipes they'd seen earlier led back to the city. That meant there might be a way through there.

"Works for me," Rodimus said. "Let's take the elevator."

They got in and set the controls. The floor began to drop through level after level. As much as Rodimus didn't want to go farther down, at least they were putting rock between them and the water. A mile farther down and they reached what appeared to be yet another service annex. Rails led away into the darkness. Bumblebee's sensors indicated that they'd been used recently to haul Energon.

"What do you think, Bee?" Rodimus asked. "Can we ride it back to the city?" Bumblebee issued a series of beeps and chirps.

"It's going in the wrong direction?" Kup said. "Oh, great."

"Maybe it runs into another junction," said Rodimus. "We can't just sit here."

Suddenly Bumblebee shifted into his scout-vehicle mode and shot off down the tracks at high speed.

"Bee! Wait!" Rodimus yelled after him. "What are you doing?"

Kup watched Bumblebee go. Then he popped open a compartment on his leg, pulled out his last fresh cy-gar, and chuckled. Rodimus couldn't believe it.

"Something funny, old-timer?"

"Oh, just taking the opportunity for a quick break." Kup lit the cy-gar. "Never thought I'd get the chance to smoke one of these again." Smoke wafted into Rodimus's face, who sputtered in protest.

"Never mind your cy-gar! Bee shouldn't just run off like that! He could get hurt! We should—"

"Wait right here until he comes back," Kup finished. "Bee knows his job. And frankly, he's a lot less likely than you to do something stupid."

"You're starting to enjoy this, aren't you?"

"Heck, sometimes you gotta laugh to keep from crying, sonny." He puffed away on the cy-gar. Not for the first time, Rodimus wondered if Kup's zest for life was what had kept him together all this time. Maybe he ought to take up the same habit. Maybe cy-gars actually tasted pretty good . . . His reverie was interrupted as Bumblebee came back around the corner, braking right in front of his companions, beeping excitedly.

"All right," Kup said, "let's go check it out." He shifted into his truck mode, Rodimus changed into a sports vehicle, and they followed Bumblebee down the tracks. Just over a mile later, they screeched to a half in front of Bumblebee's discovery: a giant set of vaultlike doors.

"Well, how about that," Kup said.

Shifting back into bipedal mode, they examined them. There was no keypad, no lock, not even a primitive counterweight system. But the tracks led directly up to the doors, so presumably they continued on the other side. Bumblebee let out a few high-pitched squawks.

"Energon," said Kup.

Rodimus stepped back and unfolded his arm bows, snapping two hi-ex warheads into place. "We need some space," he said. The three of them moved back up the corridor.

"I'm not sure this is a great idea," Kup said.

"Got a better one?"

"No, but—"

"Open sesame," Rodimus said as he let the rockets fly. The doors disappeared in a flash of light. The concussion rolled back up the corridor. When the smoke cleared, the doors were still intact, but there was a gaping hole in the center of them.

"Now we're in," Rodimus said proudly.

"And now everybody knows it," Kup said. "So much for a stealth mission."

"The stealth mission was over the moment we lost the dropship," Rodimus retorted. "All the better if somebody heard that. Maybe they'll send a rescue team or something. Now let's see what's on the other side of this door."

The three Autobots stepped through the blast hole.

"Wow," Rodimus said.

It was the largest chamber they had ever seen on any planet, so colossal that it could have held over a hundred Arks. But it was what the room contained that really got their attention: row upon row of blue-green spiny aquatic robots stretching back as far as the eye could see. They looked like the fish-bots that had accompanied the Curator but with some alarming differences. Each one sported menacing-looking fins and teeth and a veritable arsenal of missiles and guns. All of them were motionless.

"It's an *army*," Kup breathed. "Tens of thousands of them."

"Okay, this is not good," Rodimus said.

But what was overhead was even more disturbing. Weird colored patterns flickered and swirled across portions of the ceiling that Rodimus suddenly realized were in fact giant holographic screens. They were so hypnotic that it was all he could do to look away. As he glanced back at the robots, he saw that their optics were tracking every shift in the lights overhead. Kup grabbed Rodimus by the arm and started to pull him back through the breach.

"We've got to get out of here," he said grimly.

But at that moment, the holograms overhead vanished, to be replaced by a single face staring down at them.

And when it spoke, they heard nothing else.

Chapter Sixteen

CYBERTRON

"THEY'RE GOING TO PAY FOR THIS," WHEELJACK SAID.

Springer followed the direction of his gaze out across the plains of the border regions. From the cliff's edge on which they were standing they could see fires burning in several places. Smoke billowed up through shattered fissures in the ground. The Iacon skyline loomed in the far distance, all of it dwarfed by Shockwave's tower.

"They're going to pay for this," Wheeljack repeated.

"Well," Springer said, "we've been making them do that."

That was an understatement. The two of them were members of the Wreckers, the group of renegade Autobots who had been causing as much trouble for the Decepticons as possible. Outnumbered and outgunned, they survived by hiding during the day and moving only by night.

But nothing they did had prevented matters on Cybertron from going from bad to worse. Bodies littered the roads. Refugees roamed the countryside. Most of the cities were little more than wreckage filled with scavenger gangs of industrial bots preying on refugees and one another. The Decepticons recruited the most brutal of those gangs for their mercenary armies, then used the mercenaries up in search-and-destroy missions against the Wreckers. After all, they were just mercenaries, and the Decepticons could always find more.

"They're grinding us down," Wheeljack said.

"I thought it was the reverse," said Springer.

He would believe that, Wheeljack thought. Springer was a never-say-die type of bot, whereas Wheeljack tended to be more realistic. He had to be; he was an inventor, after all, and he had done much for the Wrecker cause with the devices he had unleashed upon the Decepticons. But such ingenuity came with a price, for it meant that Wheeljack was under no illusions regarding how dire the situation was starting to get.

"Hey," Springer said, "look who it is."

Wheeljack turned to see a shape flitting through the air toward them, hugging the cliff's edge to avoid detection by the Decepticons.

That was ironic, because the bot in question once had *been* a Decepticon.

Not anymore, though.

"Jetfire," Wheeljack said.

The tone in his voice suggested that he didn't appreciate Jetfire one little bit. That was understandable. Jetfire had been a member of Starscream's aerial command. It had taken Wheeljack a long time to accept that his defection to the Autobot cause was a genuine one.

But that didn't mean he had to like him.

"Wonder what he wants," Springer said.

"Must be important," said Wheeljack.

Jetfire fired his retros and alighted next to them, switching out of his jet-fighter mode to take on bot form

"Been looking for you two everywhere," he said.

"Well, now you found us," said Springer.

"We were just taking in the view," Wheeljack said, gesturing out at the blasted plain. "Admiring the handiwork of your brethren."

There was a moment's pause. "You mean my *former* brethren," Jetfire said.

"Something we can help you with?" Wheeljack asked.

"The boss wants to see you," Jetfire said.

WHEELJACK HAD PLENTY OF TIME FOR MISGIVINGS AS HE followed Jetfire through winding canyons and narrow valleys. His race-car mode was fast, but even so he could barely keep up. Given the terrain, Springer's hovercraft form was proving more effective. Wheeljack was starting to wonder if this was all an elaborate trap. Perhaps Jetfire had waited till now to show his true colors. Then again, if that had been the case, it seemed unlikely he'd use the opportunity just to bag two Wreckers. No, what really bothered Wheeljack was something more fundamental: how high Jetfire was rising in the confidences of the leader of the Wreckers. Ultra Magnus kept the location of his underground headquarters secret even from most of the Wreckers. The fact that he was confiding in Jetfire was more than a little galling. But Ultra Magnus was the boss, and it was his decision. No one was about to second-guess him. Besides—

"Flying's at a premium these days," Springer muttered.

Wheeljack nodded. Springer was probably right. Jetfire had become Ultra Magnus's personal scout, able to range far behind Decepticon lines and then report back to him directly. His former identity probably made his insights all the more useful. Jetfire darted low, landing and switching back to bot form. The others did the same and followed him into a narrow rocky tunnel whose entrance was so well concealed that Wheeljack had never realized it was there. Rock quickly gave way to metal walls; security cameras in the walls let Wheeljack know they were being watched. The corridor branched off into more corridors, but Jetfire seemed to know which way to go. It was quite the maze, and it ended in an armored door, which slid open—

"Come in," Ultra Magnus said.

The Wrecker leader stood in the center of a screen-lined control room. He looked weary, his red and blue armor battered in multiple places. But he smiled warmly as Wheeljack and Springer entered. Jetfire shut the door behind them while they saluted. Ultra Magnus didn't waste time getting to the point.

"I've got a mission for you," he said.

"Great news," Wheeljack said. "Who are we going to carve up?"

"It's not a hit job," Ultra Magnus replied. "It's a rescue mission."

Wheeljack and Springer looked at each other. "A rescue mission?" Wheeljack asked.

"You heard the bot," Jetfire said.

"Shut up," Wheeljack said.

"So who are we rescuing?" said Springer.

"Alpha Trion," Ultra Magnus replied.

That wasn't what Wheeljack and Springer had been expecting. They glanced at each other and looked back at Ultra Magnus.

"He didn't escape from Iacon?" Wheeljack asked.

"He never tried," said Ultra Magnus.

Springer looked baffled. "Why not?" he asked.

Ultra Magnus sighed. "We're not exactly sure," he said. "He may have believed he could get Shockwave to see reason."

"*Shockwave* and *reason* aren't two words that go together," Wheeljack said.

"You have to remember that Alpha Trion is a Prime," said Ultra Magnus. "That means he doesn't think the way us regular bots do. He may have believed it was his duty to stay and defend the archives. He may have been trying to stay above the fray, seeking to preserve his neutrality."

"Neutrality means nothing to the Decepticons," Wheeljack said. "You're either with them or against them."

"That is true," Ultra Magnus said. "The other possibility is that he might have felt himself constrained by the Covenant of Primus."

"How would the Covenant restrain him?" Springer asked.

"We don't know," Ultra Magnus said. "That's the point. But if it convinced him that it was his destiny to stay in Iacon even after Decepticon occupation . . . well, that might be why he elected not to leave."

"I see," said Springer, not seeing at all. This kind of philosophical mumbo jumbo didn't make much sense to him. He much preferred to just get Decepticons in his crosshairs and squeeze the trigger.

"Maybe you're overthinking this," Wheeljack said. "Maybe he lost his nerve."

"That's an unworthy statement," Ultra Magnus said sternly.

"Doesn't mean it's not true," Wheeljack persisted. "It's not like a Prime can't lose heart. Look what happened to Sentinel Prime."

"Sentinel Prime was old," Ultra Magnus retorted. "Senile, even."

"And you're so sure that Alpha Trion isn't?"

"Enough of this," Ultra Magnus said. "Alpha Trion was one of the *Thirteen*. That puts him on a level far above any appointed Prime. And it also makes him a potentially deadly tool for the Decepticons should they seek to turn him against us."

"Will they?"

"Shockwave's guards took him into custody this morning."

Wheeljack pondered this. "That isn't good."

"It gets worse," Ultra Magnus said. "They brought him to the tower, and he hasn't been seen since. The whole place is now under lockdown, and we don't know what's going on within it. But I received a report from one of my informants in the city that Shockwave has already started experimenting on Alpha Trion."

"What kind of experiments?" Wheeljack asked.

"Your guess is as good as mine. Unlock his powers . . . use him to find some of the lost artifacts . . . turn him into a Decepticon Prime. The point is, we don't know. And we can't wait around to find out. Shockwave's a mad genius, and he's capable of anything."

"Well," said Springer, "so are we."

"That's why I called you here," Ultra Magnus said, smiling grimly. "Your mission is going to be the toughest I've ever given any Wrecker. You'll infiltrate Iacon, break into the Tower of Shockwave, and get Alpha Trion out."

Wheeljack couldn't believe what he was hearing. Suicide missions were a Wrecker specialty, but this took that concept to a new level.

"Sounds like fun," Springer said.

"It won't just be the two of you," Ultra Magnus said. "You'll have a little help. Jetfire will be coming with you."

Both bots looked at Jetfire, who grinned. "Let's just say I know a thing or two about how the Decepticons think," he said.

Wheeljack chose his words tactfully. "With all due respect, Ultra Magnus, Springer and I have worked together for a long time. Talented though Jetfire clearly is, it might be difficult to make us an effective trio."

"No one's talking about a *trio*," Ultra Magnus said. "Meet the rest of your team."

A door in the far wall of the control room opened, and two chunky green bots entered the room side by side in lockstep.

Except they weren't two bots at all.

They were just one.

At first Wheeljack thought that his optics were deceiving him, that he was seeing double. But he wasn't. The two bots were connected. The right-hand bot's left arm was also the right arm of the left-hand bot. The arm was more of an axle, Wheeljack thought. He'd never seen anything like it.

"I'd like you to meet Rack," said Ultra Magnus, pointing at the bot on the left. He gestured at the one on the right. "And that's Ruin."

"Actually, *I'm* Rack," said the latter bot. "*He's* Ruin."

"How about we just call you Rack n' Ruin," Springer said.

"Works for us."

"What the slag happened to you guys?" Wheeljack asked.

"Shockwave happened," said Rack n' Ruin—or rather one of the two bots, but Wheeljack had already decided that he wasn't going to bother distinguishing between the two of them. Life was short enough as it was. What mattered more was—

"*Shockwave* did this to you?" he asked.

"We both got captured on a raid a few months back," Rack n' Ruin said. "Got tossed into the labor camps, digging some giant complex beneath Iacon. Below Shockwave's tower."

"Wonder if that's where they've taken Alpha Trion," Wheeljack said.

"Bots were dropping like flies," Rack n' Ruin continued. "Conditions were savagely bad. And then Shockwave showed up to personally inspect the work. But it turned out he was more interested in the workers. He ordered his Decepticons to transfer a bunch of bots to his headquarters up in the tower. Well, at first we thought we were the lucky ones, 'cos we weren't going to die in that camp. But maybe it would have been better if we had. We were just fodder for his experiments. Most of the results had to be put out of their misery. We escaped before that could happen. Came back to Ultra Magnus and re-upped."

"You re-upped? After all that?" Springer's tone bordered on awe.

Rack n' Ruin shrugged. "Anything for the chance to get back at Shockwave."

"Your time inside his tower will prove useful," Ultra Magnus said. "I'd hate to have to figure things out as we go."

We? thought Wheeljack. "You say that as though you're coming with us," he said.

"Of course I'm coming with you," Ultra Magnus said. "I have no right to evade the risk." He might have added that no one else was capable of leading such a motley group, but Ultra Magnus was nothing if not tactful. A commando squad consisting of himself, Rack n' Ruin, Jetfire, Wheeljack, and Springer . . . If they couldn't succeed, no one could.

"It won't be enough," Wheeljack said.

Springer looked like he wanted to punch him. "Way to boost team morale."

"I mean we could use a diversion."

Springer looked as though he'd been insulted. "A *diversion*?"

"It's just a suggestion, but we're going to sneak into the most heavily guarded fortress on the most fortified city on the planet and rescue the bot without whom we might lose this whole war. It'd be nice to get the attention of Iacon's garrison focused elsewhere."

"As it happens," Ultra Magnus said, "I *do* have a diversion in mind."

"You'd need a pretty big one," Springer said.

"*IS THIS BIG ENOUGH?*" said a booming voice.

Everyone except Ultra Magnus practically hit the ceiling. It was like they were standing in a gigantic megaphone, hearing a thunderous voice that echoed out of every speaker in the room . . . a voice that was as unmistakable as it was loud, that could only be—

"*Omega Supreme!*" Springer yelled joyfully.

"Where's he signaling us from?" Jetfire asked.

"Right here," said Ultra Magnus.

"What do you mean, 'here'? Last time I checked, he was half a mile long, kind of tough to hide."

"I thought he was out of commission," Wheeljack said. He glared at Jetfire. "Since Starscream and his air command shot him down."

"Does this room look out of commission to you?" Ultra Magnus asked.

"Wait a second," Wheeljack said, suddenly understanding. "You mean . . ."

"*We're inside Omega Supreme,*" said Springer.

"We've been doing repairs ever since the day Optimus left Cybertron," Ultra Magnus said. "And since we were doing such a good job hiding him underground, it seemed like the logical place for me to set up my headquarters."

"I've enjoyed it," Omega Supreme said. "Though the place *does* get a little noisy at times."

"Well, you'll be rid of us soon enough," Ultra Magnus said. "You'll stay here for the time being while we sneak into the city. Then, when I give the signal, show yourself. Make sure they can see you from Iacon."

"Trust me," Omega Supreme said, "they're going to do more than just *see*."

Chapter Seventeen

THE *NEMESIS* DROPPED OUT OF LIGHTSPEED AT THE system's edge, just out of range of the Autobots' long-range sensors. Megatron stood on the bridge, personally overseeing the maneuver.

"Lord Megatron, we have arrived," Starscream said.

"I'm standing right here," Megatron replied, "so you don't need to state the obvious."

Soundwave cut in. "The Autobots do not appear to have detected us."

"Have you located the Ark?" Megatron asked.

Soundwave brought the image of the greenish world up on the main viewscreen, then magnified the section highlighting the enormous Ark.

"Yes, my lord, exactly where Skywarp said they would be. In orbit around the planet . . ." Soundwave trailed off, studying the readings.

"Well," Megatron demanded, "what is it?"

"Lord Megatron, there seems to be a high amount of chatter between the Ark and some Autobots on the surface." He decrypted some of the traffic. "They seem to be searching for some missing members of their force."

Megatron almost leaped forward at the screen.

"Is Optimus among the missing?"

"It does not appear so, lord." The barely restrained emotion underlying Megatron's question was lost on neither Starscream nor Soundwave. The latter chalked it up to his master's desire to crush the Autobot leader once and for all, but Starscream knew better. Megatron was obsessed. And obsession led to mistakes. And mistakes could get Starscream killed, which was something he wished to avoid at all costs. To Starscream, Optimus was just one more piece of the puzzle, perhaps the single most important one but still a mere part of the whole. Destroy the Autobots *en masse* and you destroyed Optimus as well. But focusing primarily on Optimus left one open to unpredictable factors among the rest of the Autobots. That meant that Megatron's hatred was also his weakness. And weaknesses were something Starscream could exploit . . .

"Tell our troops to prepare for battle," Megatron ordered. "But no one is to fire a shot without my explicit command."

"Of course, my lord," Starscream answered with a deep bow. Out of the corner of his vision he caught a glimpse of dark purple and black; he turned to see Skywarp enter the bridge and give Megatron a hearty salute. Starscream glowered, less than thrilled that one of his Seekers was taking orders from Megatron directly. It was a matter of protocol. There was a chain of command, after all.

But one bot stood at its apex.

"You summoned me, Lord Megatron," Skywarp said.

"Yes. I want to commend you on the excellent job you've done."

"All done humbly in your name." Starscream rolled his optics at Skywarp's obsequiousness. He'd remember that when the time came. But for now he strained to listen in as Megatron took Skywarp aside and placed his arm around the Seeker's shoulders.

"If there's one thing I appreciate, it's a Decepticon who knows both his place and mine. You have shown great promise, and I want to reward you."

"Reward is not needed, my sovereign," Skywarp said dutifully.

"Oh, but in this case I believe it is. I have a special mission for you. One I think you will quite enjoy."

KUP WOKE TO THE SOUNDS OF MACHINES BEEPING AND A bright light shining in his eyes. When he tried to move, he realized that he was strapped into a chair that was really more of a cage; it held his arms and legs fast with a green viscous liquid that smelled even worse than it looked. He turned his head. To the right and left of him, Bumblebee and Rodimus were secured the same way, only unlike him, they were unconscious. As best he could tell, the room was some kind of laboratory.

The Curator leaned over and gave him a broad smile.

"I see you are awake. Luckily that will not affect the procedure." There was something funny about the Curator's voice. Not only was it higher-pitched, it didn't seem to be emanating from his mouth.

"Where am I?" Kup mumbled.

"In good hands," the Curator said.

"You kidnapped us."

"Well, you were snooping. Very unwise idea, my friend. Still, I'm sure we can put this opportunity to good use."

"So we were *right*," Kup said. "You're plotting against us. You've got an *army* down there—"

"Shhhh," the Curator said as though he were comforting a small child. "We never claimed to be pacifists. Would you deny us our right to self-defense?"

"Okay, have it your way," Kup said. "And while you're at it, return me to Optimus."

"All in good time." The Curator's smile grew even broader. "I don't normally do this, but time simply doesn't permit an alternative. But sometimes the traditional methods are still the best. Just hold still; I assure you this won't hurt too much." The Curator pulled open his voluminous robe, revealing what appeared to be a fist-size hole in his chest cavity out of which sprang over half a dozen red-black tentacles that wrapped themselves around Kup's head and began forcing their way into his skull . . .

"Now would be a good time to start screaming if you so desire," the Curator said.

OPTIMUS, JAZZ, AND PROWL APPROACHED IRONHIDE ON the tarmac while the rest of the Autobots prepared to split up into search teams. Ironhide had decided before they arrived that he would take full responsibility for the entire situation. He knew that he had let Optimus down. If he could turn back the chronometer, he wouldn't have been persuaded by Kup; he would have stood his ground. But the only thing he could do now was face the frequency.

"Optimus, I'm so sorry. I never should have—"

"No time for that, old friend." Privately Optimus was furious, but right now his people needed a leader, and as Prime he knew that this was one of those occasions when he had to stand tall for the rest of them. "You're chastising yourself far worse than I could," he added. "And right now we need to find them. Do you have any idea where they might have gone?"

"They wanted to take a better look at the ocean floor. To see if they could locate anything our initial scans might have missed."

"Now why would they want to do that?" Jazz asked.

"We'd already completed the reconnaissance phase," Prowl spit out, sounding insulted.

"Well, I didn't put much stock in what Rodimus and

Bumblebee thought," Ironhide said uncomfortably. "But when Kup agreed with them, I figured there might be something to it."

"Something to what?" Prowl almost growled.

"Look, they just didn't trust these Aquatronians. *I* don't trust these Aquatronians. They said this whole setup seemed too good to be true, and they wanted to take a closer look around."

"I wish they had come to me first," Optimus said.

"They violated the chain of command!" Jazz added.

"That's not the issue, Jazz." Optimus lowered his voice. "The fact of the matter is that I agree with them. There's something very wrong about this place, and I can't quite put my finger on it." He didn't add that in truth, he really wasn't sure if there *was* something wrong. He was still shaky from earlier—still convulsed by larger doubts—but he knew this wasn't the time to give voice to them. He just had to trust his instincts. "If Rodimus had come to me personally, we might have been able to make a better coordinated and more exhaustive search. A subtler one, too, that didn't require us to tip off the Curator. But as it stands, we still might be able to use this opportunity to take a closer look around."

Prowl nodded. He obviously felt negligent himself, but there was only so much a scan of the planet from orbit could accomplish. "How do you want to proceed, Optimus? Perhaps we should wait until the Curator has his search vessels ready."

"No, I don't want to use their ships." Optimus had tried to think of a way to keep the Aquatronians out of the search altogether but had decided that was impossible. If nothing else, he would still need the maps and satellite data the Curator had offered. But Optimus wanted to find his people before the Aquatronians did, and that meant he was going to have to move fast.

"Well, the combat shuttle doesn't have the same deep sea capability as the dropship. We can only use it for an hour or so of underwater use before coming back to the surface. So it's virtually useless for search and rescue."

"Maybe the Aquatronians have—"

"I said I don't want to use their equipment for this. Jazz, contact Silverbolt and find out how long it will take to prep another dropcraft for underwater use. Also, find out if there are any other ships on the Ark suitable for the search that we can deploy immediately."

"On it." Jazz stepped away, using his internal communication systems to link back up with the Ark. Optimus turned back to Prowl.

"I want you to take command of some search teams and cover the shores of this whole island. Maybe they were able to swim back. I know it's a long shot, but we've got to check every angle on this one."

Prowl saluted, then changed into his pursuit-vehicle mode and sped over to the groups of Autobots gathered around the Aquatronian holo-map projector depicting satellite imagery of the seabed. Optimus knew that Prowl was more than a little irate that Rodimus, Kup, and Bumblebee had behaved so rashly. But he also knew that if Prowl was given a specific task, he would complete it to the very best of his ability, and that was the kind of can-do attitude Optimus needed right now.

"What do you want me to do, boss?" Ironhide asked. Optimus put his hand on his old friend's shoulder.

"You stick with me, just like old times." Optimus seemed to hesitate, then said, "I've been having some issues, Ironhide."

"Tell me about it," Ironhide said. "This is a bad situation we're in."

"Not those kinds of issues," Optimus replied. He pointed to the Matrix. "In here. I'm having trouble trusting my own intuition. I need you to help keep me . . . Be my eyes and ears. Let me know if I seem to be acting oddly and not realizing it. Will you do that for me, old friend?"

Ironhide nodded. He figured that Optimus simply wanted to keep him close to keep him out of trouble; even so, Ironhide was touched that Optimus would make such a show of needing his help. After all, Optimus was a Prime and was guided by the wisdom of the greatest leaders. Why did he need the opinion of a worn-down bucket of bolts like him? Yet Ironhide was proud to stand at his leader's side regardless of the circumstances. It was the least he could do to make up for letting Rodimus and the others go off the reservation. But before he could voice his gratitude, Jazz came running back over with a frantic look on his face.

"Optimus! Sound the alert!"

"Calm down, Jazz. What's going on?"

"It's the Decepticons! They've found us!"

Chapter Eighteen

SIDESWIPE HAD BEEN GETTING BORED. THE ARK WAS now in the middle of its tenth orbit around the planet below, and he'd already seen everything worth seeing. That which wasn't wreathed in clouds was covered in ocean, and everything that mattered was clearly under that sea. The away team would have to figure out the rest, but apparently they were having some issues. Kup, Rodimus, and Bumblebee had managed to get themselves lost—or maybe there was something more sinister going on. The Curator undoubtedly was hiding something, but Sideswipe had no doubt Optimus was up to the task of ferreting it out.

"Anomaly detected," Teletraan-1 said.

Sideswipe looked up. "Where?" he asked.

"In the second planetary ring." The screens lit up with imagery showing a portion of that ring. It looked normal enough.

"Magnify," Sideswipe ordered.

Teletraan-1 obliged, zooming in, the detail becoming fine enough that if someone had just walked onto the bridge at that moment, he'd never have guessed they were looking at a planetary ring. It was more like crystal under a microscope, filled with fractal edges and intricate patterns. Accompanying readouts showed the basic structure, most of it debris, that presumably once had formed the space bridges that led to this planet. But there was something in that mass that had no business being there—blurry and indistinct yet too large to simply be more of that debris.

"Give me magnetometer readings," Sideswipe said. "And let's have spectrometers while we're at it."

Hatches on the hull outside slid open; instruments protruded and began active scanning of the anomaly. There was a disadvantage in doing that, of course, because if that anomaly was intelligent, it would know it had been detected, since now it was being subjected to a full spectrum of electromagnetic waves. But Sideswipe had to have more data.

In short order, he got it.

"Anomaly identified as the *Nemesis*," Teletraan-1 said in a dispassionate voice that utterly failed to do justice to the situation. The specs of the massive warship lit up the screen, along with the faint pulsing of its engines. It must have been making its way through the complicated ring structure for some time, Sideswipe realized, slowly creeping in toward the Ark's orbit. Now it was only a few thousand miles away.

And it was about to get a lot closer. Realizing it had been detected, the *Nemesis* gunned its engines to full blast, emerging from the ring and streaking straight at its prey, firing several barrages of missiles as it did so. Sideswipe hit the alarm; Klaxons began sounding throughout the Ark.

"Give me manual control," he yelled to Teletraan-1 as he raced for the pilot's chair. Even as he was strapping himself in, he was activating the thrusters, sending the Ark hurtling forward, moving away from the *Nemesis* at an angle. But the Decepticon warship altered its vector of approach.

As did its missiles.

"Impact in ten seconds," Teletraan-1 said.

Silverbolt came running onto the bridge.

"What in the name of Primus is going on?" he yelled.

"What does it look like? We're under attack!" Sideswipe retorted. Silverbolt glanced at the tactical display and saw the oncoming bulk of the *Nemesis* streaking toward them.

"Missile impact in five seconds," Teletraan-1 said.

Sideswipe pulled back on the stick, twisting the Ark off to the side while he deployed several packets of decoys. The Decepticon missiles exploded among them, barely a few hundred meters from the Ark's hull. Silverbolt slapped Sideswipe on the back and eyed the shipwide com-system.

"Red alert! All hands to battle stations! I repeat, red aler—"

But suddenly Silverbolt was knocked to the floor as a massive explosion shook the ship.

"Where the slag did that come from?" he yelled.

The hull cameras had the answer. Flickering suddenly into view on one of them was—

"Skywarp!" Sideswipe snarled.

The Decepticon teleportation artist removed a plasma bomb from his armor and planted it on the hull. Apparently he'd already used one to considerable effect. Sideswipe stabbed a button on his console, and the hull of the Ark magnetized; Skywarp was hurled off into space as though he'd been shot from a cannon. One of the Ark's gun batteries opened fire on him, but its shells ripped through empty vacuum as Skywarp teleported back to the *Nemesis*.

The next moment the second bomb exploded, ripping off a whole segment of the hull. Several Autobots were blown out into space even as air lock doors slammed shut to maintain pressurization.

"Damage report," Sideswipe barked.

"Hyperdrive actuator is out," Teletraan-1 replied. "Auxiliary actuator compromised."

"What does that mean?" Silverbolt asked.

"It means we can't go to lightspeed!" said Sideswipe.

"We wouldn't want to," Silverbolt said. "We can't leave Optimus!"

"Sure, but if the intake accelerators are damaged, they're going to catch us." He keyed the coms. "We need an emergency repair crew down to engineering, and we need it now—"

But Teletraan-1 was already interrupting. "Negative. Engineering room hull breach."

"Those dirty Decepticreeps!" Sideswipe cursed.

"They never fight fair!" Silverbolt yelled, slamming his fist down on his armrest. "There's no way we can outrun them!"

"Doesn't mean we're not gonna try," Sideswipe said. He worked the controls; the Ark surged toward the planet's pole, exchanging fire with the *Nemesis*, which raced after it.

"Have you tried to reach Optimus planetside?" Silverbolt asked.

"I got word to Jazz, but now the Decepticons have jammed communications. We're on our own up here."

"Same down there," Silverbolt said.

IT WAS THE MOTHER OF ALL FIREWORKS DISPLAYS, AND IT was the last thing Optimus Prime wanted to see. The Ark was a ball of fire streaking across the sky—so close to the planet now that it was touching the atmosphere as it raced across the southern pole—while behind it came the *Nemesis*, slightly higher but reflecting enough sunlight to be starkly visible. Both ships were firing away at each other with everything they had. Flashes of light roiled the sky, followed by the sound of thunder rolling over the ocean.

"This is not good," Jazz said.

"Really?" Prowl asked sarcastically.

"He looks like he's coming in to land," Ironhide said. "That's *atmospheric reentry* we're seeing—"

"It's not," Optimus said. "Sideswipe's cutting it as close to the planet as he can to get it between him and the *Nemesis*."

"But why doesn't he come down here and pick us up?" Prowl asked. "That's the *ultimate battle* going on up there, and here we are stuck as spectators at the bottom of this gravity well." He was beside himself with frustration, but Optimus just shook his head.

"Prowl, Sideswipe's making the right call. The last thing he should do now is come pick us up. Because then the *Nemesis* would just rain fire down on him from space. Destroying all of us in the process."

"So you're saying all we can do is sit here and watch," Jazz said through gritted teeth.

"Sometimes patience is the only option," Optimus told him. But the calm with which he said those words belied the emotions raging within him. How could he have been so foolish as to take so many of his key lieutenants onto the planet with him? And why hadn't he ensured that scouts were deployed throughout the system to provide early warning of any Decepticon approach? If the Ark was destroyed, they'd be stranded down here, and it wouldn't take Megatron long to figure out that Optimus was still alive down on the planet. After that, Optimus wouldn't be alive much longer, not when Megatron had the *Nemesis* and all his troops at his disposal. Optimus couldn't help wondering if his errors of judgment were due to his inner turmoil and confusion over the

Matrix and his memories. But that was no consolation whatsoever. And it certainly was no excuse. He watched as the glow of the Ark vanished over the horizon, the *Nemesis* accelerating after it; he wondered how this situation could get any more precarious.

"What's going on?" a voice inquired.

Optimus turned to see Kup rolling toward him, Rodimus and Bumblebee trundling right behind.

"You're kidding me," Prowl said. "Where the slag have you guys been?"

"Downstairs," Rodimus said, switching to humanoid form. He gestured at a doorway in a nearby tower from which they'd just emerged.

Jazz's voice was dangerously soft. "And what's downstairs?"

"All sorts of things," Rodimus said enthusiastically. "We took the pod over to the seabed and came up through the roots of the city. They've got whole chambers loaded with mining equipment, and there was one room filled with . . . with . . . how would you put it, Kup?"

"Dormant fish-bots," Kup said. He felt like he was forgetting something, but the next moment the feeling passed.

"Yeah," Rodimus repeated, "dormant fish-bots. Keeping them in reserve, I guess."

"You guys were crazy to wander off alone," Jazz said angrily.

Rodimus looked abashed. "We just thought this place was suspicious, like we should take a closer look."

"Sure, we need to take a closer look," Jazz said. "But the three of you wandering off like that wasn't the way to do it."

Rodimus ignored him. "Optimus, I'm sorry. We shouldn't have. But the place looks pretty clean from what we could see." Like Kup, he felt like there was something he ought to mention but just couldn't put his finger on it. And right now his main concern was avoiding Optimus's anger.

But Optimus showed none. "There's no time for recriminations right now," he said. "We've got bigger problems. The Decepticons are here."

MEGATRON HAD NEVER FELT SO HAPPY. HE STOOD ON the bridge watching as the *Nemesis*'s forward cannon subjected the Ark's rear shields to unholy amounts of firepower. The planet Aquatron rolled past beneath, the Ark swooping close to the atmosphere as it tried to vector below the *Nemesis*'s line of sight. But the *Nemesis*'s engines were undamaged, and the Decepticon craft was rapidly overtaking the Autobot ship. Megatron grinned.

"Today is a good day for you to die, librarian," he said under his breath.

"Excuse me, sire?" Starscream asked.

"Shut up, fool. Close the distance and prepare boarding parties."

"Standing by to activate tractor beam," Soundwave said.

"How soon?" Megatron asked.

"We're inside the one-minute window, lord."

"Hail them," Megatron said. "If Optimus has any honor, he'll accept my challenge to personal combat."

Starscream liked the sound of that. Before he and his Seekers boarded, the Ark was going to be crippled even worse than it was now. The surviving Autobots wouldn't be able to put up much of a resistance. Thus, the Decepticons' victory was assured, and the only way the situation could get more ideal would be if Optimus somehow was able to defeat Megatron in a duel. Because then Optimus would be no match for the combined

wrath of the hundreds of remaining Decepticons, and
Starscream would be left in charge of everything. He
glanced at his leader's smiling face and couldn't resist a
subtle smirk. The smartest thing to do would be to just
destroy the Ark entirely, but Megatron's ego had to be
satisfied. And that was just fine by Starscream.

Except that apparently Optimus didn't want to fight.

"DON'T ANSWER," SILVERBOLT SAID AS THE
communication line buzzed again. The *Nemesis* was
trying to hail them, and the last thing Silverbolt wanted
was any kind of dialogue.

"Why?" Sideswipe asked as he pushed the Ark's engines
into the red zone. The bridge began to shake as the ship's
metal groaned in protest. "They're right on our tail. We
might be able to buy ourselves more time."

"*Megatron* is on the end of that line," Silverbolt snapped.
"And no prize for guessing he wants to talk to *Optimus*.
Who isn't here, because he's *down on the planet*. And the
only reason Megatron didn't have Skywarp plant a bomb
big enough to destroy us altogether is so he can board
us and fight some insane duel with the only Autobot he
wants to annihilate personally. So if he finds out Optimus
is down below, he's going to stop at nothing to finish us
off and then swoop down on Optimus."

Sideswipe got it. "So you're saying the only reason
we're still alive—"

"Is that we're not answering that call. Yeah. That's
precisely what I'm saying."

"Well, that's great, but we're still about to get boarded
and massacred."

"Not if I can help it," Silverbolt said. "I've got a plan."

Sideswipe switched off the com-link. "Tell me more,"
he said.

*   *   *

"THEY'RE REFUSING TO ANSWER OUR BROADCAST," Soundwave said.

"Optimus," Megatron snarled. "You are a traitor, but I never marked you for a coward."

"Didn't you hear what Soundwave just said, lord?" Starscream couldn't resist. "Optimus isn't on the line. He's not taking your calls."

Megatron gave Starscream a look that made him glad he was on the other side of the bridge. "He's still going to die," he said. "And if you open your mouth again, so will you."

"Thirty seconds to tractor-beam range," Soundwave said.

OPTIMUS AND HIS FELLOW AUTOBOTS NO LONGER COULD see the combat, but they could certainly sense it. Electromagnetic waves rippled through the atmosphere, testimony to the titanic clash of energies taking place on the far side of the planet. Only a few more minutes passed before a glow suffused the southern horizon.

"They're coming around again," Jazz said.

Optimus nodded. From the condition of the Ark, he was surprised they'd been able to make the chase last for an entire circumlocution of the planet. But it couldn't go on much longer. The fact that the Ark was fleeing meant that it must have been damaged too badly to stand and fight; the fact that it hadn't gone to lightspeed meant that the damage extended to the engines. He begged the Matrix within him for insight, but it was the same as before: nothing. No answer.

Just when he needed it the most.

"Optimus," said a voice.

Optimus whirled to see the Curator standing there, a strange expression on his face. Then again, everything about that being was strange.

"I know," the Curator said.

"You know what?"

"You are suspicious of us. I understand that. It is only natural. But now your true enemies have come calling." As the Curator spoke, the Ark came into view again and raced along the distant horizon, the *Nemesis* steadily closing what remained of the gap. The next moment the Ark must have been struck directly by one of the Decepticon warship's shots, for an explosion engulfed it; it was so bright that Optimus had to glance away. But when he looked back, the Ark was still intact. Still fighting.

And the Curator was still staring at him.

"These are the Decepticons, no?"

"They are," Optimus said. "And when they are finished with the Ark, they will surely come for you."

"We are not without defenses," said the Curator. He looked over at Rodimus, Kup, and Bumblebee. "And it seems you are no longer without your friends."

"Your assistance was not required," Optimus said. "But thank you nonetheless."

"Perhaps we can assist in other ways," the Curator said. He gestured at the blazing dogfight in the sky. "If you want, we can help you with the Decepticons."

"You can?"

"Only if you want us to."

"Only if I— Wait a second; what do you want in return?"

"Nothing too onerous, I daresay." The peculiar earnestness of the Curator's previous cadence had disappeared; now he was all business. "But if we take time to talk terms, your ship will be lost. Your cause will be doomed. So do you want our help or don't you?"

Optimus stared at him. "I will do anything to save the Ark."

"So be it," the Curator said. He turned and began walking away. The doors of the nearby tower irised open to receive him.

"Wait a minute," Optimus said.

"Yes?" The Curator stopped in the doorway but didn't turn.

"What happens now?"

"Everything," said the Curator.

The door irised shut behind him.

Chapter Nineteen

On the *Nemesis*, one of the screens began flashing. Soundwave leaned forward.

"Lord Megatron, we're picking up multiple contacts."

"Where?" Megatron demanded.

"Just launched from the Ark. Fast attack craft, closing on us."

"Bring up the visuals," Megatron said.

"At once." The images of Silverbolt, Air Raid, Slingshot, Skydive, and Fireflight came into crisp focus on the targeting scanner. The Autobot fighters were flying fast in close formation. Starscream snorted in disgust.

"A suicide mission," he said. "Seeking to delay us from getting into tractor-beam range."

"Destroy them," Megatron said. Some of the guns of the *Nemesis* switched from the Ark to the incoming targets, but the five Autobots zigged and zagged, weaving past the bolts of energy that seared past them as they soared in toward the *Nemesis*. As they closed in—

"We should commence evasive action," Starscream said. "Target them all with all our guns."

"All they can do is strafe," Megatron scoffed. "We'll laugh off their spitballs. Stay on the Ark. We almost have them."

"Five seconds to tractor-beam range," Soundwave confirmed.

The Aerialbots dodged past the last wave of gunnery, roaring above the top decks of the *Nemesis*, heading in toward the bridge.

"Do your worst," Megatron said with a sneer.

The Aerialbots did.

Instead of opening fire, they closed on one another, simultaneously shifting into alt-mode and using their forward momentum to merge abruptly, creating a single colossal silver-and-red jet trooper that proceeded to land on top of the *Nemesis*, wielding the largest electrostatic rifle any of the Decepticons had ever seen.

Starscream's eyes practically bugged out of his head. "What in the name of Unicron is that?"

"It doesn't matter," Megatron screamed. "Concentrate all fire!"

But it was too late.

"I AM SUPERION!" yelled the giant combiner robot as it fired a bolt of energy at the *Nemesis*'s bridge, scoring a direct hit. For a moment the entire bridge was filled with lightning; electrical feedback flashed through the *Nemesis* like wildfire, blowing out consoles all over the ship. Soundwave and Starscream were hurled back into the far wall. Only Megatron remained on his feet.

"Get that scrap heap off my warship!" he yelled as he shook off the bridge's wreckage. "NOW!"

His soldiers were already on it. All over the *Nemesis* hatches opened; Decepticons poured out to face the behemoth astride their spacecraft, buzzing around Superion like angry bees while the *Nemesis*'s batteries opened up at point-blank range, sending missiles, lasers, and superheated plasma streaking toward Superion. Multiple hits and explosions knocked the massive rifle from his hands, but he just reached down, digging his mighty fists deep into the *Nemesis*'s hull, tearing off a huge piece of plated armor and using it as a shield to ward off the incoming fire. Then he strode straight toward the bridge, right at the Decepticon leader, his booming voice lost in the vacuum but vibrating through the hull of the ship.

"PREPARE TO BE DESTROYED, MEGATRON!"

"You've got it the wrong way around," said Megatron. He amped up his fusion cannon and let fly. The blast was like a supernova going off. As the glare dimmed, Megatron fully expected to see Superion's smoking wreckage.

Except there was no sign of Superion anywhere.

Megatron adjusted his optics. Had the cannon disintegrated the giant robot entirely? It couldn't have—the gun wasn't *that* powerful. Not against a bot the size of Superion, at any rate. Megatron stormed forward out of the remnants of the bridge, across the hull of the *Nemesis*. It suddenly occurred to him that there was only one place Superion *could* have gone, one single place he could have sought safety. As he reached the spot where Superion had been standing, his suspicions were confirmed: He saw the gaping hole in the hull of the *Nemesis* even as he heard the alarms wailing from deep within.

SEVERAL LEVELS BELOW, SUPERION WAS RIPPING HIS way through floors and ceilings, pulling Decepticons apart with his bare hands as he tore his way into the depths of the *Nemesis*. He was making for the ship's hangar bays, where he knew he'd have more room to maneuver. Nothing in this ship could stop him. The only thing he had to worry about was Megatron, and he had a head start on the Decepticon leader. In the meantime he was doing as much damage to the ship as he could. Once he was in the hangar bays, he'd be adjacent to the engines, and then he could quickly turn the *Nemesis* back into a glorified space station. Without propulsion, the ship's pursuit of the Ark would be at an end, and the Decepticons would be left stranded in this sector of space. Superion tore through another wall and emerged into the first of the hangar bays. The Decepticons had had enough time to get their defenses together now; they'd realized that an implacable enemy was loose inside their flagship and had taken steps to trap him. Superion smiled as he saw the several squadrons of Vehicons who awaited him.

"Let's do this," he said.

The Vehicons charged, streaking toward Superion from all sides. Shots laced in, striking the giant bot everywhere, and then it was hand-to-hand mayhem. Several Vehicons kamikazied into Superion in their eagerness to get at him, but the only bots they succeeded in destroying were themselves. After a flurry of blows from Superion had turned several more Vehicons into junk, the others pulled back, seeking to keep Superion surrounded while they fired away at him. But the monstrous bot was so well armored that their efforts were like the buzzing of flies. He strode deeper into the hangar, blazing away with his electrostatic rifle, blasting parked shuttles and fueling equipment. Fires broke out everywhere; Superion aimed his rifle at the far wall, firing and blowing a hole clean through. On the other side were the engine rooms. He raised his rifle, letting it recharge—

"Not so fast," said a voice.

Megatron emerged into the hangar bay with an enraged look on his face. But his voice was disconcertingly calm.

"I have to hand it to you," he said. "No one's done that kind of damage to my flagship in a while."

"It's not even *your ship*," Superion said. "It's supposed to be a scientific station that belongs to the people of Cybertron."

"And the people of Cybertron belong to me."

"In your deluded head, maybe. But thanks to Optimus, we all know better."

"Optimus?" Megatron's voice was cold. "Don't talk to me of *Optimus*. His words are as noble as his actions are weak."

"Weak? Leading a resistance against you is weak?"

"He's such a coward, he sent you to die in his place."

Superion laughed. "I'm not planning on dying." Abruptly he brought up his gun and fired, missing only because Megatron was already switching to spacecraft mode and roaring straight toward him. Superion didn't have time for a second shot; Megatron struck him in the chest, knocking him sprawling and sending his rifle flying. Superion lunged out to grab Megatron, but the Decepticon leader was too fast, gunning his retros and streaking back out of reach, shifting back into humanoid form and aiming his fusion cannon as he did so.

"GET OFF MY SHIP," he bellowed.

This time Superion had nowhere to hide. The shot blew him straight through the hangar door and into space, flinging his component bots out in all directions, streaming flame behind them, blaring out automated distress calls. Megatron wasted no time savoring his triumph; he stormed back to what was left of the bridge and plugged directly into a console to take personal control of the *Nemesis*. The Ark had used the distraction of Superion to pull away from the *Nemesis*, but now Megatron poured all reserve power into the forward engine banks, swooping in toward the Ark. Starscream pulled himself to his feet and looked up, dazed, through the remnants of the bridge's roof as space raced past.

"What's happening?" he asked.

"I'm winning," Megatron said as he activated the tractor beam.

*   *   *

SIDESWIPE'S SCANNERS CONFIRMED THE WORST. SUPERION'S gambit had failed, and now nothing stood between him and the *Nemesis*. The Ark was rocking under the renewed bombardment, the rear shields were disintegrating, and as smoke began to billow from the consoles around him, he came to a grim conclusion: The safety of the Ark and its crew was secondary. The primary goal was to make sure that Optimus survived, and alone down on the planet he wouldn't have much of a chance against even a damaged *Nemesis*. Sideswipe knew that Megatron would have no compunctions about raining down bombs until nothing was left, that he'd happily kill every living thing on Aquatron if he thought it would destroy Optimus Prime.

And that couldn't happen, for Optimus was the light and the hope of all Autobots. Optimus held the Matrix of Leadership, without which the AllSpark could never be recovered. Sideswipe keyed the ship's intercom and gave what he knew would be his final order.

"All hands abandon ship! I repeat all hands abandon ship!" Escape pod launch lights went green as the Autobots followed orders and ditched. The primary launch bays disgorged a wave of support craft, and even as they did so, the *Nemesis* caught the Ark in its tractor beam.

But that was just fine by Sideswipe. He was now the sole Autobot aboard the Ark; he swung the ship around, aiming it straight at the *Nemesis,* and then hit the throttle, coaxing the damaged engines to the limits of their remaining capacity, the Decepticon tractor beam inadvertently working in his favor, accelerating his kamikaze run toward the *Nemesis*. The Autobots would lose the Ark, but the Decepticons would lose everything. And Sideswipe would die free, at the helm of his beloved ship. He watched as the *Nemesis* rushed toward him.

* * *

"THEY'RE COMING STRAIGHT AT US," STARSCREAM YELLED.

That was the last thing Megatron had expected. For Optimus to get his lieutenants to embark on suicide runs was one thing, but now the entire Ark was doing it. For the first time it occurred to Megatron that Optimus might not actually *be* on the Ark, that there was some larger scheme afoot that he had missed.

But right now he had more pressing problems.

"Reverse polarity on the tractor beam!" he screamed. "Evasive action! Hit that thing with everything we have!" The tractor beam switched to repel, but the Ark's momentum was still carrying it forward. The *Nemesis* raked the Ark with withering fire, revving its thrusters in a desperate attempt to get out of the way of the oncoming Autobot ship. Megatron watched as the Ark filled his field of vision. He heard Soundwave saying something about how he was picking up an energy burst from the planetary rings—that they were changing color. Megatron marveled at his lieutenant's capacity for trivial detail, for the Ark was almost on top of them. He braced himself to leap from the *Nemesis*.

And then everything went crazy.

There was a sudden flash from the planet's innermost ring. A massive electromagnetic pulse struck both ships, which instantly lost all power. For a moment so did Megatron— then his backup systems came online. He switched on his own sensors and looked around. The darkened Ark was spinning off at an angle from the crippled *Nemesis*.

"What just happened?" Megatron demanded to know.

"Most of the ship's systems are out, my lord! The same with the Autobot ship!" Soundwave reported. "It looks like they've been knocked off their collision course as well."

"Weapons?"

"Not responding," Starscream answered.

That was when Megatron received a beacon emanating from the planet below.

"Optimus?" he growled.

"I fear you are mistaken," said the voice of the Curator.

"Then tell me who you are to dare to get in my way. What name shall we call your ashes?"

"I am the Curator, and I regret to tell you that you are violating neutral space."

"Neutral? You are now my enemy, and you will die like a—"

"I will do no such thing. Nor am I your enemy. I shut down both your ship *and* that of the Autobots because you were engaging in combat within the sovereign territory of Aquatron. Now I invite you to join me on the surface of this planet."

"You *invite* me?"

"Let me be more candid," the Curator said. "What you just experienced was our planetary defense system on its lowest setting. Should you not accept my invitation, we shall introduce you to its more advanced capabilities."

Megatron thought fast. "What lies has Optimus told you?" he asked.

"He is down here with me now, so you can ask him that yourself."

"So you *are* in league with the Autobots."

"No. As I said, I am neutral. There will be no fighting on this planet. Just talk."

"Like we're doing now?" Megatron said scornfully.

"No. This is just the preliminary discussion. Gather your lieutenants and come down to this planet. All will be explained then to both you and the Autobots under my personal flag of truce."

Megatron looked at the darkened *Nemesis* around him and realized he had no choice. For all he knew, the

Curator really *wasn't* in league with the Autobots, but in that case, the Autobots were in the same predicament he was. In order to defeat this Curator, he would have to play along. He needed more information.

And then he would crush them all.

"I accept your invitation," he said.

"Here are the coordinates," said the Curator.

THE AUTOBOT SHUTTLE SPED SOUTH TOWARD THE location specified by the Curator. Optimus had no idea what was there, but it didn't look like he had much of a choice. The Curator had kept his promise to deal with the *Nemesis*, but he'd also shut down the Ark. The leader of Aquatron held all the cards now, so he might have been forgiven a sly smile as his face appeared on a screen in the cockpit.

But Optimus refused to show any weakness. "What have you done with the Ark?" he demanded.

"You asked me to help you preserve it," the Curator said. "And I have done so."

"You paralyzed it."

"Had I not, it would have destroyed the *Nemesis*. And I never pledged the destruction of the Decepticons. I merely promised to save you from them."

"So what happens now?"

"I have spoken with both Megatron and your pilot, Sideswipe. The Autobots that evacuated the Ark have returned to it, and they will stay there for the duration of our discussions at the Pavilion."

"And what is the Pavilion?"

"A sacred place," the Curator said. "No violence of any kind is tolerated there. Please remember that during the negotiations."

"*What* negotiations?"

But the screen had gone blank.

"I don't like this one bit," Prowl said.

"He's got us by the circuits," Jazz muttered.

"But he *did* stop the *Nemesis* from destroying the Ark," Kup said. The old veteran couldn't understand how anyone could have a problem with the Curator. He'd been suspicious before his unsanctioned exploration of the undercity, but now he felt confident that the Curator had their best interests at heart.

"I guess we'll have to see what this Pavilion is," said Ironhide.

"I think I see it now," Rodimus said, staring out the window.

Everyone crowded together to take in the view. Outside lay endless ocean, yet something had just broken the surface, was rising from that sea even as the craft soared in toward it: a massive structure of all manner of levels and platforms, the base widening as the summit extended ever higher, until it became clear it was nothing less than a gigantic pyramid-island protruding from the middle of the water now pouring off it in sheets.

"They had *that* under the sea?" Prowl asked in a tone of wonder.

"They have a *lot* of stuff down there," Jazz said. "We still have barely any idea what else is—"

"*Look at the sky,*" Rodimus said.

They all saw it now: flares of light that could only be objects hitting the atmosphere. The Autobots focused their optics to reveal—

"Decepticons," Jazz said. "Heading straight for that Pavilion."

"Megatron doesn't look too happy," said Prowl.

"He's not the only one," Ironhide muttered.

*   *   *

THE SHUTTLE ALIGHTED ON THE VERY APEX OF THE Pavilion. The Autobots stepped out to find the Decepticons already waiting for them. Amazingly, no one fired at anybody. That was partly because Optimus and Megatron had both impressed upon their followers the wisdom—if not the necessity—of heeding the Curator's wishes. But it undoubtedly also was due to the sheer surrealism of the situation: the Autobots disembarking from the craft, staring at the Decepticons only about twenty meters away, at the edge of the Pavilion's roof. Though Megatron was certainly happy to try to provoke the Autobots into doing something that might bring the Curator's wrath down on their heads.

"Optimus," said Megatron, "so nice to see you."

"Megatron," Optimus said coldly, though he raised a hand in formal greeting.

"You've led us on a merry chase across the galaxy. And you might have saved us a lot of trouble."

Optimus said nothing. Megatron laughed, warming to the task of provocation. "So let's see . . . The only reason you're still alive is because the Curator took a liking to you. What did you have to do to achieve that? What favors did you offer him?"

"I offered him no favors," Optimus said stiffly.

"But maybe one of your clueless minions did?" Megatron glanced at Jazz. "Perhaps Jazz here has betrayed you the same way you betrayed me?"

"Why you—" Jazz started forward, only to be held back by Optimus's outstretched arm.

"We agreed to a truce, Jazz." Then, turning back to Megatron: "Though I would suggest you are straying dangerously close to shredding the spirit if not the letter of that law."

"*Law,*" Megatron scoffed. "A figure of speech and a maladroit one at that. What law do you speak of?"

"Mine," said the Curator.

He rose through a trapdoor that irised open in the middle of the roof, halfway between the two rivals.

"I have a confession to make," he said.

"This ought to be good," Megatron said.

"I have been less than forthcoming with you."

"Then you should tell us everything," Optimus said.

"And so I shall. I am a representative of the Quintesson Co-Prosperity Sphere, of which this planet Aquatron is a proud member."

Everyone stared blankly at him except Optimus, who looked appalled.

"The *Quintessons*?" he said. His days spent in the library had given him access to databases containing much bygone lore; he knew that the Quintessons were a race that had fought many wars with Cybertron in the distant past. They had even landed on Cybertron itself once, and had temporarily occupied the planet. Which meant that—

"You are our *enemy*," he said.

The Curator looked embarrassed. "Once that may have been true. Our ancestors were a primitive people, and like many primitives, they saw force as the only solution to problems."

"Whereas you just lie," Ironhide said.

"This is a dangerous galaxy," the Curator told him. "And like our ancestors, you Cybertronians *do* believe in violence as a solution. Can you blame us for proceeding with caution? If I engaged in subterfuge, I did it only to protect this planet."

"Which is *not* Quintessa," Megatron said, trying to get things straight.

"No," said the Curator. "It truly is Aquatron."

"So where's Quintessa?"

"Far away," the Curator said, gesturing at the stars overhead. "I see no particular reason for you to know its exact location. Perhaps that moment should await our becoming better friends."

Starscream spoke up for the first time. "So Aquatron is part of your empire?"

"Not empire," the Curator said. "Co-Prosperity Sphere."

Megatron laughed skeptically. "And what's the difference?"

"The difference is that we no longer engage in war and we no longer attempt to dominate others. All worlds within our Sphere are trading partners. Aquatron has its own self-government and is free to leave the Sphere at any time."

"Let me guess," Megatron said sarcastically. "You'd like to incorporate Cybertron into your empire—sorry, I mean Co-Prosperity Sphere."

"Only if Cybertron someday wished it. But right now your world is at war. A civil war no less, between the two groups standing here. Autobots and Decepticons."

"An accurate summary of the situation," Optimus said. "And we should not have brought our conflict to your planet."

The Curator waved that aside. "Optimus, Megatron. There is a better way."

Megatron scowled. "And that is?"

"Peace."

"A fine word," Megatron scoffed. "But only possible when every traitor has been destroyed."

"*Traitor* is just a word, too," said the Curator. "But definitions can change. As can hearts and minds. Our people are proof of that. We have spent eons trying to atone for the acts committed by our ancestors. And today I seek one more such atonement."

"Namely?"

"I have brought you both to this Pavilion so that you may sign a peace treaty."

There was a moment's stunned silence.

"Impossible," Megatron said.

"If it turns out to be so, then you may both leave freely. But I believe your differences can be resolved, and I ask for twenty-four hours to help you bridge them. You may stay at this Pavilion during that time, in luxury accommodations. Our trading expertise has made us masters of negotiation. If there is a way to solve the problems that plague Cybertron, we will find it. If there is not, then both Ark and *Nemesis* may depart with full stocks of Energon."

"What do you gain from this?" Optimus asked.

"If you are no longer at war, there is likely to be more trade. But as I said, our motives also involve less material concerns."

"My faith in peace has been battered by millennia of fighting," Optimus said. "But perhaps all the blood that has been shed demands that I be willing to at least talk."

The Curator turned to Megatron. "What say you?"

"Yes," Megatron said to everybody's surprise.

"We cannot do that," Starscream protested.

"I am in command," Megatron snapped. "And you are still under my orders. We will try for peace."

Though his mind was on anything but that.

Chapter Twenty

THE DECEPTICONS HAD FORTIFIED IACON AGAINST assault from an army and deployed their forces accordingly. That meant that sneaking inside was easier than their propaganda claimed. The trick was to go in the same way bots were getting *out*. Refugees were attempting to escape from Iacon all the time. Most of them were caught, of course, and then summarily executed or sent to the labor camps, which in practice amounted to the same thing. But Iacon's garrison had yet to come close to sealing all the bolt-holes out of the city. Thus did Ultra Magnus, Wheeljack, Springer, Jetfire, and Rack n' Ruin get in without anybody realizing it—sidling up to the walls along a fissure cracked open by a long-ago bomb and then creeping through a series of abandoned pipes, making their way through some shattered industrial plant, and climbing rusty staircase after staircase until they emerged into Iacon.

Which had changed.

"Primus save us," Wheeljack said as he gazed at the battered skyline. The only lights visible were those of the gleaming spire of the tower in the distance and—substantially closer—the Decagon, which had been turned into the headquarters of the city's defenses.

Rumor had it that they were under the control of Ratbat now, which didn't surprise Wheeljack in the slightest. That wretched little bot was the ultimate opportunist; he'd been the slimiest of politicians in the days of the corrupt caste system, and the fact that he was now loyal to Shockwave only confirmed Wheeljack's view that someone should have taken care of Ratbat a long time ago.

But now was not that time. They had more important matters to focus on. Ultra Magnus had been adamant that making straight for the tower would be suicide, that they needed more information not just on the tower defenses but also on the exact location of Alpha Trion. But they couldn't stay on the streets for long, because Shockwave had turned the city into a web of surveillance. Cameras were everywhere. So were patrols, particularly during the evening hours of curfew. The next few hours were a nightmare of crawling through ruins and sewers as the group gradually made its way across the city. Wheeljack couldn't believe how squalid life had become under the Decepticons. The Energon pools were dry. The Stellar Galleries were shattered. And gangs were everywhere, steering clear of the Decepticons while they concentrated on fighting one another and preying on the innocents who remained.

Not that there were many innocents left. Most had been corrupted by now, and it broke Wheeljack's heart to see bots crouching in the wreckage of once-great halls, furtively imbibing the Dark Energon they had purchased from the very gangs from which they were now trying to hide. He couldn't believe Shockwave wasn't trying to put a stop to this.

"He *encourages* it," Ultra Magnus said, as though reading his mind. "Helps keep the population docile."

"It's more than that," added Rack n' Ruin.

"He's evil," Springer said with some feeling.

"He's a Decepticon," Wheeljack said, glancing at Jetfire, whose attention was elsewhere. "What do you expect?"

But it was Jetfire who answered. "Shockwave is no ordinary Decepticon," he said.

"I guess you should know," Springer said.

"Stow that right now," Ultra Magnus growled.

"The typical Decepticon believes in straightforward control," Jetfire said as though neither of the other two had spoken. "Shockwave takes it a step further. He sees this city as his laboratory, just one big experiment. And seeing how Dark Energon addiction plays out in a semicontrolled environment is the least of it. Everybody here is just a rat in a maze."

"Including us," Rack n' Ruin muttered.

"We're the random factor," Jetfire said. "The ghost in the machine."

"That's great," said Springer, "but where exactly are we going?"

"There," Ultra Magnus replied, pointing.

IT WAS ONE OF THE FEW INTACT BUILDINGS IN A LOWER east sublevel that was otherwise mostly wreckage, though "intact" was probably too generous a description. The building had fallen into a bad state of disrepair. The windows were boarded up, and on the door was a sign that said PROPERTY CONDEMNED: NO ENTRY. Wheeljack couldn't imagine why they'd come here. It didn't make any sense. Ultra Magnus went up to the door and knocked loudly. The banging of his fist echoed down the deserted street, making Wheeljack look around nervously. But Ultra Magnus didn't seem to care. He just kept knocking.

And then the door opened, sliding aside automatically;

that was surprising since it barely looked like it was capable of operating manually. Ultra Magnus led the way into a darkened room. They shone their lights this way and that, revealing chairs stacked on circular tables. A canvas had been tossed over furniture that ran down the entirety of the far wall. The place was desolate.

But suddenly Wheeljack recognized it anyway.

"This is Maccadam's Old Oil House," he said.

"The one and only," said a voice.

A shadowy figure appeared in the far doorway. The lights flickered on, though the room was still lit only dully. The bot who stood there was old but squat and powerfully built. His armor was done up in resplendent purple and gold, and he sported a particularly fancy goatee.

"Close that door," he said, "or you'll have a patrol trying to follow you in."

"Maccadam," said Ultra Magnus as Springer hastily closed the exterior door. "It's good to see you." The two bots shook hands.

"Welcome," Maccadam said. Wheeljack couldn't believe what he was seeing. Maccadam had always been an enigma, lurking in the shadows of his establishment, giving rise to all sorts of rumors about which of the staff he actually was or whether he ever showed his face in the first place. But now his face was plain to see, and it was one that Wheeljack realized he'd seen many times before.

"You were the *piano player*," he said.

"I still am," Maccadam said. "Though in truth I'm not much given to music these days." He glanced at Rack n' Ruin, but if he was surprised by the composite bot's bizarre appearance, he didn't show it.

"When did the Decepticons close you down?" Springer asked.

"They never did," Maccadam told him. "I just declined to do business with them." He pulled the canvas away to reveal the bar, not to mention a full array of spigots. Rack n' Ruin eyed them thirstily.

"Let me pour you gents a drink," Maccadam offered.

A COUPLE OF ROUNDS OF DRINKS AND AN HOUR OF conversation later and Wheeljack finally was beginning to piece it together. Maccadam's Old Oil House had kept functioning during the early part of the war, a neutral ground where Decepticons and Autobots alike could rub shoulders even as they studiously ignored one another. But all that changed when the Decepticons finally got the upper hand and took over Iacon. There was no more neutrality. You either served the Decepticons or you were en route to the camps. Neither choice endeared itself to Maccadam, so he'd closed up shop.

But he'd dispensed with his neutrality, too, seeing as how the Decepticons had left him no choice. And he'd kept on doing business, only now it was an entirely different kind. What had been the center of Iacon nightlife was now the hub of a spy network dedicated to bringing down the rule of Shockwave. Wheeljack could see the logic. Maccadam knew *everybody*. He had contacts all over the city, and some of them were even Decepticons only too happy to meet Maccadam in camera-free locations over a keg or two. Some of them had been his friends before the war and simply figured they were giving him immunity from arrest in return for some under-the-table refreshment.

"They've got no clue you're guilty of far worse than bootlegging," Ultra Magnus said. The conversation had been almost exclusively between him and Maccadam while the others sipped their drink and listened. They didn't really have much to contribute. It was obvious that Maccadam and Ultra Magnus had been in surreptitious contact for a long while now, that Maccadam had placed his network at the disposal of the Wreckers and was furnishing Ultra Magnus with grade-A intelligence on events within Iacon.

"Things have gone from bad to worse," Maccadam said. "Shockwave isn't even interested in maintaining the city's population at basic subsistence levels. He's practically encouraging mass shutdown. And when bots break down, they just become scrap to feed his factories."

"You're risking the same fate yourself," Ultra Magnus said. "And I know we're dramatically increasing that risk by coming to you, but we're obviously in a bit of a bind and—"

"Don't worry about it," Maccadam said with a wave of his hand. "But the situation's complicated. Alpha Trion has been moved from the tower."

"Where to?" Ultra Magnus asked.

"That's what I'm still trying to figure out."

Ultra Magnus swore under his breath. "Shockwave's trying to keep us all guessing."

"Not just trying," said Maccadam. "Succeeding. My contacts in the tower are scared slagless. Anyone who knows what's up isn't talking. But Shockwave has disappeared as well, so it seems safe to assume that he's personally overseeing whatever's going on."

"And you don't know the what or the where."

"I will soon. I'm meeting in an hour with an engineer who helped build the tower. He said he's got something for me. He's now a member of Ratbat's staff and—"

"Can I go with you?" Rack n' Ruin asked.

"No," Ultra Magnus replied.

"Why would you want to?" Maccadam asked.

"Because I was one of the slaves who worked there. And once you're done talking with this engineer, I wouldn't mind killing him."

Maccadam's expression was a mixture of empathy and

sadness. But he shook his head. "Do you think you're Shockwave's only victim? The bot I'm talking to lost his entire family in the camps. He may be a Decepticon, but he has every reason to hate Shockwave. As does everyone in this room. And all of you are going to stay here till I get back. Are we clear?"

"We'd better be," said Ultra Magnus, looking at each member of his team. They all nodded. Rack n' Ruin emptied his can and reached for another.

Chapter Twenty-one

OPTIMUS PACED BACK AND FORTH IN THE LAVISH SUITE the Curator had given him. Night had fallen, but to say his sleep cycle was disturbed was the height of understatement. So much had happened in the last few hours that he was having a hard time processing it.

The *Quintessons* . . . So they were more than just a myth. History had come back to life, and it wasn't the most glorious of histories, either. The Quintessons really existed. They really had invaded Cybertron once. They really had occupied the planet.

But had they really changed?

Optimus walked to the balcony and gazed up into the night sky. Somewhere up there were the *Nemesis* and the Ark, orbiting the planet over and over. The Quintessons had reenabled ground communications, and Optimus had spoken at length with Sideswipe, briefing the worried pilot on the events taking place down below. There was a place called the Pavilion, he'd told him; the Decepticons were quartered in the east wing, and the Autobots were in the west. In the morning, the Curator would preside over negotiations for a treaty. Optimus had congratulated Sideswipe on his heroics in saving the Ark, but Sideswipe was more concerned about what would happen next on Aquatron. Optimus had brushed aside those concerns, keeping his doubts to himself.

Such was the burden of leadership.

That burden was getting ever heavier. There was so little that was known about the Quintessons in the first place. Where did they actually come from? How many other races had they subjugated over the centuries? Had they truly transformed an autocratic empire into a trading federation? How many Quintessons were there, anyway? The only one Optimus had met was the Curator and perhaps the doctor, Xeros. Were there others on this planet? What about elsewhere? The Curator had declined to specify the location of their home planet, though Optimus could understand that. No sensible race put *that* card on the table unless it had to. But there were so many other cards in play here. In the wake of the Curator's revelations, an emphatic Jazz had told Optimus that they weren't guests, they were prisoners. Perhaps that was true. But the Curator hadn't asked for their weapons. Both Autobots and Decepticons were still heavily armed, and Optimus had told his Autobots to maintain maximum watchfulness. Jazz had taken that quite literally, insisting on standing guard outside Optimus's suite.

Leaving Optimus to his thoughts. Deep in his Spark he knew that the Quintessons once had been anathema to all he stood for. They had subjugated Cybertron long before his time, yet here they were offering their assistance, claiming that they had changed from the tyrannical conquerors they once had been. Could he actually take the chance and accept that they had given up their ambitions of universal dominance? How could he even think about trusting the beings whose ancestors once had attempted to enslave his entire race?

Then again, perhaps the denizens of Cybertron were no better. After all, they had given rise to the Decepticons. Peace with the ones with whom war had been waged for eons . . . The Autobots might have believed it to be impossible, but Optimus was willing to give it a try because whatever anyone else might say, he knew that Megatron wasn't entirely evil. If he had been, it would have been so much easier. There would be no dilemma whatsoever. But it was Megatron who had called him brother once, who had opened his eyes to the rotting caste system and the concept that all beings had a right to rise to their natural level.

The problem was that Megatron thought his own level was above all others. Still, the idea of reaching past Megatron's bluster and finding the heroic gladiator who had inspired him to be more than just Orion Pax . . . Well, that course of action held no little temptation. And if the Quintessons truly had changed for the better, perhaps their influence would help Megatron remember the sense of brotherhood that had united him and Optimus all those years ago. The stakes were getting ever higher, the situation ever more desperate, and Optimus could only wish the Matrix would give him some sort of signal, any kind of guidance. As it stood, he'd received nothing from it since it had sent them in the direction of this planet.

That meant that perhaps the issue here was Optimus himself. Perhaps Ratchet was right; perhaps there were forgotten memories at stake here. Or perhaps it was more fundamental than that; perhaps he had simply lost faith in himself. If he could regain some sense of balance, maybe the Matrix would speak to him again. The ringing door chime drew Optimus out of his thoughts and back to his spartan accommodations.

"Who is it?" Optimus asked.

"You have a visitor," Jazz said over the intercom.

"Send him in."

The door opened, and the Curator entered with a broad smile.

"Hello, Optimus," he said. "May I speak with you for a few minutes?"

"Of course," the Autobot leader replied. He looked past the Curator at Jazz. "It's all right. You can leave us." Jazz gave him an *"if you say so"* look and closed the door. The Curator gazed at Optimus with a look of concern and extended his scaled hands.

"You look worried, my friend."

"Of course I am," Optimus said. "I'm not sure if I can trust you. No offense."

"None taken."

"And even if I can, I have little faith in the Decepticons' desire for peace."

The Curator nodded gravely. "Doubts are only natural. Doubts about peace, doubts about us. It is all right. We expected as much. We realized that if we told you too soon, you would almost certainly have rejected us outright. You would have left, and the Decepticons would have caught up with you somewhere else. And then we would not have been able to help."

Optimus shook his head. "But what makes you care? Why are you so eager to broker a treaty, Curator?"

"Because otherwise you will destroy yourselves. We almost did. For longer than we care to remember, we fought civil wars even as we fought wars of conquest. The same disease lies at the root of both kinds of conflict. Despite all your millions of years, you are still a young race. The races that survive beyond that—as ours has—owe a duty to those who have yet to reach maturity."

"Maturity," Optimus repeated.

"Please do not be offended if I use that word. I am not blind to nuances; I know there is a difference between you and Megatron. That is one of the reasons I wanted to talk to you in private."

"Because of Megatron."

"I am afraid so." The Curator cleared his throat. "Optimus, you and I both know that Megatron is far less likely than you to agree to peace—and far more likely to harbor covert agendas in his heart."

"So why even put the question to him?"

"Because our scenarios indicate that under the right conditions he will say yes."

"And what conditions would those be?"

"All of them depend on you."

"I'm not following you, Curator."

"Optimus, you are the only person in the galaxy whose opinion matters to Megatron."

Optimus laughed. "I think you grossly overestimate his opinion of me."

"No," the Curator insisted. "You are. Please don't think me condescending if I say that our science of psychology is so advanced that we can map it out in mathematics. Let me assure you, Megatron only wants to kill you because you've seen the real him. The Megatron who fought for liberty, the Megatron who wanted to be free. Now he regards that original quest as a weakness. But you can still get through to him, Optimus."

"I can *try*," Optimus said. "But that's all."

"We can help."

"You already told me that."

"We might be able to do still more."

"What do you mean?"

"Malice is very difficult to influence. But Megatron's core is not malice. It is ambition."

Optimus sighed. "There are times I have thought the same thing. But it makes no difference."

"It does."

"Why?"

"Recently, I received word from our homeworld that our scientists have made breakthroughs in somatic engineering."

Optimus searched his databanks without result. "You'll have to define that."

"It's a way to influence circuitry. Not fundamentally, of course. We can't change someone's nature. But we can—*could*—use ultrasonics in the Signature Room to make Megatron more—how shall I put it?—malleable."

"That's a drastic step," Optimus said slowly.

"I'm not about to disagree with you."

"And I'm not sure I'm about to go along with it. Free will means everything to me."

"I would only ask that you think it over. Tomorrow, perhaps your words will be enough."

"And if they aren't?"

"Then either the conference fails or you give us permission to make Megatron more amenable to listening. To both of us, Optimus. I know you believe in free will— so do we. But what matters more, the choices of a bot enraged beyond all reason or the fate of millions?"

"I'm still not sure if Megatron is beyond reason."

"Then tomorrow we will find out. If he still disagrees, then you and I will talk again."

"I'll think it over."

"You should. And while you're doing that, there is one other thing you should consider."

"Name it."

"What would you say if I told you that we know the location of the AllSpark?"

Optimus did his best to hide his surprise. "I would say that seems like another fact that you should have told me about earlier."

"It would have been premature."

"How did you even know we were looking for it?"

"By listening to your conversations, of course. Come, Optimus, you cannot blame us for paying attention to what is obvious. Ensuring that the AllSpark gets back to Cybertron and signing the treaty are the twin pillars of peace. It's impossible to separate the two factors. Cybertron without the AllSpark is like a plant cut off from water. Your world is dying, and we propose to restore it."

"Let's say I believe you," Optimus said cautiously. "Why won't you just tell me the location of the AllSpark now?"

"If we do that, how do we know you won't just return to Cybertron without coming to terms with Megatron? Trust must cut both ways, Optimus."

Optimus frowned. Something had just occurred to him. The Curator's reticence . . . the Matrix pointing in the direction of this world and then offering no further clues. Perhaps the answer was very simple.

"Is the AllSpark on this world, Curator?"

The Curator shook his head. "It is not. Nor is it in our possession; otherwise we would have brought it here, I promise you. But we will give you the coordinates once you and Megatron shake hands and swear peace. We can end your quest, Optimus. We can fulfill everything you've ever fought for. So once again I ask you: Will you help us?"

MEGATRON STOOD ON THE EAST-FACING BALCONY, barely able to keep his rage in check. The grandeur of the Pavilion was lost on him; all he could think about was the place burning down to the waterline as his proton ray set the whole scrap heap alight. How dare these Quintessons get in the way of his victory? Before this was all over, he was going to tear that smug look right off the face of the fish-bot who called himself the Curator. The sheer nerve of them interfering—they would pay. For them to think they could control the mighty Megatron was pure folly.

He would soon show them what real power was, but for now that would have to wait.

First he needed more information. It was axiomatic at this point that the Quintessons had access to advanced technology. There was no telling what else they had up their scaly sleeves. But it didn't matter; Megatron knew it would all soon belong to him. While everybody else entertained this ridiculous farce of a peace summit, Megatron's soldiers were secretly collecting the data he needed to perform a strike that would bring these fish-bots and the Autobots to their knees. Analyzing the energy sources in the planetary rings, obtaining some real data on what was going on beneath the oceans . . . Megatron decided it was time to check in again with the crew still up in the *Nemesis*. They'd already managed to restart some of the craft's systems. He was just about to establish a covert uplink when the door chime interrupted.

"Identify yourself or be destroyed," he bellowed at the doorway.

"It is I, the Curator."

"What do you want?"

"I was wondering if you would grant me a brief audience, Lord Megatron." The use of his title dampened Megatron's anger a little. At least the Curator understood his place. Megatron hit a button; the door slid open, and the Curator entered, bowing as he did so. Megatron puffed out his massive chest at the smaller robot.

"I certainly hope for your sake that this intrusion into my sleep cycle is warranted."

The Curator kept his head bowed in supplication as he spoke: "I believe it is, Lord Megatron. I come to you with an issue of the utmost gravity."

"Go on."

"My masters have long watched your conflict with the Autobots and have come to a singular conclusion."

"That conclusion being?"

"That there can only be peace through strength. Strength that only you can provide."

"I see you've been studying my speeches."

"I am merely conveying word from Quintessa itself. To some tyranny is in diametric opposition to freedom. But those who rule must have freedom, too, no? And in some cases, tyranny and freedom go hand in hand."

"*Some* cases?" said Megatron sarcastically. "How about *all* of them? I see right through you Quintessons. What you call a trading federation is nothing of the kind. This planet isn't a *trade partner*, it's a *colony world*. Don't even try to deny it."

The Curator smiled unctuously. "Your insight is precisely why I am here now. The Quintesson Imperium recognizes the same truths you do: Sentient beings need rules; otherwise there would be chaos. There must be a strong hand to guide them. In the case of Cybertron, we believe you are that hand."

"Of course I am," Megatron snarled. "You don't honestly think that librarian is capable of ruling anything, do you? It's his weakness that's brought us to this state of affairs, anyway."

"I couldn't agree more."

"So you're not telling me anything I don't already know, fish-bot."

The Curator ignored the jibe. "What if I told you there was a way for you to rule all Cybertronians without question? To end this war in a single stroke?"

"I'd tell you to stop dancing around the issue. How about you tell me exactly what it is you want before I lose my patience and throw you off that balcony?"

"It's very simple. The Autobots follow Optimus Prime not because of rank or caste or merit but because they feel that he was chosen to carry the wisdom of all the

Primes contained in the Matrix of Leadership. They believe that he has an almost divine access to the sum total of all the wisdom that ever was and ever will be. When he speaks to them, they take his words as they would those of Primus himself, because they are one and the same as far as they are concerned."

"They are weak-minded fools."

"And yet, regrettably for Optimus, his Matrix has been proving unreliable lately."

Megatron frowned. "His decisions are asinine even when it works, so how would you know it's been unreliable?"

"I have my sources," the Curator said.

"You've been disrupting it, haven't you?"

"I see nothing escapes you, Lord Megatron."

"Nothing except the point of this conversation."

"Then let me say it plainly: The Matrix is not the only one in existence."

Megatron stared at him. "You're lying."

"Am I?"

"Primus himself created the Matrix so that a single Prime could act as his instrument. So why would he have created two?"

"I didn't say he did."

"Now you're talking riddles."

"Who else besides Prime would have the power to create a Matrix of Leadership?"

"No one else," Megatron said. But then he suddenly realized what the Curator was driving at. "You don't mean—*Unicron*?"

The Curator smiled.

Megatron fought to conceal his excitement. "So you're telling me that a Decepticon Matrix of Leadership really exists."

"Not only does it exist, we can help you get it. And it would make you invincible."

"I already *am* invincible," Megatron said.

"Of course you are. That's why it's taken you several million years to win a simple civil war." Before Megatron could put his fist through the Curator's face, the Quintesson got to the heart of the matter: "Megatron, I will not bandy words. You *are* the most powerful Cybertronian alive today. But the Decepticon Matrix of Leadership would turn you into a living god. You would be the sword of Unicron himself. Why should Primus have all the advantages in the fight you've dedicated your life to?"

Megatron pondered this. "So this 'treaty' that you claimed to want—"

"We *do* want it. Just not tomorrow. Once you have your own Matrix, you can bring the Autobots the peace of the wasteland and dictate terms to the survivors."

"That is a pleasant vision. So where is this Matrix?"

"At a location that we will reveal to you once you have performed one small favor for us."

Megatron's face darkened. "I do no one favors."

"Then consider it a favor you do yourself. If you are truly worthy of the Decepticon Matrix of Leadership—or what you will soon know as the Matrix of Conquest—it will be an easy task."

"Name it."

"Kill Optimus Prime."

A broad smile crossed Megatron's iron face.

"Well, my friend, I was going to do that anyway."

"Then we understand each other."

"Indeed we do. I will kill him and take his Matrix for my own."

"His Matrix?" The Curator shook his head. "Believe me, you will discard it as a useless bauble when you have the Decepticon Matrix."

"Say I wish to claim both."

"Impossible," the Curator said.

"You dare defy me?"

"I dare explain reality. The contact of Matrix and Anti-Matrix would destroy more than just you. It would be like a supernova detonating. There would be nothing left. Content yourself with the Decepticon Matrix; grind the one in Optimus's chest to ashes."

"You wish me to destroy it?" Megatron frowned. "And here I was thinking that this was the part where you were going to say *you* wanted it."

"I have no need of such a thing," said the Curator, and he said it with such conviction that for a moment Megatron almost believed him.

Almost.

Chapter Twenty-two

STARSCREAM WAS IN THE MIDDLE OF ENJOYING THE many amenities of his lavish quarters when the knock at the door came. He cringed; only Megatron would even think of disturbing him at this time of night. He hated being at Megatron's beck and call, hated the way his master condescended to him, hated the very fact that he *had* a master.

Someday he would have to change that.

"Coming, Lord Megatron. I hope there isn't—" Starscream stopped in midsentence as the door opened to reveal the squat form of the Curator.

"Air Commander Starscream, I was wondering if you and I might talk for a moment." The Curator pushed past him without waiting for an answer.

"What can I do for you?" the nonplussed Decepticon asked.

"May I dispense with the titles and simply call you Starscream?"

"By all means. No need to stand on ceremony."

"Excellent. I took you for a no-nonsense kind of leader the moment we met. I think you are the kind of Decepticon I can work with. One I can trust." The flattery was laid on far too thickly; perhaps the Curator wasn't very good at backroom dealing. Then again, maybe he *was*. After all, here he was in Starscream's quarters talking, and Starscream was listening. Good con artists always recognize each other, and as far as Starscream was concerned, he was the best bar none. He sat down on a nearby couch, crossed his arms, and waited for the pitch.

"Do tell," he said.

"Let me be blunt with you, Starscream. I want to end your civil war. I truly do. But that objective is subordinate to my primary goal: the success of the Quintesson Imperium."

"Two hours ago it was your Co-Prosperity Sphere."

"Let's not get hung up on labels," the Curator said breezily. "The point is that our prosperity depends on peace." *Sure it does*, Starscream thought as the Curator warmed to his speech. "War has never been the answer to interstellar problems, for it only leads to destruction and death. And diaspora, too—look at the fate of your own people. We know now that subjugation and conquest of other worlds is a mistake. We want to change that paradigm for the better."

Starscream smiled. "And how do you propose 'we' do that?"

"You are extremely perceptive, so what I am going to say next will undoubtedly not be a surprise. I do not think your Leader Megatron has any intention of honoring the peace process."

"You don't say."

"I'm afraid I do," the Curator said. "Our scenarios indicate he is just biding his time until he sees an opportune moment to betray us."

"If that's so, it's the first I've heard of it." Starscream knew that at that very moment the *Nemesis* was secretly scanning the planet, looking for weak spots in the Quintesson defense grid. "Then again, Megatron plays his cards close to his chest," he added.

"He does indeed," the Curator said. "But that is precisely why I wanted to talk to you. We believe that if the Decepticons had a change of leadership, our peace process would have a much better chance of achieving success."

Starscream kept his poker face. "A change of leadership. That sounds drastic indeed."

"Sometimes drastic problems call for drastic remedies."

"Megatron is our glorious leader," Starscream said. "Who could possibly replace him?"

"We had in mind yourself," the Curator told him.

"Me?" said Starscream with feigned surprise. "Why, I'm just the air commander."

"But you could be so much more, and you know it. And we know it, too. We believe that if you were the Decepticon leader, peace with the Autobots might be easier. Megatron is obsessed with Optimus Prime. Whereas you seem to take things a little less . . . personally."

"What makes you think I would betray Megatron?"

"Must we play this game? Aren't you tired of licking his boots? You're the obvious heir to the crown. And you know where Megatron's path leads. He would sacrifice every Decepticon to achieve his one goal: destroying the object of his hatred. Burning every bot in the universe would be music to his ears if Optimus was among them. What the Decepticons need is a leader who has their true interests at heart. One who can lead them to a just and honorable peace. Hasn't this war lasted long enough?"

It's lasted long enough without us winning, Starscream thought. But he looked at the Curator solemnly. "I'm sure that if I was ruler, my policy would be one of moderation and diplomacy. But we speak of hypotheticals. Because I don't know whether you've noticed, but we Decepticons don't hold elections."

"Elections are not the only way to replace leaders," the Curator said.

"True."

There was a long pause.

"If you're asking me to kill Megatron, you can think again," Starscream said. "In open battle, he would destroy me."

"That is quite an admission," the Curator replied. "Such a far cry from the bluster of Megatron. I see it as further evidence that—"

"Let me put it this way: I'm not going to be your pawn."

"Then why don't you find one of your own?"

Starscream smiled slowly. "I like the way you think. But I feel you care more about eliminating Megatron than ensuring that I take his place."

"You wound me, Starscream."

"Because I know what I'm talking about. If Megatron were to be . . . *removed* from the game board, there would be a scramble for succession. Who is to say my rivals would not unite against me?"

"They would not dare. Because when Megatron dies— of natural causes or otherwise—we will give you the Decepticon Matrix of Leadership."

Starscream shook his head. "That does not exist."

"I can assure you otherwise. You see, we know where it is."

"Permit me to guess: You'll tell me its location after I kill Megatron."

"I shall tell you its location now. We have it in our possession." The Curator produced a small hologram projector that displayed a schematic of the Matrix in the air. It looked like the one in Optimus's chest, although whereas that one was blue, this was black, pulsating with a red glow from deep within. "At the end of our occupation of your world, we took it with us."

"That was naughty of you," Starscream told him.

"I find myself unable to disagree."

"So how do you plan to initiate the negotiations tomorrow?"

"Well," said the Curator, "I'm open to suggestions."

THE VAST HANGAR AT THE CENTER OF THE PAVILION WAS the only part of the structure where both Decepticons and Autobots were allowed. A Decepticon shuttle stood in the eastern half of the hangar; two hundred meters away was that of the Autobots. Ironhide paced back and forth in front of it. The tension was so thick that one practically could taste it. Everybody was wondering what was going to happen next. Was there really going to be peace with the Decepticons? And did anybody really believe that the Quintessons—having attacked Cybertron in the past and having deceived everybody in the present—could possibly be trusted? It was true that this planet seemed peaceful and that the Curator's explanations had a certain logic to them.

But as far as Ironhide was concerned, the whole situation stank.

He wanted nothing more than to talk things over with Jazz and Prowl, but they were giving him a wide berth. Most likely they were still mad at him for letting Rodimus take the dropship. He really couldn't blame them. They were a careful and calculating pair, and Ironhide admired them for it. Somebody had to think that way, but it certainly wasn't going to be him. Right now he was doing everything he could to keep from smashing something. A truce with the Decepticons! He couldn't see it, not after all these years. Those scrap heaps would never accept a truce; it simply wasn't in their Spark. Ironhide mulled this over while he watched Rodimus, Kup, and Bumblebee load up the shuttle with pallets stacked high with freshly minted Energon.

Ironhide supposed that was their punishment for going AWOL and wrecking the dropship.

His punishment was to sit here and do guard duty. Across the hangar he could see a group of Decepticons busily loading their own shuttle with Energon. The Curator had explained the details to everybody earlier: If ultimately peace could *not* be reached, both shuttles would depart simultaneously back to their mother ships with replenished stocks of Energon. At that point, the Ark would be allowed to continue on its way and the *Nemesis* would be held in orbit for several more cycles, long enough to give the Ark a head start. Megatron hadn't liked that at all, but the Curator had explained that allowing the *Nemesis* and the Ark to leave at the same time would simply result in an immediate resumption of the battle in orbit around the planet. The Curator added that although he wanted peace between the two sides, if they insisted on war, they could go fight somewhere far away from Aquatron.

"You okay there, sonny?"

Ironhide turned to see Kup looking concerned. "I'm fine," he told the old veteran. "What about you?"

"Never felt better. Look, I'm sorry we got you in trouble over our little excursion."

"Forget it. I'm just glad you guys came back."

"That makes two of us." Kup lit a cy-gar. "Funny thing is, we weren't down there anywhere near as long as I expected. Once we got into the infrastructure, it seemed like a quick jaunt back. Even though we must have covered miles."

"Hey," Prowl said, walking over. "You've both got things to do."

"Easy," Kup said. "I'm just taking a cy-gar break." He picked up his box of Energon and got back to it. Prowl didn't even acknowledge Ironhide, just walked straight past him. Ironhide could see that the more senior bot was on edge. In a couple of hours, it would be morning and the negotiations would begin. But really, anything could happen at any time. They would just have to wait and see.

"YOU'VE REALLY PROVED YOUR WORTH, SKYWARP. LET me be the first to say it: You've reached a potential not many thought you had in you."

Starscream had been talking for the last ten minutes. He paced back and forth like a general reviewing his troops, but the only bot in the room besides him was the nervous Skywarp. It was all that Decepticon could do to stand at attention and keep his optics looking straight ahead. It wasn't very often that Starscream spoke to him privately, to say nothing of summoning him in the middle of the night. That didn't bode well. Skywarp had heard the rumors back on Cybertron of Decepticons who disappeared after being called to duty and told to report alone. So often in the Decepticons' ranks it was a comrade who put the proverbial energy blade in your back. Skywarp searched his memory for any offense he might have given the Seeker commander, but he couldn't think of a single thing. That didn't mean the volatile Starscream hadn't taken umbrage at something.

"What was that, sir?"

"I said it's not your fault that your fellow Seekers don't respect you. You can always count on others to be jealous of power. That's one way that you and I are so alike. So feared."

"I'm feared, sir?" Skywarp asked with a mixture of trepidation and confusion. It was times like this that he honestly wished he was smarter. But he didn't like the use of the word *fear*. Not now. Not when he was experiencing it so strongly himself. Not when Starscream had that scheming look on his face . . .

"I'm not one to spread scurrilous rumors and idle gossip," the Seeker commander said. "But you must be able to see how envious the other Seekers are of you. It's not your fault that you've outshined the others. Of course they're going to be bitter. You *do* see that, don't you?"

"I suppose so . . ."

"Of course you do. You have an ability that no other Cybertronian has, Skywarp. That makes you different, and that makes people fear you. But that's why Megatron and I have been singling you out for these special missions. You're the jet trooper we turn to when we need things to get done."

"Well, I try to do my best."

"And you succeed, my friend. Which is why we need your help once more."

Skywarp's optics narrowed as he considered Starscream. Maybe the Seeker commander wasn't planning on eliminating him, after all. "My help . . . ?"

"This Pavilion we stand in is magnificent, but it is a gilded cage. These Quintessons are playing us. Megatron and I plan to turn the tables on them."

"I thought this peace treaty—"

"We don't need a peace treaty. We need victory against Autobots and Quintessons alike. Even as I speak, the *Nemesis* is preparing to strike. But at the key moment, we need our best Seeker to hit the Quintessons where they least expect it."

Skywarp was having trouble following this. Plots and intrigues just weren't his style. But fighting was. And it sounded like he was about to get called into the fray again.

"This order comes from Megatron himself?" he asked.

Starscream's face darkened. "Of course. Do you want me

to disturb his sleep cycle so he can tell you that personally?"

"No, no, no," Skywarp said quickly. "That won't be necessary. Tell me what it is you require."

THE CURATOR WAS GLAD TO LEAVE THE PAVILION. IT was intended to make the Cybertronians feel comfortable, but to him it was a monstrosity. Everything about its architecture was wrong, though that wouldn't matter shortly. Returning across the Kraken Sea aboard his personal craft, he was only too happy to get back to his inner sanctum, where he found Xeros waiting for him.

"How have matters gone?" the junior scientist asked.

"Excellently well. These Cybertronians are a painfully simple lot. The current progression of events is well within the margin of error of all the simulations we played out. My calculations now place our probability of success at 84.5 percent."

"Even though we have revealed our identity?"

"That was a necessary step at this juncture. The timing demanded it. There is no way a backwater planet like this could have access to the weapons that we just neutralized their ships with. We had to tell them who we are or else we had to tell them some wild story that could be disproved—or that would simply raise more questions than it answered."

"But to admit that we are their ancient nemesis—"

"*Were*," the Curator corrected him. "That's all we've admitted."

Xeros didn't seem convinced.

"Surely some of these bots will suspect our ultimate intent."

"All of them suspect *something*," the Curator said. "But none of them know for sure. And the bait dangled before each of them is too great. Each one thinks he can still outwit me if necessary."

The doctor nodded slowly. "When really you have trumped them all."

"Let this be a lesson to you, Xeros." The Curator was in an expansive mood. "The key to realizing a plan is to avoid trying to control the exact paths by which that plan is realized. Indeed, sometimes one sets those paths at odds with one another, as I have done tonight. Never tell one falsehood when you can deploy several contradictory ones. Sometimes you can even tell your victims the truth. It doesn't matter. Each player in this game is still hooked by his own desires. The fact that their agendas clash only strengthens our hand. No matter what transpires tomorrow, we shall win. Then we can proceed to Stage Two."

Xeros raised an eyebrow. "So events on Cybertron—"

"Continue to proceed on schedule."

"You are not concerned that the scientist Shockwave might discern our plans?"

"What these primitive bots call science is mere fumbling in the dark," the Curator said scornfully. "We have taken Shockwave's measure without him even knowing it. There was a 96.7 percent probability that he would tamper with Vector Sigma and a more than 80.0 percent likelihood that he would use Alpha Trion to do it. He thinks to create something that will make him a god; little does he know that he is merely forging the chains with which we will bind his race. But the maturity of that particular vector is still a few days away. The primary vector on *this* world will come to fruition tomorrow, and you and I will enjoy the spectacle from here."

"I applaud your genius," Xeros said with a graceful bow. "I must admit that to see a plan as complex as yours achieve fulfillment like this is simply . . . breathtaking.

There surely is no doubt you will be asked to report back to Quintessa when your work here is done."

"Should that happen, you will be accompanying me."

"You do me too great an honor," Xeros protested.

"Not at all. Your work here has made mine possible. It is only right that you share in my success." The Curator went over to the glowing replica of the Matrix of Leadership and began to make adjustments to various wires and conduits to the apparatus.

"The real thing will be infinitely more useful," Xeros said.

"This has proved its worth. We've replicated enough of the codes to be able to interfere with the actual one, and that is no small feat."

"But the genuine one can be used to find the AllSpark itself. We can breed whole new armies—uncover the remaining secrets of the Primes—"

"I am fully aware of that," the Curator snapped, and Xeros cringed visibly. "I estimate the chances that the Matrix will be destroyed tomorrow at less than 2 percent. It is far more resilient than the one who carries it, who has at least a 65.3 percent chance of termination."

"Optimus Prime truly doesn't suspect we have been manipulating it?"

"No. The complexity of the circumstances has provided us with the perfect cover. He believes that the Autobot Matrix of Leadership is malfunctioning due to his own self-doubt. The effect is self-reinforcing. That said, I intend to make a few minor adjustments before tomorrow."

"He wears his virtue as though it were the heaviest of burdens," Xeros said. "It weakens him. Makes him more susceptible."

"I couldn't agree more. In the meantime, have the required amount of Energon moved from the refineries to the holding tanks in preparation. In the wake of tomorrow's events, we must be ready to launch Stage Two without delay."

"I anticipated your desire and already gave the order."

"Excellent. Now we have merely a few more hours to wait." The Curator turned back to the glowing Matrix replica and began to ponder what dreams Optimus Prime would have next.

Chapter Twenty-three

CYBERTRON

"DISTURBING," SHOCKWAVE SAID.

That was as emotional as he ever got, but it was quite enough. Things just weren't working out as planned. He prided himself on his objectivity—the essence of the true scientist—and he was increasingly realizing that the gap between what he'd thought was going to happen and what was actually taking place had diverged to the point where he was going to have to do the unthinkable, violating a key principle of his methodology.

By talking to a subject in the middle of an experiment.

"Remove consciousness locks," he said to the drones that buzzed around Alpha Trion's prone form, attending to the interfaces with the glowing mouth of Vector Sigma. "Reinstate consciousness along the following parameters." He reeled off a series of numbers. Halfway through them Alpha Trion's eyes opened.

"Shockwave."

"Alpha Trion. I trust you are in no pain."

"Considering you've removed most of my external sensors, I'm far less concerned about pain than I am about damage."

"Damage," Shockwave said in a tone so devoid of feeling that it would have made any psychiatrist in the room rush for the exit. "Damage. No. I have spared you that."

"I'm not talking about damage to me. I'm talking about damage to reality itself."

"Oh," Shockwave said lightly, "that. Well, I wouldn't worry. Reality has a way of looking after itself. But I will confess to some small difficulty in harnessing Vector Sigma."

"Small enough to make you seek my counsel?"

Shockwave ignored the jibe. "I need your fail-safes."

"My fail-safes . . . ?"

"You've put a code around the core of your cortex."

Alpha Trion looked amused. "And you can't break it?"

"I'd prefer to have the key rather than force the lock."

"That's going to be difficult given that I haven't used any such codes."

"You lie."

"The only one dissembling in this room is you, Shockwave. Why don't you tell me what's really got you concerned?"

"I just did."

"But you're holding back. What do your energy readouts on Vector Sigma show?"

"They are strange," Shockwave admitted.

"Was that so hard to say?" Alpha Trion chided.

Shockwave fought down the urge to slap him. "There are surges in areas where there should be none and no energy in areas which should be awash with it."

"And what does that tell you?"

"I thought you might be able to speak to that."

"How long has passed between you starting this experiment and now?"

Shockwave frowned. "You mean to say you don't know?"

"You removed my consciousness filters. I have no idea."

"Consult your chronometers, then."

"All my monitors are frozen."

Shockwave frowned. "That wasn't supposed to happen."

"*None* of this was supposed to happen. I repeat: How long has passed?"

"Twelve hours."

"And besides the anomalous energy readings, what are you finding?"

"That the structure of Vector Sigma is not precisely what I was anticipating." He gestured at a screen; readings chased themselves across it. Alpha Trion studied them closely, and his eyes narrowed.

"Someone is interfering with you," he said.

"*You* are interfering with me if you continue to obfuscate."

"Shockwave, put aside your egotism and listen to me. You think that I could be a back door to Vector Sigma, but once you open the door, it may be another that passes through it."

"I have shut down all interfaces to the rest of Cybertron. And besides, no one on this planet could possibly rival me for—"

"What makes you assume they're on this planet?"

"What are you rambling about, old man?"

"Think of the universe as a dark and endless forest, Shockwave. What you are doing is lighting a fire in the middle of it. You will draw in any predator that can see the blaze."

"We're thousands of miles beneath the surface of Cybertron, Alpha Trion. No one can *see* what we're—"

"I'm not talking about visuals, you fool. I'm talking about the *fabric of space and time*. Since you persist in being so willfully obtuse, I will employ another metaphor. You are sending out vibrations like a fly struggling in a spider's web. So do not curse me if I cannot tell you the identity of the spider."

Shockwave laughed. "You tell me fairy tales in the desperate hope of dissuading me from going further? I suppose it's a step up from begging."

"I'm no longer begging. You are so blinded by your own narcissism that I doubt I can convince you of anything. But since you are *asking* me, I am *telling* you that this data is clearly being manipulated remotely. Someone else has found a conduit to Vector Sigma, and they are piggybacking on your efforts. That is why you must not resume this process."

"Nonsense," said Shockwave. "I simply need more power to break through your codes."

"I already told you there are none. And as to power, you're already feeding in as much as this room can stand."

"I will pour in still more. Break through your resistance and reformat Vector Sigma's operating protocol so that I can override all—"

"You are insane, Shockwave."

"Am I really?"

"Not to mention impractical. Where will you get the needed energy? Overriding Vector Sigma would require ten times the power grid of Cybertron itself."

"I'm not intending to draw upon the power grid."

"Then you are talking fantasy."

"Dark Energon isn't fantasy."

Alpha Trion looked at him in horror. "Now I know you've taken leave of the last of your senses."

"Said the Prime so long past *his* prime that he's become a living relic. I have three heavy-class refineries within ten miles of this room. And many more than ten miles of pipes at my disposal." He signaled to the attendant drones. "Resume the process."

"Shockwave," Alpha Trion said as the conduits clamped around his head, "you would bring down all of creation just to satisfy your own ambition." But then he fell silent as cognition left him once more. Shockwave smiled as the Dark Energon began pumping.

"I would indeed," he said.

AND IN THAT INSTANT ALPHA TRION KNEW THE TRUTH of it.

He didn't lose consciousness down there. He just forgot it all when he was revived. Now he was a chained Prime, a tool in theory but bait in practice, surrounded by mathematics as the equations at the root of all reality spun about him. Somewhere out there a hunter was closing in, something so malevolent that it made the hostility between Autobot and Decepticon look like the squabbling of toddlers. Something ancient and terrible, half a galaxy away.

But right next to him all the same.

Chapter Twenty-four

IT WAS MORNING.

The roof of the Pavilion's hangar slid back to reveal a verdant dawn sky. Jazz and Perceptor made a final inspection of the Autobot shuttle and then crossed the hangar floor quickly. They needed to talk to Optimus.

Scarcely had they departed the hangar than the huge room's far door opened and Megatron stepped into the room. Bemused Autobots paused momentarily from their task of loading to watch the spectacle while dozens of Decepticon warriors fell on their knees in front of their leader.

"Hail Megatron!" they yelled in unison.

"Rise!" Megatron said, spreading his arms wide. Starscream, who stood a half step behind his leader, tried not to appear bored as Megatron reveled in the pomp and glory. Things were going to change soon enough. Thundercracker stepped forward and knelt at the foot of his master.

"My lord, we hear rumors of a treaty. Tell us they are lies. We hunger for war."

"Spoken like a true Decepticon," Megatron said as he looked out over his minions. "Brothers! I know what you desire. But today we do indeed seek peace with our Cybertronian brothers." He gestured to the Autobots across the chamber while a confused murmur went up among the gathered Decepticons. "I know that to many of you peace seems like an unexpected destination, but it is one to which we must venture. The future of the planet Cybertron depends on our mutual cooperation. No longer can we remain divided. When Autobot and Decepticon stand side by side in battle, there will be no force strong enough in the universe to oppose us. No power shall stand in our way." The last line drew an appreciative rumble among the Decepticons; this was closer to the red-meat rhetoric they expected from Megatron, who sensed their mood and figured this was a good time to wrap it up: "We will bring this weak universe to bended knee and make it realize who its true masters are. We were born to lead, and lead we shall. United we will rule for all eternity!"

But the cheer that rose up from his troops was still a little muted. Nor could Megatron blame them. His soldiers might not be a hundred percent behind the idea, but it didn't matter. The audience for this speech wasn't the Decepticons but rather the Autobots. Before the assembled troops could ask him any embarrassing questions, he turned and left the room, accompanied only by Starscream.

"Excellent speech, my lord," Starscream said.

"Spare me your flattery, dolt. It was the worst speech I've ever given."

"Very well," Starscream agreed. "It was terrible."

Jazz and Perceptor found Optimus in his quarters, staring out the window, deep in thought, watching the sun sparkling over the ocean. He turned in surprise to see his two lieutenants.

"What are you doing here?" he asked.

Jazz placed his hands on his hips. "Telling you not to go through with this," he said.

Optimus nodded. He'd been wondering who would tell him that. "Right now Megatron seems to be abiding by the rules of the truce," he said.

"Yes," said Jazz, "but for how long?"

"I guess we'll find out," Optimus replied.

"But what about the Quintessons?" Perceptor asked.

"What about them?"

"I still don't trust them," Jazz said.

"Some of the energy readings from this planet don't make any sense," Perceptor added. "I'm worried you're just stepping into a trap."

"We're not *stepping* into it," Optimus told him. "We're in it already. Do you truly think I don't see that?"

Perceptor looked abashed. "Optimus, I didn't mean—"

"Of course you did. And you should. But here's what you should consider: If the Quintessons wanted to destroy us, surely they could have done so already. The weapons in the planetary rings could have obliterated Ark and *Nemesis* alike and then rained fire down on those on the ground. So why didn't they?"

Jazz and Perceptor had no easy answer for that. Optimus gestured out at the ocean. "This planet possesses a technology more advanced than ours. And no sane bot wouldn't be scared by that. But if this really *is* part of some greater game, all we can do is play along and look for some way to get off the board altogether."

"And that's what you're doing," Jazz said, sounding utterly unconvinced. Optimus was glad he hadn't mentioned the Curator's offer to reveal the location of the AllSpark. That probably would have made Jazz laugh. But that didn't mean it wasn't true.

"What's the situation up on the Ark?" he asked.

"Sideswipe has the repair crews working around the clock getting the backup systems running," Perceptor said. "And installing extra shielding to act as conducting rods. We think we might be able to vent the pulse back into space if they hit us with it again."

Optimus nodded. "Good. That's the key. We have to get the ship operational. But I want you two to bring another shuttle down from the Ark and take it back into space. Before these negotiations are over, I want you back on the Ark."

Jazz was taken aback. "I don't follow," he said.

"If this really *is* a trap, then the Ark might escape. But those of us down here won't."

"The Ark will evacuate you, Optimus. Get you off the planet."

"Too great a risk. If we have to face Quintesson weapons again, the Ark is to make for deep space. Put this place in the rearview and never come back."

"No Autobot will ever abandon the Prime," Jazz insisted.

"It's precisely *because* I'm a Prime that you will carry out my orders. Get Sideswipe on the com-link and tell him to continue repairs and monitor both this planet and the *Nemesis*. No doubt the Decepticons are thinking along the same lines, so we need to keep a close eye on them."

Jazz looked as conflicted as Optimus had ever seen him. "Fine," he said. "But take some protection to the negotiations. Ironhide, maybe. Or Kup."

"The Curator wants Megatron and me to meet with him alone. Just the three of us."

"A trap," Jazz repeated, practically grinding his teeth.

"As I said, if it was, they could have sprung it already."

"But why do the negotiations have to be between just you and Megatron?"

"Because that's literally the only way he's going to listen." Optimus didn't tell his lieutenants about the Curator's offer to deploy somatic engineering. But that bot's words had been ringing in his head all night. *A way to influence circuitry . . . make Megatron more malleable . . .* Optimus felt that such tampering would violate something sacred. But was it more sacred than peace?

"At least let someone escort you down there," Jazz said.

"No. If there are distractions—no matter how well-meaning—it could upset everything."

"If you say so, Commander." Optimus wasn't used to seeing Jazz so reluctant to accept orders, but these were unusual times. And then there was the question of what would happen if peace actually became a reality . . . Perhaps that was the real reason for the Autobots' disquiet. To have to acknowledge that they hadn't beaten the Decepticons after all this time. To be forced to coexist with them . . . Were they prepared for that?

"Don't worry, Optimus," said Perceptor as though in answer, "we're ready for anything."

"I know you are," Optimus said. "I'll see you when I get back. Believe me, whatever Megatron's got planned, I can handle him." With that Optimus stepped into the elevator at the far side of his suite. Jazz couldn't suppress a feeling of dread as the doors slid shut. He and Perceptor turned away, and even as they did so, one of Soundwave's mini-cons silently landed on the roof of the elevator, an invisible companion to Optimus as the elevator plunged into the depths of the Pavilion and the answers the Prime was seeking.

ON THE FAR SIDE OF THE COMPLEX, MEGATRON REACHED another elevator. He turned to Starscream.

"All is in order?" he asked.

Starscream nodded. "Yes, my lord."

"How go the repairs on the *Nemesis*?"

"Almost ready for battle, sire. Even damaged it stands as a formidable opponent."

"And are the warriors I requested properly briefed?"

"Of course. They are waiting as per your request."

"What about Soundwave's spy?"

"In position. Soundwave confirms that Optimus is on his way to the Temple of Peace alone."

"Very good. When this is all over, you will be properly rewarded, Starscream. You have served me well."

"Reward is not necessary, my lord. I have merely done my duty."

With that Megatron strode into the elevator. As the doors closed, Starscream could not help thinking of a tomb slamming shut forever.

It was a thought he found immensely comforting.

SKYWARP WORKED IN SILENCE AS HE MADE THE FINAL modifications to the cluster mine with which Starscream had provided him. The air commander had told him he'd stolen it from the Aquatronians. Skywarp didn't give much thought to how he'd done that; undoubtedly Starscream had pulled another of his scams. No, he was more interested in the weapon itself, which he estimated was several times more powerful than the bombs he was accustomed to using. Starscream also had given him a detailed schematic of the Pavilion and precise coordinates on where the Curator would be. The fuse on the warhead would give Skywarp just enough time to teleport in, set the bomb, and teleport to safety. After that he would join the Decepticons in the final slaughter of Autobots and Quintessons alike. He was honored that Megatron and Starscream had such confidence in him. There was no way the plan could fail.

* * *

WATCHING THE TWO CYBERTRONIAN FACTIONS PREPARE for the peace summit, the Curator was glad he was nowhere near the Pavilion. Xeros pointed a long scaly finger at instrument readings alongside the main viewscreen that showed exactly how much Energon each of the ships had placed in its respective hull.

"Their vehicles are fully loaded," he said. "Seems they just couldn't get enough of it."

"Don't be so hard on them," the Curator said. "Who could resist such a generous gift? The chance they would have left the energy behind was minuscule. All we need now is one last insurance policy."

"An insurance policy?" Xeros was puzzled. "But your plan is perfect."

"No plan is perfect," the Curator snapped. "And while Stage One now has less than a 3 percent chance of failing, Stage Two's variables still need strengthening."

"What are you suggesting?"

"That we activate Tyrannicon."

Xeros paled. "Are you sure that is wise?" he asked. "That seems to be a bit . . . premature."

"The sooner we bring him into the picture, the better. If we truly intend to utilize him in Stage Two, this will be a suitable test of his leadership capabilities."

"It's not his leadership capabilities that worry me. It's that—"

"Your concerns are well known to me." The Curator looked Xeros square in his dark green eyes. "And utterly irrelevant."

Xeros stepped back abashed as an honor guard of Aquatronians entered the room, bearing a gigantic cryo-unit as though it were an oversized coffin. Ice crusted its windows, concealing what lay within. The honor guard set the unit down on a pedestal in the center of the chamber and left quickly. The Curator stepped

forward and keyed in a security code. The cryo-unit
started to hum.

"You're activating him *here*?" Xeros asked.

"Why not?" The Curator gestured at the ceiling, and a
hatch slid away. A sizable laser cannon descended from it
and swiveled to aim straight at the coffin.

"Always put insurance polices on your insurance
policies," the Curator said as steam poured out of the
unit's venting system, filling the room with a light fog.
A sine curve appeared on a screen and began oscillating
more quickly as a heartbeat accelerated. As the ice
melted, water beaded and ran down the glass. One at
a time, the security latches released; a lump formed in
Xeros's throat as lights atop the cryo-unit went from red
to green. The unit's huge door slid back with a hiss of gas
and the crunching of ice breaking away. Xeros felt like he
was staring into the heart of an ancient casket filled with
long-dead evils. A huge pair of green scaly metal claws
gripped the sides of the box, grasping for leverage as the
massive bulk to which they were attached began rising
from within. Xeros stepped back, trying not to cower, but
the Curator simply stood there calmly, staring up at the
thing that now stepped from its place of slumber.

"General Tyrannicon. Welcome back to the world of
the living."

A bloodcurdling roar filled the room.

Chapter Twenty-five

THE ELEVATOR DOORS OPENED.

Optimus emerged into the center of an enormous circular chamber in the Pavilion's basement. With the exception of another elevator directly opposite him, the walls consisted of a single wraparound window through which was visible nothing but oceanic abyss. He estimated that he was at least a mile beneath the surface. The floor and the ceilings were covered with the most ornate runes he had seen yet. Works of art depicted ferocious battles between disturbing-looking sea creatures. Maybe it was the history of Aquatron, Optimus thought, though it was an odd choice for a place called the Temple of Peace.

Before he could further contemplate the meaning of the elaborate murals, the doors of the far elevator slid open to reveal Megatron. Optimus held his ground but did not offer his hand. He knew Megatron would see it as a sign of weakness.

"Megatron."

"Optimus. Aren't you glad to see me, old friend?" Megatron wore his trademark sneer.

"I suppose that depends."

"On what?"

"Whether you truly desire peace."

Megatron laughed. "Of course I do." He advanced

farther into the room. "Just not the kind that you and I are likely to agree on."

"I refuse to believe we can't come to some kind of understanding. Where is the Curator?"

"I suppose he's running a little late." Megatron shrugged. "Such a shame. I was so looking forward to having an audience for your execution." On the last word, a concealed third elevator door slid open—this one was set within the window-wall, and it made Optimus wonder just how much of the room was screen rather than aperture. Six burly Vehicons stepped out, their weapons ready.

"What sort of treachery is this, Megatron?"

"The best kind, of course."

"What did the Quintessons promise you?"

"Nothing I can't claim for myself."

"They're playing you, Megatron. You must see that."

"They're next on my list. Right after you."

"It doesn't have to be this way."

"Oh, yes, it does. But never let it be said that I don't appreciate your consistency. Right up until death, you remain the fool you've always been. Look where your eternal optimism has gotten you." Megatron's troopers moved in toward Optimus. "Any final words of wisdom you'd like to share?"

"How about this?" Optimus said, whipping out his energy ax and decapitating one of the Vehicons. As the head flew across the room, the others rushed him. Only Megatron hung back.

"Kill him slowly," he said. "I want to savor every moment."

The room resounded with the clash of steel.

* * *

SKYWARP EXECUTED HIS TELEPORTATION WITH PINPOINT precision, appearing on the underside of the lowermost part of the Pavilion, grasping the metal support bulwarks and stabilizing himself. According to the schematics, the Curator's inner sanctum was right above him. Below him was nothing but oceanic abyss. Skywarp set the mine in place, activating its magnetic clamps. He'd set the bomb on a ten-second counter, but as he reached out to activate it, he realized that someone must have overridden that counter.

Because it had already started counting down.

Nine seconds ago.

In a single brutal moment, he realized the sickening truth. Starscream had set him up. Because Skywarp needed at least five seconds to fully plot out the coordinates for a successful jump. And he had way less than that now. As the final second clicked onto zero, Skywarp did the only thing he could.

A blind jump.

That was as last-ditch as resorts got. He could end up inside the sun or half phased into a rock. For a teleportation artist, there was nothing worse than a blind jump.

Except clinging to a bomb while it detonated.

Just as the warhead went off, Skywarp's teleportation system kicked in. He felt the first particles of detonation brush against him, with nothing but a wave of white-hot heat behind them—and then he was gone. Transitioning momentarily through phase space, he had time to swear a quick oath to the great destroyer Unicron that if he should somehow survive this, he would not rest until he had Starscream's head on a platter.

And then he was back.

Several hundred meters above the ocean.

To make matters worse, he was a burning wreck; he'd

taken severe damage from the bomb. He plummeted
down toward the green sea, spewing smoke and debris.
All his systems were malfunctioning; there was nothing
he could do but wait to hit the water—smashing into it
with such force that pieces of him flew even as sea doused
flame. But it did little to stop his fall; he plunged ever
farther downward, ocean seeping in through the cracks
and holes in his armor. His systems were shutting down
altogether now, and with them all hope of revenge. Or
life, for that matter. Just as his waterlogged optics went
dark, a giant shadow fell over him. The last thing he saw
was a tooth-filled mouth coming toward him . . .

A HUGE BOOM SHOOK THE HANGAR.

"That came from somewhere below," Prowl said.

Jazz keyed up his communicator. The negotiations had
barely started; he and Prowl hadn't even had time to do
as Optimus had commanded and bring down another
ship. "Optimus! Do you read me?"

"I sense treachery," Prowl said, raising his Investigator
Special. "We've got to—" But before he could finish the
sentence, the Decepticons on the far side of the hangar
opened up with everything they had. Rockets and lasers
whipped in toward the Autobots, who ran for cover
and returned fire. As they did so, they heard Starscream
yelling at the top of his voice.

"I knew we couldn't trust them! They just killed our
lord Megatron! Destroy them!" Thundercracker and his
attack wing of Seekers took to the air, gaining height
and then roaring in toward the Autobots. The rest of the
Decepticons weren't that far behind.

"I can't reach Optimus!" Jazz yelled.

"Never mind that!" Prowl shouted back. "We've got
more immediate problems!"

The Seekers swooped in; Bulkhead crushed the first of them with his battle mace. Ironhide grinned as he reached up and caught hold of a low-flying Decepticon's wing, smashing him nose first into a nearby bulkhead. This sure was a lot more fun than peace, he thought. Jazz barked out commands; Rodimus switched to his sport-vehicle mode, popping up on two wheels and performing a wild stunt jump that catapulted him into the air and onto Thundercracker's back, causing them both to crash into the side of one of the shuttles. The remaining Seekers landed, shifting back into their jet-trooper mode. Kup let loose a bracket of shots, bringing one of them down.

"I guess the negotiations failed," he said to Bumblebee.

But before the scout could answer, the floor beneath them suddenly shifted. The entire Pavilion began to list to the side.

"I think we're sinking," Prowl said as he shot a Decepticon in the face. "That explosion down below—"

"Starscream!" Jazz yelled, his voice carrying above the fray.

"Do you want to beg for mercy?" Starscream called out.

"I want you to listen to reason! We don't know what's going on downstairs, and if this place is going under, we need to work together on getting out of here!"

"That starts with you surrendering," Starscream yelled—but that was when he noticed something bizarre about the shuttle he was standing next to. Hundreds of tiny porelike holes were appearing in the ship's hull, each one shining with an eerie bluish glow. Just as he realized that the same thing was happening to the Autobot shuttle, the Energon loaded within burned through the floor of the hangar beneath.

"*Look out!*" Jazz yelled. The next moment, the unstable Energon went critical. Both shuttles in the room exploded, sending sheets of blue flame and shrapnel in every direction. The entire floor began disintegrating like so much burning paper.

"Autobots!" Jazz yelled. "Make for the roof!"

"Every Decepticon for himself!" Starscream yelled into his com-link. And with that, he took his leave, fleeing through the smoke, making for the exit. He could guess what had happened: The Quintessons had tampered with the Energon, turning the precious substance into a time bomb. Staying in the Pavilion seemed like a really bad idea. Reaching a window, he climbed through and then fired his engines and took off for orbit as if his life depended on it. Let the others stay behind and fight it out. For the next several minutes they did just that, slugging it out even as the Pavilion sloped ever farther to the side, the balls of molten Energon sizzling as they dropped through floor after floor, down toward the deadly struggle far below . . .

IT HAD STARTED OUT BADLY AND GOTTEN WORSE FROM there.

Optimus had fought, of course—sliced his sword through another Decepticon's faceplate—but as that bot twitched and sparked, the rest were on him, burying him under the force of sheer numbers. Megatron stood back, laughing while two of his henchmen held Optimus's arms. A third prepared to ram an energy spear through his torso.

But then everything went white as Skywarp's explosion blew through the floor, folding back the wall. Thousands of tons of water poured in, hurling everyone in the room against the far wall. The video of the ocean flickered out amid electrical shortages, and as the blast of real ocean intensified, the Decepticons were swept one by one from the wall, hauled toward a watery grave. The pull on

Optimus intensified; he searched for someplace on the wall he could grab on to and find purchase. But there was nothing. So he made his own, punching into the wall and holding on as the water roared past him—and with it the last of the assassins.

Megatron.

What happened next was pure instinct. Optimus reached out and grabbed Megatron with one arm, then used his legs and other arm to climb, pulling them both out of the rising white water. A dazed Megatron looked around.

"What are you doing?" he yelled.

"Saving your life," Optimus told him.

"You're an idiot, librarian."

"Thanks for your opinion," Optimus said as they reached the ceiling; he smashed through it with his power ax, clambering into the elevator shaft, which was now tilting diagonally as the Pavilion listed ever farther. He and Megatron heard more explosions far above.

"My people are slaughtering yours," Megatron proclaimed.

"That may be so," said Optimus as water poured into the shaft. "But how about we suspend our own quarrel until we get up there and see?"

"Agreed," Megatron said. They began to clamber up the shaft. And as they did so—

"So what *did* the Quintessons promise you?" Optimus asked.

Megatron shrugged. "The Decepticon Matrix of Leadership."

"And you believed them?"

"What did they tell *you*?" Megatron snarled.

"That if I couldn't convince you of peace, they could control your mind."

"What? And you believed *that*?"

And suddenly Optimus realized that he really did. And

that the Quintessons had already been doing that. But not to Megatron.

To him.

A way to influence circuitry . . . make the subject more malleable . . . Optimus knew in that instant what he had to do. Something that his whole being rebelled at. Something he never would have contemplated doing until now. He reached into his chest cavity.

And switched off the Matrix of Leadership.

As the artifact went dark, all of his doubts fell away. None of it was left—just him. He had no idea where the AllSpark was. No clue to what Prime really wanted. But he knew for certain that he faced a foe far worse than the Decepticons: an ancient enemy that once had enslaved his race and had almost enslaved him and somehow managed to corrupt the Matrix itself. Because now that it was dormant, everything was clear. He remembered everything about the Quintessons now. Somehow they had manipulated the Matrix to lure him to this planet. Somehow he had to defeat the Curator and get his people to safety. He and Megatron kept on climbing, water lapping at their heels as they clambered desperately upward. But as they did so, Optimus heard something coming down toward them—a hissing noise . . .

"Do you hear that?" Optimus asked.

"That's the fighting," Megatron said.

"No, much closer—" Then the ceiling ruptured, and molten Energon poured down toward them. Optimus and Megatron hurled themselves aside and were engulfed in steam as the Energon hit the water rushing up beneath them. They made it through into another corridor and kept on heading toward where they thought the surface was. Another thunderous explosion echoed down to them.

And then all the sounds of combat stopped.

* * *

RECOGNIZING THEIR COMMON PREDICAMENT, THE Autobots and Decepticons had combined their fire on the hangar ceiling, blowing it open. Water poured in, but so did light. As the Seekers flew out, the remaining Autobots and Decepticons scrambled along the walls and onto the part of the hull that was now the roof of the Pavilion. It wasn't a pretty sight. Unbroken ocean lay all around. Everyone was just taking this in when a hatch opened and Optimus and Megatron climbed out.

"Optimus!" Jazz yelled. "Thank Primus you made it!" He said nothing about Megatron, nor did he express surprise that the two were working together. Necessity had a way of throwing enemies together. Yet necessity was nothing if not capricious, and Jazz braced himself for Megatron to order the Decepticons to get back to the task of finishing off the Autobots.

But what happened next was even worse.

"Look!" Ironhide pointed at waves churning toward the remnants of the wrecked Pavilion, closing from all sides. The next moment, hundreds of gigantic manta ray–shaped ships broke the surface and moved in at high speed.

"A full-scale battle fleet," Ironhide breathed.

Several hundred meters out, the noses of the warships peeled back and spit forth thousands of terrifying sharklike robots bristling with weapons and oversized razor-sharp dorsal fins. Both Decepticons and Autobot stared in amazement at the sheer number of new arrivals. To Kup, Bumblebee, and Rodimus the new robots looked very familiar, but they couldn't quite remember where they'd seen them.

A hatch opened on the bow of the flagship, and a huge blue-green behemoth emerged. A king-size version of his Sharkticon army, the newcomer wore a scaled red cape and a giant squid-shaped battle helm; he carried a titanic trident. The tentacles that draped down his chest and back might have been extra armor, but they writhed like snakes and probably could lash out like them, too. Sharp jagged-edge fins protruded all along the creature's back, forearms, and calves. He handed his trident to two members of his honor guard—that was how many it took just to hold it up—whereupon three more of them placed a giant conchlike object into his open palm. He held the device to his mouth and began to speak through it. A monstrous voice boomed and echoed over the sea.

"You have the honor of hearing the voice of Lord General Tyrannicon, the First of the Many. As supreme commander of the Aquatronian Defense Force, I hereby place you under arrest in the name of the Quintesson Imperium. Surrender now or prepare to be utterly destroyed." As if to drive his point home, thousands of Sharkticons began gnashing their teeth and thrashing their powerful tails. But an undaunted Megatron stepped forward and waved his fist at Tyrannicon.

"Who dares speak to Megatron that way? I'll tear you limb from—" Optimus grabbed Megatron's shoulder and pulled him back. Megatron shoved him away.

"Get your hands off me, librarian!"

"Megatron, there's no way we can win this one. You have to stand down."

"I never stand down."

"Hate to break it to you, but this might have to be the exception."

Megatron looked back over the endless mass of Sharkticon warriors.

"I guess we *are* slightly outnumbered," he muttered.

Not only that, but the few troops he still had were exhausted from combat with the Autobots. For that matter, so was he. And he could only guess at what this maniac of a shark boss could do. Megatron longed to go out in a brilliant blaze of glory, but there was no honor in going down at the hands of these fish-bots. He was going to get out of this and wreak his vengeance on everybody. But the only way to do that was to do what he'd never done before.

Megatron raised his hands in surrender.

Chapter Twenty-six

CYBERTRON

"I HAVE IT," SAID MACCADAM.

Wheeljack looked around, startled. He hadn't even heard the old bartender enter the room. Apparently Maccadam still knew how to keep a low profile. He'd been gone for several hours, to the point where Wheeljack was wondering if he should suggest to Ultra Magnus that they head elsewhere, that Maccadam might have been captured by the Decepticons, might have been forced to tell them that a team of Wreckers was hiding out at his bar. But Wheeljack had said nothing. And he knew why: If they were going to rescue Alpha Trion, they had no other choice than to hope Maccadam came through for them.

Now apparently he had.

"What's the story?" Ultra Magnus asked.

But Maccadam was taking his own sweet time about it. He went behind the bar and began to pour each of them a cup of oil. That done, he set about cleaning another cup. That cup was already sparkling, but for an old-timer like Maccadam it was as much about the ritual as anything else. He'd been out on the streets, risking his life. Now he needed a few seconds to process everything. Finally he looked up.

"Shockwave is trying to use Alpha Trion to harness Vector Sigma."

Ultra Magnus looked stunned. "I thought Vector Sigma was a legend," he said.

"It is," said Maccadam. "It also happens to be quite real. And every bit as potent as the stories say."

"What's Shockwave intend to do with it?"

"Whatever he wants, presumably," Springer said.

"True," Maccadam said. "But my contact has heard something more specific—that he's attempting to build a superweapon. But he didn't know more than that."

Ultra Magnus's face was grave. "Does your contact know where all this is taking place?"

"Fortunately, yes." Maccadam unfurled an electronic map and folded it out across the bar. The screen showed the subbasements beneath Iacon. Maccadam hit a few buttons, and the view of those subbasements shrank toward the minuscule while a larger area below the planetary crust came into focus.

"He's down near the core," the bartender said. "It's one of the access points to Vector Sigma. Shockwave obviously has been planning this for a while, because he's constructed an entirely self-sufficient bunker down there with at least two fully functioning Dark Energon refineries."

"And we've never heard of any of this before?" Jetfire asked. "How could he keep all this under wraps?"

"Every worker who took part in the construction has been sent to the furnaces."

"That slag heap," said Rack n' Ruin. Everyone nodded in agreement.

"Shockwave is still down there," Maccadam told them. "So whatever he's trying to do, he has yet to succeed. Meaning there's still time if you hurry."

"How do we get there?"

"This," Maccadam said, tracing a vertical red line

that cut from the basements beneath Shockwave's tower straight down to his secret bunker. "Shockwave's personal maglev transport. That's the most direct route."

"So you think we should break into the tower and—"

"Everything around the tower is too well guarded. No, what I'd recommend doing is breaking into the maglev tunnel a few miles down. Jack one of the trains, travel in style the rest of the way. Otherwise—well, most of that area isn't even mapped. We don't know what parts are undercity and what parts are solid rock. You'd never get there in time."

"Got it," Ultra Magnus said. Maccadam rolled up the map and handed it to him.

That was when all hell broke loose.

The entire bar shook with the rumble of an explosion right outside. A barrage of shots crashed into the building and would have perforated the walls if they had not armored and reinforced them. Maccadam brought up the security camera feed on the screens to show Decepticons taking up positions in the streets outside.

"They've found us," he said.

The blaring of a megaphone sounded from the Decepticon positions. "This is Ratbat, commander of the city garrison. You're all under arrest. You have thirty seconds to come out with your hands up before we demolish that whole place."

"This is all my fault," Maccadam muttered. "They must have followed me."

"Your contact sold you out," said Rack n' Ruin.

"Unlikely, given that he's been passing me information for years. If they've gotten to him, he's dead, too. No, I tripped a curfew. Or got spotted by a camera."

"Or *we* did," Ultra Magnus said. "Look, there's no use in recriminations. We need to get out of here, and we have to do it fast."

"Sure, but how?" Springer asked as he gestured at the screen.

"I'm going to make a call," Ultra Magnus said.

RATBAT HAD SET UP HIS COMMAND POST SEVERAL BLOCKS away, well out of line of sight of anyone inside Maccadam's who might be inclined to take a potshot at the Decepticon forces outside. And he had reason to believe it wasn't just Maccadam in there, either. If the reports of a Wrecker commando force entering the city were true, it might have holed up there. If that was the case, Ratbat would have good news to tell Shockwave. That was excellent, because Shockwave hated hearing anything else. Ratbat had no intention of telling Shockwave about the Wrecker team until he had it in custody.

Not that Shockwave was available right now, anyway. He was somewhere deep beneath his tower, engaged in one of his experiments, and had given orders that he wasn't to be disturbed except in the event of a dire emergency. Which this wasn't. That suited Ratbat just fine. The less he saw of Shockwave, the better. The two bots had been working together for only a short while now, but Ratbat had quickly come to realize just how unpredictable and dangerous Shockwave was. He almost longed for the days when Megatron was running things.

Almost.

"Time's up," he said to the Decepticons nearby. "Stand by to commence ground assault." There was a clanking noise, and several giant Decepticons that looked more like tanks than bots rumbled past as smaller Decepticons scrambled to get out of their way. Gaining speed, the Decepticon assault units roared up toward the door of Maccadam's like battering rams.

But suddenly there was a distant shrieking noise, a sound that grew steadily louder, building to an overwhelming level as incoming shells streaked in and hit the leading Decepticons, smashing them to bits and sending pieces of metal flying for hundreds of meters. More shells kept raining down; more bots disintegrated, along with several buildings. Ratbat was still spluttering with shock when his bodyguards seized him and started dragging him away.

"Who's firing?" he screamed.

"It's coming from outside the city," yelled one of the bodyguards.

Two miles away, Omega Supreme continued to fling all manner of rockets and shells over the walls of Iacon on the precise trajectories that Ultra Magnus had just given him. He hadn't enjoyed himself so much for a long time. The only thing more fun than shelling the city was watching the Decepticons get the surprise of their life. He could see lights flashing along the walls, could hear the noise of Klaxons and sirens going off across the city. For several more seconds he was able to continue shelling with total impunity, and then, finally, Decepticon gun turrets along the walls began swiveling in his direction. Ultra Magnus had told him that would be a good time to leave, but as he reversed at full speed back into the wastelands, he switched his attention to those wall turrets, targeting them with withering accuracy. As turret after turret exploded, Omega Supreme permitted himself a moment of grim satisfaction. He just hoped he'd bought Ultra Magnus whatever breathing room his mission needed.

*   *   *

ULTRA MAGNUS EMERGED CAUTIOUSLY FROM THE BAR and looked around.

"All clear," he said.

"Impressive," Wheeljack said. The smoke-filled street was littered with craters and smashed Decepticons.

"They didn't know what hit them," said Springer.

"That's the way it should be," Rack n' Ruin said.

Jetfire nodded. "Omega Supreme's a good friend to have."

"But not an omnipotent one," Ultra Magnus said. "We need to move quickly."

"Yes, you do," Maccadam said as he emerged from the bar, locking the door behind him. "They'll be back shortly."

"What about you?" Ultra Magnus asked.

"I'll be just fine," Maccadam said. "Got plenty more places I can lie low. Once the heat dies down, who knows? Maybe I can even sneak back here."

He and Ultra Magnus shook hands. "Good luck," said Maccadam. "Everything depends on you now."

"I just pray we still have time," Ultra Magnus told him.

Chapter Twenty-seven

THE WAITING WAS DRIVING EVERYBODY CRAZY.

The portholes still showed nothing but the black of deep underwater. Hours had passed since the prisoners had been taken into custody by the Sharkticons. They'd spent most of that time in the hold of one of the manta ships, Autobots on one side of the room and Decepticons on the other. Optimus knew that imprisoning them together was a deliberate gesture intended to add insult to injury. Both sides would have to suffer the humiliation of close-quarters incarceration after a fight. No doubt the Quintessons wanted to observe them and file away the reactions. So far there had been no incidents; both sides were still licking their wounds and trying to figure out what had happened. As to what the Quintessons had in store for them, well, that was anybody's guess, although it didn't take a genius to figure out it wasn't going to be pleasant. The reasons the Quintessons would want them alive were few, and every one Optimus could think of gave him a chill. It didn't help matters that he knew everyone else was thinking the same thing.

"Optimus."

"Yes, Jazz?"

"Where do you think they're taking us?"

"I don't know. Just stay alert." Optimus was trying to keep up a good front. His men needed him to be strong.

He didn't need a Matrix of Leadership to tell him that. He wished he'd never had the Matrix in the first place, wished he'd never listened to its siren song of duty, because then he would never have led his people into this mess. Duty had led him astray—or was it glory? Was that the real temptation to which he had succumbed?

"Why do I feel so weak?" Rodimus asked. "I can barely move."

"I can't activate my weapons," Prowl said while trying to pop his Investigator Special. Perceptor pointed to the glowing lights embedded in the ceiling.

"I think they're using an energy-dampening field," Perceptor said. "I hate to say this, but they were probably able to tune it to our specific physiology because of the scans we let them take of Optimus. It's my fault. If I hadn't been in such a hurry . . ."

"No sense in crying over spilled oil, Perceptor." Ratchet was trying to console his friend but wasn't really succeeding. "Right, Optimus?"

Optimus chose his words carefully. "The Quintessons are masters at blending fact with fiction. They tricked us into disregarding our own instincts."

"You sound like you know these Quintessons well."

"Not well enough. They managed to hide my own memories from me. I knew them millions of years ago, back in the days when I was just Orion Pax. They enslaved our world—"

"They admitted as much," Ratchet interrupted.

"They ruled us mercilessly. Eventually Sentinel Prime rose up and defeated them, drove them from Cybertron. We thought they would never return. We forgot them and went on with our lives. But they seem to have forgotten nothing."

Jazz couldn't believe what he was hearing. "Why didn't the Matrix alert you to any of this?"

226 David J. Williams and Mark S. Williams

David J. Williams and Mark S. Williams

"They've been manipulating it, Jazz. They drew us here, making us think the AllSpark lay somewhere along this vector."

"They got to the *Matrix*?" Ratchet asked. "Then we are truly lost."

"We're lost only if we believe it," Optimus said. "And right now I choose not to."

Perceptor's brow furrowed. "So where *is* the AllSpark?"

"That's the least of our problems," Optimus told him. He didn't even want to speculate; he was all too conscious of unseen listening devices all around. "Right now we need to focus on the here and now. Quintessons hide their moves within moves, bury their plans within plans. There's some larger game in play here. It can't just be about the trap they set for us. There's something more to it."

"Even if there is, that doesn't explain why they would blow up their own temple," Rodimus said.

"What makes you think it really was a temple?" Jazz asked.

"I know what happened," Bulkhead answered as he staggered to his feet. "Those Decepticons tried to kill us!" At the sound of the challenge, Thundercracker stood up and wobbled toward Ironhide. A few Decepticons behind him started to stir.

"You miserable scum! You were the one who tried to kill our lord Megatron!" Thundercracker rasped.

"Say that again, you scrap heap!" Ironhide yelled. But Optimus managed to get between the would-be combatants.

"Enough!" he said. "Fighting among ourselves isn't going to change anything!"

Megatron's laughter rang out. "Always the voice of reason, aren't you, librarian? Did it even occur to you that maybe you're responsible for the situation we are in?

You were the one who fell for this whole peace nonsense in the first place."

"Whereas you just planned to betray us all," said Ironhide.

"Shut up, fool; I'm talking to your sniveling excuse for a leader. Optimus, would it surprise you to know that the Curator came to me and spoke at length about how weak you are? How much contempt he has for you?"

"I'm sure the Curator told you all sorts of things," Optimus said drily. "And you were far too eager to listen."

Megatron shook his head. "Don't try to change the subject, clerk. Wasn't your Matrix of 'Leadership' supposed to keep you from making these kinds of rookie mistakes?"

Optimus was too weary to indulge in recriminations. "You're in the same cell with the rest of us, Megatron."

"Not for long." But Megatron's bravado rang hollow in that cramped hold. Some of the Autobots laughed openly at him. Optimus simply shook his head sadly.

"Megatron, don't you realize who the Quintessons are? They're the very same race who sent you to toil in the mines millions of years ago! If I'm a fool for believing them, then what does that make you?"

Megatron smashed his fist against the floor. "Come here and I'll show you."

The manta ray ship suddenly ground up against something solid.

"We're docking!" Perceptor said. There was a rush to the portholes on either side as Autobots and Decepticons crowded around them, trying to get a look at their destination. The ship had surfaced in a massive undersea grotto, a gigantic military staging area. Multiple industrial cargo elevators ran back and forth between other manta ships while maglev cargo trains hauled Energon and weapons out of the room and into tunnels. Sharkticons were everywhere, some standing guard and others loading. Still others stood in long lines, where they were being issued with weapons and supplementary armor before marching into the open holds of the manta ships.

"Looks like they're getting ready for a war," Rodimus said.

"Sure," Ramjet said, "but with whom?"

"The Sharkticons in this room already outnumber us twenty to one," Dirge muttered. "They didn't need all this for us."

"So who are they planning on fighting?" Ramjet repeated.

"Someone else on this planet?" Rodimus suggested.

"I think they've got this planet locked down pretty tight."

"So who are their neighboring star systems?" asked Jazz.

"We didn't see any," Optimus said.

"Because you didn't *look*," Megatron said. "You were so eager to rush in and find the AllSpark, so trusting in your precious Matrix. That's Optimus's leadership for you, everybody! Fling the most important artifact in history into the cosmos just so you can spend your entire life running around looking for it!"

"While you'd rather just spend your entire life running your mouth," Ironhide said.

"Impudent whelp!" Megatron snarled. "Your days are numbered!"

But even as he said it, the holding cell doors slid open to reveal a squad of Sharkticons wielding laser whips.

"Check out the welcome wagon," Rodimus snarked. His comment was immediately met with a laser whip that lashed out and sent him sprawling on the ground.

"NOT TO TALK!" a Sharkticon screamed at him. Another cracked its whip and pointed to the open hatch.

"YOU, THIS WAY! NOW!" Both Autobots and

Decepticons fell into line as their Sharkticon guards marched them out of the manta ship and onto the docks, where a maglev train awaited, its hatches open.

"Looks like we're going for another ride," Ironhide said. A Sharkticon guard raised his whip threateningly.

"YOU GET IN! NOW!"

As they filed aboard, Optimus looked up and saw the huge Sharkticon general overseeing the entire process from an observation deck on his flagship. For a moment he and Optimus met each other's gaze, and then Optimus stepped inside to join his companions. The Autobots and the Decepticons were loaded into separate train cars this time. That came as a big relief to the former, especially because the Decepticons were starting to be less than cooperative as they reached their designated car on the train. Megatron's voice boomed and echoed through the cave.

"I demand to know where you are taking us!"

Megatron got his answer in the form of several laser whips cracking over his head.

"SHUT UP! MOVE ON TRAIN! NOW!" At least some things were consistent, Optimus thought. Even in the face of the unknown and adversity Megatron remained a pompous scrap pile. But Optimus was thinking that maybe—just maybe—there might be a way to turn that arrogance to their advantage.

THE TRAIN SPED THROUGH A ROCKY TUNNEL FOR A couple more hours. Optimus did his best to maintain his bearings, but with all his systems frozen at such low power, it was all he could do to keep from falling asleep. At least this time they didn't have to spend the trip watching their backs for Decepticon treachery, though perhaps leaving the Autobots alone with their thoughts was even worse.

Optimus was glad when he detected a change in the train incline, which sloped ever more steeply, rising steadily from the level of the seabed. He went to a window to get a better look, half expecting to see that they were back in the water again. To learn that this train was partially aquatic would have been the least surprising thing that had happened that day.

But he was wrong.

Bleak landscape stretched off in all directions, punctuated by distant mountains, their peaks shrouded in low-hanging clouds and mist. A steady rain beat down. The only signs of life were overland power lines and pipes that crisscrossed the barren lands. Huge lightning rods rose up from the rails at regular intervals, no doubt to counter the constant storms. It was one of the most desolate wildernesses Optimus had ever seen, and it went on for mile after mile, until finally the weather began to clear a little and through the clouds up ahead Optimus caught sight of a distant city skyline.

"Guys," he said. "I think we're here."

As everyone pressed up against the window, it quickly became apparent that this was no ordinary city. In fact, it might have been the largest city Optimus had ever seen, several times bigger than Iacon. There was no doubt this was the Aquatron capital. And it was set in the middle of a vast lake; as the train raced onto a causeway that stretched out over the water, Optimus studied the approaching buildings. They almost seemed more organic than mechanical, curving into and around one another as if they were enormous crystal growths. Optimus could make out flying versions of the Sharkticons weaving their way in and out of the skyscrapers. It stunned him that the city had gone undetected during the scans from orbit. Clearly the weather had been a factor, but there must have been additional shielding at work here. As the train passed over the lake, Optimus could see down into the clear water; bots sped this way and that, busily working on infrastructure just below the surface. Optimus could only wonder what else was down there as the train raced off the causeway and into the city.

Unlike the one at the pole, this place was crowded. Aquatronians were everywhere. But now that the subterfuge was over, it was clear what a cowed lot they were. They were the planet's worker class, whereas the Sharkticons were the warrior caste. The latter were a constant presence on the streets, their macelike tails bouncing along behind them. The population showed no curiosity at the prison train thundering past them. Perhaps it was a routine occurrence. The train traveled a considerable distance into the city and then came to a stop in front of a grand cathedral-like structure. Huge flying buttresses carved from sea stone held up a magnificent archway in which stood statues of huge trident-wielding Sharkticons. The runes indicated that the building was the Hall of Justice. Optimus had a feeling that justice would be the last thing they would find in it.

"I hate this place already," Ironhide said.

The train doors slid open, and Sharkticon guards marched the Autobots and Decepticons out of the train and down onto the platform. Waiting for them there were—

"Not these guys again," Rodimus said.

The Curator and Xeros were surrounded by a Sharkticon honor guard. Both looked pleased with how the situation had turned out.

"KNEEL!" One of the Sharkticon guards cracked his whip. The Cybertronians reluctantly obeyed and dropped to their knees. It was one of the most painful things Optimus had ever done, but he knew he had to stay alive if his people were to have any chance at all.

Trumpets sounded as General Tyrannicon appeared in the doorway two cars back. He marched up to the Curator and dropped to one knee before him.

"May the light and hope of Quintessa shine down and empower your humble servant," he said formally.

The Curator smiled and beckoned the general forward with his scaly hand.

"You may rise. General, allow me to congratulate you on apprehending these . . . malefactors. We can only shudder to think what further damage they would have caused had you not acted quickly. You have done well, and now that you have brought them to our great city of Hydratron, we can administer justice as the law requires."

"Thank you, my lord. I live to serve."

"See, Xeros?" The Curator turned to the taciturn scientist at his side. "I was right to return the Sword of Sharkticons to his rightful place."

"Of course you were, my lord." Xeros glanced at Tyrannicon with more than a little trepidation. "How could I have not seen how essential his role would be?"

Tyrannicon puffed out his chest and spoke in his imposing baritone. "These cretins surrendered without a fight once they saw the majesty of my battle force."

"Liar!" Megatron screamed. Then, turning to the Curator: "You! You set us all up! I'll rip you limb from limb for this." His words were cut off as Tyrannicon stepped over to him and delivered a powerful backhand blow that sent the Decepticon leader flying into the side of the train. Not content to stop there, Tyrannicon lifted his huge scale-covered foot and placed it on Megatron's throat.

"Another word from you and I shall permanently deactivate your voice circuits," he said.

For once, Megatron shut up. "You should let me kill them now," Tyrannicon said to the Curator.

"Your enthusiasm is commendable, General. But these

Cybertronians must formally account for their hubris."
The Curator then turned directly to Optimus. "To think I
thought you Cybertronians were ready for peace. Instead
you've proved yourselves totally unworthy."

"You deceived us," Optimus said.

"No," the Curator insisted. "You deceived *us*. You defiled
our temple, and you disgraced yourselves. I gave you the
benefit of the doubt when I should have known better."

"You little two-faced *snake*," Ironhide said. A whip
knocked him sprawling.

"You see?" the Curator said. "Even now your people
can't control themselves. You're primitives. But you still
must answer to the law."

"And what does *that* mean?" Optimus asked.

Tyrannicon stepped in. "You dare take that tone of
voice?" he rumbled. He was about to give Optimus the
same treatment he'd just meted out to Megatron, but the
Curator raised his hand.

"He has the right to speak, General. Or rather, he will
inside the Hall of Justice." Then, turning back to Optimus:
"You see, Optimus, we Quintessons place a premium on
truth and justice. Unlike you, I might add. But despite
your many transgressions against us, you are still entitled
to certain protections under our ancient code. Despite
your proclivity for destruction and mayhem, we will treat
you in a way that befits your status. Despite the fact that
you do not deserve it, you will still receive a fair trial."

"A fair *trial*?!?" Jazz shouted incredulously. "But we've
done nothing wrong!"

Xeros snickered. "Of course you would think that. You
have no true concept of what is right and what is wrong.
Empathy and reason are empty words to you."

"I've heard enough," Optimus said, facing the Curator
directly. "Not only are you our mortal enemy, you can't
even admit that to my face. You hide behind this talk of

justice, and you're laughing all the time. You've deceived us, but I promise that the one who will pay for his crimes will be you—" He was cut off as Tyrannicon raised a fist and smashed him to the ground.

"For shame," said the Curator. "Every word you say can and will be used against you. But in the end, I have no doubt you will recognize the gravity of your transgressions. Mark my words, Optimus Prime. In the end you will beg to be forgiven. General, take them in to meet the justice they run from all their lives."

Tyrannicon smiled the smile of a pure predator. "At once, my lord."

Chapter Twenty-eight

STARSCREAM STRODE ONTO THE NEMESIS'S FRESHLY repaired command deck with a newfound air of confidence. Fleeing the Pavilion had been instinctual, but it had been one of the best moves he'd ever made. Because now the ship was undeniably his, and it was almost operational again. To be sure, he was short some of his key Seekers and a few others, but no matter. As far as Starscream was concerned, there was no reason to remain out here in the middle of nowhere, especially not when he could return to Cybertron and rule it himself. That mad scientist Shockwave would put up little opposition. Besides, if he waited here long enough, the Quintessons would finish him off, too. After all, that was exactly what he would do if the situation were reversed. The best answer he could think of was to be someplace else entirely, and that someplace undoubtedly was Cybertron.

"Soundwave," he demanded, "what is the status?"

"Regrettably, I have been unable to reboot several of the Nemesis's computers. However, I have managed to link new circuitry directly to the engines and devised a series of manual workarounds."

Starscream looked impatient. "So can we fly or can't we?"

"We can. Just not as well as I should like."

"Excellent. Plot a course back to Cybertron. We're

leaving this place immediately."

"But what about Lord Megatron?"

"Megatron is dead." Starscream figured that would be the last time he'd need to hear *that* name. He congratulated himself once more on using Skywarp so deviously to eliminate the Decepticon leader. He began thinking about his plans for Cybertron. First of all, it would be necessary to rebuild Iacon entirely from the ground up. And there would need to be some suitable monuments. Perhaps a giant image of himself, three hundred meters tall, carved with laser on stone . . . Starscream became aware that Soundwave had said something.

"What was that?"

"I said Megatron isn't dead, Air Commander."

"Impossible."

"It's true, my lord. Let me show you." Soundwave pulled up the video footage taken by the *Nemesis* of the sinking Pavilion. The two Decepticons watched the drama unfold. Just when it looked like there'd be no survivors, the Autobots and Decepticons crawled out and were rounded up by the Aquatronian fleet. Both Megatron and Optimus were among them.

"By Unicron," Starscream said.

"Excuse me, Air Commander?"

"I meant, thank Unicron he's alive." Starscream simply could not believe his bad luck. This was a serious monkey wrench in his plan: The remaining Decepticons would no doubt think it was their sacred duty to attempt to rescue Megatron from the clutches of these fish-bots. What angered him even more was the certain knowledge that they would never dream of doing the same thing for him. Starscream figured that for now he would have to play along and give the impression that he wanted to save their dear leader, too.

"I knew he was too tough to fall before those insipid

fish-bots and their Quintesson allies," he said. "Where did they take them?"

Soundwave brought up his scans of the planet and pointed to a large island in the south; it was so big that it might have been classified as a small continent. Most of it was shrouded in bad weather. Soundwave must have been hard at work reversing the planetary defense system's scramblers, since it hadn't been visible earlier.

"They took them all there," he said. "For what purpose I do not know."

"What can you tell me about that continent?" Starscream asked.

"The weather has impeded our scans, but it seems to be the largest single landmass on the planet. Also, there is substantial electromagnetic activity, which further inhibits my efforts. That said, irregular breaks in the storm systems have allowed me to get a glimpse of what appears to be a huge city-island in the middle of a lake in the planet's center. We think Megatron is now someplace within—we received a quick glimpse of his signal about twenty minutes ago. We also detected what appears to be a huge energy source beneath the city, which might be the source of all the electromagnetic activity."

"Presumably their Energon facilities."

"I don't think so. It is far more concentrated than that. Take a look at this scan." Starscream leaned in for a closer look. "As you can see, that is not an Energon signature. It is something else entirely."

"So what do you think it is?"

"I do not know. But whatever it is, Megatron and the rest of our soldiers are standing right on top of it."

"Continue your scans. I don't want to attempt a rescue until we know more about what these Quintessons are hiding."

"Of course."

"Now, what's the status of the Ark?"

"The Autobot ship remains on the far side of the planet. But we have to assume that they're trying to figure out how to launch a rescue mission. If nothing else, I very much doubt they will allow the Matrix of Leadership to remain in Quintesson hands."

"Any sign of Quintesson moves against us or the Ark?" Starscream asked. He eyed those planetary rings nervously.

"They seem to still believe they have us in stasis. And the Ark may still *be* in stasis for all we know."

"Excellent, Soundwave. You have done well." Starscream turned on his heel and strode off the bridge, his body language radiating the anger he dared not put into words.

As soon as the door closed, Soundwave moved to another screen and brought up his mini-con's footage of the fight on the Pavilion. His spy's purpose had been to make sure that Optimus Prime went down to the Temple of Peace by himself, but the spy had captured much more than that. What was particularly troubling was that just before the combat in the Temple of Peace began, another energy signature appeared on the exterior hull of the Pavilion. Soundwave had been trying to decode it for some time, and now at last he had an answer.

Skywarp.

Right before it had been destroyed, the mini-con had transmitted X-ray data that indicated that the Decepticon teleporter had appeared on the hull and attached an explosive device, which promptly exploded, disintegrating him in the process.

That made no sense whatsoever. Skywarp was a lot of things, but he wasn't a suicide bomber. So why would Megatron give such a risky order? He already had Optimus cornered, and the bomb easily could have killed everybody in that room. Soundwave had combed through the ship's database looking for whatever information he could find on the Quintessons, but there was virtually nothing. It was as though somebody had erased much of the data. All signs pointed to them as somehow being the instigators behind all this, but there was precious little hard evidence to support that theory. Had Skywarp turned traitor? Or been under their control the whole time? The immediate problem was how to rescue Megatron, of course, but now there was a second challenge behind that one, for Soundwave intended to unravel the mystery of just what had set this lethal chain of events in motion. And if it turned out he couldn't save Megatron, Soundwave knew what his duty demanded.

Vengeance on everybody involved.

THE INTERIOR OF THE HALL OF JUSTICE LOOKED LIKE A cross between an ancient gladiator pit and a modern opera house that sloped down to transparent holding cells, allowing an audience of thousands to enjoy a good view of the captives. Aquatronians packed those seats, sitting in attentive silence, waiting for the spectacle to begin. In front of the cells was a circular sunken area surrounded by a half circle of five viewscreens that stretched from floor to ceiling. A defendant's box stood in front of those screens, and a dais had been placed opposite the box, with a witness stand off to one side. The entire room was resplendent in eerie green and black with gold highlights here and there. The Sharkticons who stood guard everywhere wore elaborate armor that matched the color scheme and design aesthetic of the hall. In a peculiar way, it made the short fat killing machines seem almost regal.

"I don't like the look of this one bit," Jazz said. He and

the rest of the Autobots were in one set of holding cells; the Decepticons were in the other. Everybody was glaring at one another, wondering what was going to happen next.

"You and me both," Ironhide replied as he looked for a weakness in the cell. He grabbed the bars and pulled. A Sharkticon guard slapped his hands with his tail.

"GET BACK!"

"It doesn't do us any good to antagonize them," Ratchet said.

"I'd say they're already pretty antagonized," Ironhide replied.

All at once the lights dimmed. Deafening horns sounded throughout the chamber. A figure wreathed in shadow appeared on the dais opposite the defendant box. It was hard to make out the details, but from the way it flickered, it was obviously a holographic projection.

"Guess that's the chief," Perceptor said.

"Guess again," Prowl said as the five screens suddenly came to life. On each screen was another shadowy figure, five in all. Only they weren't figures. They seemed more like disembodied heads floating in midair, each face contorted into a skull-like grimace. It was impossible to make out more than that, and the overall effect was more than a little eerie, an effect that intensified when one of the heads began speaking. A low hollow voice seemed to echo from a place beyond all space and time.

"By the power of the Quintesson Imperium, I call this high court to order on the city of Hydratron, in the province of Aquatron, and do hereby stand before you as chief magistrate."

Megatron chose that moment to start yelling. "Chief coward is more like it! Why don't you show yourself instead of hiding behind that screen!" The Sharkticon guards promptly knocked Megatron to the ground with their maces and whips. The chief magistrate let the beating go on for a while before resuming his speech.

"Another outburst from the defendant will result in him being found in contempt of court. Prosecutor, are you ready to commence your case against the defendants?"

"I am," said the figure on the dais.

"Do you swear to present that case with neither malice nor prejudice?"

"I do," the figure said.

"Then proceed."

"Your honor, I shall begin with the charges against their leader, Optimus Prime."

Megatron looked outraged. "Optimus isn't our leader"—but his words were cut off as a Sharkticon smashed him back onto the ground. More Sharkticons grabbed Optimus and led him to the prisoner's box. He stood there for a moment regarding the screens. He suddenly realized that he was looking at some kind of long-range communication system, that whoever was running this trial was offworld, perhaps on Quintessa itself. That meant they had to have a space bridge nearby to enable faster-than-light communication. It also meant there had to be a considerable power source close at hand. Perhaps they could turn that power source against the city's defenses. If he could only find a way out from under the thumb of this sham of a court . . .

"State your name for the record," the prosecutor said.

"I am Optimus Prime, and I refuse to recognize the legitimacy of this court."

"Your recognition is not required," said the prosecutor. "Are you ready to hear the charges?"

"Go ahead," Optimus said wearily.

"The charges against you are as follows: destruction of public property, criminal mayhem, high treason, war crimes, and galactic blasphemy. Do you have any questions regarding these charges?"

"You're charging me with *treason*? Against whom?"

"Are you not a native of the planet Cybertron?"

"Yes. Which means that—"

"It means that treason is applicable. The other charges reflect the destruction you have wrought on Aquatron and your past crimes against the Quintesson Imperium committed by both you and your minions—" He broke off as the Autobots and Decepticons started howling in outrage. The Sharkticons had to restore order; by the time they were finished, many of the Cybertronians were unable to do anything more than watch the proceedings from a prone position. After that there were no more interruptions, and the prosecutor got on with his hatchet job.

"You have the right to know the evidence," he said to Optimus. "Are you prepared to hear it?"

"I'm prepared to hear it, but I doubt you're going to listen to me."

The prosecutor ignored him. "First, as to mayhem and blasphemy. The following is indisputable: that you did willfully engage in violent combat in an area designated as a sacred neutral zone. This combat did result in the destruction of our Temple of Peace. The following footage will be labeled as Exhibit A." The image on one of the screens was replaced by a scene of Autobots and Decepticons battling savagely at the Pavilion. It was followed by another of Optimus desperately fighting for his life in the Temple of Peace before the bomb on the hull detonated and turned the screen white.

"This was instigation," Optimus said. "A setup. The Curator orchestrated all this, and you know it."

"I know nothing of the kind," said the prosecutor. "Do you see this 'Curator' in the courtroom today?"

Optimus looked around, but the Curator had remained outside. "No, I do not."

"Then we regret that we are unable to call him as witness."

"He's right outside!"

"But not present. And thus legally not relevant."

Optimus ground his teeth. Obviously this was a kangaroo court, and the ending was preordained. He forced himself to listen as the prosecutor continued: "Your wanton desire to wage war on Aquatron itself is beyond dispute. However, these incidents pale in comparison to the ancient and long-standing vendetta you have harbored against the Quintesson Imperium. May it please the court, we turn now to the war crime and treason charges."

"Proceed," said the chief magistrate.

"I wish to introduce Exhibit B." The face on another screen faded, to be replaced by an image of a barren and rocky Cybertron. "Millions of years ago we found your planet a barren wasteland. In our infinite wisdom and benevolence, we Quintessons gave life to both Autobot and Decepticon. We brought forth your race and gave you the gift of intelligence, along with the spark of life itself."

Down in the cage Prowl looked at Perceptor. "That's not the creation story I was told," he said in a low voice. Now the screen gave way to bots changing into jets and vehicles while an automated assembly line installed cockpits on them and shadowy figures climbed in.

"And after we gave you all these gifts, you chose to reject our love. You rose up against us and drove us from your planet. You betrayed us and set yourselves on a path to never-ending war and violence. And look where it has gotten you. Millions of years of fighting later, it was inevitable that you would return to us—and now that you have, we demand that you account for your disobedience."

Optimus's head was spinning. Was all this true? If

the information had been presented to him in any other way, he might not have taken it so seriously, but there was something about the visuals that had the spark of truth to them. Or maybe it was just the entire spectacle of the court; maybe he was meant to be taken in by all the pageantry. Surely this was just propaganda, pure and simple. But in that case why was the pressure in his head building? Why did it feel like he was about to have another seizure? What if the Quintessons really *had* created the Cybertronians? Through the haze that engulfed him he could hear the prosecutor continuing:

"Thus is Optimus Prime guilty of blasphemy," he said. "Guilty of rebelling against his own creators."

"So a video constitutes proof?" Optimus asked.

"More blasphemy," said the prosecutor. "You condemn yourself with your own words."

"I thought you said the blasphemy charge was for fighting in your temple."

"I didn't say it was limited to that," the prosecutor shot back. "During our rightful rule of Cybertron, you spoke against us. *That* was blasphemy. Then you acted to thwart us. *That* was treason. Both are capital crimes."

Both sounded virtually interchangeable to Optimus; he suspected that there was no real distinction in the Quintesson legal code. Either that or they were making all this up as they went along, given that the outcome was so certain. Then again, they seemed to attach inordinate importance to the proceedings. Perhaps they were seeking to get him to admit guilt. Perhaps that was what they regarded as victory. The pressure in Optimus's skull was getting ever worse; the prosecutor spoke with such a forked tongue it almost made Optimus forget what was really at stake here—that he had let his people down. He had walked into a trap, and now there was no way out. He searched his mind for some way to respond, and a single obvious thought rose to the surface.

"But I wasn't there," he said.

"But you were," said the prosecutor.

"This was before my time."

"Was it really?"

Suddenly it all came rushing back. Optimus remembered things he would rather have forgotten: remembered the Quintessons' rule of his homeworld, remembered them presiding over courts just like this one, handing out their brand of justice, deciding who lived and who died. He *had* been there, after all. Ratchet had been right.

Or had he? Had the Quintessons merely put those thoughts into his head just now? Agonizing pain gripped Optimus, and he sank to his knees; he heard a murmur of horror from the watching Autobots. As blackness rushed up to claim him, two words floated into his head—two words that were like life rafts in a sea of agony, two words that he reached for as though they were his sole chance at salvation. It was the only way out. Perhaps mercy would be shown to the Autobots, but he knew there would be none for him. Nor did he wish for any. He pulled himself to his feet.

"I confess," he said.

The prosecutor smiled. "Go on," he said.

Optimus could barely speak, but he knew he had to: "I confess I rebelled against you."

"And blasphemed."

"And—" Optimus stopped, for now he remembered a world without the Quintessons, a world *before* the Quintessons. He had been a data clerk that whole time. And he had seen what had happened, seen the Quintessons come down from the sky in their silver ships and take custody of Cybertron.

Without firing a shot.

That was the part Optimus could scarcely believe even

as he saw the truth of it. The Quintessons had arrived on Cybertron at the dawn of spaceflight. They were the first creatures from another world ever to visit Cybertron, and so it was easy for them to proclaim themselves to be superior beings. They had been the first to explain to Cybertronians the mystery of the T-cogs, had shown them how to change themselves into other modes. After that, it was easy to pass themselves off as gods. They had brainwashed the entire population, just as they were trying to brainwash Optimus now.

"I confess I should have done more," he said.

"What?" The prosecutor's face went dark, but Optimus finally had seen the light.

"I should have done more to fight you," he said. "I didn't do enough. I was a data clerk; I just sat in the archives. All I could do was record the truth of it and help reveal to the people the lies that you were telling us. You never created us, much as you might claim it. You Quintessons are the ultimate megalomaniacs. You want a universe filled with slave races, all of them believing themselves to be your creations. Perhaps in the absence of all dissenting voices you'd start to believe it yourself. Perhaps that's what you believe even now. Maybe there are no limits to your self-deception. But I won't be a party to it. You may kill us all, but you won't kill the truth."

The prosecutor's face was grim. "So you wish to take the path of agony?"

"Apparently *you* do," Optimus said. "You could have just executed us all, but instead you seem compelled to make us go through this mockery of a trial, yet all the while the only ones you're fooling are yourselves."

"Is that so?" The prosecutor laughed. "A moment ago you were denying everything, and now you've just confessed that you did indeed carry out seditious activities against us."

"And I'm proud to admit it," Optimus said. "But I never led the resistance. That was Sentinel Prime, and he's dead."

"And not honorably, either," the prosecutor said.

"He lived long enough to grow old and decline," Optimus admitted. "But the final stage of his life cannot take away the years of his glory. And you can't take them away from him, either. That's why you're striking out at me, isn't it? I'm just a convenient proxy for the one who exposed the truth and threw you off Cybertron."

"You underestimate yourself," the prosecutor said. "We have witnesses that will testify to the full magnitude of your crimes."

"Sure you do," Optimus said. "Witnesses with fins who know loyalty only to you."

"No," said the prosecutor, "witnesses from among your own followers."

That was news to Optimus. "What?" he asked. "Who?"

But the prosecutor was milking the moment for all it was worth. He turned to the magistrates. "It is time to learn of the true nature of Optimus Prime. Bring forth those who would testify!" The Sharkticon guards gathered at the Autobot pen, opened it, and dragged out Rodimus, Kup, and Bumblebee.

"Why them?" Jazz muttered.

"I don't know," Ratchet replied. "But I've got a feeling that none of us are going to like the answer."

"The witnesses should be aware that they can speak freely without fear of reprisals," said the prosecutor. "We only want you to tell us the truth. For only the truth can set you free from the shackles of your oppression. State your name for the record and begin."

Rodimus stepped forward and fell to one knee in front of the shadows on the viewscreen: "I am Rodimus. Optimus Prime is obsessed with one thing: destruction of the Decepticons and anybody who would try to oppose him. He will go to any length to destroy a Decepticon regardless of any innocent who might be in the way. The only thing that drives him is the destruction of his enemies. He has been fighting for millions of years and sees war as the only form of diplomacy worth practicing."

"Then why did he agree to the peace talks?" the prosecutor asked.

"He confided in me that he agreed solely in order to create an opportunity to strike at the Decepticons when their guard was down. He never intended for there to actually *be* peace. He is a cruel tyrant who yearns for the day when he will be the sole power in the universe."

"Rodimus!" Optimus yelled. "What have they done to you?" But he could guess. During the excursion that Ironhide had foolishly allowed, the three bots must have come to considerable grief. Quintesson brainwashing had been at work. But why would the Quintessons go to all this trouble just to contaminate witnesses? Did the sham appearance of justice matter so much to them? Or did they truly think this *was* justice? If so, it was the most warped view of reality Optimus had ever encountered. But then again, he'd been naive in more ways than one today.

"Next witness, state your name for the record and begin your testimony."

Kup stepped forward. "I am Kup. Life means nothing to Optimus Prime. He rebelled against Cybertron's rightful masters and did all he could to ensure civil war. He proclaimed that he jettisoned the AllSpark into space in order to keep the Decepticons from getting their hands on it. But the truth is that he wishes to possess it free from all interference so that he can rule this galaxy and all the creatures who dwell in it."

"And what of your comrade's testimony regarding the peace process?"

"Under the flag of truce, Optimus planned to steal your Energon production technology. Once he had the ability to produce limitless Energon, he planned to make himself tyrant beyond all measure."

"Indeed. And what does the last witness have to add?"

Bumblebee stepped forward; he raised his yellow arms high to the shadowy figure, pointed at Optimus, and let loose a series of beeps, squeals, and high-pitched tones.

"Despicable," said the prosecutor. "Absolutely conclusive testimony. The court will note that even his own men recognize that Optimus Prime is a depraved maniac with no regard for anybody's rules except his own. If left to his own devices, he will continue to be a danger not only to the peaceful people of Quintessa but to thousands of other races as well."

"Agreed," said the chief magistrate. "Do you have further questions?"

"Your honor, I have one final witness." A larger than normal Sharkticon emerged into the courtroom and strode to the center of the floor.

"*This* is your witness?" For the first time, the chief magistrate sounded surprised.

"No, your honor," replied the prosecutor.

The Sharkticon opened his gaping maw and dumped pieces of the bot that had been Skywarp onto the floor.

"*That's* my witness," the prosecutor said.

"Very good," said the chief magistrate. "The witness will state his name for the record."

Much of Skywarp was gone, but the torso and head were still functioning. The eyes glowed faintly, and the mouth moved slowly. "Skywarp," it said.

"Begin your testimony."

The testimony didn't just sound brainwashed; it rang so rote that Skywarp might have been taking dictation. "Before the peace conference began, Optimus Prime approached me," he said in a monotone. "He told me that if I killed Megatron, I could be the new leader of the Decepticons. He provided me with a bomb and schematics of the Temple of Peace. As you can see from my sorry state, he tried to double-cross me and set off the bomb while I was planting it. He is a ruthless killer, a deceiver of the lowest kind."

"Whereas you are just a ruthless killer," said the prosecutor. Skywarp said nothing. He probably hadn't been given any more lines to say. "Take him away." The Sharkticon scooped the pieces of Skywarp up into his mouth and left, and the prosecutor turned back to the judges.

"I think we have heard enough. The testimony that has been provided seems quite sufficient to make a prima facie ruling. So I turn now to the honorable magistrates and ask that they—"

"Wait," Megatron said.

Everyone looked at him.

"I, too, wish to testify."

"Very well," the prosecutor said. Sharkticons led Megatron onto the stage.

"State your name for the record."

"Megatron. I wish to say that the fact that you charge the librarian with crimes against your illegal rule is beyond laughable." The crowd audibly gasped. "The sniveling data clerk known as Orion Pax never did anything to you; he never fought in the war against you. He was too busy counting data chips. I have never had much use for the past, but now as I am forced to listen to you, some of it is coming back to me. *I* was the one you sent to the mines. *I* was the one you could not control. *I* was the one who took up arms alongside Sentinel Prime and drove you slime back to where you came from. I should have remembered your stench the moment I saw you, but now—in the light of this mockery of justice—I see you precisely for what you are. I do not recognize this court. You have no power over me, no power over any of us. All of your so-called evidence is nothing more than lies. Your judgment is beyond worthless."

Most of the latter part of this speech was drowned out by Aquatronians yelling at Megatron from the galleries. Optimus figured that Megatron would receive yet another beating, but apparently the Quintessons adhered strictly to their view of legal niceties. "Thank you for your testimony," the prosecutor said gravely. "Though I should warn you that it shall be used against you in your own trial."

"Use away," Megatron said contemptuously as the Sharkticons hauled him back to the cage. The prosecutor turned back to Optimus.

"Our legal system does allow for a statement from the accused. Never let it be said that this high court is anything other than a paragon of justice. Do you have anything to say for yourself, Optimus Prime?"

Optimus paused; he looked at Megatron and then back at the Autobots he had failed so badly. Surely there was still some way to save them. But if there was, he had yet to see it. He turned back to the prosecutor and the magistrates.

"Though I wouldn't quite use the same language, for once the sentiments of Megatron and myself overlap. I oppose you and everything you stand for. And as I said, it is to my shame that during your occupation of Cybertron, I did not personally lead the battle against you. But that was a time when we were scholars, scientists, philosophers . . . when we pursued the arts and sciences and all the wonders they contain. If anything, your desecration of our world turned us from clerks to warriors. I don't know what you did to my Autobots to make them say such outlandish lies, but don't think

I don't realize that you Quintessons are masters of manipulation. Eventually the truth will be known, and it will undo all of your plans. You accuse me of doing all these things against you; I wish I had. My real crime was not doing more to fight you. And I swear that I will find a way to atone for that."

"Your own words serve as a fitting condemnation." The prosecutor turned to the screens. "I move that the magistrates pass judgment based on the evidence I have presented."

"We have heard all and have weighed its veracity and value," said the chief magistrate. "We are indeed ready to pass judgment." The other four nodded.

"What is the judgment of the court?" asked the prosecutor.

All five judges spoke at once: "We find Optimus Prime to be . . . *innocent*."

Chapter Twenty-nine

THE REBOOTED TELETRAAN-1 HAD NOTHING ON FILE about the Quintessons except that they had indeed occupied Cybertron millions of years past, yet the computer's databanks seemed to regard the whole period as a minor footnote in Cybertronian history and had very little to say about it. To Sideswipe that seemed strange. Having your planet subjugated should have merited more than just a few annotations. But apparently there wasn't anything more in Teletraan-1's ancient memory circuits.

"Scrap it," Sideswipe mumbled to himself. He would have loved to know more about the enemy, but as it stood, he would have to operate in the dark. So he dived back into something he *did* know about: the Ark. All the backup systems were functioning perfectly. Even better, he'd finally been able to locate the island where Optimus and the others had been taken. But rescuing them was going to be tricky. In fact, it might be downright suicidal, for a lightning-fast strike through inclement weather against unknown planetary defenses seemed like an invitation to a fast demise. The Aerialbots were still nursing their wounds from the last fight with the Decepticons; it didn't seem right to ask them to be in the vanguard of another risky mission. But what other choice was there? The Ark was too clumsy to use as an orbital dropship. It just wasn't designed for that kind of attack maneuver. Sideswipe's contemplation of the matter ended abruptly as the bridge door slid open and Sunstreaker entered.

"So what's the plan?" he asked. Sideswipe tried his best to hide his irritation at his brother's nonchalance about the predicament they were all in. Calling him on it never worked. It was easier just to meet Sunstreaker on his own insufferably glib ground.

"I'm still coming up with one."

"Know what your problem is?"

"Tell me," Sideswipe said wearily.

"You think too much. Give me Bluestreak, Trailbreaker, Mirage, and a combat shuttle, and we'll go down there and snatch the big OP back, no problem."

Sideswipe knew that it was precisely this attitude that kept his brother from having too many friends in the Autobot ranks. Nobody could live up to the legend that Sunstreaker was in his own mind. Sure, he was one of the best, but that didn't mean he had to remind everybody about it constantly. "You really think it's going to be that easy?" Sideswipe asked.

"Um, yeah." Sunstreaker nodded. "I think it should be pretty straightforward. This is me you're talking to. A card-carrying member of the Magnificent Six, and I don't make claims I can't back up." Sunstreaker was having a hard time damping down his enthusiasm, and Sideswipe could guess why. Fighting Decepticons was par for the course, but the chance to get to grips with a whole new foe was too good an opportunity to miss. Sideswipe suspected it was all Sunstreaker could do to stop himself from commandeering a shuttle and heading down to the surface with all guns blazing. He shrugged and turned away.

"Well, thanks for the perspective. Now if you'll excuse me—"

"Look," said Sunstreaker. "I know you're under a lot of

pressure here, but you've got to believe that we'll prevail. After all, we Autobots always come out on top."

"I wish I shared your confidence."

"Yeah, you and half of Cybertron. Come on; give me the green light."

Sideswipe sighed. "We're not doing anything until I can get more intelligence on where they're being held. And figure out what the *Nemesis* is up to. We can't afford to make any more mistakes as far as the Decepticons are concerned. Last thing we need is to end up getting caught with enemies on both flanks."

"Sound thinking," Sunstreaker admitted.

"Gee, thanks for saying so."

Sunstreaker was about to retort when Hubcap entered carrying a datapad. With Bumblebee down on the planet and Hound lost back on Cybertron, Hubcap was the best scout remaining. Sideswipe knew he could count on Hubcap to give him an honest assessment even if it was a truth he didn't want to hear.

"This is the best we could do, boss." By *we* Hubcap meant he and Teletraan-1; between the two of them, they'd coordinated a deployment of semi-intelligent sky spies into orbit around Aquatron. In normal circumstances Hubcap would have left the whole operation to Teletraan-1, but in this instance hands-on piloting expertise had improved the satellites' chances of evading detection. Hubcap handed the pad over, and Sideswipe took a look at the incomplete schematics of the Aquatronian city. "We think they're keeping them all *here*—at this large building in the city center."

"Good work, Hubcap."

"Yeah, well, don't thank me yet. As you can see, that's probably one of the most defended places on the whole scrap yard of a planet. Getting in there won't be easy. Especially with the weapons systems still active in the ring. We're going to need to do something about that."

"I've seen worse," Sunstreaker chimed in.

Hubcap looked scornful. "Oh, really? Even if we got down there in one piece, those fish-bots have the numbers. We counted up to about fifty thousand Sharkticons in the city alone—never mind the sea fleets and Primus knows what else."

"Quantity is no match for quality, buddy."

Sideswipe decided to nip this in the bud. "What about the *Nemesis*?" he asked Hubcap.

"She's still on the other side of the planet. Impossible to tell what's going on inside."

"Do they seem to be making repairs?"

"Can't tell. Which means the Quintessons can't, either."

"Okay," Sideswipe said. He made a decision and keyed the ship's intercom. "Listen up, everybody. Here's what's going to happen."

OPTIMUS WAS LED AWAY FROM THE PRISONERS' BOX AND pushed back inside the pen.

"I thought they said you were innocent!" Jazz yelled.

"Apparently they define that word differently than we do."

"Maybe you should have pleaded guilty."

"I don't think that was an option." Optimus looked around to see Perceptor in the process of examining Rodimus, Kup, and Bumblebee, who had been returned to their cells. Now that they'd given their testimony, those three bots stared straight ahead, blank expressions on their faces.

"So what's wrong with them?"

Perceptor turned. "Their minds seem to be stuck in a repeat pattern. Almost like their brains are on standby."

"They'll probably remain that way now that the

Quintessons have no more use for them. See if there's something you can do, Doctor."

"I'll try my best," Perceptor said.

Optimus turned back to Jazz and Prowl. "We've got to figure a way out of here. We're running out of time."

Back on the stage, the prosecutor was addressing the magistrates again. "May it please the court, I wish to invoke Article 7B384 and declare the entirety of the Cybertronian group before you bound together as a criminal conspiracy. Since Optimus Prime has been found innocent, it follows that all those who were carrying out his orders are innocent as well."

"Agreed," said the chief magistrate.

"Wait a second," Optimus said.

But the prosecutor ignored him. "Will you therefore pronounce the verdict?"

The chief magistrate nodded. "This high court finds all Cybertronians arraigned before us to be innocent of the following charges: destruction of public property, criminal mayhem, high treason, war crimes, and galactic blasphemy, with the appropriate sentence to be carried out forthwith. This court is hereby adjourned."

The five screens went blank, and the prosecutor disappeared as well. Suddenly the whole atmosphere changed. The audience started cheering as though they were taking in a circus, and that cheering grew louder as a squad of Sharkticon honor guards opened up the cells and began driving Autobots and Decepticons back with whips.

"START WITH THOSE TWO!!!" the guard captain yelled.

The Autobot Brawn and the Decepticon Ramjet were pulled out of their cages and marched to the dais where the prosecutor had just been. The noise of the crowd became deafening.

"They found us innocent and they're still going to

sentence us? I don't get it," said Brawn.

"Don't look at me for answers, Autobot. This whole thing stopped making sense a long time ago."

A voice boomed down from above.

"You have been found innocent by the Quintesson Imperium. Prepare for judgment." Without warning, the floor opened up beneath them and they fell several hundred meters down into a water-filled pit. Ramjet started thrashing around, screaming the whole while.

"I can't swim!" he yelled. But Brawn felt his feet touch the bottom, and he helped Ramjet get his bearings. Far above them, the two Cybertronians could see the narrow circle of light that was the mouth of the pit. Their predicament was projected on all five viewscreens so that Cybertronians and audience alike were able to see what was happening at the bottom.

"The water's not that deep," Brawn said. "I guess they don't expect us to drown."

He was right. Suddenly, multiple hatches in the walls opened up and hundreds of ravenous Piranhacons poured in. It was like a wave of nothing but razor-sharp teeth; Brawn and Ramjet barely had time to scream before they were pulled beneath the water. A few more moments and oil slicks rose to the surface. The crowd applauded wildly while the Autobots and Decepticons reacted with sheer consternation.

"By Primus! They didn't stand a chance!" Bulkhead cried in disbelief.

"This is barbaric!" Megatron yelled.

Optimus said nothing. He couldn't bear to. The crowd noise swelled again as Sharkticon guards pulled out Hotlink and Blaster, dragged them over to the pit. Hotlink struggled the whole way, imploring Megatron to help him, while Blaster remained cool and calm even in the face of certain death.

"Hey, Hotlink, you want to die with a little bit of dignity?"

"I'd rather live with none at all!"

The Sharkticons tossed the Cybertronians over the edge with relish.

THE WINDOWS OF THE CURATOR'S INNER SANCTUM afforded an excellent view of the city of Hydratron, but the Curator and Xeros were focused on a more immediate spectacle: the courtroom proceedings, projected on a screen that dominated the entirety of one wall. Another wall contained two smaller viewscreens; Tyrannicon's face was on one, and Commander Gnaw was on the other. Gnaw had been the one assigned to carry Skywarp's parts into the courtroom. He was happy that he could swallow again and even happier now that Thundercracker's screams were echoing from the speakers. Gnaw had always found the screams of others extremely satisfying. Tyrannicon, though, seemed less than thrilled.

"Pathetic," he said. "And these Decepticons are supposed to be fearsome warriors?"

The Curator looked amused. "Don't underestimate them, General. They are far more resourceful than you might think. After all, they were able to accomplish what you people never could."

On the screen, scales flared around the general's gills. Xeros didn't like the way the Curator kept baiting Tyrannicon. Sure, all the Sharkticons were under neural conditioning controlled from this chamber, but Tyrannicon's will was particularly strong. That was why Xeros had been so hesitant at the idea of bringing him out of cryo. But the Curator had assured him that Tyrannicon's anger would be easy to channel. All the same, Xeros didn't enjoy the way Gnaw kept looking at him like he was gourmet food laid out on a platter. He was glad Gnaw wasn't in the room with him; he did his best to ignore Gnaw's gaze, focused instead on the death throes of the Cybertronians on the large screen. But the Curator was concentrating on another screen, one that swam with readouts. A look of concern crossed his face.

"We are getting a high-energy output from these executions, but at the current rate, there is a 78.2 percent chance that we simply may not have enough to initiate Stage Two."

"Surely you jest," Tyrannicon said.

"I never jest, General. These Cybertronians have already depleted much of their energy fighting each other."

"Fighting that you encouraged."

"You draw perilously close to insubordination," said the Curator. For a moment the two bots stared at each other. But then Tyrannicon drew back in deference.

"Forgive me, lord. I seek the same victory you do. Perhaps if we could harvest the bots aboard the two crippled ships in orbit . . . ?"

"I would rather not do that unless we have to," the Curator said. "Xeros and I were saving them for experiments."

"You may have to forgo that luxury," Tyrannicon said.

"Perhaps. But there is an alternative solution that I suspect will solve our energy requirements."

Tyrannicon looked skeptical. "To what are you referring?" he asked.

The Curator waved his hand over a control panel, and the room filled with a reddish light as the simulacrum of the Matrix of Leadership rose from the floor.

Tyrannicon looked unimpressed. "That's a fake," he said.

"It's a replica," the Curator told him. "There's a difference."

"That difference being?"

"This is more than just a stage prop. I haven't simply been using it as bait to dangle in front of these Cybertronians. This device replicates key elements of the Cybertronian computer systems, allowing us to hack into them as needed."

"Such as Optimus's Matrix," Xeros added.

"I thought he shut that down," Tyrannicon said.

"I believe there is a more than 80 percent probability that he's going to find himself in a position where he needs to start it back up again," said the Curator. "Commander Gnaw, you will report back to the Hall of Justice and redirect proceedings there."

"At once," Gnaw said. The screen flickered out. Tyrannicon looked annoyed, and Xeros could guess why. He didn't like the Curator going over his head to give orders to his subordinates. The Sharkticon general opened his mouth to protest, but the Curator beat him to it.

"General, report attack readiness."

Tyrannicon stiffened with the reflexes of a born soldier. "We are at total readiness," he said. "But again, we still don't have the requisite energy for—"

"Leave that to me."

Tyrannicon saluted. "The fleet awaits your command," he said.

As Tyrannicon's face disappeared from the screen, Xeros stood up. He knew what was about to happen, knew he wasn't invited. That was fine by him. He didn't envy the Curator one bit. He left the room. As the door closed, the Curator sighed heavily and then adjusted the settings on the screen that showed the courtroom. For a moment, there was static.

And then his masters appeared.

Skull-like visages regarded him coldly. "Report," said one.

"Stage One is complete. May I congratulate you on

your mastery of the courtroom just now—"

"Do not presume to comment on our legal expertise. Confine yourself to the science. What is the status of the energy readings?"

If the Curator had sweat glands, he would have been using them now. "Everything is under control. I hope to report initiation of Stage Two within minutes."

"Have there been any complications?"

That was a trick question. There were always complications, but the Curator's masters never wanted to hear about them. They certainly didn't want to hear that despite all his maneuverings, it was going to be touch and go whether he achieved enough energy for Stage Two. As always, it came down to what the Prime would do. The Curator longed for the days when Primes would no longer be a factor in anybody's calculations. He stared at his masters and forced himself to be calm.

"No complications," he said. "We cannot fail."

"*Cannot* is a strong word. Are you compensating for a lack of confidence? Do you need reinforcements?"

The Curator knew what *reinforcements* meant. It meant *shall we replace you with someone more capable?* It would be his body in the Piranhacon pit if he went down that road. He shook his head.

"There is no need for reinforcements. We are more than equal to the challenge before us. The Cybertronians still have inklings of what they are facing. They possess no idea our real trap has yet to be sprung."

"Let us hope you are correct, Inquirata." The Curator stiffened to hear himself addressed by his proper name. "Much depends on your success."

"A success we must have," said a second voice.

"For the sake of our ancestors," added a third.

"And our descendants," said a fourth.

"We rose," said a deeper fifth voice. It was that of the

chief magistrate. "We rose, and we fell. Now we rise again, and this time we shall not falter. Nowhere will escape our reach. All the universe will be gathered up under our sway."

"For the greater glory of Quintessa," the Curator intoned.

"For the greater glory of Quintessa," the magistrates repeated.

The screen went blank.

For a few moments, the Curator stood there, breathing heavily. It all came down to his next move. Everything was at stake now. He longed to get off this useless backwater world, longed to be recalled to Quintessa itself. Or perhaps he would resume his Curator status on a more important world. That was its own kind of promotion. Especially with the right kind of world. Something strategic. Something valuable. Something worth planning for eons to dominate.

He had one in mind right now.

Chapter Thirty

CYBERTRON

IACON WAS A CITY OF MANY LAYERS.

There was the surface, of course, that once-proud skyline laid bare by war and now eclipsed by Shockwave's tower. There were the sublevels stacked beneath that, many of them still buzzing with industrial activity. But as you kept going lower, that activity died down. The corridors grew emptier, the echoes were louder, and the infrastructure was in ever greater disrepair. There was no one point where you could be said to have entered the undercity, but once you got there, you weren't going to quibble. Lighting flickered sporadically when it flickered at all. Corridors lost that distinction and became tunnels. Steam hissed erratically. Elevators no longer worked. Ladders ended halfway down chutes. The place was an utter maze.

The denizens weren't really under anybody's control, either. Maintenance droids gone rogue, digging machines with glitched programming, rat-bots of all sizes, gladiators who had escaped the pits and gone feral somewhere along the way . . . They kept out of sight mostly, although Wheeljack wouldn't have wanted to come down here by himself. He could hear them scuttling here and there in the dark, just beyond the range of his lights, and the only reason he wasn't seeing them was that no one down here was foolish enough to mess with a heavily armed team of Autobots. Predators preferred easier meals, and the prey now passing looked anything but easy. Wheeljack had never dreamed that such anarchy existed so short a distance below civilization. It seemed strange to him that even though the ancient castes had been overthrown—rejected with such alacrity by Autobot and Decepticon alike—the lowest rung of that system had persisted almost unnoticed throughout the war that followed. These creatures down here were the true untouchables, not even worthy of classification in the heyday of the caste system and certainly not meriting any attention now. It made Wheeljack question many of his most cherished assumptions. All the more so as none of his teammates seemed to notice the irony. They were focused on more tangible issues.

That was understandable enough.

"We must be at least four miles below the surface," Springer said.

"More than that," Ultra Magnus said. He was the only one who seemed to have an exact sense of their bearings. There was a lot of magnetism down here, and it was playing havoc with the compasses. But Ultra Magnus had the map Maccadam had given him, and it was proving far more trustworthy than their instruments. After their escape from the bar, he'd picked the nearest manhole and kept their course as vertical as possible for at least a hundred levels, pausing only to sow false trails off to the side every once in a while. It must have worked, too, for there had been no sign of any meaningful pursuit. Then again, there'd been enough chaos up on the surface to keep everybody busy. Omega Supreme had seen to that. By now, he was probably retreating at speed into the polar wastelands, daring the Decepticons to come after him so that he could ambush them in that desolate terrain. Wheeljack envied the giant bot. He had the simpler task. Then again, if truth be told, right now Wheeljack envied anybody who wasn't having to crawl like a mole-bot beneath the surface.

"Up ahead," Ultra Magnus said. They waded through a corridor that was waist-deep in chemical sludge and climbed a staircase, and then that corridor suddenly ended in a convex steel wall that looked more than a little out of place down here.

"It's *new*," said Rack n' Ruin.

It was so shiny that they could see their own reflections. Quick sensor readings indicated that the barrier curved away on either side of the crumbling corridor walls and was at least several meters thick: too wide for the sensors to say what was on the far side of it.

Though it was easy enough to guess.

"The train route," Ultra Magnus said. "This is the way to Shockwave's bunker."

"So now what?" Jetfire asked.

"What do you think?" Rack n' Ruin asked. One of his arms extended a welding torch, and he began slicing through. Blue flame stitched into steel; shadows played across the faces of those watching. But several minutes went by, and Wheeljack could see that the torch had made it through only a few inches.

"There's got to be a faster way than this," he said.

"You're right," Rack n' Ruin told him. His other arm sprouted a drill that whirred to life and began plowing through half-melted metal. Wheeljack could see why Ultra Magnus had brought this peculiar bot along. Rack n' Ruin switched back to the torch and then kept alternating between his two tools. In short order, he had to climb into the hole he was carving to keep extending it. And shortly after that—

"Paydirt," he said.

"Good work," Ultra Magnus said. "Wheeljack, you take over."

Rack n' Ruin clambered out of the cavity he'd dug, and Wheeljack climbed in. Crawling forward to the rear of the area Rack n' Ruin had sliced out, he found himself staring through an opening into a wide vertical tunnel covered with cables and wiring. Opposite him were rails that ran down the wall and disappeared into the darkness below.

"Well?" Ultra Magnus demanded.

"Looking good," Wheeljack said. He reached out and removed the cover from one of the cables before slotting in one of his input jacks. There was a click.

And then he was in.

In a single instant, the physical world dropped away and the datanet expanded inside his head. Only it wasn't the datanet he was used to. That was an endless grid of wires and conduits that stretched throughout Cybertron and covered the planet in a wireless cushion. This was much smaller, extending only to the tower that lay four miles above and down to more facilities many miles below.

It was Shockwave's private net.

It was isolated from the rest of the communications links on the planet so that intrepid bots like Wheeljack couldn't get in and hack it. The only way to do that was to do what Wheeljack was doing now: get past the armored walls that protected Shockwave's personal domain and gain physical access. With the ease of the practiced hacker, Wheeljack bypassed security protocols and worked his skills. The rails hummed to life.

Two minutes later, a rumbling echoed down the shaft. A shape appeared in the darkness above, coming rapidly down the shaft toward him. He hit the brakes, and a two-car train, empty of personnel but by no means bereft of purpose, clung with electromagnetic clamps to the rails opposite him. Wheeljack smiled in satisfaction.

"Our ride's here," he said.

Chapter Thirty-one

OPTIMUS MADE HIS DECISION.

He stepped to the gate, determined that no more
Autobots would die. When that gate opened next and the
Sharkticons came for their next victims, he was going to
make a move. He didn't care what the odds were. One
way or another, this farce had to end.

"Optimus, what are you doing?" Jazz asked.

Optimus didn't answer. It was all instinct now. As the
Sharkticon guards approached the gate, he braced himself.

But suddenly doors beneath the giant screens slid
open. Commander Gnaw entered the courtroom,
flanked by more Sharkticons. They stopped in front of
the pens with crisp military precision. Gnaw stepped
forward and brandished his war baton. He pointed at
Optimus and Megatron.

"Secure the leaders." The guards pulled Optimus
and Megatron from the pens and led them toward the
Piranhacon pit, but as they approached, a metal cover
slid across it. But it wasn't the same flooring as before;
it was an odd kind of shimmering material that Optimus
had never seen before. An excited buzzing went through
the watching crowd. Gnaw cleared his throat.

"Optimus Prime, Megatron, it has been decided that
mercy will be shown." Megatron wanted to tell Gnaw
what he thought of his mercy, but the nearby whips

caused him to hold his tongue for once. "You have the opportunity to save your people."

"I feel like I've heard this one before," Optimus said.

"You haven't. The high magistrate of Quintessa is considering commuting the sentence to banishment."

"Banishment?"

"You leave and never return to this planet."

"A tempting offer," Megatron said.

"It's not an offer. The commuting of the sentence will occur in tandem with a separate sentence for you and Optimus Prime."

"Namely?"

"Trial by combat."

"Really?" Megatron said. Now he was interested. He got even more so as Gnaw continued.

"The two of you will fight to the death to see whose people we will set free. The winner will get to choose whether the loser's people face the Piranhacon pit or are simply melted down for scrap."

"I like the way you think," Megatron told him.

Optimus shook his head. "Megatron, this is clearly yet another trick."

"Are you a coward even now, librarian?"

"Here are the rules," Gnaw said. "Both of you will remain within this circle. None of your energy weapons will be repowered or given back to you. All fighting must be hand to hand. You will begin when I give the word. Do you accept?"

"Absolutely," said Megatron.

Optimus bowed his head; if this was the only way out of here, then so be it. "Trial by combat it is," he said.

Sharkticons tossed a variety of archaic weaponry at the feet of Optimus and Megatron and then retreated. Megatron picked up an enormous battle-ax lined with armor-tearing metal teeth.

"This is it, librarian. Your doom has finally arrived."

"Megatron, are you blind? They're still lying to us."

"You know what, Optimus? I don't even care anymore. Because even if they kill me, it won't be before you meet death at my hands."

Optimus picked up a pair of short swords and pointed them at Megatron in an ancient Cybertronian gladiator salute. "So be it, then."

"Begin," said Gnaw.

The two bots leaped at each other.

THE NOISE WAS DEAFENING. THE SCREENS IN THE Curator's chamber were filled with close-up video of Optimus and Megatron battling each other like there was no tomorrow. Which there really wouldn't be—not for either of them. But the Curator was unconcerned about the details of the combat. He turned down the volume so he could focus on the only thing that mattered now: the rising power gauges on his instrument consoles. The metal on which the Cybertronians were fighting represented the very latest in Quintesson technology, and it functioned as an almost perfect energy sink. Not only was it slowly absorbing the life force of both combatants, the harder they fought, the faster the process went. And in their frenzied efforts to bring each other down, Optimus and Megatron were both expending enough energy to power many a factory; sparks of Energon literally flew off each of the combatants as they twirled and writhed in the deadliest dance there was. If the Curator had had more of a taste for combat, he would have recognized what was going on in the pit as sheer ballet. Certainly the roaring crowd of Aquatronians had never seen anything like it. As the fight became ever more savage, the Curator smiled as the power readings climbed higher and higher.

"It is exactly as you predicted, master," Xeros said. "This is a far better option than just throwing them into the pit. And much more entertaining as well."

"If you say so. I never developed a taste for physical combat. I suppose I always thought of it as uncivilized."

"Uncouth in the extreme," Xeros agreed quickly. "But useful. A Prime and the greatest gladiator in Cybertron's history . . . with so much personal animosity between the two . . . No wonder the power gauges are already passing 40 percent. Such irony that it is their very skill in the martial arts that will help us destroy them. Which one do you think will prevail?"

"Do I look like I care?" the Curator asked. "Get Tyrannicon on the screen."

THE SHARKTICON GENERAL STOOD ON THE BRIDGE OF his flagship as the Curator's face appeared on one of the dashboards. Tyrannicon saluted reflexively.

"Command and I obey," he said.

"The energy threshold will be crossed within moments," the Curator said. "Start your engines and stand by for the final attack order."

"At once, my lord." The screen went dark, and Tyrannicon began barking out commands. A rumbling filled the vast chamber as thousands of ships powered up. Each vessel was loaded with a full complement of heavy weaponry and Sharkticon warriors, and all were impatient for battle. Tyrannicon's heart beat faster as he surveyed his armada. The fleet had been primed for combat for hours now, and everyone was hungry for action, Tyrannicon most of all; he hated waiting—particularly waiting on Quintessons—but like any good general, he knew that timing was everything. It would be the height of folly to let his impatience rule him when he was so close to his birthright, so close to fulfilling his ultimate purpose as a warrior.

"Open a channel to the fleet," he said. He stood up and extended his massive arms. His two bodyguards stepped forward. One placed his ceremonial battle trident in his hand; the other presented him with the battle horn. His voice echoed across the fleet.

"Brother warriors! Today is the day that we etch our superiority into time itself. Suns may dim and planets may crumble, but the cosmos will know that we were here—that once we lived, walked, and conquered. When they tell their children the stories of the warriors who swept away their puny civilizations, they will whisper our names in awe and know that we were never defeated— that we are the ultimate fighting force. Now we fight the ultimate battle. When you hear my horn sound, follow me to glory. All hail!"

"ALL HAIL!" The noise rang throughout the huge cave. The underground lake on which the fleet rested glowed and flickered as lights flickered over the huge metallic hoop that dominated the entirety of the chamber's far end. The lights started to move ever faster as the energy poured down through conduits from the city twenty miles above. The space bridge technology had been primed by massive infusions of Energon and fueled even further by the sparks of the Cybertronians devoured in the pit. Now it was being driven to still greater heights by the titanic battle under way above. The noise from both bridge and fleet was thunderous now. Tyrannicon stepped over to his flagship's pilot chair and prepared to release the brakes . . .

"THAT'S STRANGE," SAID SIDESWIPE.

Hubcap glanced over. "What's strange?"

"We're picking up huge spikes of energy beneath the

Sharkticon capital. So strong that they're reflecting off the atmosphere. Easily discernible from the far side of the planet."

"What's causing it?" Hubcap asked.

"Don't know. Teletraan-1 is still running scenarios. But it's absolutely off the charts."

"All the more reason to hurry," Hubcap said.

"I know that," Sideswipe replied. The last of the repair crews had reported in, and the Ark was as ready as she'd ever be. Teletraan-1 put her fighting ability at just over 81 percent. After the beating she had taken earlier, it was going to have to do. Sideswipe had set all the boards to green; they were hoping that the old girl was ready once again to do the impossible. He keyed the com-link.

"You guys ready back there, Sunstreaker?"

"Ready as we'll ever be," his brother replied. He was back in the cargo area with the main force of Autobots, completing the final checks on their weapons and swapping stories about the last time they had been in a tight spot like this. Overall their spirits were high considering the possibility that what was about to take place would be their final fight.

"Great. Now hold on; it's going to be a bumpy ride."

"The bumpier, the better."

"Great," Sideswipe said. He hesitated, then said: "Until all are one—"

"Save the prayers," Sunstreaker said. "Let's get this show on the road."

THE CROWD WENT WILD AS OPTIMUS SWEPT MEGATRON off his feet with double blows from his swords. Both combatants were leaking oil and lubricating fluids from deep gashes in their armor. The weapons were razor-sharp and were inflicting devastating damage when they made contact. Megatron struggled to get back to his feet, adjusting his chest plate in an effort to keep his key components from spilling out. Optimus pivoted on his one good leg to receive Megatron's next flurry of blows, grinning as he did so.

"You're getting slow in your old age, Megatron!"

Megatron quickly brought the ax up, clipping Optimus's faceplate and sending him staggering. "Shut up, upstart! I'm done playing with you!"

Optimus spun to the right, but his blade hit nothing but air. Megatron was already shifting to the side, using his ax as a staff to deflect the next blow. Before Optimus could compensate, Megatron stuck his foot out and tripped him, sending him sprawling. In one smooth motion, Megatron raised the ax over his head and sliced it back downward in a crushing two-handed blow. But Optimus had already rolled out of the way, and then he was back on his feet again, one of his blades slicing across the Decepticon's midriff, a blow that might have been fatal if Megatron had not stepped back in the nick of time. The crowd was approaching a state of frenzy. As the noise washed over the combatants, Megatron grinned.

"Seems I've underestimated you, librarian. You've become quite the soldier. I always said you would have done well in the pits had you started out there. You've learned much from me over the course of our conflict."

"As always, it all comes back to you," Optimus said sarcastically.

"Make no mistake, you're going to lose. But I'm offering you a genuine compliment: I'm impressed."

"Then let me impress you some more," said Optimus, moving forward.

* * *

THE CURATOR WATCHED THE NEEDLE AS IT CLIMBED steadily into the red. It was almost at the requisite threshold.

"Lord," Xeros said, "the Autobot spaceship is on the move."

"*What?*" The Curator was as dismayed as he was surprised.

"They must have made repairs. Shall I order them destroyed?"

"We're channeling every drop of power from the planetary rings to the bridge. If I back that off now, we might lose our window. What's their heading?"

"Powering away from the planet at speed." Xeros pulled up the projections, showing the Ark vectoring out from its current orbit, a course that would take it over the pole and out into space. The Curator breathed a sigh of relief.

"They're running away," he said. "A wise decision."

"So we do nothing?" Xeros asked.

"Not right now. We'll hunt them down and destroy them later."

"By which point they'll be the last survivors of their race," Xeros said.

The Curator slowly nodded.

"LORD STARSCREAM," SOUNDWAVE SAID.

"Yes, what is it?" Starscream said impatiently.

"We are picking up more energy spikes from the city."

"You already told me that."

"These are the most intense yet. There seems to be a generator of the first magnitude somewhere beneath the city itself."

"Does this have anything to do with whatever's going on in that building?"

"I'm not sure, lord," Soundwave answered. There

was a certain edge to his voice, and Starscream could guess what it was: Soundwave was getting tired of Starscream's constant requests to keep studying the situation. Perhaps he was even starting to realize that Starscream was just trying to delay things so long that no rescue of Megatron would be required because they'd get proof that he was dead. Starscream would far rather get a lavishly detailed report on the death of the Decepticon leader than launch the mother of all last-ditch rescue operations.

The doors to the bridge slid open. Headstrong, Rampage, and Tantrum stood in the doorway. Behind them were several more Decepticons. All looked more than a little annoyed.

"Why the slag are we still here?" Rampage asked.

"You want to leave?" Starscream asked him. "I suppose that could be an option."

"We want to go rescue Megatron," Tantrum rumbled. "And we're tired of your telling us you're 'assessing the situation.'"

"One might almost think you didn't *want* to rescue Megatron," Headstrong said. The Decepticons crowded into the room, and Starscream had to think fast. He had a mutiny on his hands, and history showed that if one of those got out of hand, it could be a very quick route from command chair to air lock. But if you couldn't beat 'em, it was better to just get on out in front.

"On the contrary," he said. "I was just about to give orders to—"

"Lord Starscream," Soundwave shouted. "The Autobots' Ark has left orbit!"

"What are its coordinates?"

"It's heading past the pole, out toward deep space." A rumble of contempt rolled through the Decepticons.

"Fleeing for their lives," said Headstrong. "Typical

Autobots. Cowards, each and every one." He looked at Starscream. "What was that you were about to order?"

"That it's time to free our glorious leader!"

Everyone cheered. Soundwave prepped the controls while Starscream smiled outwardly and inwardly mulled his options on how to avoid being Megatron's savior. He wasn't done yet. Friendly fire happened all the time. Especially in chaotic rescue missions.

MEGATRON'S POWERFUL WHEEL KICK SENT OPTIMUS skidding toward the edge of the gladiator pit with a huge dent in the side of his head. Through his blurred optics, Optimus caught sight of Megatron bearing down on him, dragging the ax behind him, sending sparks flying in all directions.

"Say good night, librarian!"

But Optimus leaped backward and out of the way as the ax smashed down into the floor, sending sparks everywhere. Optimus brought both swords down on the haft of the ax, slicing straight through it. The blade spun through the air; Megatron ducked inside Optimus's guard and grabbed his arms, twisting, forcing the Autobot leader to drop both swords. It was hand to hand now. Optimus slammed his shoulder into Megatron's already wounded chest, but Megatron grabbed his neck and got him in a headlock.

"Did you really think you could beat me, librarian? This is where it ends."

Optimus suddenly realized that Megatron was almost certainly right. Now that the weapons were gone, Megatron's natural brute force was giving him an advantage that was steadily increasing as he tightened his grip on the Autobot leader. Optimus felt like his head was about to come off his shoulders. He struggled to free himself but couldn't. His optics were flickering, on the point of going out.

He did the only thing he could.

The Matrix of Leadership: He'd sworn to never use it again, at least not until he could defeat the Quintessons and purge the Matrix of the corruption they'd inflicted on it. But right now he didn't need to ask it any questions. He didn't need to listen to it. He just needed to defeat Megatron. With the last of his strength, he switched it back on—and felt a blast of energy surge inside him. Everything around him seemed to glow. He grabbed Megatron's arm, shifted his great weight, and flipped Megatron over his shoulder and onto the floor with such force that the whole room shook. Waves of energy pulsed across that floor.

Which then shattered.

THE CURATOR SPARED OPTIMUS AND MEGATRON BARELY a glance as they tumbled into the pit. His focus was on his systems as they at last attained full power. The Matrix replica's normal reddish glow changed to a bright white light that filled the entire inner sanctum. Xeros cried out as he covered his face to ward off the intense and burning light.

"We've done it!" the Curator yelled. "Now channel all power on my command!"

"At once!" Xeros said, recovering and rushing to the consoles. The Curator brought Tyrannicon up on another screen.

"GENERAL TYRANNICON! INITIATE LAUNCH SEQUENCE!"

"Forward for glory!" Tyrannicon yelled. He released the brakes, and the flagship thundered into motion, followed by the entire armada, all of them making straight for the vast hoop of fire that was the now-activated space bridge. Tyrannicon howled a battle cry as the fire filled the screens, engulfing his vision. He braced himself.

And then they plunged through.

Chapter Thirty-two

CYBERTRON

Shockwave frowned.

A moment ago he thought that he'd at long last attained what he'd been seeking, that he'd successfully broken through to the core of Vector Sigma. But now the energy readings were going haywire. Lightning crackled over Alpha Trion's prone form. For one brief crazy moment, Shockwave considered bringing Alpha Trion back to consciousness and asking him for advice on what to do. But he knew that that old relic would subject him to another stupid lecture, one that probably would contain the words *I told you so*.

Shockwave didn't need that. What he needed to do was ride it out. He furiously made adjustments to the consoles around him and ordered his servitor drones forward into the glowing furnace that Vector Sigma was rapidly becoming. Shockwave wondered if it was actually possible for Vector Sigma to experience meltdown. If so, the incandescent mainframe might burn straight through the core of Cybertron, all the way down to the Well of All Sparks. Would it release Primus from his eon-long slumber? Would there be anything left of the planet? Shockwave had no idea. He didn't want to find out, either. He brought up a screen showing the overload patterns and began to initiate fail-safes, trying to damp down the overflow. But what he was seeing on the screen just didn't make sense. This room wasn't the source of the energy.

Somewhere else on Cybertron was.

"Impossible," he breathed.

His fingers flew over a keyboard; a schematic of the entire planet appeared on the screen. It was a simple enough matter to map things out from there, to track the source precisely: a burning line that cut through the equator of Cybertron, a line that could represent only one thing . . . something that was no longer functional . . . something that *couldn't* be functional.

And yet it was.

"The space bridge," he whispered.

An explosion shook the room. The vault doors at the far end of the chamber blasted open. Shockwave looked up to see a figure standing in that doorway.

It was Ultra Magnus.

"This ends now," he said.

"With your death!" Shockwave yelled. He waved a hand; Insecticons and drones swarmed from the walls, moving straight in at Ultra Magnus. But as they did so, four other Wreckers appeared in the doorway behind Ultra Magnus: Wheeljack, Jetfire, Springer, and some misbegotten dual-bot Shockwave vaguely remembered from one of his less successful experiments. As all of them opened fire, Shockwave ducked behind Alpha Trion; that was the only place in the room that was comparatively safe. But only for a moment, because Shockwave was under no illusions about the outcome of the firefight now raging through the chamber. His guards didn't stand a chance. He had no idea how these interlopers had managed to get in there. This bunker was supposed to be impregnable. But Shockwave hadn't lasted this long by believing the hype of defense contractors. That was why

Wheeljack set to work, reversing the locks Shockwave had placed on Alpha Trion's mind. The others stood there and waited.

"Why would the space bridge be operational?" Jetfire asked.

"Maybe Shockwave was trying to contact Megatron," Springer said.

"Maybe Megatron's come *back*."

"Everybody shut up and let Wheeljack do his stuff," Ultra Magnus said, and Wheeljack most certainly was. It intimidated him more than a little to be working on a Prime, but he was too proud to admit that. Because really it was the greatest honor he could possibly have, the ultimate test of his skills. Wheeljack expertly removed the circuit clamps from the conduits that linked Vector Sigma to Alpha Trion, letting the parts of the Prime's brain that controlled consciousness rev up, reboot—

Alpha Trion's eyes opened.

"Ultra Magnus," he said.

"Alpha Trion," Ultra Magnus said. "It's okay; you're safe now."

"Where is Shockwave?"

"He won't be troubling you anymore."

Alpha Trion shook his head. "You don't understand."

"It's all right," Ultra Magnus said, his tone almost soothing. "We're here to rescue you."

"It's not me that needs the rescuing."

"What?"

"It's our world," said Alpha Trion.

Chapter Thirty-three

Optimus and Megatron both came to their senses at the same time. Their predicament was about as bad as it could get. They were at the bottom of the Piranhacon pit, up to their waists in water and all too close to the myriad holes through which the Piranhacons would come. Far above, they could hear the roaring of the crowd.

"There's got to be a way out of here," said Optimus.

"Logic would dictate that we go back up," Megatron said.

"I don't think that's possible." As he spoke, Optimus saw the glowing eyes of the Piranhacons approaching. Megatron grinned.

"I hope you have some fight left in you, librarian," he said. The next moment, Piranhacons surged into the room from all sides. Megatron met them head-on, plucking them from the water and hurling them against the walls and against one another, sometimes tearing them in half. Optimus opted for an alternative approach, moving straight into the mass of fish and lashing out on all sides, metal crunching under his feet. But sooner or later the sheer numbers of robotic fish would overwhelm them. Probably sooner . . .

"We can't keep this up!" Optimus said.

"Speak for yourself, librarian!" Megatron was in his element; if he had to die, there was no better way to go out than to do so while killing. But that was when Optimus grabbed him by one of the power couplings on his back.

"By Unicron, this is no time to continue *our* fight." Then Megatron felt it: a sudden surge of power ripping through him. The blast of energy was so intense that he barely heard Optimus's voice.

"Fire your cannon! NOW!" A minute earlier it wouldn't have been possible. But now he had the necessary power, and he used it. The noise was deafening inside the cramped pit; the point-blank shot tore a hole straight through the wall. The water started to drain from the chamber.

"What in the name of all the galaxies did you just do to me?" Megatron asked him.

"I transferred some of the Matrix's energy directly into your system."

"I didn't know that was possible."

"Neither did I. I played a hunch."

"Extreme risk taking," Megatron said as he shifted back to robot mode. "I can still feel the energy. It's like I'm fully charged again. We make a great team, librarian."

"Don't push your luck." Optimus looked through the smoking hole to see an underground passage, half filled with water, in which floated hundreds of scorched Piranhacons.

"Where do you think that goes?" Megatron asked.

"I don't know." Optimus glanced up at the top of the pit hundreds of meters above, where Sharkticons already were starting to peer down. "But I do know this: Anyplace is better than here."

SIDESWIPE LET THE ARK THUNDER OUT TOWARD DEEP space. Every instinct in his body screamed at him to just keep going, to get this accursed planet behind him. But he wasn't listening to instinct right now. He had a plan, and he was going to stick to that plan. What mattered was the planetary ring they were about to roar past, the one that housed the weaponry that had crippled the ship earlier. Right now that ring was crackling with energy that seemed to be linked to whatever was going on down on the planet.

Not for much longer, though.

Sideswipe keyed the intercom. "All hands, prepare for action," he said.

"Ready when you are," said Sunstreaker's voice over the speakers.

Sideswipe opened fire. Heavy lasers ripped against the ring, and then a bracket of torpedoes hit home. The ring lit up with thunderous explosions.

THE POWER READINGS IN THE CURATOR'S INNER SANCTUM began fluctuating wildly. The Curator looked from screen to screen in near panic. Had he made a miscalculation regarding the power matrix? Had the circuitry overloaded? Had one of the batteries blown?

The truth was far worse.

"Lord Curator, we are under attack!" Xeros yelled.

"What? Impossible!"

But the cameras showed otherwise. The first and most powerful of the planetary rings had just sustained fatal blows from the Ark. Even as the Curator and Xeros stared, the ring began to crumble into its component pieces. Very soon the planet of Aquatron would be the proud owner of a brand new asteroid belt.

"Those treacherous dogs!" the Curator snarled. But he took heart from knowing that the Autobot attack had come too late. Tyrannicon and his legions already had crossed through the space bridge. The invasion of

Cybertron was under way, and there were now more than enough Sharkticon forces there to conquer the entire planet, ravaged and divided as it was by civil war. That meant the Curator could focus on problems closer to home.

"Target all gunnery on the Ark," he hissed.

"Yes, lord!" Xeros began reeling off the necessary orders.

SIDESWIPE FIRED TWO MORE VOLLEYS AT THE RINGS, but he wasn't waiting around to see the results; instead, he turned the Ark around at the sharpest angle possible and vectored straight back toward the planet. Although he was much farther away than he had been before leaving orbit, he was now on the side of the world that mattered. What the Quintessons initially had thought was a craven attempt to flee was actually a gambit intended to give the Ark line of sight on the capital city of Hydratron. Sideswipe engaged the afterburners and thundered in toward it. They were going to rescue Optimus or die trying.

But up ahead was the *Nemesis*, still in near orbit above the city. Sideswipe could only hope that the Decepticons weren't going to interfere with him. Or that they wouldn't interpret his closing in as an attack on them. He was going to find out in a few moments.

STARSCREAM AND SOUNDWAVE WERE COMPLETING THEIR final system checks when the Ark shot the ring to pieces and did its about-face. Now it was bearing down on their position at several thousand miles an hour.

"Destroy them!" Starscream yelled, happy to have a distraction. He'd far rather fight Autobots than rescue Megatron.

"They're not coming for us," Soundwave shot back. "They're obviously making for the city! Which is what you said we were going to do!" Before Starscream could protest, Soundwave revved up the *Nemesis*'s engines and sent the Decepticon warship screaming down into the atmosphere. The fire of reentry licked past the window; the weather buffeted the ship violently, but the howl of the engines was drowned out by the noise blaring from the intercom: the roar of hundreds of Decepticons cheering at the top of their lungs throughout the ship. Soundwave brought up the targeting system and put the approaching city in his crosshairs . . .

XEROS NO LONGER HAD THE PLANETARY DEFENSES OF the first ring at his disposal, but he had plenty of other resources to draw on. All across the planet, ground-to-space batteries whirred to life. But even as he began targeting them on the Ark—which had turned around, he noted—the alarm lights began flashing as a new and far closer menace swooped in.

The *Nemesis*.

"Recalibrate defense parameters on the following lines!" he yelled, barking out a series of coordinates.

But it was too late.

Long tongues of flame streaked in across the sky toward the city. The incoming *Nemesis* had barely reached the lower atmosphere, but it was already opening fire with everything it had. Explosion after explosion rocked the Aquatronian capital. Through the window, the Curator watched in horror as a torpedo hit the roof of the Hall of Justice. A column of fire roared across the sky, and then the view was blotted out as armored plates slammed into place across the inner sanctum's windows.

"Lockdown complete," said an automated voice.

The Curator turned to Xeros with murder in his eyes. "I told you to do something about those ships!"

"Lord, I was trying—"

The Curator cuffed Xeros hard enough to send him sprawling. Xeros started begging for mercy, but the Curator stepped past him and keyed a mike.

"Commander Gnaw, report!"

The face of Commander Gnaw appeared on the screen. He was in his command tank, presumably somewhere near the Hall of Justice. "I am yours to command, my lord!"

"I am moving the inner sanctum into fortress mode! You are hereby placed in charge of the city's defenses! Concentrate all fire on the incoming ships!"

"I hear and obey, lord!" The screen went blank. The Curator hit a lever, and the inner sanctum began to descend from the skyline, trundling on vertical rails as it dropped beneath the streets. Clearly, it was no time to be anywhere near the surface.

INSIDE THE HALL OF JUSTICE IT WAS PURE PANDEMONIUM. The audience barely had time to process the fact that Megatron and Optimus somehow had escaped the pit; the next moment, the whole building shook and part of the roof caved in as the *Nemesis* strafed the city. As the power died, Aquatronians poured through the exits, only to be shot down by Sharkticon guards who had taken up position outside the building with orders to let no one escape lest some of the prisoners get away in the confusion. Now free of the energy-dampening field, those prisoners were working on finding a way to do just that. Using all his strength, Jazz managed to bend one of the bars enough to get through; as the Autobots followed him, Dirge was doing the same thing for the

Decepticons. The Sharkticon guards still in the chamber found themselves in hand-to-hand combat with scores of Cybertronians. For once Autobots and Decepticons weren't fighting one another; they'd watched on video screens while their leaders teamed up and figured now it was time to do the same thing. They could always settle their differences later, if they lived through this. Outside the building a screaming filled the sky: the vast roar of an incoming warship . . .

THE NEMESIS EMERGED FROM THE LAST OF THE CLOUDS and hurtled toward the city.

"Where shall we land, lord?" Soundwave asked.

Starscream scoffed. "Who said anything about landing? Keep giving them a taste of our firepower. They'll be begging us to negotiate in no time."

"We're taking a considerable amount of ground fire," Soundwave said.

"Put the shields into the red!" Starscream gripped the back of Soundwave's chair as the metropolis ripped in toward them; building after building disintegrated as Soundwave strafed away at point-blank range. But that cut both ways, for the Nemesis's initial bombardment had left the city with plenty of defenses, and now every antiaircraft gun Gnaw had was opening up on them. On the scanners, Starscream could make out a honeycomb of ground defenses that hadn't shown up on the original schematics. Apparently someone who knew military tactics had made some last-minute adjustments; the view from the bridge of the Nemesis showed a curtain of laser fire rising toward them, smashing against them like a driving rain. The bridge's windows shattered. The ship shuddered. Alarms went off.

"Shields up!" Starscream yelled.

"They're all knocked out!"

"You incompetent fool!"

But Soundwave said nothing. He was too busy trying to keep the craft level.

"I'm losing control," he said.

Starscream resisted the urge to strangle him. What was happening was the entirely predictable result of their being stupid enough to try to rescue Megatron. Not only were they going to die, they were going to die uselessly. Smoke billowed as engine after engine flamed out. As more shots crashed home, the *Nemesis* dipped dangerously low, almost crashing into the buildings. But Soundwave managed to engage the auxiliary power and keep the nose up, firing off another round of missiles and lasers into the nearest antiaircraft defenses. All that was visible from the ship's bridge was the skyline of the Aquatronian capital wreathed in palls of smoke. The topmost part of the Hall of Justice had been shot off, but there was still enough of the structure left to make it the highest point in the city.

"Set us down as close to there as possible!" Starscream bellowed.

"I think you're overestimating how much control I have," Soundwave shot back.

"Do it or I'll kill you myself."

Not that Soundwave really needed any extra motivation. He was trying for a crash landing, with an emphasis on the word *crash*. Starscream caught a glimpse of Aquatronians running in all directions as the ship just missed the top of one of the buildings, smashed through a series of light rails, and then skidded down a wide ceremonial avenue, plowing through all manner of vehicles and bots as it gradually slowed, crunching through the front wall of the Hall of Justice and coming to a halt. Starscream was amazed they were still alive but figured it wouldn't do to act surprised. He stepped out onto the nose of the *Nemesis* to see Autobots and Decepticons alike staring at him.

"Consider yourself rescued," Starscream said.

Chapter Thirty-four

SIDESWIPE LET THE ARK GAIN INCREDIBLE SPEED AS IT hurtled down through the atmosphere, firing its main missile launchers into the heart of the Aquatronian city. Ground-to-air defenses opened up on him, but the *Nemesis* already had absorbed the brunt of the damage, managing to take out large portions of the city's defense network while doing so. Now it had crashed straight into the Hall of Justice, creating chaos in the Sharkticon defenses. Sideswipe made a mental note: *Always get someone else to go first.* Especially if that someone was a Decepticon. One of his rockets sliced through a central power junction, rewarding him with a deadly light show that flared over a whole quadrant of the city.

"That ought to keep them occupied for a bit." He keyed into the main com and gave the order he'd been waiting to give: "Strike Force Zero—you are a go!" With a flick of the switch he deactivated the locks on hatches all along the hull.

"Let's see how you punks like this!" he said as he leveled off over the center of the city and dumped his deadly cargo. Led by Sunstreaker, more than two hundred Autobots floated down toward the city like deadly snowflakes. Some were equipped with rocket packs that allowed them to descend gracefully and land with precision all around the Hall of Justice. Others, of greater bulk and sturdier construction, dropped like stones, crunching through buildings to cushion their landings. Still others just hit the ground hard, emerging from their impact craters and unleashing the full measure of their firepower against the Sharkticons, sending rockets, missiles, and bolts of superheated plasma in all directions. Their erstwhile commander was too busy landing to keep an eye on his troops; Sunstreaker bounced against the side of a building, smashed his fists and feet through the stone, and rode the tidal wave of wreckage down to the city streets. Then he switched to sports-vehicle mode, gunned his engines, and roared toward the Hall of Justice, blasting Sharkticons as he went. Bluestreak and Mirage swung in on his flanks; together the three carved their way forward, straight over a shattered wall and into the hall itself. And as they got inside—

"Glad you could join us," Starscream said.

Sunstreaker looked around to see Decepticons pouring out of the crashed *Nemesis*. As the Autobots who had just landed entered the building, a palpable tension gripped the wrecked courtroom.

"We need a truce," said Jazz, "until we beat the Quintessons and get off this planet."

Starscream nodded. He'd already decided that was a great idea. A firefight here would merely increase his chances of being killed. That would be just his luck: He'd get blown to bits, and then Megatron could take over once again. Because he couldn't help but notice that the glorious leader wasn't here.

"Where's Megatron?" he asked.

"Never mind Megatron," Sunstreaker said. "Where's Optimus?"

"They both went down the pit," Jazz said. "They're somewhere beneath this city."

"Maybe they're dead," Starscream said. "I mean, that sounds like a lot to survive—"

"Optimus is *alive*," Jazz insisted. "And until I see a body, no one's going to say otherwise. Least of all any Decepticon."

"Agreed," said Ratchet. "We don't leave until we find him."

"We don't have much time," Hubcap said, consulting his datapad. "This city's crawling with Sharkticons. We may have taken care of those in the immediate vicinity, but there are a lot more where they came from. If we don't find Optimus soon, we're going to be up to our armpits in sharp teeth and lasers."

"We're still pretty weak," Jazz said. "That inhibitor field may be gone, but it's been a while since we—"

"I anticipated that," Sunstreaker interrupted. His strike team unpacked its satchels and began handing out fresh cubes of Energon from the Ark's replicator to both Autobots and Decepticons.

"Now you're talking my language!" Kup said as he grabbed one.

Perceptor looked at him quizzically. "You okay there?"

"Never felt better."

"Even though you testified against Optimus?"

"What are you talking about?"

Perceptor frowned. "What do you remember about what happened? As in before right now."

"Well, the three of us went exploring and . . ." Kup's voice trailed off.

"Then we were in the cage here," Rodimus said. "And then there was a big explosion, and then you guys showed up." Bumblebee clicked and whirred in agreement.

Ratchet and Perceptor looked at each other. "When that energy inhibitor went down, it must have let their circuitry go back to default mode," Perceptor said.

"Default mode?" Kup asked. "What other mode have we been in?"

"The Quints did something to your neural architecture to get you to testify against Optimus."

"I would never do that!" Rodimus yelled in horror. Bumblebee bleeped in agreement.

But Kup took one look at everybody's face, and the awful truth dawned on him. "When we took that dropship," he whispered. "That's when they must have done it."

"Probably," said Perceptor.

"We *really* stood up there in the trial and condemned Optimus?"

"You really did. Listen, for what it's worth, you didn't have much of a choice."

"Primus take them," Kup muttered. "They're going to pay."

"Whatever they did to us has worn off," Rodimus said. "Give us a chance."

"So you're okay to fight?" Ratchet asked.

"Give us some more Energon and we'll show you," Kup told him.

Sideswipe circled the capital city well out of range of what was left of its guns but close enough to maintain contact with the ground force. His radio crackled.

"Sunstreaker to Sideswipe, objective secure."

"Great. I'll circle back and pick you all up."

"That's a negative. We don't have Optimus. We're going to need a little more time."

"How much time?"

"Not sure. He and Megatron went down into this city's cellars."

"He's with *Megatron*?"

"Look, it's complicated down here. Just give us a few more—"

"Complicated up here, too," Sideswipe interrupted, eyeing his instruments. "My radar shows Sharkticon fleets closing on the island from all directions."

"I'm more worried about the Sharkticons right outside this building," Sunstreaker said.

COMMANDER GNAW FINALLY HAD BEEN ABLE TO RALLY his troops, forming a steel ring around the Hall of Justice. His recon drones showed that the Cybertronians were trapped in the heart of a city they didn't know, with no way out—a major tactical mistake. They still had one ship flying around up there that was proving tough to bring down thanks to the damage to both the rings and the city's strategic weaponry. But once the Sharkticon reserve fleets had taken up position around the island, that ship was going to get shot out of the sky fast.

Gnaw had to admit some grudging admiration for the boldness of the Cybertronian onslaught. Most beings who came face to face with Sharkticons were so overcome with fear that they were incapable of doing much else besides dying fast. But these Cybertronians were fighters. Gnaw respected that. Besides, fighters were the kinds of beings he enjoyed slaying the most, and there were few instances here on Aquatron in which he was able to indulge that habit. His Sharkticons weren't exactly original thinkers, and as a result they rarely had disciplinary issues. Gnaw's secondary occupation as head of the police security force was even more boring. Aquatronians were so terrified of being dragged off in the middle of the night to be experimented on by Doctor Xeros that breaking the law never crossed their minds. And then, just when something big was finally on the menu—just when the Quintessons got ready to invade a whole new *planet*—of course it had to be Tyrannicon who got the plum assignment. No, there were very few opportunities for Gnaw to sharpen his claws, and he wasn't going to let this one go to waste. He keyed up the central command channel.

"Attention all units, this is Commander Gnaw. The Cybertronians are pinned down in what's left of the Hall of Justice. Divisions Razor and Claw, set up your main forces at their right and left flanks and prepare to counterattack. Division Incisor, you will move into the city cellars and cut off any escape from below. Division Dorsal will cut the causeways and block any attempt to get out of the city."

"Sir," said the commander of Dorsal Division, "won't cutting the causeways trap the civilians in the city, too?"

Gnaw grinned. "And?"

The commander of Dorsal Division said nothing.

"That's what I thought," Gnaw said. "Commence the attack."

Chapter Thirty-five

CYBERTRON

Shockwave sat in his personal maglev car, racing along a set of rails that cut through a tunnel leading off from the one the Wreckers had used to get into his bunker. There was no way they were going to be able to catch up with him, and if they were foolish enough to try, they would trigger a pair of king-size remote mines that he'd rigged at the tunnel entrance.

Not that Shockwave seriously thought the Wreckers would pursue him. They'd come for Alpha Trion, and now that they had him, they were going to do what they did best: make themselves scarce. That was the only consolation Shockwave had. Other than that, the situation was a complete disaster. The Wreckers had deprived him of the single factor most likely to help him win the war and face down Megatron upon his inevitable return. The whole thing was so depressing, it was several moments before Shockwave registered the early-warning system bleeping frantically on his dashboard.

Suddenly all his calculations were forgotten as he snapped back to the present moment. There was something ahead on the tracks, about a mile up, and it was literally up, as he was heading back toward the surface. Something that just shouldn't be there. His maglev's sensors went to full resolution. For one terrible moment he thought that it was the Wreckers, that somehow they'd managed to get ahead of him, had smashed through the wall of the tunnel and were waiting for him to come this way. But when his onboard computer made a positive ID, it didn't show any Wreckers. It showed something else altogether.

Something called Sharkticons.

Shockwave had no idea what they were, and he wasn't waiting to find out. Chain guns sprouted from the nose of his maglev and lit up the tunnel, shredding the bots to pieces. As the train ripped past the place where the Sharkticons had appeared, Shockwave caught a quick glimpse of a larger cave adjacent to the tunnel that was swarming with those bots. Some of them fired at him, but he was already shooting past, opening the throttle as he surged toward Iacon and the surface. His mind was racing as fast as his vehicle. Who the slag were Sharkticons?

And what were they doing on *his* planet?

"THE BEST TRAP IS ONE THE VICTIM SETS FOR HIMSELF," Alpha Trion muttered.

That was the first coherent sentence he'd uttered since they'd dragged him out of the command bunker and back into the maglev train in which they'd arrived. They'd accelerated away at supersonic speeds, only this time they were running in reverse, back toward Iacon, Wheeljack driving while Ratchet manned the guns. Ultra Magnus was doing his best to get Alpha Trion to elaborate on what was going on, but that venerable robot seemed to be in something approaching a state of shock. And no wonder: He'd obviously been tortured at length by Shockwave, and now he seemed to have lapsed into some kind of paranoid fugue state, babbling about how Cybertron itself was lost.

That was bizarre, because as far as Wheeljack could tell, things had never looked better. By rescuing Alpha Trion, the Wreckers had scored their biggest victory against Shockwave yet. Surely they'd turned the tide of the war tonight. He slowed the train, approaching the point in the tunnel where they'd entered. It seemed an eternity ago. Wheeljack braked the train and opened the doors. Ultra Magnus and Jetfire helped Alpha Trion out while Wheeljack, Springer, and Rack n' Ruin moved in front, their guns out. The denizens of the undercity hadn't messed with them on the way in, but that didn't mean they weren't going to hassle them on the way out. Wheeljack was ready for anything.

Or at least he thought he was.

The entire undercity was a chaos of noise and motion. Every ladder and stairway and shaft seemed to be crowded with bots, and none of them were trying to stop the Wreckers. In fact, none of them paid any attention to the interlopers. Nor were they fighting one another. It was several seconds before Wheeljack realized exactly what they were doing.

"They're *fleeing*," Ultra Magnus said.

Just what had them so scared, Wheeljack didn't know. But the rumbling of machinery was echoing from somewhere deep below, and at the limit of his sensors Wheeljack could make out what might have been shots. Incredible as it seemed, there was heavy combat going on deep in the undercity.

"What the slag is going on?" Springer asked.

"Does it matter?" Jetfire said. "We've got to get upstairs."

SHOCKWAVE WAS MORE THAN A LITTLE RELIEVED WHEN he got back to the surface, and his guards were more than a little surprised. They hadn't even realized there was trouble down in the bunker, so compartmentalized was the hierarchy that Shockwave had imposed.

Though they were starting to get it now. Alarms rang throughout the tower as Shockwave soared up through the levels in his personal elevator. Sirens sounded across the city as he strode into his luxurious penthouse and called up wall-screen readouts in an attempt to get a grip on what was happening.

The view from the windows told its own story. The horizon flushed with the light of explosions just beyond them. Iacon's defenses swung into action—lasers powered up, missiles aimed skyward, guns loaded—but there wasn't anything to shoot at yet. There was just confused babbling on every Decepticon channel:

"Under attack—under attack—Unicron help us!"

"Repeat, we are surrounded, request reinforcements—aarrgh!"

"Identify yourself, identify yourself, I said—*noooo*!!"

"They're everywhere! Every bot for himself!"

Schematics on the wall gave Shockwave some insight into the overall situation. It was a total mess. Most of the datanet was down, half the cities on the planet were no longer reporting, and he still didn't understand the nature of the attack. Except that it was overwhelming and was falling on his garrisons like the mother of all storms. As though in a dream, he heard himself giving orders to all units that could still hear him to fall back into Iacon, to man the walls, to seal the undercity. Shockwave wasn't a bot given to introspection—and certainly not to self-doubt—but in the back of his head was the dawning awareness that he just might be responsible for the disaster now unfolding.

Yet what he needed most was hard data. He was relieved to see that his mainframe still had access to the archives beneath Iacon. Forcing himself to remain calm, he called up all the data he could find on Sharkticons. To his surprise, there was only one reference, and it wasn't very helpful: Sharkticons were the warrior caste on a world on the far side of the galaxy known as Aquatron. That was it. That and a single cross-reference to another creature entirely. Shockwave called up data on that entity, trying to remember just why the word *Quintesson* seemed so eerily familiar.

TYRANNICON STOOD ON THE BRIDGE OF HIS FLAGSHIP. Of course, technically it wasn't a ship anymore, since Cybertron had the misfortune of being almost exclusively land. But that didn't matter; the myriad vessels in the Sharkticon fleet had sprouted treads and wheels and were rumbling forward, armored leviathans crushing everything in their path. The invasion was going like clockwork. The attackers had achieved complete surprise and were ahead of schedule both above and below the ground. Within minutes of exiting the space bridge, Sharkticon commandos had seized the Well of All Sparks. The Cybertronians had contaminated it with Dark Energon, presumably as a scorched earth strategy. Not that it would matter. Once all resistance on the planet had been crushed, Quintesson scientists would arrive with the requisite technology to clean up the well, remove the stains of Dark Energon, and start harnessing its secrets. It was said that the Cybertronians' god was chained somewhere below the well. If that was true, so be it, for Cybertronian religion would prove no match for Quintesson science. The Quintessons had faced down creatures that called themselves gods before, and they hadn't lost yet. They didn't intend to do so this time, either.

Especially now that the computer known as Vector

Sigma was in Sharkticon hands. Another team of commandos had captured it mere minutes after the Cybertronians who were there had fled. Apparently they'd been fighting among themselves—one more way in which Tyrannicon's Quintesson masters had turned Cybertron's civil war to their advantage. The Decepticons had enjoyed the upper hand in that conflict; they'd become complacent and thus had received a very rude awakening when the dormant space bridge suddenly had revved up and legion after legion of Sharkticon troops had poured out. It was ironic, really: The Cybertronians had fought a war among themselves for millions of years, but the war now under way would be over within hours.

That was a pity, because Tyrannicon enjoyed a good fight. And he hadn't yet given up on getting one here. Most of the resistance was coalescing around Iacon, which was precisely what the Curator had told him to expect. Not only was that the capital, but all remaining key objectives were there: the Hall of Records, the vaults, and the last of the Primes. Tyrannicon wasn't so sure about that last one, but the Curator had been emphatic that one of the Thirteen—whatever that meant—was still alive on Cybertron and had to be captured. The Curator had said this with enough of an edge that Tyrannicon realized that these orders were coming from way up the food chain, that this Prime—who went by the unlikely moniker of Alpha Trion—wouldn't just be sent to Aquatron, he'd be going all the way back to Quintessa for close analysis from the very top Quintesson scientists. The Curator's tone made it clear that he hoped to count himself among that elite group one day. Tyrannicon could barely suppress his contempt for such piddling ambition. He had no interest in climbing any ladder or licking the boot of any bot. He was achieving his ambitions right now, carving out his legacy in smoke and flame. He gave orders to his pilots to pour on the speed as the fleet moved out over the shattered polar badlands. Ahead lay Iacon.

Chapter Thirty-six

"THIS PLANET DISGUSTS ME," MEGATRON SAID.

Optimus wasn't about to disagree. For several minutes now, he and the Decepticon leader had been making their way through a maze of service tunnels and natural caves. Some were filled entirely with water, but most ranged from half flooded to just very damp. Many of the caves had deep tidal pools that were teeming with lesser forms of Aquatronian life—small blind crabs, eels, weird little fish. Many were albino. None of them were remotely intelligent or strong enough to be interested in the two Cybertronians passing through their habitats. That was good, because the last thing Optimus wanted right now was yet another fight. He had enough to worry about with getting through this quasi-aquatic warren and back up to the surface so that he could rescue his men.

The problem was that as far as he could tell, he and Megatron were moving away from the Hall of Justice. The challenge of navigation was compounded by the high iron content in the area. Their compasses weren't much help at all, and Optimus knew better than to trust the Matrix. He'd left it on, of course, since it was providing him with valuable energy. But as to listening to what it had to say . . . Well, listening was all he was going to do. And even that was a little hard to take. Right now it was projecting images into his brain showing the birth of the Cybertronians. Quintesson scientists presided over assembly lines to produce Autobots and Decepticons alike. Optimus watched in horrified fascination while each Cybertronian vehicle received a final modification: a cockpit within which a Quintesson pilot could sit.

"It's a lie," he said out loud.

"Are you talking about your leadership?" Megatron asked sarcastically.

"The Matrix is trying to tell me that it wasn't Primus that created us. That it was the Quintessons themselves."

"They claimed that during the trial, remember? Doesn't mean it's true."

"What about our cockpits? Ever wondered about those?"

"Sure I have," Megatron said. "But if they conquered Cybertron, they could have made those modifications then."

"Maybe."

"Definitely. Look, Optimus, I don't know if you've noticed, but these Quintessons are really good at lying."

"That says a lot coming from a Decepticon."

Megatron ignored the jibe. "In fact, they're so good that my advice is to believe the *opposite* of anything they're telling us. If they say they created us, that's the best argument I can think of for assuming they didn't."

Optimus mulled that over. "You're probably right."

Megatron laughed. "I'm impressed, librarian. I know how much it pains you to admit that I'm right about anything."

"That's not true," Optimus said. "You were right about the old caste system. You were right when you said every Cybertronian has a right to chart his own destiny."

"So in that case why did we ever go to war?"

"You know why, Megatron. Because you think that all

destinies aren't created equal. That the strong should rule the weak."

"It's not a matter of *should*, librarian. It's just what happens naturally."

"I couldn't agree more," said a deep voice.

There was a rumbling, and several cave walls collapsed at once, revealing a much larger chamber, most of which was filled by a large tidal pool. Emerging from that pool was a monstrosity like nothing Optimus had ever seen.

"What in the name of Unicron is *that*?" Megatron blurted out. Half metal, half flesh, it seemed to be an enormous mutant lobster. The creature's semitranslucent body was made up of three key segments: a massive tail covered in spikes, a midsection resting on six legs, and a front section sporting four giant claws and a gaping mandible-covered maw. Two dark yellow eyes glared down at Optimus and Megatron from the ends of long stalks.

"They told me lunch was on the way," said the creature, saliva dripping from its maw.

"Who dares challenge Megatron?" Megatron asked, dropping into a combat stance.

"It's one of the Curator's creations," Optimus said.

"The most successful of them all," said the lobster-bot. "I'm the Gamekeeper. This is my lair."

It was quite a place. The walls were covered with kelp-stained carvings even weirder than the ones Optimus and Megatron had seen earlier. Phosphorescent fungi grew in tufts from fissures in those walls, emitting a glow that bathed the whole room in an unnatural light. The lobster-bot heaved his bulk farther out of the pool, moving toward the two Cybertronians . . .

"I tend to the creatures down here," he said. "The Piranhacons, the Eelcons, and anything else used for the pit and the trials. But very occasionally, some of the innocent escape their punishment, forcing me to become involved more . . . directly. And you have special distinction, since you are the last of the Cybertronians."

"What do you mean, the last?" Optimus's heart sank. "Our men on the surface have been executed?"

The Gamekeeper chuckled, a horrible burbling noise. "Dear me, no. At least, not yet. I think they're still holding out, actually. Putting up quite a fight from what I hear."

"So what are you talking about?"

Now the Gamekeeper was laughing openly. Saliva dangled down onto the rocks. "You mean you haven't heard?"

"Heard what?" Megatron demanded.

"Your planet. The Quintessons are invading it even as we speak."

And in one terrible instant Optimus understood. *This* was why they had been lured to Aquatron. *This* was why the Quintessons had played such games with him and Megatron. This was why they'd woven a web of such sick manipulation, why they'd been so eager to manipulate the Matrix and toy with his mind. Because it wasn't about him. It was about something much, much larger.

"You lie," Megatron said slowly. "Your kind always lies."

"No," Optimus said, "he speaks the truth."

"There is a space bridge far beneath this city," said the Gamekeeper. "The Curator opened up a door; Tyrannicon and his legions went through. Your planet will have no chance against their might. The Quintessons have sought retribution against your kind for eons, and today they will have it at last. Soon Tyrannicon will begin sending the first batches of captured Cybertronian slaves back through the bridge. Some will be fodder for the pits. Some will be food. Some will be experiments. But all will be doomed. Because this time there will be no liberation."

"We'll see about that," Megatron snarled as he aimed

his fusion cannon. But a giant claw swung out, knocking him against the wall. Suddenly it was all too clear that the painstaking way the creature had hauled its bulk from the pool had been just for show; a second giant claw snatched up Optimus and hurled him into the ceiling with no little force. A third claw sliced through the air to finish off Megatron, but he'd already rolled out of the way.

Optimus wasn't so fortunate. As he landed with a thud, the creature held him down with his fourth claw and went for the kill; Optimus looked up to see the monster's toothy mouth descending toward him; long sinewy tendrils slid out of that mouth and reached for him. Thinking fast, he kicked up his legs and braced them against the sides of the mandibles, managing to hold the beast's snapping jaws a few feet from his head. But the lobster-bot was exceptionally strong; Optimus knew he couldn't hold out for long. And he knew, too, what would happen when he lost. From his position right beneath the creature, he could see a gelatinous sack filled with what looked like the half-digested remains of its previous meal. And past that he could see—

Megatron.

Charging in at the underground fiend, yelling a gladiator's battle cry. The thing swung its great bulk to meet Megatron head-on; four claws lashed out, a virtual buzz saw of death as they sought out the Decepticon leader, but Megatron anticipated the claws' movements, vaulting onto one of them and leaping from there onto the lobster's back. The creature reacted instantly, arching its huge spiky tail like a scorpion in an attempt to sweep away the nuisance, but as it did so Optimus grabbed on to that tail, pinning it against the lobster's body. The creature thrashed frantically, trying to reach the two Cybertronians with its claws. Optimus felt himself losing his grip on the tail; as soon as he did, he knew he was going to be battered against the floor with a force that almost certainly would be lethal.

"Can't hold much longer." He grimaced.

"You don't need to," said Megatron, who reached forward and plucked off both eye stalks as if he were picking a couple of flowers. The creature howled; Megatron jumped from its back, ripped a stalagmite from the floor, and drove it straight into the monster's heart. The lobster convulsed and emitted a horrendous death rattle. Optimus let go of the still-quivering tail.

"Maybe you're right," he said to Megatron. "We do make a pretty good team."

But Megatron didn't answer. At first Optimus thought he was injured, but then he realized that the Decepticon leader's attention had been caught by something on the far wall: one of the more striking carvings. It was a particularly bizarre one, to say the least. A giant bot stood there, covered in shark fins, its arms raised in triumph, hapless opponents at its feet. Optimus thought there was something familiar about that bot, and as he studied it more closely, it occurred to him that it bore more than a passing resemblance to—

"*Me*," said Megatron. "That's me."

"Don't be ridiculous. Why would it be you?"

"I don't know, but you have to admit the similarities are rather striking."

"So are the differences. Notice the fins? Notice how you don't have them?"

Megatron shrugged. Optimus knew that the Decepticon leader was such a narcissist, he was fully capable of seeing his own reflection in virtually any image that was put before him. Though it did occur to Optimus that the carving might have been added at the eleventh hour by the Quintessons as still more psyops warfare. After all, they'd used the Matrix to mess with *his* head; why shouldn't they have come up with some way to mess with Megatron's? He became aware of a burbling voice that was half whisper, half gasp.

"Sharkticon superstition," the dying Gamekeeper muttered. Optimus was surprised he wasn't dead yet. There must have been more of his blood in the tidal pool than there was left in his body. Optimus stepped past a weakly grasping claw and placed his boot on the creature's head.

"Care to tell us what you mean?" he asked.

"The Sharkticons . . . they were conquered long ago by . . . Quintessons . . ."

"We figured that out already," Megatron said.

"They were brainwashed . . . conditioned. But some of them once told stories . . . of the one who would come to free them . . ."

"And that's the guy on the wall?" Optimus asked.

"The Sharkticons who drew that were killed long ago. I . . . consumed them personally. There has been no talk of freedom since. But . . . but . . ."

"But what?" Megatron demanded.

"They tasted sweet," said the lobster—and died.

"I still think that looks like me," Megatron said.

"Never mind that," Optimus said. "We've got to somehow find this bridge, defeat the Quintessons, and save Cybertron."

"It may already be too late," Megatron said.

"It's never too late. Are you with me or not?"

Megatron raised his fusion cannon in the old gladiator salute.

Chapter Thirty-seven

CYBERTRON

IACON WAS IN A STATE OF NEAR PANDEMONIUM. THERE
had been no official announcement, but by now everyone
was aware the planet had been invaded. Scarcely anyone
outside Shockwave's high command knew the identity
of the invaders, but that didn't really matter. Rumors
were sweeping through the city like wildfire. Megatron
was back and had turned against Shockwave! Optimus
had returned with the AllSpark and was thrashing the
Decepticons once and for all! But anyone who got past
the surface level of the rumor mill knew that something
far worse was afoot. Something alien had landed on
Cybertron, something no one had seen for many millions
of years.

"Those slagging *Quints*," Maccadam said.

Ultra Magnus nodded as if he understood what that
meant. Wheeljack and Springer refrained from asking
the obvious question, waiting to hear more. But Rack n'
Ruin had no such patience.

"Who are the Quints?" he asked.

It was Alpha Trion who answered. He'd been sitting
in the corner of Maccadam's ever since they'd got here.
Coming back to the bar was the last thing Wheeljack
would have expected them to do, but all the tunnels

that led out of the city were being rapidly sealed or blown up by Iacon's defenders. Alpha Trion's eyes were scarcely focusing, as if he were still having trouble processing events.

Or else was way ahead of them.

"The Quintessons are an ancient evil who once enslaved us," he said slowly. "They've returned to finish what they started."

"Okay," said Wheeljack. "In that case, why is all the radio chatter talking about *sharks*?"

"Not sharks," Springer said. "Land sharks. There's a difference."

"*Sharkticons,*" Alpha Trion said. "They are the servants of the Quintessons, who have sent them across the bridge."

"So when do we see the Quintessons?"

"You don't," Alpha Trion said. "That's the point. They always work through proxies." He drew a deep breath. "I am to blame for all of this."

"It's not your fault," Ultra Magnus said. "Shockwave used you."

"I should have self-destructed rather than fall into his hands."

"Well, you're here now," Maccadam said. "And frankly, we could use your advice."

"Advice?"

"What do we *do*?"

The room shook with a deep rumbling. For a moment, Wheeljack thought that Maccadam's was under attack once more, a suspicion that seemed to be confirmed when the camera feeds showed Decepticon battle tanks on the street outside. But they weren't stopping. They were trundling past, rolling toward the city walls.

"Shockwave's moving up his reserves," Springer said.

But no one listened to him. They were all still focused

on Alpha Trion, wondering whether he had an answer, whether he could give them any hope at all, no matter how slender. He took a deep breath.

"We need to get to the Hall of Records," he said.

No doubt about it; this had been the worst day of Ratbat's life.

Mere hours ago, it had looked like he was going to capture the leader of the Wreckers. But then Omega Supreme and his long-range cannon had intervened, and things had been going downhill ever since. Faced with the prospect of telling Shockwave that not only had he let the Wreckers get away but the forces he'd sent after Omega Supreme had been ambushed and destroyed by that giant robot . . . Well, Ratbat had been worried about more than just his career. And now a remorseless enemy was closing on Iacon, and he was in charge of stopping it. Shockwave had made it very clear that if the invaders got past the walls, he'd personally perform a very special experiment on Ratbat aimed at discovering just how long a bot could survive when it was sliced into several thousand pieces.

Ratbat was thus doing his utmost to bring some order to the city's defenses. So far he was failing. He'd set up his command post at the city gates, which were still in a state approaching anarchy. The defenders weren't even bothering to try to stem the tide of refugees flooding into the city. Once the enemy came into sight, the gates would have to be shut, of course, but right now Ratbat doubted that he could get his soldiers to fire on the refugees. They'd be just as likely to shoot him, and they'd probably enjoy it a whole lot more. A vid-screen on the wall started buzzing. Ratbat picked it up.

"Yes?"

"Report," said Shockwave.

"Everything's under control," Ratbat said automatically.

"That's not what I'm hearing."

Then why are you asking me? Ratbat wanted to say. But a lifetime of deference had trained him in the art of not uttering the first thing that popped into his head. "Lord Shockwave, I just arrived at my command post. I assure you the defenses will be at peak performance momentarily."

"For your sake," Shockwave said, "they had better be."

IN HIS TOWER, SHOCKWAVE SWITCHED OFF THE SCREEN and went back to studying the map of Iacon and the surrounding area. He knew that Ratbat's assurances were worthless. Frankly, Shockwave had never expected that Ratbat would have to contend with a situation this grim. If he had, he would have picked someone more capable. But skill in battle meant a potential rival, and Shockwave's whole regime was based on the principle of divide and conquer, making sure that no one bot ever attained enough power or prestige to challenge him. That had worked well enough for dealing with sporadic guerrilla warfare, but the current threat was a different story altogether.

Then again, even if he'd had the right officers in place—and Megatron had taken all the best ones with him anyway—Shockwave doubted it would have made much difference. The last thing anyone had been expecting was a full-scale invasion fleet to roar out of the dormant space bridge. Shockwave stared at the flames darkening the sky around Iacon and mulled over his fast-dwindling options. Most of his bots had been ground to powder already. All his remaining reserves had been moved to the walls and were waiting for what was probably going to be a fairly quick demise. Shockwave studied video imagery of the invaders: their manta ray crafts, their finned troops. They all looked like they'd been run off the same assembly line.

Except for one.

The leader wasn't exactly keeping a low profile. Obviously, his approach was very different from that of Shockwave, who preferred to stay in the most fortified place possible while others did the fighting. The Sharkticon leader stood resplendent on the exterior part of the bridge of his flagship, at the very front of his onrushing forces, his scaled cape streaming in the wind. Shockwave stared for long moments. An old aphorism came to mind:

Kill the head and the body will die.

Shockwave had in mind just the bot to do it, too. Even if that bot wasn't loyal to him, he knew its general location, in the vicinity of Iacon.

And Tyrannicon was heading right for it.

"THE CITY IS SURROUNDED, LORD."

Tyrannicon nodded. His armada had spread out, extending its flanks on precise vectors so that it enclosed the entire area around Iacon. Now it only remained to tighten the noose. He gave the order to advance; his flagship rumbled forward through the jungle of metal that constituted the polar badlands. Far ahead, he caught a glimpse of a tower protruding from the far horizon. Presumably that was the Tower of Shockwave: the highest point of Iacon's skyline. Tyrannicon smiled to himself. There was nothing that could stop him now.

That was when the ground below his battle craft began to shake and splinter open; a titanic rocket poked out of the growing hole, followed by what appeared to be a number of rail tracks that folded and converted into a huge hand that grabbed the front of Tyrannicon's ship, twisting the entire vessel and pulling it downward.

Tyrannicon was thrown clear, but most of his crewmen were crushed as the ship smashed into the bottom of the gully. Simultaneously, high-altitude Decepticons began dropping smoke bombs onto the fleet; in short order, visibility dropped toward near zero. Tyrannicon heard terrible rending noises as his ships struck one another. But he knew that the real target wasn't his fleet.

It was him.

The Cybertronians were going to do their best to kill him in the confusion. It was a sound plan; in fact, it was exactly what he would have done. He wasn't surprised when a huge shape shambled out of the smoke and loomed before him.

"Who dares defy General Tyrannicon?" the Sharkticon general yelled.

"THE MIGHT OF OMEGA SUPREME!" The bot's voice was so loud that it practically shattered Tyrannicon's sensors. He quickly searched his database. The lumbering giant in front of him was one of the last of the ancient Guardian robots. A true challenge if ever there was one. But maybe it was possible to win the bot over with reason. Or at least confuse it.

"Omega Supreme," Tyrannicon said. "You are no Decepticon. There is no need for you to defend this city."

"I AM CYBERTRONIAN. THAT IS ENOUGH."

Sharkticons appeared at the edge of the canyon and opened fire on the Autobot behemoth. It was like watching peashooters in action against a brick wall. Omega Supreme stood there, absorbing the damage, and then he swung his rocket cannon up and disintegrated the enemy forces with a single devastating blast before turning back to Tyrannicon.

"LET'S GET THIS OVER WITH," he bellowed.

*   *   *

FROM THE ROOF OF HIS TOWER, SHOCKWAVE TRAINED his telescope on the unfolding carnage outside Iacon. What was taking place was so far away that it wasn't even visible from the walls; it was beyond the horizon of every structure in Iacon except the very summit of the tower. Shockwave stood there alone, letting the wind whip across his face. Through the barrage of smoke bombs, he could see plumes of fire where the Sharkticon ships had collided with one another. The exact extent of the damage was impossible to determine. All he knew was what he was picking up from the intercepted chatter on the Sharkticon com-links: that the Sharkticon fleet was in disarray, that Tyrannicon and Omega Supreme were battling for supremacy out there, that everything hung in the balance . . .

OMEGA SUPREME SMASHED HIS FIST DOWN, JUST MISSING Tyrannicon, but the sheer force of the impact against the ground was enough to send the Sharkticon leader flying against the wall of the gully. For a moment, all Tyrannicon could see was static. His systems were so overloaded that he couldn't even think. He shook his head, clearing his vision. To his surprise, he wasn't dead.

Just very angry.

"You're the best Cybertron has?" he said. "No wonder we're winning so easily."

Omega Supreme raised the giant blaster on his left hand and fired, but Tyrannicon had already leaped to the side. Omega Supreme changed the beam setting to wide burst and tried to reacquire the smaller target, but the wily Sharkticon general apparently had ducked behind some nearby boulders. Omega Supreme advanced on them.

"THERE IS NO ESCAPE!"

"Who said anything about trying to escape?"

Omega Supreme turned to see that Tyrannicon had skittered up the rock face and was staring him right in the eye. The laser cannon on Omega's head swiveled, but Tyrannicon thrust his battle trident straight into the weapon's power supply, detonating the gun and sending Omega Supreme staggering backward. Tyrannicon leaped onto Omega Supreme's shoulder and yanked his trident free. Omega Supreme tried to swat Tyrannicon off like he was an annoying insect, but Tyrannicon vaulted deftly over Omega Supreme's head, straight onto his other shoulder; as he did so, he thrust the trident into Omega Supreme's right optic, penetrating his neural circuitry. There was a terrible crackling noise; sparks flew everywhere; the huge bot staggered and then started to fall. Tyrannicon rode his toppling adversary all the way down, sliding down the massive chest, stabbing it over and over with his trident. Omega Supreme hit the ground with a boom that reverberated all the way to Iacon. Sharkticons peered over the edge to see their general standing atop Omega Supreme's chest.

"Well, don't just stand there," Tyrannicon said. "We've got a planet to conquer."

Chapter Thirty-eight

THE WALLS OF THE HALL OF JUSTICE SHUDDERED beneath the impact of the Sharkticon guns. Most of the Autobots and Decepticons had taken up positions around the perimeter and were firing back at any Sharkticon that stuck its head out. Yet even as the bombardment intensified, Starscream and Jazz were engaged in a heated argument that was increasing in volume rapidly. No doubt about it, the uneasy alliance between the recently freed prisoners was starting to fray. But from the noise of the guns outside, if they didn't get a plan together soon, it wasn't going to matter.

"I'll have you know my rank is *air commander*," hissed Starscream, practically spitting in Jazz's face. "That means I outrank you."

"I've got news for you," Jazz shot back. "You're not in the air anymore. And we don't need anybody to be in charge; we just need to cooperate. See the difference?"

From the expression on Starscream's face, he didn't. "So what are you proposing?"

Jazz gestured at the pit into which the Quintessons had tossed their victims. "We have to go down into the undercity and look for Optimus."

"I'm not sending any of my people down into that death trap! And certainly not to search for the leader who led you into this mess!"

"It's not just Optimus," Prowl yelled. "*Megatron's* down there, too."

"He's a big bot. I'm sure he'll be able to find his way back here. But if you Autobots want to get down there and take a look, be my guest."

"And here I was thinking we were supposed to be working together," Perceptor said.

"We are!" Starscream said. "We'll stay up here and guard the high ground while you Autobots go dig our leaders out of the rubble. Seems pretty straightforward to me."

"What's straightforward is you're a coward," Prowl told him.

"Say that again," Starscream said. "Go on, say it—"

Jazz stepped between the two.

"Listen, Starscream, we need you to send at least *some* of your troopers with us. We've got no idea what's down there."

"Exactly why I'm not sending anybody. For all we know, you could be trying to send us into a trap. Divide us and then pick us off one by one."

Perceptor's face went red. "Unlike you Decepticons, we Autobots keep our word!"

"You dare to insult the honor of the Decepticons?"

"You mean to say you have honor?" Before Starscream could react, Jazz suddenly saw movement in the bottom of the pit. For a moment, he thought that it was Optimus and Megatron, that they had returned.

But then he realized otherwise.

"Sharkticons!" he yelled even as the Sharkticons who had entered the bottom of the pit started firing upward. Simultaneously, explosive charges went off beneath the Hall of Justice, ripping away part of the floor. The next moment, Sharkticons began pouring from the smoking hole, swinging their mace tails and firing lasers from their shoulder-mounted weapon packs.

"They're inside the perimeter!" Ironhide bellowed as he grabbed a nearby Sharkticon, tore its mace tail clean off its body, and proceeded to use that mace to smash another Sharkticon to bits. Hand-to-hand combat broke out everywhere.

"We'll finish this later!" Starscream snarled at Jazz, and then: "Decepticons to me! Decepticons to me!" But none of the Decepticons were paying much attention; they were too busy fighting for their lives. In normal circumstances, Starscream immediately would have ordered his jet troopers into the air, but he was wary of the still-active ground-to-air defenses out there; anybody who decided to take off would be an easy target. That meant he was trapped on the ground, fighting side by side with Autobots against impossible odds. He heard more shooting as a second wave of Sharkticons rushed the building from the streets outside.

"Here they come!" said Prowl. He and Jazz and Ratchet were falling back into one of the corners of the Hall of Justice, trying to hold on. Meanwhile, Sunstreaker, Hubcap, and their strike force were coalescing in an arrowhead formation, advancing on the pit, shoving the Sharkticons that were coming out of it back in. As their opponents tumbled to their doom, Sunstreaker whirled around and let loose a barrage of rockets that blasted the Sharkticons emerging from the rift in the floor.

"Hubcap!" he yelled. "Find us a way out of here!"

But Hubcap already had consulted his datapad. "There may not be one! They're coming in from the undercity! That means we're trapped!"

"We've got to drive these creeps back! Follow me!" Sunstreaker leaped over a Sharkticon, shooting it with his electron-pulse blaster, and as he landed, he switched into vehicle mode and took off at full speed, smashing through still more Sharkticons. Rodimus also shifted into vehicle form and got a good head of speed, running over Sharkticons while Bumblebee and Kup gave him covering fire. But more swarms just kept coming.

Two blocks away, Gnaw watched the battle on the main monitor in his massive command tank. He was amazed how much of a fight the Cybertronians were putting up. Surely they had to realize they were outnumbered at least ten to one. That they were trapped like rats with no way out. But Gnaw understood that kind of thinking. If the situation had been reversed, he, too, would have chosen a fight to the death over an ignoble surrender. Why capitulate to an enemy without making him pay as high a price as possible?

The Cybertronians were certainly making this a costly battle. The Hall of Justice destroyed, thousands of Sharkticons knocked out of the action—and this was the extent of the bloodletting just on Aquatron. Gnaw could only guess what kind of resistance the general must be running into on Cybertron itself. But if the Cybertronians wanted annihilation, well, Gnaw was more than happy to oblige. The faces of his divisional commanders appeared on the screen.

"Report," he said.

"Dorsal Division. All causeways have been cut. There is no way out of the city."

"Incisor Division. We have secured the area beneath the Hall of Justice and are attempting to break out onto the surface."

"Razor Division. Our second wave is meeting heavy resistance."

"Claw Division. Our second wave is being forced back."

Gnaw turned to an aide-de-camp. "And what of the

remaining Cybertronian spaceship?"

"Currently five miles above the city, sir. If it comes in for another strafing run or attempts an evacuation, we won't be caught napping."

"Good." He turned back to his division commanders. "I will personally lead the final assault on the Hall of Justice. But first I will attempt to make these Cybertronians see reason."

The commanders saluted; the screens went blank.

Gnaw picked up his battle mace and switched channels to address his team of handpicked warriors packed into battle tanks behind his own. "Sharkticons, your hour of glory is here! We will strike at their weakest point and hold it as a beachhead for the other divisions. We will overwhelm and destroy them! Let no Cybertronian remain standing. Forward for victory!" The warriors shook their maces and growled in agreement. Gnaw slapped his helmsman's shoulder.

"I want you to bring us right to the edge of their defenses. Turn on the speakers and broadcast this message on all channels."

The helmsman obeyed; the battle tank ground toward the Hall of Justice. As it closed in, Gnaw started telling the Cybertronians what was what:

"Attention, worms; your fight is over. We have you surrounded. Even if you escape, you have nowhere to go. The city of Hydratron is cut off, and your planet is under assault by our mighty legions! I am giving you this one chance to surrender. You have ten seconds to reply."

The reply came in far less time than that.

"Well?" Gnaw asked.

The communications technician looked puzzled. "They say . . . 'bolts' . . . ?"

"Bolts? What does that mean?"

"I . . . I don't know."

Gnaw pulled his blaster and shot the communications technician dead on the spot.

"Begin the assault," he said. "No prisoners."

EXPLOSIONS ROCKED THE HALL AS THE MAIN WAVE OF Gnaw's forces triangulated their firepower. Those Sharkticons who had already stormed forward suddenly found themselves caught between the Cybertronians and their own comrades. They went down like the cannon fodder they were. Ducking another round of blasts, Jazz switched off the com-link and turned to some of the Autobots huddled together under some wreckage.

"I guess he got the message," he said.

Even Starscream seemed amused. "Well played, Autobot. Let them know none of us is going to roll over and make it easy for them."

"It may not be that hard," Jazz said wryly. "They've got us pinned down here, and there's no way we can hold out for long under this firepower." As if to punctuate the point, a near miss showered them with debris. "So if anybody has any bright ideas, now would be the time to propose 'em."

"We should take cover in the *Nemesis*," Starscream said, gesturing at the nose of the starship, which still protruded through the far wall.

"We're not leaving Optimus!"

"Will you shut up about your precious Optimus?" Starscream said. "The *Nemesis crashed*. Meaning it *can't fly*. But it's got to be more defensible than what's left of this building. A good place for a final stand."

"Who's talking about a final stand?" Ratchet asked. "We need to bring the Ark back in here, take some of the pressure off us."

"Do you think what Gnaw said about invading Cybertron was true?" Prowl asked.

"*Nothing* these guys say is true," Jazz answered. "Don't even give it another thought. I hate to say it, but Starscream's right—we need to fall back to the *Nemesis*."

"That's the smartest thing you've said today," Starscream told him.

"I'll cover your retreat," Jazz said. "Now go! All of you!"

Starscream and his Decepticons didn't need to be told twice; they took off like they were trying to break the lightspeed barrier. The rest of the Autobots fell back in more measured order. Ratchet remained where he was, staring at his old friend with considerable concern.

"You don't expect to hold them off by yourself?"

Jazz picked up a laser and a Sharkticon mace. "Get out of here," he said. "I'll be right behind you."

"No, you won't," said Ironhide.

"You'll be right alongside us," Ratchet said. Bulkhead raised his battle mace.

Jazz grinned. The four Autobots gathered their weapons and turned to face the oncoming Sharkticon tide.

INVASION!

The word detonated in Sideswipe's mind like a bomb. Teletraan-1 had managed to hack into the Aquatronians' communication net and was piping their every word into the Ark's bridge. Not that the data was doing them any good; in fact, all it seemed to do was reinforce what dire circumstances they were all in. And Sideswipe had more immediate challenges, anyway, such as keeping the Ark in the air. He was dealing with the damage from braving the city's gunnery earlier; already he'd had to shut down one of the four thrusters. He was keeping away from most of the ground-to-air defenses, but the long-range cannon remained dangerous. He was debating gaining even more height when—

"Jazz to Sideswipe! We could really use some help down here! We're pulling back to the *Nemesis* and need some serious air support."

"The city's air defenses are too tough," Sideswipe said. "I can't get any closer; you saw what happened to the *Nemesis*."

"Well, if we don't get a break down here, we're finished!"

"Copy that." Sideswipe realized he had very little time to come up with a working plan. He knew that even if the Ark deployed all of its remaining shuttles and dropships, they would still be no match for the withering fire of the city's defenses.

"I hear you could use some assistance."

Sideswipe turned to see the recently repaired Silverbolt enter the bridge with a slight limp. "Aerialbots ready for duty," he proclaimed.

"I thought you guys were smashed up pretty badly. I can't ask—"

"You don't have to," Silverbolt said. "What's the situation?"

"Our guys down in the city center are about to get overrun, and there's no way we can get to them." Sideswipe brought up the city map on the viewscreen. Silverbolt studied it for a moment.

"Piece of cake," he said.

JAZZ, RATCHET, BULKHEAD, AND IRONHIDE KEPT MOVING, bringing Sharkticons down with precise shots as they gradually fell back toward the *Nemesis*. Though it was plain the situation wasn't much better there. Only the *Nemesis*'s weaponry deployed at point-blank range was keeping the onslaught at bay; plasma cannons unleashed torrents of liquid fire, melting onrushing Sharkticons. But the four Autobots were about to get cut off. They had a company of Sharkticon commandos on the right and an unknown number on the left; at this rate, their chances of rejoining the forces at the *Nemesis* seemed negligible. At least they had given the others a chance.

"Stop," Jazz yelled. "We'll make a last stand here."

Ratchet popped his blades. "I guess this is as good a place as any," he said.

Ironhide cracked a smile. "One thing's for sure— they're going to know they've been in a real fight." And then the Sharkticons were on them, charging into the four Autobots' kill zones, those behind climbing over the corpses of those in front until finally they were close enough to engage in savage hand-to-hand combat. Through the swinging mace tails and whirling blades, Jazz could make out still more Sharkticon reserves bearing down on them. *This is it*, he thought . . .

But from out of nowhere a pair of rocket arrows knocked two Sharkticons out of the way, freeing a path for a speeding yellow blur to smash over several more, giving the three warriors space. Only when Jazz heard the recognizable sound of Kup's ancient battle laser did he realize what was happening. The next moment, Bumblebee resumed bot form and fired his photon cannons while Rodimus leaped in and continued to fire rocket arrows into the oncoming horde, which wavered and drew back.

"You disobeyed orders!" Jazz yelled.

"Only to save your iron butts!" Rodimus retorted.

They heard what sounded like a thunderclap and then another. As a third blast resounded, the nearby Sharkticons went up in flames and the rest broke and scattered in all directions. Roaring into the Hall of Justice were the Aerialbots.

"We'll cover you," Silverbolt said. "Meet you at the *Nemesis*!"

Jazz shifted into his pursuit-cruiser mode; Ratchet,

Ironhide, and Bulkhead hopped on while Kup and Rodimus leaped onto Bumblebee. They sped across the floor of the now-cleared hall toward the *Nemesis* as Silverbolt and the rest of the repaired Aerialbots streaked back out of the gaping hole where the roof had been, skimming the top of the city's skyline, strafing Sharkticon troops and knocking out more of the city's air defenses. Then the Aerialbots swung back toward the crash site, joining together at the last possible moment and forming Superion before touching down as a single giant bot next to the *Nemesis*. Autobots and Decepticons cheered as Superion brought his awesome weaponry to bear, incinerating nearby Sharkticons in a hail of rocket and laser fire. For a moment it almost looked like the tide was turning in their favor.

Almost.

Ironhide was the first to see it. A street rose up on hydraulic lifts and folded back into compartments; vents opened up all along the walls throughout this section of the city. The next moment, water jetted out of those vents at full force.

"What the slag's going on?" Jazz yelled.

They got their answer a moment later. The floor of the Hall of Justice shuddered—and not just the floor but the entire surface level of the city. A terrible rumbling filled the air.

Then huge waves of water poured down the streets.

"The city's submerging!" Ironhide yelled.

He was right. Scores of Sharkticons were knocked out of the way, dashed into walls before they could switch to shark mode. Only those advancing in tanks were safe from the deluge, for those tanks quickly switched to hover mode and sped in across the water. Superion turned to face the rushing water and was shoved back into what was left of a building, smashing it entirely.

Autobots and Decepticons climbed atop the back of the crippled *Nemesis*, firing their weapons in every direction. Inside the ship, Starscream started yelling at Soundwave.

"Talk to me, Soundwave! I need some answers!"

Soundwave studied the readouts. "They're flooding the island."

"They're not just flooding it, it's sinking! This island's artificial!"

"Maybe," Soundwave said. "I need more data. All I can tell you is that in less than two minutes, our position will be submerged completely."

"And the *Nemesis*? Will she float?"

"We'll find out in another hundred seconds," Soundwave said. "Maybe you can be the first Decepticon naval commander."

Starscream punched Soundwave so hard that he knocked him onto the ground. Out the window he could see Commander Gnaw leading the final assault himself, riding on the back of what looked like a giant aquatic war turtle.

"Now we have them!" Gnaw yelled over his communication channel to his forces. "Kill them! Kill them all!"

Sharkticons swam in from every side, eager to oblige.

Chapter Thirty-nine

"DID YOU FEEL THAT?" OPTIMUS ASKED.

Megatron looked scornful. "You're imagining things, librarian."

But then the corridor shook again, this time violently enough for it to be unmistakable. There was a noise in the distance that sounded like a thousand whispers, all of them getting gradually closer. And louder.

"Okay," Megatron said. "Maybe you're not imagining things."

"Something's out there," said Optimus.

"Just as long as we don't have to fight another overgrown lobster."

"Will you shut up about that lobster? The water level's rising."

It had been a factor they'd had to contend with as long as they'd been down there. They had been doing their best to pick the passages that seemed the least waterlogged. But now Optimus could plainly see that the water lapping around his ankles was rising toward his knees. And that noise in the distance was growing thunderous.

"Run!" he said. He and Megatron started sprinting, and as they did so, a deluge of water poured into the corridor behind them. The two Cybertronians made it another hundred yards before the force of the deluge started to lift them off their feet. It was obvious they had only a few more seconds before they lost traction altogether and were swept away. Optimus reached up with his energy blade and sliced a hole in the ceiling to reveal a corridor immediately above theirs.

"Get on my shoulder!" he yelled to Megatron. Megatron did just that, clambering onto Optimus's shoulders and into the upper corridor. He looked down at Optimus, who was holding on to the wall to keep his balance against the rising tide.

"This is the part where you help me up," Optimus said.

"Is it really?"

"Megatron, don't be an idiot. We can continue our quarrel once we beat the Curator, but if you abandon me like this, you're just decreasing your own chances of survival."

Megatron seemed to ponder this. Then he extended his hand. "I'm just joking with you, librarian."

Optimus had his doubts about that. He suspected it was the raw calculation he'd just suggested that had persuaded Megatron. He'd have to watch his back from now on. Not that that came as news in working with the Decepticon leader. He scrambled up, and the two bots continued down the new corridor, making as much haste as they could, because it was only a few more minutes before water started to pour past their feet once more.

"They're flooding the whole place," Optimus said.

"Probably to try to drown us."

"They're going to succeed unless we hurry."

"Maybe this means we're getting close to that space bridge. They're trying to keep us away from a key objective."

But Optimus didn't buy that. This had to be about more than just getting him and Megatron. And as for the space bridge's location . . . well, he didn't believe in torture, but he was starting to wish they'd asked the Gamekeeper a few more questions before he died. All the monster had told them was that the bridge lay somewhere below. Presumably the Quintessons weren't flooding the bridge's infrastructure—they'd want to keep it operational—but the rising water was certainly going to make it difficult to keep going in that direction. So maybe the flooding *was* intended as a defensive measure against him and Megatron. Optimus realized that his thoughts were starting to go in circles; he wondered how this could get any worse.

"Duck!" Megatron yelled.

It was said with such urgency that Optimus didn't think twice about Megatron's out-of-the-blue command—he just followed it instinctively. He was glad he had. The Sharkticon that had been stalking them just missed him, instead landing right in Megatron's waiting arms. The Decepticon threw the monster to the ground, held its jaw open with one foot, and then effortlessly pulled the top of its head clean off with a resounding crack before hurling the skull at another Sharkticon bounding down the corridor toward them. Optimus couldn't help noticing the scores of gleaming eyes behind them . . .

"I think it's time we started running," he said.

"No disagreements there," Megatron said. He and Optimus sprinted down the corridor as fast as they could with the chatter of gnashing Sharkticon teeth behind them. As the water level rose, some of the Sharkticons began to swim and were all the faster for it.

"The Gamekeeper's starting to look good by comparison!" Megatron yelled.

"Complain about it later!" Optimus shouted, and then they rounded a corner and skidded to a stop. A heavy metal door blocked the way. There was no time to lose; the two Cybertronians shoved against the door for all they were worth while the Sharkticons closed in. The door started to give way, but not enough.

"Pull, Optimus! Scrap you, pull!"

"Save your breath," Optimus breathed. They weren't sure which would give first, their steel joints or the door. The Sharkticons were almost on them, but then they were rewarded with a cracking noise followed by the shriek of iron tearing as the great door came off its mooring.

And tumbled into an abyss.

Nothing could have prepared them for what they were looking at. It was a huge room with neither floor nor ceiling, and Optimus realized it was actually a circular shaft some hundred meters across, dropping like a spine down the length of the island to depths too far below to see. Water slopped around their feet and fell past them into darkness.

Then the Sharkticons were on them. Optimus and Megatron battled it out hand to hand, dodging mace tails and razor-sharp teeth while they punched and kicked and sent battered Sharkticons flying. The one advantage of fighting in this cramped space was that only a few Sharkticons could get to grips with them at any one moment. But there were more coming up all the time, pressing against the ones in front of them, and the sheer weight of numbers meant that Optimus and Megatron were being forced steadily backward to the very edge of the precipice.

Suddenly Optimus heard a creaking noise behind him. Even as he parried a Sharkticon blow, he glanced around and saw movement in the shaft above. Descending into view on cables was the most heavily armored and largest elevator car Optimus had ever seen. It was the size of a small house, and as it reached their level, it became clear that the door they'd just broken through wasn't intended to provide access to it, for the elevator car was more than ten meters away, dropping farther down the gigantic

David J. Williams and Mark S. Williams

shaft. Optimus processed all this in a moment while the Sharkticons regrouped and surged forward once more.

"Only one way out of this," Optimus shouted, shoving Megatron off the edge and jumping down after him. They both dropped more than fifteen meters out into the shaft, landing on top of the descending elevator. Megatron rose up, furious.

"You pushed me!"

"Couldn't take the time to explain, and this thing is going down fast." Optimus broke off as a Sharkticon plummeted past the elevator, followed by still another. The two Cybertronians looked up and saw water and Sharkticons pouring out of the passageway where they'd both been standing, tumbling down toward them.

"By the eyes of Unicron!" Megatron said as a Sharkticon hit the elevator roof next to him, splintering into pieces. The fall was too great a distance now for anything to survive, but that didn't seem to worry the Sharkticons, who were raining down like bombs. It was the most effective lemming strategy Optimus had ever seen, and it was only a matter of time before one of the plunging kamikaze bots hit paydirt.

"We need to get inside this thing," Optimus said.

"Agreed," said Megatron as he and Optimus leaped around the roof of the armored car, dodging the plummeting Sharkticons. Quickly studying the metal plates, Optimus found what he was looking for: an emergency hatch. He ran over to it, evading falling Sharkticons, and grabbed it with both hands.

"Give me the strength!" he muttered to himself, and with considerable effort pulled the hatch open. Megatron ran over and dived through the hatch headfirst. Optimus followed suit and slammed the panel shut from the inside. He then activated his energy blade and used it as a welding torch to fuse it shut before turning to find

Megatron holding the being called Xeros by the throat, pressing him against a wall.

"Where is the Curator, you spineless worm?"

"Not here," Xeros said, looking more than a little scared. Evidently this was the Quintesson command center, the Curator's inner sanctum. The walls of the chamber were filled with viewscreens showing scenes from the battle raging around the Hall of Justice. To Optimus's horror, he could see that the place was almost entirely flooded, that scarcely any part of the city remained above water now. There was fighting, but he couldn't make out which of his Autobots were left. It was a disaster.

But it was nothing compared to the screens on the adjacent wall.

They showed live images of Cybertron: Sharkticons slaughtering the population . . . Tyrannicon's battle fleet shelling Iacon . . . smoke and flame and carnage everywhere. Optimus felt himself going numb and turned to Xeros.

"You'll pay for this," he said.

"We already *did*," Xeros shot back. "You wreaked slaughter upon us when you threw us off your dirtball of a planet. So this time we're not going to make the same mistake of trying to turn you into slaves. This time we're going to wipe you scum from the stars. Your destiny is extinction, Prime! Tell me, how does it feel?"

Megatron threw Xeros onto the floor, kicked him in the chest, and was about to kick him again when the sound of Sharkticons impacting the roof grew more frequent. And at least some of those Sharkticons were still alive, because now everyone in the elevator chamber could hear the whine of power tools starting up.

"They must be sliding down the cables," Optimus said.

Megatron drew back his foot, bracing himself to put a

lethal kick through Xeros's head. *"Where's the Curator?"* he repeated.

"I'm so terribly sorry," Xeros told him. "He took a different route to the bridge. A faster route."

"Leaving you to manage the situation."

"I'm expendable," Xeros said, summoning his courage. The volume on the roof increased further. "But he did want me to give you both a message."

"Namely?"

"He hopes you die badly—very badly indeed." Xeros's insane laughter filled the chamber. It was all Optimus could do to keep Megatron from killing him right there on the spot. Instead Megatron turned and smashed his fist into one of the consoles out of sheer frustration. There was a whirring, and a panel slid back. Inside was an incandescent red object that looked exactly like—

"The Matrix of Leadership," Megatron breathed. Confusion and greed warred on his face. He turned to Optimus: "But I thought you had—did they steal it from you?"

Optimus patted his chest. "You know as well as I do that mine's still here. Just tampered with."

Megatron mulled this over, and then understanding suddenly dawned in his eyes. He pulled Xeros to his feet, grabbed him by the shoulders, and pulled his face up against his own. "This is the *Decepticon* Matrix of Leadership! The one the Curator promised me! Admit it!"

"You're crazy," Xeros said.

"And you're lying!"

"The Curator was lying to *you*," Xeros told him. "That's just the computer he was using to—" He looked at Optimus. "—influence you. And augment the bridge activation. He transferred all the codes there when he left. So he still has everybody right where he wants them. All this does now is assist me with coordinating Sharkticon movements."

"The same ones who are trying to break their way in here now?" Optimus asked as the noise above grew still louder. The ceiling was starting to glow.

"Those are beyond my control, alas." Xeros shrugged sarcastically. "The Curator programmed them to destroy any intruders who penetrated his inner sanctum. This device won't help you."

"We must destroy it anyway," Optimus said.

"It won't do you any good," Xeros said.

"It's going to do me a world of good!" Megatron yelled. "For once you Quintessons told the truth, and now you seek to bury it in still more lies!" He ripped the Matrix replica from the console and tore off the wires. Optimus tried to grab the object, but Megatron slugged him hard, sending him staggering backward.

"Megatron, don't do this!" Optimus yelled. "It will unleash still more madness!"

"You're slagging right it's going to unleash madness!" Megatron screamed. "The madness known as *ME*!"

He shoved the Matrix replica into his chest.

Chapter Forty

CYBERTRON

SHOCKWAVE WATCHED TRANSFIXED AS THE SHARKTICON armada roared in toward the walls of Iacon. Its ranks had thinned slightly, and many of the ships that remained bore the damage of collision or bombs dropped by high-altitude Decepticons. But the bulk of the invaders were still operational, and from Shockwave's vantage point he could see that they were attacking the city from every side. The guns of Iacon opened fire. A wave of lasers and shells lacerated the initial ranks of the oncoming forces, but then hatches opened on all those manta ray craft; cannons protruded and let rip. The walls of Iacon disappeared in sheets of flame and fire. Some of the more high-trajectory shots sizzled past the tower; Shockwave knew it was only a matter of time before they found the range and started to knock his stronghold to pieces. There was only one place in Iacon that might save the situation now—and only one bot. He sent out orders to that bot, then stepped inside the nearest turret and set the elevator controls for maximum speed. He descended the depths of the mammoth structure even as shells began to crash against him.

* * *

RATBAT HAD NEVER SEEN ANYTHING LIKE IT. THOUSANDS of manta ray craft were sprouting battering rams, accelerating as they made their final rush toward the walls, and it seemed like they were all coming straight for him. He couldn't even make himself heard over the roar of the bombardment. The sky was one huge mass of smoke and flame. He did the only logical thing he could think of.

He deserted.

Straight out the door, past his shocked troops, and into his staff tank, which was waiting with the engine running for just such an occasion. As they hurtled away, Ratbat imagined what he was going to have to say to Shockwave. Something along the lines of *I was the only survivor, and I escaped to bear you these grim tidings,* but then he realized that he was just in denial. Shockwave no longer mattered. Nothing did. In the rearview he could see clouds of dust as the Sharkticon juggernauts hit the walls.

THE WRECKERS MADE THEIR WAY THROUGH THE panicking crowds. Decepticon soldiers mingled indiscriminately with civilians, all hierarchy dissolving as every bot looked for sanctuary that wasn't there. The city walls were breached. The war was lost. It didn't even look like the Sharkticons were taking prisoners. This was shaping up to be a total massacre. But Ultra Magnus seemed as calm as ever, leading his team along a side alley and down a series of staircases and ramps, letting the noise subside until it was only a distant rumbling somewhere above. And somewhere below, too—the Sharkticon forces that had infiltrated the undercity were obviously climbing higher. The portion of the city that remained free was dwindling rapidly.

But so far the Wreckers were still within it. They passed through a double-vaulted set of doors and into the vast labyrinth that housed the Hall of Records. Files, computers, and consoles of every description were stacked everywhere—every medium imaginable, even old scrolls and paper. Wheeljack caught a glimpse of Alpha Trion's face; he could only imagine what it must feel like to be returning to the place where he had spent so much of his life. Now it seemed that life had reached its final chapter. Unless Alpha Trion had one more trick up his sleeve . . .

"What's the plan?" Ultra Magnus asked.

"There must be something here about the Quintessons," Maccadam said. "Something we can use to destroy them. Something—"

He broke off as he saw Alpha Trion's face.

"We can't destroy them," the ancient bot said.

Wheeljack was shocked. "Why not?"

"It's far too late for that."

"Then why did you say we had to come here?" Maccadam asked.

"Because there is something we can do to wound them."

SHOCKWAVE'S ELEVATOR REACHED THE BASE OF THE tower and kept plunging through several more levels. As soon as it stopped, Shockwave leaped out, racing down metal corridors into the basement beneath the High Council Pavilion, which had to be nothing but wreckage by now. He could hear the roar of the Sharkticon machines above him. But up ahead were the double doors to which he alone had the key and that gave way to the vault that housed the relics that might yet save him. The Forge of Solus Prime . . . the Star Saber . . . several canisters of Tox-En . . . and several other weapons that might be used to turn the Sharkticon tide. His fingers flew over code keys. There was a buzzing noise, and the doors slid open. He entered.

TYRANNICON GAZED AT THE DEVASTATED CITY. HIS NEW flagship was almost as good as his old one, only slightly smaller. But its crew was no less eager to please than the ones who had been destroyed in Omega Supreme's ambush. The manta ray craft smashed its way through Cybertron's buildings, grinding the smaller ones beneath its treads, punching straight through the walls of the larger ones so that they collapsed around the ship like a falling house of cards. Gunners all along the length of the hull were having a field day blasting fleeing Cybertronians. Tyrannicon suspected that most of the city's population was now hiding underground, but that wouldn't save them. His Sharkticons were closing in from all sides. What was left of the garrison kept fighting, but their defense was as hopeless as it was heroic.

That was when an enormous purple and green bot leaped down onto the hull of the flagship and put its foot straight through the bridge. Half the bridge crew was crushed instantly; glass and metal flew everywhere as Tyrannicon hastily leaped aside. The bot began to tear its way into the flagship, screaming that it was Devastator and assuring them that they were all going to die. Tyrannicon had to admit that the bot seemed to be specifically designed to rip things apart; he suspected that it might have been involved in construction before the war. But he wasn't hanging around to study it; he moved aside to let several squads of marines past and then stepped out onto the hull and leaped onto the ground, rolling clear. Gunfire echoed from within the craft that had been his replacement flagship; the ship trundled forward out of control, swaying from side to side while Devastator tossed marines out the portholes. Tyrannicon watched it go.

Then he took out a remote control and hit a button.

A huge explosion shredded the erstwhile flagship; what was left was tossed about fifty feet into the air and landed on its back with a sickening crunch. Tyrannicon smiled the smile of a bot to whom collateral damage was an alien concept. If Devastator was still intact in the smoking wreck, they could dig him out later and harvest the scraps. He strode away.

But as he did so, the wreckage started to rumble. Before Tyrannicon could process what was happening, several smaller vehicles erupted from the remnants of the flagship and sped toward him. Tyrannicon realized that Devastator had separated into his component bots, which were now busy smashing their way through buildings and rubble as they zeroed in on him.

As far as the Constructicons were concerned, Tyrannicon was going to be easy meat; Scrapper flashed his lights, and his fellow bots flawlessly rolled into an arrowhead formation as they closed on Tyrannicon's position, sounding their horns and sirens while they circled Tyrannicon.

"Okay, let's put this fish-bot down!" Scrapper broadcast.

"You got it, buddy!" Mixmaster responded. "Do it by the numbers."

The Constructicons picked up speed, broke their formation, and started driving figure eights around Tyrannicon, dashing in and out, conducting hit-and-run attacks against the mighty general's imposing form. Tyrannicon was surprised such heavy vehicles could move so fast; the next moment, Mixmaster sped past him, spraying a blue adhesive gel from his cauldron. Tyrannicon pulled free, but in the time it took him to do so, Hook snared him by the armor, ground forward, and smashed him into a nearby building while Long and Scavenger closed in from the sides. They whirled and dumped debris and fuel down onto Tyrannicon, whereupon Frontloader streaked by and ignited the pile. Tyrannicon, wreathed in flames, emerged from the debris with his fire extinguishers working overtime and a furious expression on his face. He had to admit he was impressed with his adversaries' skills; the close order with which they fought was a sight to behold even if they were trying their best to eliminate him. He shook his war trident in their direction.

"Vermin," he said. "All you've done is get me angry."

If he was trying to provoke the Constructicons, he succeeded. They converged on him, slamming on their brakes and converting from their vehicle modes back into robot form as they trained their lasers on their target.

"Give it up, scaly," sneered Bonecrusher. "This is a fight you can't win."

Tyrannicon answered by doing a ten-meter somersault, landing in the middle of their line, after which he tripped Hook with his war trident and then grabbed Mixmaster by his arm and executed a throw that propelled the Constructicon into a nearby building. Then he did the same to Scrapper, using him as a club to send Scavenger sprawling. The latter was trying to get a clear shot and wasn't succeeding. Scrapper couldn't believe how bad this fish thing was making them look.

"That's it!" he yelled. "You asked for it! Constructicons to me!" The bots seamlessly synced together, each one taking on the requisite component as they shifted back into the giant green-and-purple chrome form that was—

"DEVASTATOR!" yelled the enormous bot, bellowing his name as he slammed both fists into the ground with a seismic force that sent Tyrannicon sprawling. Devastator then proceeded to snap a massive antenna off the top of a nearby building and hurl it like a spear at Tyrannicon, who ducked at the last moment. He was showered with shrapnel as the projectile smashed into a nearby wall and exploded. But as Devastator closed in, Tyrannicon snagged an oil conduit with his trident and directed a geyser of fuel upward, temporarily blinding the lumbering titan and enraging him even further.

"A LITTLE OIL WON'T STOP ME, PUNY BOT!" Devastator sputtered.

Maybe not, Tyrannicon thought, but it might buy some breathing room. While Devastator flooded his optics with cleansing fluid, the Sharkticon leader turned and sprinted down an alley, smashing against buildings almost at random. To an unwitting observer, it might have looked like he was damaged beyond repair, that he was malfunctioning so badly that he was unable to run straight. Devastator's vision cleared just in time to see Tyrannicon turn a corner and vanish from sight, but the size of the bots meant that the head start wouldn't last for long. Devastator strode after the Sharkticon leader, following him into an area of the city where the buildings crowded particularly closely. Yet getting to grips with Tyrannicon proved to be more difficult than expected; Tyrannicon kept turning, dashing down alley after alley, his path so unpredictable that it bordered on the random, even though it was anything but that. Tyrannicon danced an acrobatic circle around the enraged giant, finishing with a series of leaps that brought him to the top of a nearby roof. Devastator saw him and turned to grab him.

"NOW YOU ARE MINE," he said, but that was when the charges Tyrannicon had been placing along his route all detonated simultaneously. This time the gambit

THEME: TRANSFORMERS: RETRIBUTION 349

worked perfectly as several skyscrapers collapsed on Devastator, burying him beneath thousands of tons of metal. Tyrannicon breathed a sigh of relief as he scanned the rubble, and then he clambered down. But as he reached the ground—

"Congratulations," said a voice.

Tyrannicon looked down to see a bot with batlike wings, very sharp teeth, and a devious smile on his face.

"I'm Ratbat," he said. "Commander of the city garrison."

"*What* garrison?" Tyrannicon said. He raised his trident—

"Wait," said Ratbat.

"Better talk fast."

"To continue your massacre would merely deprive you of valuable slaves." Tyrannicon frowned. "You *are* going to need slaves, aren't you?"

"Some," the Sharkticon leader replied. "Are you volunteering?"

"I'm volunteering to order the garrison to surrender."

"And what else?"

"That's not enough?"

"Not really."

"What if I could tell you where Shockwave is?"

"What about the bot they call Alpha Trion?"

"Him, too." Ratbat hesitated, thinking fast. "There's two places left that matter. All you have to do is check them both."

Tyrannicon grinned. "Are you willing to bet your life on that?"

WHEELJACK FELT ILL. THE ARCHIVES CONTAINED ALL THE information ever compiled across the long history of Cybertron: every scrap of data, every particle of knowledge. Regardless of their differences, all

Cybertronians had the same history—the history that was held in these rooms.

Now Alpha Trion was proposing to erase it all forever. But Ultra Magnus and Maccadam had both agreed to his proposal immediately. The team of Wreckers had gotten rapidly to work, rigging charges throughout the labyrinth. When they detonated, they weren't just going to destroy the Hall of Records; they would take half of Iacon with them.

Not that there would be much left of Iacon by now, anyway. They could hear the rumble of the Sharkticon juggernauts above them, drawing ever closer. Alpha Trion had declared that he would sooner forswear Primus than allow the Quintessons to capture the knowledge of the Cybertronian people. No one had disagreed. All of them knew it was their own deaths they were undertaking. They would perish in the explosion; there was no doubt about that. And Wheeljack had to admit that at this point he wouldn't have it any other way. Better to die cleanly than live under Quintesson slavery or, even worse, be given to the Sharkticons as playthings. Wheeljack attached one final charge, then went back to join the others in the main hall. On the way, he met Springer.

"Looks like this is it," he said to his old comrade.

Springer grinned wanly. "You always knew we weren't going to die of natural causes."

"Didn't expect it to be under these circumstances, though."

"Hey, if we're going to go out, we may as well do it with a bang."

"You got that right, friend. It's been an honor."

"Maybe there'll be an afterlife where we can kick Decepticon tail forever."

But Wheeljack wasn't really in the mood for jokes.

They reached the main hall to find the others waiting.

"Everything ready?" Ultra Magnus asked.

Everybody nodded. Ultra Magnus picked up the detonator, but Alpha Trion shook his head.

"The responsibility is mine," he said. Ultra Magnus handed him the detonator. Alpha Trion took it and looked at all those gathered.

"I want to thank all of you," he said quietly. "And seek your pardon that it's come to this."

"There's no need to say that," Ultra Magnus told him.

"I disagree," Alpha Trion said. He flipped the fail-safe off the detonator. But just as he was about to hit the button, the doors to the Hall of Records flew open.

Shockwave stood there, several bodyguards crowding behind him.

"What do you think you're doing?" he yelled.

"Blowing this place sky high," Ultra Magnus replied.

"You're going to destroy our sacred Hall of Records?"

"Like you hold anything sacred," Rack n' Ruin snarled.

For once Shockwave had no quick rejoinder. Instead he seemed to be genuinely upset. He entered the room and looked around, his gaze flickering from database to database. When he spoke next, his voice approached the desperate.

"There must be something in here that can save us."

"All the history in the world cannot give us a future," Alpha Trion said.

Shockwave looked like he wanted to rip the Prime's head from his shoulders. "I should have guessed, Alpha Trion. Our people are being *wiped out*, and all you've got to dispense are more of your stupid aphorisms."

"You say that as though you think I'm the one who set all this in motion," Alpha Trion said calmly.

"You *did*, you senile idiot."

"Because I failed to persuade you to listen to me?"

"Because you emptied out the vault!" Shockwave turned to Ultra Magnus. "Where I've just come from! Do you realize what was in there? Artifacts of the Primes that might have allowed us to defeat the invasion!"

Ultra Magnus was impassive. "And how do you know Alpha Trion—"

"Because the records of the vault show it," Alpha Trion said. Everyone looked at him in astonishment. "It is true. I cast the artifacts in the vault into space long ago. Back when the Autobots left the planet and the Decepticons took over. Because I could not allow such a precious cargo to fall into the hands of a maniac like Shockwave."

The scientist could do little more than splutter furiously. "And now you have consigned this planet to maniacs like—"

"Me," said a voice.

Tyrannicon stood in the doorway, scores of Sharkticons crowding behind him. The invasion leader was battered and covered with the oil of those he'd killed. He looked every inch the conqueror of Cybertron. The fact that the diminutive Ratbat was standing beside him did not diminish that image in the slightest.

"I suggest you surrender now," Tyrannicon said.

Ultra Magnus shook his head. "We will fight you to the last—"

"You *are* the last," Tyrannicon told him. He gestured at Ratbat. "This bot has already been kind enough to surrender the city to me."

"You traitor," Shockwave shrieked.

"On the contrary," said Ratbat, "*you* are the traitor. Tyrannicon has made me temporary governor of all Cybertron."

"The key word in that sentence is *temporary*," Ultra Magnus muttered.

"Wait a second," said Ratbat. "Let's not be too hasty."

Alpha Trion held up the detonator. "Long live Cybertron," he said.

And pressed the button.

Chapter Forty-one

AUTOBOTS AND DECEPTICONS WERE HUDDLED IN THE crippled *Nemesis*, firing from open hatches and portholes. The ship was floating right now but slowly taking on water through the holes it had sustained during the crash. It wasn't going to stay above the surface for long. Nor was what remained of the city, for that matter. The tops of a few buildings still protruded above the surface; Sharkticon heavy guns had been set up there and were blasting down at the Cybertronians. Superion stood next to the spaceship, up to his waist in water, firing wildly as Sharkticons crawled all over him in an effort to bring him down by sheer force of numbers. Gnaw's battle turtle was making a beeline for him. On top of the *Nemesis*, Kup, Rodimus, and Bumblebee were blazing away at it.

"Looks like this is it," Kup said.

"Never say die," said Rodimus.

Bumblebee chirped and beeped and pointed. Rodimus and Kup looked up to see—

"*The Ark*," Rodimus said.

Like a gigantic bird of prey, it roared down from the sky, evading the missiles that streaked in toward it. Though he should have been jubilant, Rodimus watched its approach with a sinking heart. He knew what Sideswipe was trying to do: get them off the planet with or without Optimus. But it was a suicide run: The Ark was far less maneuverable than the Aerialbots. Already the guns on the city towers were tracking it, lining up their target. At this range they couldn't miss.

MEGATRON CONVULSED.

As soon as he slotted the device inside his chest, it began to consume him. It was as if his whole torso was on fire; heat radiated out along his arms and down his legs, rising up into his head, setting his brain alight.

He fell to the ground gasping, struggling to maintain his sanity.

"Megatron!" Optimus yelled.

"Stay back," Megatron gasped. He felt like he was fighting for his very life now, as if he was going to explode any second and scatter pieces of himself all over the room. Was this how Optimus had felt when he received his Matrix? No, Optimus had had it easy. Optimus always had it easy. Then again, Optimus had been given a real Matrix. Perhaps this really was a fake. For the first time it occurred to Megatron that he might have made a mistake, that he might be in his death throes even now. All of existence was shrinking to a single point, all his past and future bound up in a single present moment— but in that point was clarity. This *wasn't* the Decepticon Matrix of Leadership.

It was something else entirely.

Suddenly it all made sense. All the runes, all the cave drawings, everything that had happened up till now; all of it clicked into place like the turning of a great key. This was his moment. He was on this planet for a reason. The Quintessons had tampered with Matrix technology, but in so doing they had created a device whose purpose even they didn't fully understand, a device whose repercussions would shake the universe. Insight blasted through Megatron's head, practically frying his circuitry, as he took it all in: The cosmos spun around him, the eons spread out before him, the epic struggle between Primus and Unicron that had spawned the Thirteen, that had given rise to the Cybertronians themselves.

As well as the Sharkticons.

For Aquatron was one of the lost Cybertronian colonies, after all.

Only it had never shaken off its Quintesson rule and thus had been lost to history. The knowledge was as clear to Megatron as if Unicron himself had spoken in his ear. Or Primus—he no longer cared who was saying what, because the heat in him was intensifying further. He was melting from deep within. His steel was turning molten. From somewhere far away he heard Optimus yelling at him to remove the abomination from his chest, and he dimly wondered what Optimus was referring to. He saw Xeros frantically punching buttons on the console and laughed to see such flailing impotence. He saw the roof fall in, saw the Sharkticons dropping into the room.

Then he couldn't see a thing—the object in his chest was glowing so brightly that it was blinding him. Or maybe his optics were gone. Maybe he would never see again. Something was building up inside him, wreaking havoc on his circuits, rewiring his alt-modes, playing hell with his mind, building up until he couldn't take it anymore, until he was ready to—

Energy poured out of him with a clap of thunder that shattered every screen in the room, hurling the Sharkticons, Optimus, and Xeros back into the walls. For a moment all was still.

Then Megatron slowly got to his feet and laughed.

For now he was reconstructed.

Vibrant blue and red had become the blue-purple of this planet's people. His chest plate now resembled the head of a giant open-mouthed Sharkticon, frozen in an open snarl, showing row after row of teeth. His armor had been augmented by razor-sharp scales that glittered even in the dim light of this chamber. Huge fins protruded from his forearms, and his eyes glowed a horrifying deep sea green.

It was Optimus who broke the stunned silence.

"Megatron . . . ? Is that you?"

"Yes, librarian. It is I." Megatron crossed the room and took Optimus by the shoulders. Optimus looked at his old nemesis with a mixture of awe and fear, but as Megatron made contact with him, something happened: Optimus's Matrix stopped broadcasting gibberish. The Quintesson influence that had corrupted it dissolved like shadow before sunlight. Whatever steps the Curator was taking to control Optimus had failed, just as he had failed to anticipate Megatron's sudden mutation—a mutation driven by Megatron's own impulsiveness and arrogance. Optimus was about to thank Megatron when his old adversary reached out and placed his finger on his lips as though to hush him.

"I told you the power would be mine," he said. "Our conflict is at an end, Prime. Good-bye, my brother."

Before Optimus could react, Megatron hefted Optimus over his head and hurled him straight through the wall of the command center, sending him plunging to his doom down the endless shaft. Then he turned to Xeros, who backed away, a terrified expression on his face. Xeros had been ready to face death. But this was something far worse.

"Who . . . who are you?" the stunned scientist asked.

Megatron thought about it. He wasn't sure yet. All he was sure of was the new power coursing through his circuitry. He felt as if he were one with all the life on Aquatron. Perhaps that was what bots meant when they said *until we are all one*. Perhaps they'd been talking about him all along. He saw another wave of Sharkticons pour into the room through the ripped-up ceiling, heard Xeros ordering them to kill him.

"No," Megatron said, turning to them.

The Sharkticons stopped, stared, and then knelt, row after row.

Xeros could not believe what he was seeing. The programming he and the Curator had created to control the Aquatronians had collapsed. The law of unintended consequences had played the cruelest joke of all. No longer would Sharkticons or any of the other people of this planet worship faraway Quintesson gods.

Because now their god was far closer.

"You can't," he heard himself say. "It's not possible! You're not supposed to—"

"Don't talk to me of *possible*," Megatron said. "Instead talk to me of last words."

"What?"

"And here I was expecting something more eloquent." Megatron stepped out of the way and let his Sharkticons rush forward and eat their fill.

OPTIMUS PLUMMETED DOWN THE SHAFT. HE WAS TOO far from either side to grab hold of anything; all he could see was blackness beneath him, and all he could hear was the whistle of the wind as he fell. So this is it, he thought. After all this time, Megatron had been right and he had been wrong. Though he hated to think of what Megatron would do with his newfound power. The only solace Optimus could take was that the Matrix was at last free of Quintesson manipulation. In his last moments, he let his mind go, basked in the Matrix, gave himself over to it completely . . .

And all at once his mind filled with light.

He was back on Iacon in the Chamber of the High Council, only it was the way the chamber had looked millions of years ago, before the Golden Age. It was as if he was gazing at one of the pictures he'd seen in the ancient tomes of the archives, but now he was inside that image, a part of it. Thirteen shadowy figures were seated in thrones around the room. Optimus decided they were there to show his Spark the way. All his fear was swept aside in the consolation that at least his experience would be added to the ancient collection, his advice would inform future leaders, future Primes . . .

It is not your time, Optimus Prime.

The voice came from all around. Optimus saw that the thirteen figures had vanished. All that was visible was a glowing light, and out of that light came a voice he had heard only once before, back at the core of Cybertron . . .

You have yet to fulfill your destiny. It is not yet time for you to pass on this burden. You are exactly where you should be.

"But—"

Now go. Until all are one.

Optimus opened his eyes to find that he was still tumbling down the shaft. He'd hoped that he'd be miraculously transported elsewhere, but there were no miracles to be found here. Just the strength to live or die as required. Now the bottom of the shaft was dimly visible, rushing up toward him. At the last moment, Optimus realized it wasn't solid at all.

It was water.

Even so, the impact would have shattered a lesser bot. He plunged into it, sinking downward, away from a metal hull that stretched out in all directions—and he realized in that moment that the island that he'd been in and that housed the capital city of Hydratron was actually nothing of the kind; it was a huge machine that floated on the surface of the lake. But topographical niceties didn't matter right now. What mattered was that he was continuing to sink fast. As he struggled to get his bearings, he turned to see an enormous pair of jaws closing in on him.

THE SHARKTICONS THAT HAD SURVIVED THE FALL AND chewed their way into the command center fell to their knees in front of their new god-king. They chanted that they had been delivered, that their liberator had come down from the stars and set them free of the yoke of Quintesson oppression. But most of all they chanted a single name:

"MEGATRON! MEGATRON! MEGATRON!"

Megatron basked in the adulation for a few moments. It was even better than it was with the Decepticons, because their loyalty was so total. There was no Starscream among these subjects. None of them were plotting against him. They were ready to do whatever he ordered without question.

"Rise," he said. They rose as one. "You owe your freedom to me and me alone. And now you will serve me and me alone."

"As you command!" they replied in unison. Megatron smiled. With both Sharkticons and Decepticons at his back and Optimus no longer a factor, he would lead an army that could subjugate entire galaxies. A new force for a new age, ruled by Megatron and Megatron alone. But first things first; he had to subjugate Aquatron, and then he would complete the invasion of Cybertron under his own rule. With the space bridge open, he wouldn't need to rely on overambitious lieutenants like Shockwave anymore.

"What are your orders?" the Sharkticons asked.

"My orders are to shut up for just a moment," Megatron told them. He studied the various readouts in the control center. The screens were all broken now, but enough of the instrument readouts remained to show him how Xeros had been orchestrating the Sharkticons' movements from this location. It was like being handed a gift from Unicron himself. Megatron used the command override provided to him by the Sharkticon Matrix and proceeded to issue new orders to his fishy legions. He listened over the speakers with satisfaction as the word spread. There was only one being that could stop him now. Megatron worked the controls of the elevator car to bring it adjacent to a wall. A door opened. He turned to his new minions.

"Find the Curator and kill him!"

"As you command, lord!" Sharkticons stumbled over one another in a mad rush to fulfill the wishes of their new ruler. Megatron decided to stay in the inner sanctum so that he could monitor the situation. It wouldn't surprise him at all if the Curator still had a few tricks left to play. Megatron knew better than to underestimate an enemy who had been planning for this moment for millions of years. Particularly since none of the Sharkticons knew where their former leader was.

The now-deceased Xeros wasn't any help, either. Megatron hadn't bothered to torture him because he figured there were more reliable ways to get information. After the Sharkticons' devouring of every part of the Quintesson except his head, Megatron had personally searched through the circuitry in his skull only to discover that he hadn't known where the bridge was or that the Curator had wiped that information from his memory banks. The Curator kept his operations very compartmentalized indeed. But the bridge couldn't be far away. And when the Sharkticons found it, Megatron would be heading there, too. In the meantime, he worked the consoles and gave orders to Sharkticons all across Hydratron, humming as he did so an old song he'd learned as a fighter in the gladiator maze beneath Kaon:

Come out, come out, wherever you are . . .

KUP COULDN'T BELIEVE HIS EYES. THE SHARKTICON cannons aimed at the Ark were suddenly lowering their trajectory, all of them pointing at a single target. For the briefest of moments he thought that it was Superion—that the giant robot was about to wither under the rain of laser blasts—but then he realized they had in mind something entirely different.

Commander Gnaw.

As the lasers struck him, he and his gigantic sea turtle caught fire. Kup doubted he even knew what had hit him. The Sharkticon subcommander disintegrated entirely; the guns switched off, and Kup realized that all the Sharkticons were making themselves scarce: swimming away, diving beneath the surface, withdrawing from the fight. Victory had been theirs for the taking, and they were throwing it away like they no longer cared.

"Doesn't make any sense," Rodimus said.

"Who's arguing?" Kup said as the Ark fired its retros and floated in.

OPTIMUS SAT ASTRIDE THE SILVER BACK OF THE MASSIVE whale-bot as it dived deep into the sea. Moments before he had thought he was a goner. But at the last moment, the creature had swerved aside, losing all interest in consuming him. Optimus had grabbed onto one of its fins, hoping to hitch a ride back to the island above him.

But instead the creature began talking to him.

"Who are you?" it asked. The voice was deep, reverberating through the vibration in its metal, but it sounded like it was talking in Optimus's ear anyway. He realized he could communicate back through radio.

"My name is Optimus Prime," he said. "Who are *you*?"

"My name is Leviacon." There was a pause, then: "But I did not know that until you just asked it. I have the strangest feeling that I just woke up."

"The Quintessons enslaved you."

"The who?"

"Listen," Optimus said. "What are you doing down here, anyway?"

"Swimming," Leviacon said. "It's what I do best. In fact, I never want to do anything else."

"I mean, what were your orders?"

"Orders?"

"Someone told you to be here, Leviacon. The same someone who controlled you up until a few minutes ago. I need you to try to remember."

"I seem to remember . . . something about defending a place. Somewhere below here."

Optimus thought about that. "How far down is the lake bed?"

"Two miles."

It all made sense now. Beneath the lake bed was a far better place for the space bridge infrastructure than in the floating city overhead. It would be much more secure; even if a bomb entirely destroyed the city-island, the space bridge would be safe. And two miles of water meant that creatures like the one he was riding could provide an additional layer of defense. He wondered why these bots weren't under Megatron's control now. Perhaps because the Decepticon leader hadn't known about them, hadn't given them any orders.

"Do you mind taking me down there?" he asked.

"No problem," said the Leviacon, and plunged into the depths.

Chapter Forty-two

WHEELJACK BRACED HIMSELF AS ALPHA TRION HIT THE detonation button. *It's been real*, he thought to himself . . .

And realized he was still thinking.

Alpha Trion hit the button again. But once again nothing happened.

Tyrannicon laughed and held up a second device. "Ever heard of a wireless jammer?" he asked.

"How did you hack our frequencies?" Shockwave muttered.

"Same way I hacked everything else, Shockwave— thanks to you. My masters have been studying this planet's datanet by looking over your shoulder. Surely you've realized that by now."

"You're lying," Shockwave said. "Ratbat gave you the codes."

"You want to blame all this on *me*?" Ratbat asked.

"I can certainly try."

"You're in denial," Springer said.

"I know traitors when I see them."

Tyrannicon smiled mirthlessly. "Ratbat may have given me the keys to the city, but you gave us the keys to the planet, Shockwave."

Ultra Magnus turned to Shockwave. "Don't you get it? You've destroyed us all."

"And here I was thinking Alpha Trion was the one trying to blow us up."

"He was trying to make sure our precious data didn't fall into enemy hands," said Maccadam. "Which he wouldn't have had to do if you hadn't let these monsters in."

"And I suppose that's the *other* reason you've lost," Tyrannicon said. "You Cybertronians just can't stop bickering among yourselves, can you? A bunch of children is what you are."

"Go slag yourself," Rack n' Ruin retorted eloquently.

"Funny you should say that," said Tyrannicon. "Because that's what I've been turning your planet into. Now are you going to surrender, or would you rather go down in a blaze of glory?"

"I think you know the answer to that," Ultra Magnus said. The Wreckers brought their guns up—

But as they did so, the Sharkticons around Tyrannicon suddenly went haywire.

Two of them leaped at Tyrannicon, who easily countered their blows before finishing them off with his fists. Some of the others started attacking one another. Others just ran in all directions. As the Wreckers shot down the ones dashing forward into the Hall of Records, Tyrannicon and Ratbat took to their heels, sprinting back up the stairs. Strategic retreats were an option of last resort, but having one's forces lose it so completely certainly qualified. The Wreckers got off a couple rounds in Tyrannicon's direction, but he was gone too fast for anything to strike home decisively.

Then the Hall of Records was silent once more.

"Will someone tell me what just happened?" Springer asked.

"I'm not exactly sure," Wheeljack replied.

"Well," said Rack n' Ruin, "whatever it is, it's still going on upstairs."

He was right. The combat in the city above them had started back up, but the only audible weapons were Sharkticon ones. It sounded like a total free-for-all.

"Primus has intervened to save us," Alpha Trion said slowly.

Wheeljack looked skeptical. "What, you mean he's risen up out of the core?"

"Nothing so direct. We can't pretend to understand how he works, save that it is as mysterious as it is miraculous. But I sense long chains of events that stretch across this galaxy and back."

"So in other words, you have no idea," Rack n' Ruin said.

"You don't talk like that to a Prime," Ultra Magnus warned.

"He can say whatever he wants to," said Alpha Trion. "He's earned that right."

"Hey," Springer said, "where's Shockwave?"

They looked around. There was no sign of him.

Maccadam sighed. "He must have fled deeper into the archives."

"Well, what are we waiting for?" Wheeljack asked. "Let's go after him."

They did just that, fanning out as they went, but Alpha Trion already knew they were just going through the motions. They weren't going to find Shockwave. This place was riddled with secret passages, and Shockwave probably knew at least half of them. No, the scientist had gotten away again, had once more managed to salvage the thing that mattered most to him: his own hide. But as to whether he was going to salvage the overall situation on Cybertron, not if the Wreckers had anything to say about it. Fittingly, it was Ultra Magnus who called the search off.

"Let's get back up to the surface," he said. "No sense in staying here."

THE SURFACE WAS THE LAST PLACE TYRANNICON WANTED to be.

"Take me to Shockwave's tower," he told Ratbat.

"I think we might stand a better chance of survival in the undercity," that bot replied.

"There is no *we*," Tyrannicon said. "But *you'll* stand a better chance of survival if you do exactly what I say. Now, where's the best route to the tower?"

Ratbat showed him. It wasn't that far, particularly since Ratbat had the necessary security clearances to take shortcuts and avoid setting off the automatic defenses. He led Tyrannicon through some maintenance ducts that once had serviced the Energon pools and then headed beneath the vaults whose contents—or lack thereof—had caused Shockwave so much anguish. In short order they were in the basements below the tower. All the guards had fled. The Sharkticons hadn't reached the place yet. Tyrannicon was trying to raise his officers on the com-link, but he hadn't had any success. His mind was working overtime trying to figure out what was going on.

"Shockwave's elevator," he said. "Where is it?"

"Right here," said Ratbat. Tyrannicon stepped in and then stopped Ratbat from following him.

"I'll take it from here," he said.

"Are you going to kill Shockwave?" Ratbat asked.

Tyrannicon looked puzzled for a moment but then started to laugh. "I'm not interested in him. Wherever he's gone, he's nowhere near his tower. He'll have made himself scarce. And I suggest you do the same."

Ratbat nodded agreement as the elevator door slid shut. As the elevator carried Tyrannicon upward, he wondered why he hadn't killed the slimy little bot. Was he starting to go soft? More likely, he had too many other things to worry about. He needed more data. That his Sharkticons would mutiny . . . it was unthinkable. But then again, it *couldn't* be mutiny. It was something far worse. They'd gone absolutely berserk. The elevator doors opened, and he emerged onto the roof of the tower, the city stretching below him. What he saw confirmed his worst suspicions. His once-great fleet was a complete shambles. Manta rays were on fire everywhere, and the ones that weren't were busy turning their guns against one another, ramming one another, running down Sharkticon platoons as though they weren't all on the same side. They were on no one's side now. Someone had messed with their programming.

But there was no one on this planet capable of doing that.

That meant that someone had sent an override across the space bridge. Perhaps the Curator had been overthrown by Xeros. It seemed unlikely, but even if it was so, why would it have changed the basic strategy? An override transmitted over the space-time distortion of a space bridge was incredibly dangerous. Even if someone back on Aquatron was attempting to assert control over the Sharkticons here, he ought to have known better than to try it from halfway across the galaxy. It could lead to exactly the pandemonium that he was witnessing. As far as Tyrannicon could tell, he was the only member of his army who was not affected.

That didn't surprise him, because the truth of the matter was that he *wasn't* conditioned: his leading of military campaigns depended on his maintaining complete tactical initiative. He would have been useless to the Quintessons as a mindless slave. Instead, he was their finest creation. Whereas the Sharkticons had been a race forced into servitude, Tyrannicon was the product of Quintesson science, engineered to be the leader of a captive race. Xeros might have doubted his reliability, but that was his fear talking, for the Curator never had. No, at least until now Tyrannicon had been utterly reliable, literally built to lead Sharkticon armies wherever the Quintessons might deem. That didn't mean he *liked* the Quintessons, of course. He didn't have to like them. He just recognized strength when he saw it.

But right now he saw chaos all around him.

Tyrannicon knew where his duty lay. Cybertron was no longer the priority. As he suspected, the roof of the tower contained Shockwave's personal ship, loaded with enough fuel to reach anywhere on the planet. And Tyrannicon knew exactly where he needed to go.

ULTRA MAGNUS AND HIS TEAM SAW SHOCKWAVE'S SHIP roar overhead and speed off toward the south. They had a clear view of Tyrannicon at the controls.

"Maybe *he* killed Shockwave," Wheeljack said.

"I doubt it," said Ultra Magnus. "I suspect he's got other things on his mind."

The Wreckers had made it back to the surface of Iacon fairly easily. It was straightforward enough to keep a low profile while they snuck out, since everyone was more than a little preoccupied. Crazed Sharkticons continued to fight Decepticons and one another, but their numbers were thinning rapidly. Most of the city was burning. The only structure that didn't seem to have sustained much damage was Shockwave's tower. The Wreckers watched from the now-deserted southern wall as the stolen ship vanished over the horizon.

"Where do you think he's going?" Springer asked.

Wheeljack pulled a piece of a Sharkticon mace out of his armor while he mulled it over. Truth be told, he was just as confused as everybody else.

"It doesn't make any sense. They had us all dead to rights."

For the first time that day Alpha Trion actually smiled. "Their plan to make our world theirs failed. That's all we need to know for now. The rest will surely reveal itself in due time."

"Speaking of time," Springer said, "right now we've got to get out of here before the Deceptigoons regroup and come looking for a fight."

Ultra Magnus's arms transformed into two laser cannons as he prepared to take point. "Exactly," he said. "We can't stay here much longer. Let's roll."

That was when Springer noticed something.

"Hey," he asked, "has anybody seen Rack n' Ruin?"

SHOCKWAVE DIDN'T BELIEVE IN LUCK, BUT HE HAD TO admit that he'd been more than a little fortunate to stay alive so far. He had no idea what had happened to the invasion, but it was obviously falling apart all over the place. Something had gone badly wrong with the Quintesson plan; his relief at that fact was mitigated only by the knowledge that they'd played him like a fiddle. He was too much a scientist to remain in denial about that; obviously, his attempt to plumb the secrets of Vector Sigma had been an overreach. The worst of it was that Vector Sigma was *mobile* . . . He had spent long years tracking the computer down and finding a way to freeze it in place, but he was under no illusions that the catastrophe that had shaken Cybertron almost certainly would have allowed Vector Sigma to retreat farther into the depths of the planet.

Still, all wasn't lost. The Sharkticons were beaten, and he hoped there were still enough Decepticons for him to pick up where he'd left off before the invasion: in control of the planet. As he approached his tower, he contemplated his next steps. First he'd order a search and destroy mission on Ultra Magnus before he could get too far from the city. Maybe he could even recapture Alpha Trion and resume his experiments, albeit along more straightforward lines. This time he would focus purely on that Prime. He wouldn't try to hook him up to anything. Nothing fancy; he'd just take him apart and find out what made him tick. As he rounded a corner and walked toward his tower, he saw that it was virtually undamaged. The shells had left scars on the walls, but undoubtedly all the laboratories inside were still intact. Shockwave practically rubbed his hands together with glee; as long as he had his research, life was going to be all right. He headed in toward his tower.

Which suddenly lit up like a flaring star.

RACK N' RUIN HAD BEEN BUSY. WHILE HE AND THE Wreckers had been searching the vaults for Shockwave, he'd taken the liberty of collecting the explosives with which they'd rigged the place. And then on the way out, while everybody had been preoccupied with rogue Sharkticons, he had managed to split off from the group and head someplace else entirely. After all, it would be a shame to let good bombs go to waste when there were still Decepticons that needed destroying.

One Decepticon in particular.

Of course he knew that the honorable Ultra Magnus would never have given him this chance at revenge if he had just come out and asked for it. Assassination just wasn't the Autobot way. Sure, killing a Decepticon in a fair fight was smiled upon and even encouraged, but at their core they eschewed trickery and low blows. Funny how a little time in Shockwave's lab could change a robot's perspective on the world. He didn't expect anyone else to understand. No doubt about it, this was one of those cases where it was better to do it and ask forgiveness later. He hummed to himself as he thumbed the detonator's safety off and hit the button.

FOR A MOMENT, SHOCKWAVE'S TOWER SEEMED TO RISE into the air like a giant rocket, only to crumple back and collapse in on itself, coming down like a huge house of cards. Debris blasted across Shockwave, smashing him to the ground. All he could hear was ringing and all he could see was dust, and when that cleared, there was no tower left, just a huge pile of rubble. Any other Decepticon in Shockwave's position probably would have gone insane with rage at that point, but Shockwave was nothing if not dispassionate. This was a minor setback, no more. After all, another minute and he would have been inside the tower; he'd be dead under all those rocks.

But he was still alive. He still had time. Time to rebuild, time to plot. Time to devise new ways of making the Autobots suffer. And suffer they would.

ON HIS REAR VIEWSCREENS, TYRANNICON CAUGHT A glimpse of a tremendous explosion back at Iacon. Getting out of there had been a smart move. The place was probably total anarchy by now. He accelerated, flying at supersonic speed back toward the equator, trying not to look at the carnage unfolding beneath him: the plains littered with his Sharkticon dead and their burned-out war machines. He even wondered if the whole exercise had been a particularly elaborate Quintesson experiment; perhaps *he* was the one being experimented on. It certainly felt like he was being messed with. Or had the Quintessons decided he was no longer worthy? The mere idea made him almost crazy with rage. He wondered what he would find when he went back through the space bridge and returned to Aquatron. Because whatever was happening there, one thing was certain.

Somebody was going to pay.

Chapter Forty-three

THE CURATOR'S WARTIME COMMAND POST HUNG UPSIDE down like a bubble on the ceiling of the massive underwater cave that housed the space bridge. Through one window could be seen that enormous hoop, still operational and glowing. The energy needed to maintain the link was a mere fraction of that required to switch it on. And thus far that energy continued to flow.

That was basically the only thing going right at the moment. Not only had the Curator lost contact with Xeros, the Sharkticons were having what the computer euphemistically called mechanical difficulties. That could mean anything, but before the Curator could get more details, the Sharkticon interface had gone offline as well.

As had Commander Gnaw. That was the point at which the Curator started to wonder whether it had been such a wise idea to send Tyrannicon through with the first wave. It would have been reassuring to have him by his side, ready to respond to whatever contingency was unfolding. Especially because the computer had just detected anomalies in the signals pulsating through the space bridge. They had been brief, but they seemed to coincide with loss of contact with the Sharkticons. The timing made the Curator more than a little uneasy. He could not quite put his scaly finger on it, but he sensed that the percentages that formed the basis of his operating assumptions might be a bit off.

But before he could order the computer to run full-scale diagnostics, the readouts from the gate indicated that a large number of beings were coming back through from Cybertron. That made no sense at all. No one was supposed to withdraw; all assault forces were to take up garrison duties on the conquered planet until further notice. The Curator turned from the computer to the wraparound window to get a better look, and much to his dismay, hundreds of angry Sharkticons poured through, diving into the water as they chanted and screamed in their brutal native tongue.

"KILL THE CURATOR! KILL THE CURATOR! KILL THE CURATOR!"

The Curator got the message. It was reinforced further as the Sharkticons began climbing out of the water, skittering up the cave walls by using their sharp claws, shooting their lasers at the command blister. The Curator watched in stupefied fascination as the heat began to smear the outer layers of that blister. It would take several minutes of sustained fire to melt it, but from the looks of the Sharkticons closing toward him along the cave roof, they weren't going to have the patience for that. They were going to do their best to tear their way in.

And that just wouldn't do.

The Curator's hands flew over the controls. A turret lowered from the command blister, swung in the direction of the Sharkticons, and began spraying them with sheets of plasma, burning them right off the wall. Even before the charred bodies could hit the water, the Curator was lowering the angle of the gun, raising the temperature of the water toward the boiling point, frying the Sharkticons still swimming around down there. They didn't seem to realize what was happening. So determined yet so very stupid, mused the Curator. He'd been so looking forward to the new Cybertronian slaves he would soon have—primitives, yes, but undeniably smarter than these fishy idiots he'd had to work with for so long. But now something had gone catastrophically wrong.

Naturally, that was the moment when the console chimed, alerting him to an incoming priority message from Quintessa. The Curator's subordinates might not have been answering him, but if he didn't answer his bosses, there was going to be real trouble. He composed himself as best he could and prepared to receive the signal. He found that proximity to the space bridge's energy made communicating with his masters on Quintessa easier, although in truth this was the one time he wouldn't have minded a little interference.

"Hail Quintessa!" the Curator said as his shadowy masters came into view. "I was not sure if I would be able to receive your transmission. We have been having some solar activity that—"

"How proceeds the invasion?" The voice was colder than tundra.

"Excellently well," the Curator said, trying to make his voice sound calmer than he was feeling.

"We detect plasma residue in the chamber behind you. Why is that?"

"Ah, yes, just a bit of light housecleaning. Nothing to worry about."

"It would appear you have been under attack. Have hostiles reached the bridge?" It was a different voice speaking now, a voice that never spoke . . .

"Mere target practice. A drill that got out of hand. But it turns out my defenses are working just fine; in fact, they are more than up to snuff." To his horror, the

Curator realized that he was starting to babble. He was almost glad when he was cut off:

"Inquirata. Our calculations show a greater than 85.3 percent chance that you are not telling us the entire story."

You got that right, thought the Curator. He took a deep breath. "A few minor missteps, nothing more. The conquest of Cybertron is almost complete. Why, an hour ago I received word from Tyrannicon that the assault on Iacon was under way."

"And what word have you received from him since?"

That was the decisive moment. The Curator could obfuscate and spin all he wanted; he could lie through omission and distort the truth to his heart's content, but a direct lie would register automatically on at least a hundred different instruments. There was only one way out. He began slowly switching frequencies, ad-libbing while the static grew overwhelming. "I regret to say it seems that the solar interference has returned," he said. "Another flare, most likely. I will report back as soon as I can." With that he switched off the transmission and disconnected the line.

And took a deep breath.

The Curator knew that his only chance for survival now lay in being able to call back with a message of total victory. And he would need to do it soon. He turned back to the diagnostics he was running. The story they told sent a chill down his spine. The Sharkticons' programming had been overridden. Someone had gained control of the replica Matrix and countermanded his orders. Had Xeros betrayed him? It seemed incredible, yet by this point nothing would have surprised the Curator. But whoever it was, they were in the city above, turning all systems against him.

There was only one way to stop them.

It was the greatest gamble of them all, but it was his only chance. With trembling hands, he removed the fail-safes and keyed in the activation codes. The schematic of the city above him appeared on a screen, its surface almost completely submerged by the defense mechanisms Xeros had set in motion, its corridors teeming with furious Sharkticons and fleeing Aquatronians. The latter were in a state of panic; they had no idea what was happening to the only city they had ever known.

Nor did they know that it was no city . . .

THERE WAS NOWHERE FOR THE ARK TO TOUCH DOWN, SO Sideswipe kept the retros flaring, letting the craft hover right above the sinking *Nemesis*. He scanned the flooded cityscape, but there was nothing to shoot at. All the Sharkticons had made themselves scarce, and it wasn't clear where they'd gone. Superion stood nearby, up to his waist in water, keeping a watchful eye on the flooded cityscape while Autobots scrambled onto the roof of the *Nemesis* and up ramps that were lowering from the Ark's belly. The bridge of the *Nemesis* promptly hailed the Ark.

"What do you think you're doing?" Starscream asked.

"Evacuating our people," Sideswipe said.

"Our ship is sinking! You can't just leave us here!"

"Can't I?"

"We have a truce, Autobot!"

"Do you see me violating it, Decepticon?"

"You might see *us* violating it if you don't help us." The guns on the *Nemesis* swiveled to aim at the Ark. "We need you to keep us from going under while we make engine repairs. Our truce ought to hold until we get off this confounded planet."

Sideswipe considered that. It was tempting to settle

things with the Decepticons here and now. He could drop a bomb straight on the center of the *Nemesis* and send it to kingdom come. Then again, he was so close that the resultant explosion might take down the Ark as well even if the Decepticons didn't have time to fire their guns. Besides, technically, Starscream was right. There *was* still a truce in place.

"All right," he said. "We'll help." He lowered the Ark still farther, extending clamps, going into docking mode, letting the Ark's engines run to keep the *Nemesis* level.

"What are you *doing*?" asked Sunstreaker, entering the bridge.

"What does it look like I'm doing? I'm keeping the *Nemesis* afloat while they make repairs."

"We should just leave 'em!"

"They'll do their best to shoot us down if we try that."

"Everybody stow this talk of shooting," Jazz said as he came onto the bridge, Ironhide just behind him. "For all we know, we might still need the Decepticons. I don't know what's up with the Sharkticons or this planet's defenses, but this may all be part of some Quintesson trap. We'll help the *Nemesis* until it gets back into orbit."

"Besides," said Prowl, "it's the honorable thing to do."

"And we know the Decepticons are all about honor," Sunstreaker said sarcastically.

Soundwave ignored him and kept scanning through the windows for any more signs of Sharkticons.

STARSCREAM PACED UP AND DOWN ON THE BRIDGE OF the *Nemesis*, yelling at the engineers belowdecks to hurry up with the repairs. The holes beneath the waterline had to be sealed, water had to be pumped out, and the second engine needed a replacement fuel line. But now that they weren't fighting Sharkticons, it wasn't going to be too long before they could head back to orbit. Deep-space travel might be a different story, but they could make more extensive repairs once they were off this planet. That meant that for now he wasn't going to fire at the Autobots and they weren't going to fire at him. Or so he hoped . . . The buzz of an incoming transmission sounded on the bridge. Soundwave put the call through.

It was Megatron.

Or at least it *looked* like Megatron. But it also looked like he'd had an accident in a teleport machine with at least a dozen Sharkticons. He was done up in Sharkticon colors now; his chest looked like a shark's jaws, and fins were studded down his back. But though his eyes were now deep green, his face was unmistakably that of Megatron. And when he spoke, it was with Megatron's trademark sneer.

"Starscream! Give me a status report!"

"Megatron . . . what happened to you?"

"What happened is that I am now lord of this planet! Where are the Autobots? Where is the *Nemesis*?"

"Just above where the Hall of Justice used to be. The Ark is docked to us, my lord. The Autobots are keeping us afloat while we make repairs."

"What?!? No!! Attack them immediately!"

"My lord, it's a delicate situation."

"I'll show you delicate, Starscream. Not only is Optimus no more, but I now control every Sharkticon in existence! I have only to give the signal and they will swarm to do my bidding!"

"Uh . . . really?"

"You dare doubt me? Now that they've killed their officers, they are loyal only to me. Stay there, fool. I'm coming up there to personally deal with the Autobots, and I'll be bringing about a thousand of my finest Sharkticons with me. Is that clear?"

It wasn't, but Starscream nodded anyway. The screen went blank. Starscream turned to Soundwave. "Did any of that make sense to you?"

"He is our lord and master," Soundwave said tonelessly.

He's also achieved a whole new level of crazy, Starscream thought. But he kept that one to himself.

Chapter Forty-four

MEGATRON HIT THE CONTROLS ON THE INNER SANCTUM; the elevator car began climbing back up the shaft. Loyal Sharkticons stood at attention throughout the car, but it was the ones Megatron couldn't see that he was most focused on. Now that he had them completely under his control, he was coordinating vast armies throughout the city. The search for the Curator had yet to bear fruit, but Megatron wasn't going to wait for that before he took care of the Autobots once and for all. Especially now that Optimus was finally out of the way. The Autobots were going to get the surprise of their life when Sharkticon legions began swarming all over them. It made perfect sense to Megatron that the final defeat of the Autobots would coincide so directly with the forging of his new identity. To think he had been so narrow-minded as to believe that his destiny was limited purely to the Decepticons! He would gather all the lost Cybertronian colonies across the galaxy under his sway and proudly wear his Sharkticon colors while he did so. He was just admiring those colors in the reflection of a shattered viewscreen when the voice of the Curator came over the loudspeaker.

"Megatron. I should have known."

"Nice of you to call," Megatron said. "Why don't you do my Sharkticons a favor and come out of your little hidey-hole?"

"Where is your friend Optimus Prime?"

"He met the same fate you're about to."

"I have to congratulate you, Megatron. You turned out to be far smarter than I gave you credit for. But you're still a fool if you think my downfall can be engineered through a few disloyal Sharkticons."

"A few? Try *all* of them. Why not surrender now? I promise to grant you a quick death."

"I was about to make you a similar offer," the Curator said. "But your insolence demands that your destruction be as unpleasant as possible."

"And when does this 'destruction' start?" Megatron asked.

"That would be now," said the Curator. Suddenly the elevator stopped climbing as though it had smashed against a barricade. The next moment, a huge slimy translucent tentacle slid through the hole in the wall through which Megatron had thrown Optimus. Megatron lunged backward instinctively as it grabbed a couple of Sharkticons and dragged them from the room. A second tentacle slithered in, and he blasted it to bloody flesh with his fusion cannon. But now the inner sanctum was rocking back and forth; more tentacles were tearing still more pieces from the walls. Megatron didn't hesitate. He raced forward and leaped out of the inner sanctum, his momentum carrying him across the elevator shaft and onto the wall. As he held on with his hands, it took him only a few seconds to use his razor-sharp fins to carve his way through, and during that time another tentacle grabbed him. He severed it with his ax and rolled into a corridor that was shaking like the worst kind of turbulence. Water was pouring down from the ceiling.

Except it wasn't water.

Megatron's sensors registered the high acidic composition even as he kept running down the corridor, blasting away at tentacles the whole time. The voice of the Curator echoed from a speaker at the passage's end.

"That's right, Megatron. Those are *digestive juices*. Most predators have to catch their prey, but *you're already inside this one*."

Megatron aimed his next shot at the speaker. Anything to shut the Curator up. He fired again, shooting his way into the next corridor, knowing that his only hope now was to keep moving.

STARSCREAM WAS JUST STARTING TO WONDER WHAT WAS taking Megatron so long when hordes of Sharkticons broke the surface and began swimming among the protruding city towers toward the *Nemesis* and Ark.

"Just as Megatron promised," Soundwave said.

Starscream keyed the ship's intercom. "All hands, stand by to board the Ark. The Sharkticons are on our side. Repeat, the Sharkticons are on our—" He broke off as the *Nemesis* shuddered as if it had been punched.

"What the slag was that?" he asked.

He got his answer as an enormous tentacle smashed through the bridge's window. He and Soundwave opened fire instinctively, their lasers cutting straight through it, and as the severed tentacle dropped to the floor of the bridge, pandemonium broke out in the waters around them. Masses of tentacles were appearing everywhere, sprouting from the sea, grabbing Sharkticons and pulling them down. The *Nemesis* began rising into the air; as Starscream dashed to the window, he could see it was caught on top of a gigantic balloon-like sac filled with unsavory-looking green fluid, which then gushed down onto more hapless Sharkticons, melting them almost instantly. Jazz's face appeared on a screen.

"Are you seeing what we're seeing?"

"This whole city's alive!" Starscream yelled. More balloon sacs were bloating into view everywhere; the tentacles continued to snatch up Sharkticons, throwing them into those rancid-looking pouches for quick digestion. Tendrils were coming at the Ark and the *Nemesis* from all sides now. The gunnery on both ships opened fire. Starscream turned to Soundwave.

"We need to get airborne right now!"

"And I'm telling you we can't!" For once Soundwave's voice was breaking from its customary monotone. "We lack the thrust to reach orbit!"

Starscream cursed. Whatever Megatron had been trying to do had gone horribly wrong. The only good news in all of this was that the Decepticon leader was assuredly dead, but Starscream knew he was unlikely to survive him by more than a few minutes. He blasted away at the tentacles trying to force their way inside the bridge, swearing as he did so that whatever happened, he wasn't going to end up getting digested alive. He'd put a laser through his own head first. He just wished he'd done the same thing to Megatron while he'd had the chance. Because the only chance they had now was that the Ark would prove strong enough to lift them both.

WHILE JAZZ AND SUNSTREAKER FIRED AT THE TENTACLES hammering on the bridge of the Ark, Sideswipe wasn't waiting around. The threats of Starscream paled by comparison to what the vast entity awakening around them could do. He rushed to the consoles, undocked from the *Nemesis,* and fired the engines. The ship rumbled as the thrusters came online. Sideswipe amped up the motors. The Ark began to shake violently, rising slowly into the air.

Way too slowly.

"Those Decepticons have clamped onto *us*!" Sunstreaker yelled.

That made perfect sense, Sideswipe thought. Starscream undoubtedly was figuring that if the Decepticons had to die, so would the Autobots. And if the Autobots made it out of here, so would the Decepticons. Still more tentacles hurled themselves against both the Ark and the *Nemesis*, grabbing both ships and pulling them downward. Jazz keyed the com-link.

"Jazz to Superion, do you—"

"I'm on it," said the great voice. Thunder rolled against the window as the giant bot flew past, firing at the waving tentacles, trying to sever enough of them so that the Ark could gain height. But then more tentacles slapped against Superion, and it was all he could do to keep himself out of trouble. Sideswipe put the ship's engines into the red and began to steer amid the writhing pseudopods. But the Ark was still way too low, and it was reaching the limit of its power. There was a terrible shuddering noise, and then the Ark-*Nemesis* combo began to sink inexorably toward the myriad maws below.

THE LEVIACON HAD DESCENDED ONLY HALF THE DISTANCE to the lake bed when Optimus felt ripples through the water; looking up, he caught sight of an amazing scene high above him: The base of the floating city was lighting up in a dazzling display of colors. Streams of bright light flowed out from it like star-filled tendrils. Optimus was almost lost in the dazzling display of color; it seemed for a moment that he was drifting free of the Leviacon, floating up toward a kaleidoscope of sheer beauty.

"Don't look directly at it!" the Leviacon said. "That's how it snares its prey!"

Optimus shook his head violently as though to clear

it and grasped onto the Leviacon more tightly as the great bot steepened the angle of its descent, plunging downward, just missing a gargantuan tentacle that swept by them and wrapped around a whole school of fish-bots. Optimus could almost hear their terrible screams as they were crushed mercilessly. And now he saw more tentacles coming in behind them.

"What are they?"

"It is the drinking doom," the Leviacon moaned. "The most ancient of all Aquatronians, that which was never meant to awaken! The Hydratron itself!"

"I thought Hydratron was the name of the city."

"The city *is* the Hydratron," the Leviacon said. "And now it hungers!"

Optimus adjusted his optics and finally got a clear view of the nightmare above. The city had transformed into the most monstrous of all jellyfish, a man-o'-war several miles across. Every creature caught inside it was surely just meat now. And its tentacles were coming down like the wrath of some ancient sea god.

"This is the Curator's work," Optimus snarled as the whale-bot's dive steepened into the vertical. It was all he could do to hold on as the Leviacon did its best to outrun those unfurling tentacles. Below him, he could see glowing lights: the entrance to an underwater cave.

AS STOMACH JUICES CHURNED DOWN CORRIDORS THAT were folding up and twisting like tangled intestines, Megatron's Sharkticons rallied to him, leaping onto him and clinging to him, serving as an outer shield of armor against the burning acid. They were literally dying to save him, yet their efforts would be in vain unless Megatron got out fast. He was blowing his way through corridors as quickly as he could, making for the nearest outer wall, but he wasn't going to get there in time. He felt like he was dissolving in his own arrogance; he'd believed for one shining moment that he was a god, only to find himself being digested inside the belly of a real one. The last of the melting Sharkticons fell away from him; he could feel the acid start to wash across him. He was going to die, yet in the back of his mind was a single fleeting thought, an imperative that had become second nature on the floors of the gladiator pits eons ago and a galaxy away: Never give up.

Never.

Megatron summoned all his remaining strength, making one last herculean effort, stumbling forward, ripping through the outer wall with his bare hands, letting a tidal wave of pure water pour in, an inundation that would have destroyed the old Megatron but now was his salvation. He was staring out into the ocean, gazing at swathes of tentacles. He fired his laser through the water, severing the nervous system of one so that it unfurled limply. Then he reached out, grasped it, and began sliding down that tentacle, gathering speed as he plunged into the depths below.

MORE AND MORE TENTACLES WRAPPED AROUND THE Cybertronian ships as they sank back toward the horror beneath them.

"We need more power!" Starscream yelled from the bridge of the *Nemesis*.

"Thanks for helping!" Sunstreaker shot back.

"Everybody shut up and let the pilot fly!" Jazz shouted.

Sideswipe was doing his best. Lights throughout the Ark dimmed as he pushed the motors way beyond the red. But the ship kept dropping. Sideswipe felt like he was sliding inexorably down a mountainside. Teletraan-1's consoles flickered; the engines were about to burn out. Something massive hit the *Nemesis* from below; the reverberation rippled through both ships. It was too big to be a tentacle; it had to be the monster's jaws. But then something entirely unexpected happened.

The ship began to rise.

"*It's Superion,*" Jazz breathed.

He was right. The gigantic robot had managed to get beneath the *Nemesis* and was acting as an additional engine. The *Nemesis*-Ark combo continued to climb, gaining height, the guns of both ships frying the tentacles that still grasped them. Then there was nothing left holding them back, nothing above them except sky. Sideswipe hit the throttle and was pushed back in his seat as they thundered upward toward the heavens.

Chapter Forty-five

LEVIACON DESCENDED EVER FARTHER, WITH OPTIMUS holding on while they dropped through cave after cave, all of them filled with water. The whale kept on telling him they were almost there, but it seemed like he'd been saying that for miles. Yet all at once Leviacon changed direction and started swimming upward. Optimus saw a glowing light shimmering above him, a giant circle reflected in the shimmering surface toward which Leviacon was now surging up.

And breaking.

But only barely. Only the Leviacon's eyes protruded. Optimus crawled carefully up the creature's back, sticking his head above the water to try to get a sense of what was going on in this chamber.

It turned out to be a lot.

An enormous cave with a titanic glowing hoop of fire covering the entirety of the far wall. Pouring through that space bridge were hundreds of Sharkticons, swimming out into the chamber, scurrying up the walls, trying to get at the command module that hung from the center of the ceiling. But the plasma cannon on the bottom of that module was spraying out death in every direction, knocking Sharkticons into the water and raining fire down on them. It didn't take a genius to guess where the Curator was. Optimus patted the whale's back.

"Thank you for everything, friend. I'll take it from here."

The Leviacon rumbled dissent. "There is no way you would get close to that alone. Together we have a chance to defeat the being that tried to enslave both our planets."

"What do you suggest?" Optimus asked.

"I'm not *suggesting* anything," said the whale, and abruptly submerged, diving while Optimus held on for dear life as it picked up speed, arcing back toward the surface, changing into a gigantic humanoid robot as it fired rockets that sent it streaking out of the water, reaching up with its mighty hands and pulling the control bubble clean off the ceiling, flinging it against the side of the cave. The module slid down the wall, coming to a halt upside down where a ledge met the water. As the Leviacon somersaulted and dived back toward the surface, Optimus caught a glimpse of masses of Sharkticons closing on the disabled module. The water closed in over his head; he figured that it was all over for the Curator.

He was wrong.

Suddenly the bridge glowed with the brightness of the sun as a surge of energy radiated out from it, frying the circuitry of everything that happened to be above the water's surface at that moment. That included every Sharkticon. Its lower half still exposed to air, the Leviacon was burned badly. It transformed back into whale mode, thrashing in pain, retreating to the bottom to nurse its wounds. Only Optimus was left unscathed. As the bridge reverted to its normal energy output, he let go of the crippled Leviacon and swam quickly toward the command module, scrambling onto the rocks and vaulting inside.

The Curator was crouching on what had been the module's ceiling, a self-satisfied smile on his face. Apparently he'd been protected by the shielding in the module's walls. Or he was simply immune to the more lethal effects of the bridge. After all, he'd built the thing. He straightened and gazed up at Optimus.

"Well, well," he said. "Miracles never cease. Megatron told me you were dead."

"Megatron has a bad habit of exaggerating."

"And you have a bad habit of surviving where so many others don't," the Curator said. He eyed the hundreds of dead floating Sharkticons in the water. "I really didn't want to do that."

"You mean destroy them wholesale?" Optimus was puzzled. "They'd have chewed you to pieces otherwise."

"I mean push the bridge to the limit like that. A portal through space-time might harness considerable energies, but what I just did had a 30.4 percent chance of shutting it down altogether. And I happen to still have need of it."

"I don't think you understand, Curator." Optimus towered over the smaller bot. "It's all over."

"Over?" The Curator laughed. "It's just *begun*. I trust you met my pet."

"You mean that city-size jellyfish?"

"The Hydratron. I'm going to be sending it through the bridge to consume everything on your planet, Optimus. It may be the largest jellyfish ever created, but on the plains of Cybertron it'll be more like a spider. And it will hunt your people down like the insects they are."

"The caves leading here are too narrow, Curator. There's no way you could get that monster—" But even as Optimus spoke, he heard a distant rumbling. The ceiling began to vibrate faintly. "Oh, no," he said.

"Oh, yes," said the Curator. "It's tearing its way through the lake bed to get to me. Such loyalty. Would that all my servants showed the same."

"This has gone far enough," Optimus said. He stepped forward, ready to rip his foe apart. But just before Optimus's fists connected, the Curator produced a wandlike object and pointed it upward; Optimus suddenly felt energy flowing out of him. It was as though the Matrix of Leadership was expanding in his chest to the point of bursting. He sank to his knees as the Curator smiled.

"How do you think I opened the link to Cybertron in the first place?" he said. "Your Matrix was an essential part of the equation. And although whatever you and Megatron did to the Matrix replica means I can no longer manipulate you remotely, you've made the mistake of coming down here. This is the heart of my power, Prime."

"Primus . . . curse you," Optimus muttered. The Curator flicked more buttons, and he slumped forward, fighting for consciousness, his optics dwindling to the point where all he could see was the Curator's cackling visage.

"It's fitting it should come to this," the Quintesson said. The rumbling overhead grew louder. "Without our wisdom, without our brilliance, your race would amount to nothing more than an elaborate wind-up toy! We gave you purpose! We gave you a chance to serve! And look how you paid us back!"

"You claimed to be . . . creators." Optimus could barely talk now. "Claimed dominion. You lied. You had no right . . ."

"Don't talk to me of *rights*," said the Curator. "Don't talk to me of *lies*. We Quintessons create our own reality, and our slaves dwell within it."

"Not anymore," said a voice.

The Curator and Optimus looked up to see a battered and bloodied Tyrannicon emerging from the glowing hoop, striding along the ledge toward them, his trident on his back. Pieces of his armor were missing, and he was covered with tooth marks. But he was still very much alive.

"Ah, General," said the Curator. "You've arrived just in time to—" But before the Curator could finish his sentence, Tyrannicon had closed the distance between them and grabbed the Curator by both arms.

"What do you think you're doing?" the Quintesson screamed.

By way of answer, Tyrannicon tore the Curator in two.

Or rather, he tore the Curator's shell. From within fell something far smaller: a fleshy black cephalopod whose mantle was covered with red splotches and beady eyes. The thing was covered in a disgusting slime, and before it could skitter away on feeble tentacles, Tyrannicon scooped it up in one of his massive fists.

"I should have known you would try to have me done away with," he thundered. "Turning my own forces against me in my hour of victory. Did you not trust me?"

"No! I had nothing to do with that!" the Curator squeaked, his voice high-pitched now that he'd lost his shell. "You're crushing me—*urrrghh*!" Tyrannicon kept squeezing more tightly, cutting off the Curator's shrill pleas. All that was audible was the intensifying rumbling of the approaching Hydratron, and Tyrannicon was far too angry to notice that. The only thing he cared about now was wringing the answers he wanted from the hapless Curator.

"Give me back command of my soldiers," he demanded. *"Give me back my armies."*

"Please, please, believe me—"

"Believe a Quintesson who's begging for his life? Never."

"But you should," Megatron said.

Everyone turned as he emerged from the water, which poured off his fins in sheets. Tyrannicon's face went dark as he saw how the Decepticon leader had changed. His eyes locked on Megatron's shark-jaw chest plate.

"What abomination is this?" he asked.

"It is I, Megatron, the First of the Many. Be grateful you have the good fortune to witness my true incarnation."

"You seek to usurp my rule," Tyrannicon growled.

"Megatron," Optimus said, "we've got to—"

"Save it, librarian. I'll deal with you in a second. Tyrannicon, your legions are now mine. But perhaps we can strike a deal."

"A deal?" Tyrannicon repeated the word as though it were a curse.

"Yes. You may serve me and lead my Sharkticons. You've been a minion all your life; why change now? Trust me, you'll enjoy being my general."

"Is that a fact?" said Tyrannicon. He stepped into the water, striding through the shallows toward Megatron, still gripping the Curator in one hand. Megatron moved slowly to the side, clearly seeking optimal ground as the two opponents squared off. The whole room was shaking now; the Hydratron was drawing ever closer. But both bots seemed to think the vibration was purely the result of their own stomping around the chamber. Optimus tried to mutter a warning, but no one was listening to him anymore. Tyrannicon reached Megatron and looked down at the Curator.

"Have you heard this farce, Curator? Megatron tells us to bend the knee for all eternity. How do you think we should reply, hmm? How shall we answer?"

"Please, Tyrannicon, show mercy."

"I give you the mercy you gave the innocent!" Tyrannicon clenched his fist until the Curator was crushed completely. Juice ran down the Sharkticon general's arm as he stared coldly at Megatron. "Such is the fate of any who would claim to be my master."

"I'm going to do more than just *claim*," Megatron said, stepping forward and swinging his fists. Tyrannicon lowered his head, charging Megatron like an enraged bull. There was a thunderous crash as the two giants clashed, locking arms, each trying to rip the other apart, shove the other beneath the water.

"Imposter," Tyrannicon said through his teeth. "You may as well give up now."

Megatron laughed. "I was fighting in the pits a million years before they built you. You can't possibly hope to defeat—"

But Tyrannicon's helmet shot a corrosive mixture of black inky acid right into Megatron's eyes. Megatron broke away, stumbling backward as his optics tried to cope with the toxic substance. Tyrannicon pulled his trident from his back and swung it around so that the hooked pommel caught Megatron under the arm, knocking him sprawling down in the water; then he reversed the trident in a blur, stabbing out with a thrust that would have speared the Decepticon if he had not rolled to the side, diving beneath the surface. Tyrannicon leaped forward, submerging; only the general's fins were visible as he closed on where Megatron was. Thrashing filled the water as the two bots furiously battled on the rocky bottom. Watching the fight, Optimus figured it could go either way. But the intensifying vibration now shuddering through the chamber told him that neither was going to win.

That was when he noticed something.

The Curator's wand. Mere feet from him. The Quintesson leader must have dropped it when Tyrannicon had seized him. Gathering what strength remained to him, Optimus reached out and grabbed it. He could feel the whole room shaking now as though it were in the throes of an earthquake. Chunks of rock were tumbling from the ceiling. The Hydratron was almost upon them. Optimus had no idea how the wand worked, but he knew he couldn't simply turn off the bridge. That wouldn't be enough. He had to destroy it, had to stop that thing from reaching Cybertron at any cost.

Including his own life.

The Energon stockpiles that were fueling the bridge . . . that was the key. Optimus set all the controls for maximum and watched as the wand began flashing bright red and the bridge started to pulsate. Out in the water, Megatron hauled Tyrannicon to his feet, grabbing him with one claw while a buzz saw protruded from his other. The saw roared to life as Megatron shoved it toward Tyrannicon's face. It was mere feet from those cold fish eyes. Now it was inches . . .

But at the last moment, Tyrannicon kicked out with one clawed boot, knocking Megatron backward toward the cave wall, just far enough to swing the trident around and fire the triple blades off like a missile. They struck Megatron right in the chest, pinning him against the cave wall.

"You were saying something about your expertise in the pits?" Tyrannicon asked as he put his giant hand around Megatron's throat.

"It isn't possible," Megatron murmured. He was struggling desperately, but the energy-powered trident blades had him stuck fast. "*I'm* supposed to be the chosen one."

"Then I guess I shouldn't be able to do this," Tyrannicon said. He punched straight through Megatron's chest plate and seized the Quintesson-made matrix. Blue lightning erupted from Megatron's body and arced into Tyrannicon as Megatron convulsed, reverting to his normal form. The vast room was shaking as though it was about to collapse. Tyrannicon shuddered as though he was being torn apart. But then he held the blazing object in the air above him—

"The power is mine!" he screamed.

—and plunged it into his own chest. Blue-green energy enveloped him as he looked at his trapped opponent.

"Foolish Cybertronian. What misbegotten notion made you think this power belonged to you? This was mine by birthright." As he spoke, Tyrannicon grew taller, the fins on his arms and legs larger. His squid helm turned black, and his scales started glowing a translucent blue. The war trident sprouted new blades that glowed with fresh energy. He was too caught up in the rush of his transformation to notice the rocks falling all around him.

"Welcome to the reign of Tyrannicon the First," he said. "Any final words, gladiator?"

"I've got two," Megatron snarled. "Scrap you."

Tyrannicon raised his trident to deliver the killing blow, and the ceiling blasted open to reveal the hideous countenance of the Hydratron. Dozens of tentacles swarmed down, enveloping the tallest target in the room, pulling Tyrannicon up toward all too many maws; he bellowed furiously, swinging his war trident desperately, but for every tentacle he sliced, two more grabbed him as the monstrosity inexorably drew him up and into one of its mammoth gullets. The concentrated acid must have been potent indeed; there was a blue flash so bright that it was dimly visible through the semitranslucent flesh. Lightning flickered through the creature's body and erupted from the tips of myriad tentacles, bouncing around the cave, shearing off slices of the cave walls. For a moment, Optimus hoped that the blast had killed the creature, but it didn't seem to be affected in the slightest; instead, it kept trying to force its way down into the chamber. With sickening clarity, Optimus realized that he and Megatron were both helpless, about to be eaten alive.

"Optimus," a voice whispered.

Optimus looked up to see the Leviacon peeking above the surface, mere feet from his face.

"I thought you were dead," he said.

"I've had better days," the Leviacon whispered. "Now get on." Optimus crawled desperately toward the whale; it seemed like an eternity while Megatron roared and struggled against the far wall, and the glowing on the bridge intensified and the Hydratron forced its way ever farther into the chamber. Its terrible bulk seemed to writhe with excitement as it spotted the bridge, an entire portion of its body extending out toward the portal like a gigantic pseudopod. Optimus reached the Leviacon at last and rolled onto its burned back. The Leviacon began swimming desperately for the exit; half the chamber was now filled with the Hydratron's mass. Tentacles draped down toward Megatron. He and Optimus locked eyes.

Optimus knew he couldn't let him die like this.

"We need to take a detour," he told the Leviacon.

"We don't have time!"

"We'll make it," Optimus said as he guided the Leviacon to the side wall where Megatron was. The colossal gelatinous sack strained against the rocks above them. The pseudopod had almost touched the bridge's blazing energies. The entire portal was going critical. Optimus reached up and tried to pull the trident blades from the wall, but he was too weak.

"Nice try, librarian," Megatron muttered. "Save yourself while you still can."

"I can't leave you."

"Sure you can."

Optimus stared at him. The Leviacon slapped the trident from the wall with his wounded tail; Megatron fell forward onto the back of the whale. The Leviacon dived and swam desperately for all their lives. The last Optimus saw of the bridge chamber was through dark shimmering water, a circular glow slowly being eclipsed by a titanic bulk. Tentacles unfurled through the water toward them, but the Leviacon plunged farther, ever deeper, through a maze of passageways that Optimus was certain wasn't the way they'd come in.

"Where are we going?" he asked.

"Deep as we can go," said the Leviacon. "We've got a minute at most."

It turned out they had a lot less.

THE ARK AND THE *NEMESIS* HAD JUST REACHED ORBIT when they picked up the explosion on their scanners. It was a force ten blast, wiping Aquatron's only continent clean off the map, sending up a mushroom cloud that reached to the very edge of space.

The Autobots, stubborn beings that they were, detached the Ark and proceeded to reenter the atmosphere, running low-level search and rescue passes for their missing leader, hoping against hope. Nor were they alone in their quest. Starscream had announced that he would remain in orbit supervising repairs on the *Nemesis*, but most of his Seekers flew alongside the Ark, scanning the ocean. The sight of bots such as Skywarp and Dirge cruising in formation next to the Ark made for an unusual sight from the Ark's bridge, which was packed to capacity with many of the day's combatants. Jazz and Prowl stood right behind Sideswipe's command chair, scouring the readouts for any sign of Optimus. Sunstreaker and Bulkhead paced up and down while Ratchet and Perceptor ran every possible scan and then some. Ironhide sat at the back of the room with his massive arms crossed, insisting that if Optimus was gone, they would all have felt his passing, that it couldn't be any other way with a Prime, that it just couldn't . . . But he was in denial, and they all knew it. Kup consoled him with the last cy-gar he had stashed in his quarters before they'd left Cybertron. For once Rodimus and Bumblebee were silent; they just looked on as Hubcap went over his maps again and again, trying not to look at the pillar of smoke rising from the horizon. Was there something he had missed? Anything . . . ?

But all at once an elated scream from Sideswipe pierced the air.

"There! Down there!"

He magnified the image and put it on the main screen. It was a giant battle-scarred whale shark, and riding on its back like a knight of old Cybertron was Optimus Prime. The bridge erupted in shouts of elation and joy, a jubilation that barely wavered when they saw Megatron holding on to the whale's tail. The Seekers whooped and streaked down toward their leader, the Ark moving down with them. With a feather touch, Sideswipe set the craft to hover mere meters from the Leviacon. A ramp lowered toward the huge whale. Optimus watched it descend toward him and felt strength return to his limbs. Since the destruction of the bridge and all the Curator's foul works, the Matrix had surged back to life within him, burning with rejuvenated insight. Optimus had never felt better. Especially now that he knew his soldiers were alive, too. He patted his new friend on the back.

"Thank you for all your help, Leviacon."

"Thank *you*, Optimus Prime. If it had not been for your efforts, Aquatron would still be a slave world."

"And now it's practically been depopulated," said a weary Megatron as Ramjet and Slipstream moved in to assist him. But he shook them off, clearly meaning to travel under his own power in spite of the pain he was in.

"That is not true," the Leviacon said. "Most of my people dwell near the seabed. We rarely venture to the surface. It was only under Quintesson compulsion that we did so."

"Well, welcome to freedom and thanks for the lift," Megatron said sarcastically. He turned to Optimus. "I'll be seeing you again shortly, librarian." And with that, he changed into his spacecraft mode and roared off into the sky, his Seekers following him, leaving fiery trails behind them. The Ark's ramp reached Optimus. Naturally, Jazz was right there at the forefront with a hearty handshake for his old friend.

"Glad to see you, boss. You really had us worried there for a second."

"It's good to see you all," Optimus said with heartfelt relief. He looked out across their jubilant faces, felt sweet relief flood through him. He barely heard Ironhide's question and had to ask him to repeat it.

"So you and Megatron were working together? Is that how you got out? You and him, you were a *team*?"

Optimus stepped onto the ramp. "We had a common foe," he said.

"And now?" Jazz asked.

"Now it's up to Megatron," Optimus replied as he led his men back up the ramp. "Perhaps one day he will realize how much stronger we are united."

"That'll be the day," said Ironhide.

"It may yet be," Optimus said. "But right now we've got a mission to complete. Autobots, roll out!"

The Ark fired its engines and soared back toward the black of space.

Epilogue: Alpha Trion

AND SO IT COMES FULL CIRCLE.

Yet so much remains untold. The AllSpark remains unfound. The conflict that tears our people asunder continues. And Cybertron remains a blighted land. Even as I write this, smoke still rises from the shattered ruins of Iacon. I am in a place of safety, for now at least. Ultra Magnus will not leave my side, will not risk my becoming a tool in the hands of those who would play dice with the fortunes of our people. For he knows that Shockwave is reasserting control across our planet, that he is rebuilding his tower, that soon the days of guerrilla fighting will begin once more, only burdened with new complications. Devastator was successfully recovered from Iacon's wreckage, and Wheeljack is busy making repairs to Omega Supreme. There are reports that some of the invaders remain, scattered here and there, fighting all the harder now that chaos has gripped their minds. I do not know whether to believe this.

But this much I do know: The enemy that set this invasion in motion is still out there. My time within the mind of Vector Sigma opened up broader vistas within me. I saw our galaxy spread before me, saw the duel between Optimus Prime and Megatron the gladiator swept aside for the briefest of moments as they battled a foe that history itself had forgotten. No longer; the Quintessons will be a *factor in everybody's calculations now. As assuredly we are a factor in theirs—somewhere out there, on a faraway planet drifting around an alien sun, the masters of that race are setting in motion plans to harvest the seeds they sowed so many eons ago. Theirs is a people who combine the cunning of the lowest beasts with the remorselessness of a machine that thinks a million moves ahead. I cannot tell you how much I fear them.*

Yes, fear. Primes can know that, too. Or at least I can. I cannot speak for my brethren of the Thirteen lost among the stars . . . except to wish that those who gave way to malice will never return and those who still seek the good will also seek the home that needs them so desperately. Yet I know better than to expect them. For now, legend will remain just that. Perhaps it is better that way. The heroes of yesteryear will not save us; only those of today can. Optimus Prime has become every inch the leader I hoped he would. He has learned that he is more than just the sum of the Matrix, and that is a lesson he will surely need in the days ahead. For just before I was cut loose from Vector Sigma, I glimpsed something.

A blue-green world.

Out on the fringes of the Orion Arm. I have seen it before. I sent the contents of the vault there, after all. Wreathed in atmosphere, orbiting a yellow dwarf star, the third of eight major planets and countless minor ones; I cannot say if Optimus goes there next, but go there one day soon he surely will. For this planet is somehow bound up in his quest in some way I had not at first anticipated. Nor do I know precisely what this planet means—cannot tell what evil or good it might portend. Only the pages of the Covenant of Primus to which I have yet to turn can do that.

So turn to them now I shall.

About the Authors

DAVID J. WILLIAMS was born in Hertfordshire, England, and is the author of *The Mirrored Heavens*, *The Burning Skies*, and *The Machinery of Light*. He has previously worked as a writer and concept developer for the award-winning Homeworld franchise of videogames.

MARK S. WILLIAMS studied poetry at the University of Maryland before joining the corporate world as a security professional. His previous collaboration with David J. Williams was the short story "Maze Run," which appeared in *Star Wars Insider* magazine. He currently lives in the Midwest, where he can often be found haunting bookstores and pizza parlors when he's not writing.

More thrilling Transformers™ novels
available now from Titan Books

Transformers: Exodus by Alex Irvine
Transformers: Exiles by Alex Irvine

Transformers: Ghosts of Yesterday by Alan Dean Foster
Transformers: The Movie Novelization by Alan Dean Foster
Transformers: Revenge of the Fallen by Alan Dean Foster
Transformers: The Veiled Threat by Alan Dean Foster
Transformers: Dark of the Moon by Peter David

TITANBOOKS.COM